LIBERTY

LIBERTY

JAY TAVERNER

Tollington

For Judith
at long last

First published in 2021 by Tollington Press, Machynlleth, Wales
www.tollingtonpress.co.uk

A catalogue record for this book is available from the British Library.

ISBN 978-1-909347-20-5

Cover image: 'The Love Letter', François Boucher,
courtesy National Gallery of Art, Washington, USA

Designed and typeset by Helen Sandler

Printed and bound in the UK by Biddles Books Ltd

CONTENTS

PROLOGUE

1789

Early Spring

The *Robin*: two-masted coasting vessel out of Salem, walloping southwards before a following wind off the Carolinas. The *Robin*: shabby, worm-eaten and stinking, laden with oak staves for sugar casks and fusty rice to feed slaves in the British colonies. The packet plodded along, more Dobbin than Robin, Rebecca thought: an old nag bound head-down for its stable. But she did not care. She loved the ugly little ship. For her, everything – salt spray and heaving deck, swearing sailors and puking passengers – was insignificant in the face of the huge shining sky and the swooping, thrusting flow of brilliant air. And every day of rolling progress brought her nearer to her new, half-guessed future.

She sat each day on a pile of spars in the steadily strengthening sun, breathing deeply and, with each long breath, letting go of another link that chained her. On the ninth morning, the new warmth seeping into her back through the serviceable grey wool of her winter gown made her wonder for a moment whether she might go barefoot, as the sailors did; she had not felt the world through her toes since she was a wild child running in the summer woods, twenty years ago.

It had taken some persuasion to make the captain take her as a passenger. She knew that her appearance had hardly recommended her – a tall, spare woman dressed in Quaker grey, past her youth at eight-and-twenty and, she thought ruefully, with all the marks of an old maid. But she'd fixed him with a steady gaze and made him listen to her carefully prepared speech about needing a passage to England, via Jamaica. Captain Singleton had clearly been unhappy about an unaccompanied woman traveller; but it was not entirely unprecedented, for the Friends did quite often go forth alone, to bear witness in distant places. By a stroke of good fortune, Captain Singleton's wife's parents were already on board, bound to see a new grandchild in Jamaica. They had agreed, a little reluctantly, to take Rebecca under their protection, and so the problem was solved.

In the event, she had seen very little of these other passengers. Since the *Robin* had sailed, Rebecca had spent every day on deck, mostly gazing out eastwards towards her distant destination; she rarely entered the cabin. She had watched Salem dwindle out of sight as they left the harbour and, as they sailed on, watched the crew at work. They watched her in return, grinned, and answered when she spoke to them. She had stood out of the way while they kicked the poxy old tub into shape, and now she strode the length of the deck without so much as holding to the rail. She had stood by the man at the helm for two days, asking questions, which he answered with surprised politeness. Now the sailors tipped their caps and she smiled as they passed by.

On the tenth day they left American waters, sailing out into the Gulf, the last leg of the trip to Jamaica. The sun grew hotter and, by the time Rebecca went down to her cot in the narrow cabin, the wind seemed to have dropped to a lulling whisper. But when she woke, too early, before light, she could feel a strange shift in the motion of the ship. The other passengers were both sound asleep on the other side of the cabin, their sickly faces pale in the surging sea-light that slapped against the porthole. Rebecca sat up. The everlasting wallow of the ship had changed to a choppy, gut-wrenching rhythm. Rising quickly and wrapping her woollen shawl over her shift, she made her way across to the companion-way, holding on against the unnatural buck and rear of the deck.

Above, in the midst of the turbulent motion, there was a strained stillness about the crew. She could see three men holding on by the port rail, and the captain at the wheel; all were staring into the east, as if to catch the rising dawn. Rebecca turned her head. The easterly sky was livid, with green-tinged rays of light rising eerily from the coming sun. Singleton caught sight of her at the companion-head and called out, gesturing for her to go down again – but his voice was lost in the wind, and in the disaster that fell upon them. A screaming, twisting squall swept down on the ship, tossing it madly like a nutshell in a waterfall. As Rebecca clung to the rope at the stairhead, a wall of water wrenched her sideways, completely off her feet. The icy wave knocked all the breath from her body, but she clung on, pressed against the companion housing for what seemed an age, banging helplessly in the wall of water that swept across the deck. The sound of crashing, splintering timber deafened her.

Then the surge of the sea dropped her abruptly and spewed out of the bilges. Men ran by shouting, laid hold of ropes and began working like demons with knives and axes to free the cumbered ship as she thrashed like a terrified horse tied by the head. Tons of broken wood and sail trailed away in the water. The mast, Rebecca realised – the main mast – had gone by the board. She ducked down the stairwell out of the screaming wind, but darkness and enclosure filled her with terror and she scrambled out again, watching as the crew slashed and chopped to clear the rigging, while two men struggled with the wheel. The captain was gazing away from the rising sun now, westwards, and she pulled herself along by the rail to see what he was watching.

It was land. A rocky coast, green cliffs incredibly near. She had imagined them still out at sea, swept by this twister in mid-ocean; but they were hard by the shore. Her heart leapt. Then, as she turned back to watch the struggle to master the ship, the deck shuddered and rose under her feet, freed from some of the dragging debris. A man screamed. Horrified, she watched him fly by, mouth open and hands clutching, caught by the leg in an escaping mass of rigging that he had cut free. The ship seemed to right itself, pulling upright before the wind, almost as if it answered to the helm; but as she drew a stunned breath, the air exploded into wet chaos again and she was flung aside, up and away as, quite unmistakably, the hull struck a rock.

She knew she was swept overboard, striking her side on the rail with a force that emptied her completely. She gasped as the water closed over her, and dropped through the roaring depths to a green silence. But she felt herself stop and begin to rise, and she struck out for the surface. She shot into the wet air above, in time to see the ship tilt wildly away, its bottom rearing up like a barnacled cliff from which the tide streamed as fast as a river in spate. The ship was turning turtle, was about to go down; gasping, Rebecca kicked out in panic, struggling to get out of its wash. A deck spar hit her in the back and she turned and clung to it. With a wet-throated roar and then a series of splintering explosions, the ship pulled back, grounded, lifted and settled, breaking up on the invisible rocks beneath the waves. Rebecca closed her eyes.

... And opened them on brilliant whiteness, a blank wall of light and silence. Far, far away, a black dot shaped itself into first a pulsing seed and then a frame, a tiny picture that grew as she looked at it until she could see a flight of steps – a doorway – the door of Cousin Richard's house in Essex Street, and someone – herself – running up the steps.

She is seven years old and angry, because she wants to go fishing in the brook, but Dorcas has said she must stay home and help with the laundry. Dorcas says fishing is boys' work, and girls must attend to their duty indoors. So now Rebecca feels guilty as well as angry, because she has been very rude to Dorcas, who doesn't deserve it on account of being so good and working so hard always, and looking after Rebecca all year since her mother died. Rebecca's father has explained to her more than once that Dorcas has more than enough to do and that Rebecca is obliged not to add to her burden in this world, but rather to show her obedience and loving-kindness like a good Christian and a sister. Instead of which, Rebecca has thrown a pot of fresh-made starch across the wash-house, and her clean white cap after it, and said a most unchristian word. And now she has run away, to the only person who can right her and make her good again.

Cousin Richard is her best friend, even though he is so old – as old as her father, and white-haired already. Richard says he was white before he was old, because of having red hair before. But she cannot imagine that; she thinks of him having always been as he is now, with his brown eyes, clever and kind, and his thick white hair tied behind with an old-fashioned black ribbon. He is sitting in his high-backed wooden armchair. He looks at her without saying anything and closes his book. (When she asked her father why Richard was always reading, he said it was because he was a lawyer and they loved books.)

She pants to a halt and looks at him, scowling.

Richard smiles, though she knows she doesn't deserve it, and says in an everyday voice, 'Good day, friend Judith. What brings you here so early?'

'It's me – Rebecca! Why do you call me Judith?' She runs towards him, alarmed, reaching for a reassuring hand. Then she stops. 'Judith is my other name – I am Rebecca Judith Wiston.' She drops her head and looks up at him with narrowed eyes. 'What do you mean?'

He is not smiling now, but thoughtful. 'It has often occurred to me, Rebecca Judith Wiston, that your two given names are alarmingly different. Rebecca, as I'm sure you know, was a good, obedient woman. A willing helpmeet to Isaac her husband. A kind and patient mother, I warrant also, to Jacob and Esau, her troublesome sons.' He puts the book carefully aside. 'Beside which, of course, it was the name of your good grandmother Beeston in England, who was a loving neighbour and a pattern of virtue.'

Is he mocking her? She shuffles her feet crossly on the boards of the porch. 'And Judith?'

'Oh, a very different kind of heroine. Angry. And cunning.'

He looks at her mildly. '*She slew a man. The commander of the Assyrian army, no less.*'

Rebecca is interested in spite of herself. '*How?*' she demands.

Now she is sure that he is trying not to laugh. 'No doubt your sister Dorcas will upbraid me for sharing these apocryphal horrors with you, but they do say' – and he lowers his voice as if it is a secret – '*that she cut his head off. With his own sword.*'

There is silence while Rebecca Judith contemplates this picture of her second namesake.

'*But, friend, wasn't that breaking the seventh commandment?*'

'*Well observed. A nice point.*' *He always talks to her like this, as if she were as old and wise as himself. It is one of the reasons she loves him.* 'But this was in a time of war, when men in general hold killing to be excusable – noble, even. Certainly, in a time of peace, such fury would not be held to be a virtue. Particularly in a woman.'

Rebecca looks up at him. 'I see. So, I should try not to be Judith, even though I am.' *It is a new and interesting idea, that she might be more than one person. She considers it and puts it away for another day.*

A roaring of dark water and a tug at her heart. The light dwindles and she is deathly sick. She turns, wallowing in the tide. She is going to die. Something within her, some demon of resistance – the spirit of Judith, perhaps – flares up. She kicks and kicks, until her head breaks the surface. Choking out a shuddering breath, she tries to tighten her grip on the spar to which she is still clinging; but the pain in her side takes her breath and the spar turns, tipping her headlong into the waves again.

And again, the blank white light. She wills herself to resist, to stay in the present, in the sea, but she cannot. Memory has become a tide as irresistible as the ocean and she is watching again. This time the square of light is not a door, but a window.

It is the window of her own attic room. She is taller now, so that her old spy-glass rests in the bottom corner of the top right-hand pane, where it always did. She is looking out to sea, as she used to do; but this is no ordinary morning. She knows, with a shooting lurch at the heart, that if she turns round, she will see Lizzie, in her bed. And then she hears her voice.

'Come back to bed.'

Rebecca lowers the spy-glass and turns. After the brightness outside, the attic room is dark. Lizzie's face is a pale oval in the gloom, her shoulders white above the shadow-patterns of the quilt. So beautiful. As always, Rebecca's spirits soar at the sight of her. Since Lizzie has come into her life, everything has been different.

'What were you looking at?' *Lizzie asks.*

'Awake at last?' *Rebecca sits on the end of the bed, unwilling to turn entirely away from the window.* 'There's a ship in the offing. I've been watching the sun come up, and suddenly there she was – hull down, but she's coming in, I'm sure of it.'

'Hull down?' *Lizzie sits up straighter.* 'You mean she's sinking?'

Rebecca laughs. 'No, I mean she's right out beyond the horizon. You can't see her hull at all, only her masts. She's a three-master, I think, an ocean-going vessel. I wonder who she can be.' *She puts down the glass.*

Lizzie pouts. 'Are you surprised I can't understand you, when you talk more like a sailor-boy than a respectable person? You even look like a sailor, with that spy-glass stuck in your eye all the time.'

'If I were a sailor, do you think I'd be wasting my life gazing at ships from a window, when I might be on board one, and voyaging over the world?' *Rebecca's voice rises.* 'Or fighting the British, taking back all the taxes they took from us? Now that's a life!'

Lizzie looks shocked. 'What foolishness! You would not say such things in front of your brothers. Whatever the British have done to us, you know that war is no answer. Sometimes I think you choose to be odd.'

Rebecca raises an eyebrow.

'Well, do you know any other girls who want to be sailors?

Or who keep a telescope in their chamber window? You are impossible!'

Rebecca's good humour is not to be dented. She grins. 'Sailor or no, you liked me well enough last night,' she says, moving the quilt aside.

Lizzie wriggles down the bed and looks up at Rebecca through her lashes. 'Perhaps I did,' she says. 'Are you coming aboard?'

Rebecca groaned and willed the scene away. The pain of it merged into the throb of her head and her labouring heart. She was getting cold, which was strange since, when she opened her eyes, she saw the sun was coming up, a glimmering green; it blurred the waves between her and the rocks. She felt tears well up, though whether she cried for herself now, weltering helpless on this black shore, or for the odd, awkward girl she had once been but had so long forsaken and forgotten, she did not know.

She began, very slowly, to ease her grip on the spar. There was a crack and a jolt, and she felt the heavy, slippery timber wrenched from her arms. Her knees hit something beneath the water, and she cried out, or thought she did; but her voice was lost in the hissing invasion of the sea as she tumbled forward, face down, and all the light went out.

PART ONE

1789

Winter into Spring

1

The winter Richard Farley died was the coldest anyone in Salem could remember. The gales that blew in off the Atlantic locked up the town in a freezing prison. Doors and windows were sealed with ice each morning; boxes and barrels were frozen to the boards of the pier; frost thickened the rigging of the ships along the wharf until each vessel was veiled with hard white lace. In the town, icicles a yard long hung from gutters and broke with a noise like gunshot, birds fell dead out of the trees and children were put to bed in the daytime simply to keep them warm. Even the mildest New England winter took its toll of the old and weak, and Richard had become frail of late. Yet Rebecca had never allowed herself to think of his not being there, and the news of his death took her unawares.

She was not given to weeping. She had not wept since that springtime, long ago, when Lizzie was married. The day that Elizabeth Haraden married Ben Pickering, the lad who had sailed the town's first British prize into Salem harbour, Rebecca had lain face down in the grass on Naugus Head and wept, and forsworn love forever. She was sixteen years old, and she had not known that anything could hurt so much. She had thought she would die, for how could she live without love? And she would never love anyone else; that part of her was dead.

No one had noticed. Life in the Wiston household went on as if nothing had happened. Rebecca helped her sister-in-law Dorcas to wash and cook; she sat at Meeting with the family and wished good day to their neighbours afterwards; and slowly, as the years went by, she deserted the parlour, and the walks, and her school friends deserted her. In the end, she mostly spent her days on a high stool in her brothers' shipping office, entering the details of their transactions in the account book. The world at large was too busy with war and politics to notice that a light had gone out in Rebecca Wiston.

She did not let herself think about that summer – the summer of love and danger when she had been so full of strength, of wild, totally unreasonable self-confidence, when she had thought that Lizzie loved her. Their passion had been a secret, an unspoken pact against a world which would not have understood; but she had thought it would last forever. Or perhaps she had not thought at all. In any case, she would not make the same mistake twice. She took care not to give her heart again, or to show her feelings to anyone. And she gave away the spy-glass. A ship standing in with the tide between Winter Island and Naugus Head would be reported soon enough by one of the wharfingers; for herself, she had no more need to look beyond the horizon.

Setting her jaw against grief, Rebecca walked behind Richard's coffin to the burying-ground, though she knew her brothers would have preferred her to stay at home with Dorcas and leave this ritual to the men. She stood, stone-faced, on the high slope of the little Quaker graveyard behind the town, looking out over the heads of the mourners, beyond the houses and wharves, out beyond the harbour mouth, as the wind whipped white horses across the bay and the familiar silence took hold and lengthened. She tried to pray, but her mind was as frozen as her fingers. She found herself remembering other deaths. Both her parents lay in this same graveyard: her mother, taken by fever when Rebecca was six; her father, suddenly old and tired, only three years later. She remembered how lonely she had felt then, a frightened child in a house of solemn adults; and how Richard had been there to listen and to understand. He was her mother's cousin, and Rebecca had loved him since childhood, each of them recognising in the other a friend and kindred spirit, in spite of the long gap of years between them. She could talk to him about anything at all and know he would take her seriously. The only thing she had never spoken to him about was Lizzie. To her horror, Rebecca felt tears burn behind her eyelids.

At last someone began to speak. Gratefully she wrenched her mind away from the losses of the past. In measured tones, the Elder told of their friend Farley's good life, his works, his piety. Rebecca had to put a hand over her mouth then, to stop herself from shouting out. Piety? A cold, strangling word for the fire against all suffering and injustice that had burned always in that bright soul! Mercifully, the eulogy did not last long – it was too cold to stand still for many minutes together. The coffin was lowered into the hole which had taken two days to hack out of the frozen ground and, as the icy soil rattled down, Rebecca excused herself and hurried home.

She knew only one way to dull pain, and that was by working. Passing by the front of her brothers' house, she let herself in at the side door which led straight into the office. Still wrapped in her winter cloak, for the stove had not been lit, she climbed on to a stool, drew on the clerk's linen sleeves she wore to protect the cuffs of her gown, and pulled the great leather-bound Day Book towards her. Methodically she sharpened her pen, inked it and began to write.

16th February. Cold still, and the wind north-easterly. The Grand Turk and two other merchantmen lie at Derby's wharf, China-bound on the spring Trades and buying cargoes now. Our ships idle still. No Business done this day, the Office being closed and all the Family gone to the burial of Richard Farley.

Outside it was already near to dark. Two men hurried by in the street, huddled against the wind that swayed and rattled the frozen rigging of the great ships moored tight against the wharf. A last seagull swooped low, heading along the quay towards the house with the white porch where Richard Farley had lived, and where now no light showed between closed shutters. Rebecca closed the Day Book and turned with a sigh to the ledger. She was deep in a calculation of next month's interest on their ever-growing debts, when the house door behind her opened.

She looked round, suppressing a sigh. Samuel was clearly out of temper. His frown brought his black hat down over his nose; he fussed into the room like a wet hen, shaking his annoyance all over her. Rebecca helped him out of his coat, hanging it to dry on the wooden peg behind the street door before she spoke.

'Is all over at the law office, then, Brother? Your supper will be a while yet, I fear – we had no notion of how long a will-reading would be.'

He did not immediately answer, but busied himself putting something into his own desk, not meeting her eye.

He looked his age today, she thought. As the eldest and youngest of a long family, she and Samuel were separated by more than a score of years. He was near fifty now, old enough to be her father, and Barnabas only a year younger. Old men. She set her lips. 'Is ought amiss?' she asked, eventually.

He turned. 'Rebecca, child, come into the house – you may leave the books, surely, on such a day?'

Pausing only to wipe her pen clean and take off her sleeves, she followed him through the wide hall and up the stairs. He obviously had something solemn to say. Had it to do with the will? Maybe Richard had left them something. She realised now that she had never considered this possibility or wondered what would happen to his possessions when he died. His gift to her had been given long before: her hand stole now to her throat, where the locket lay hidden inside her high-necked gown. No Friend would wear such an ornament, and she had not told anyone of the gift, but it comforted her to know it was there.

The candles were already lit in the parlour. Barnabas, suffering from his perpetual winter rheumatics, was tucked up in his leg-comforter by the fire. Indeed, he must have been home a while – long enough to have a steaming bowl of punch and an empty glass on the small side table beside his chair. Samuel took up his usual place on the hearthrug, his back to the fire.

As Rebecca took her seat beside the candles, he finally began upon his speech. 'Sister, I have something to tell you. As I am sure you know, Richard Farley had no close family. He was a single man when he came from England with our mother and father, and remained a bachelor all his life, so there was no one to whom he might decently leave all he had. Even so...' Samuel cleared his throat uncomfortably and filled his glass before beginning again. 'His house was his own, of course, and he was free of debt, so he was at liberty to leave it where he would. But one might have thought – after all, our mother was his cousin, however distant...'

'Samuel!' Today Rebecca could not show forbearance with her brother's mean pomposities. 'I will hear nothing against any choices Cousin Richard might have made. His belongings were his own – such as they were, for they are much diminished, I have no doubt, by the large charities of his life. To whom has he left his house?' But before he could answer, a thought occurred to her. She smiled. 'Not to Tabitha Gates?'

Samuel reddened and glanced sharply at her. 'Did you know he intended this?'

'No – but it is like him. I am so glad.'

He regarded her as though she was mad. 'What does an elderly black woman want with a house? She was his housekeeper! It is not a fitting thing. Had he heirs, they might –' He paused, and turned to Barnabas. 'Indeed, brother, now I think of it, might not we –?' But Barnabas frowned, and Samuel turned back to Rebecca. 'And that is not all, sister. If, as you say, you were ignorant of this, then you will not know either that, apart from the shocking matter of the house, he has made you' – he swallowed as if the news might choke him – 'his sole heir.'

Rebecca stared.

Barnabas smiled a somewhat creaking smile. 'It is true. When any outstanding debts or obligations are met, and the expenses of his funeral deducted, all the residue of his estate passes to you. I understand that a substantial part of this, amounting to perhaps as much as two thousand dollars, is in good sound coin. The rest is in property and rents; the lawyers will draw up a more detailed account of those in due course.'

'*Two thousand* dollars?' She struggled to gather her wits.

Samuel broke in again. 'Even if we leave aside the value of the property, the money could not come at a better time. Two thousand will go a great way to help in our present difficulties. A little rejoicing is called for, is it not? Barnabas, will you pour our sister a little punch?'

Barnabas reached for a third glass and lifted the ladle in the bowl, but Rebecca waved the offer away. She must keep her mind quite clear. 'What do you mean?' she asked carefully. 'Samuel, what do you mean? Did Richard leave his money to the business, or to me?'

Her brother flushed slightly as he answered. 'You are named in the will, as I told you, but we should regard it as a family legacy, of course. No doubt he thought it best not to give scope for idle tongues to say we were in need of Richard Farley's charity; a thoughtful act, and like his sensibility. It is a charitable deed, after all, to leave money to a young girl, one who is like a daughter, to set her up in life. But it remains with her friends and relatives to see to it that the money is wisely invested.' His voice wavered very slightly as he finished.

Now she saw clearly. Struggling to keep her voice steady, she said, 'Samuel, I am not a young girl.'

'Hush, my dear. Since our father's death you are our responsibility. And although you are our sister you are, after all, young enough to be a daughter. Have no fear. We both have your best interests at heart.'

'I am eight-and-twenty, brother.' She stood up. 'I am eight-and-twenty and, since our father's death, the responsibility, as you call it, for this family and its affairs has to all intents and purposes rested on me. No – listen to me! Our trade, or such of it as remains, rests on my intellects, brother, my head for figures. Had I the seniority of you – and were I a man – the business would not, I venture to say, be in the sorry state it is. So, if Cousin Richard left his money to me, then it was because he wanted me to have it. What I might choose to do with two thousand dollars in good coin, left to me in my own name, is – forgive me – for me to decide.'

Even in her anger, she saw that she had made a mistake. A

muscle in Samuel's jaw jumped, and his fingers tightened on the arm of his chair as he rose to face her.

'Since, as you say, Rebecca, you know so much about our trade, you must know how sorely we need this money. Your duty is clear.' He stopped, turning from her fierce gaze, and strutted away across the carpet, hands thrust under his coat-tails, looking like an old turkey-cock. Without turning towards her, he said, 'I see that the strain of this sad day has been too much for your nerves. Leave us now, my dear, and go to your duties in the kitchen. I am sure your sister Dorcas will help you to see the right of this matter. We will discuss it again when you are more yourself.'

2

The matter of the inheritance hung like a storm cloud over the household. If Rebecca had disagreed with her brothers in the past, she had kept her opinions to herself. They were glad enough of her good head for business when she confined her skills to neat book-keeping; but she had discovered long ago that any other topics or triumphs were best not mentioned. They seemed not to know – or perhaps simply chose to ignore – the reputation she had gained throughout Salem for driving a hard bargain, even though the savings she made had become more and more necessary as the shipping business struggled. New ideas, seeds of change, were sure to fall on stony ground, and she had long since ceased to offer them. But now she had spoken her mind about the bequest, and the peace of the house had been broken.

She tried the next morning to reason with Samuel. 'Say that I do put all this money into our trade account. Granted it will pay off most outstanding charges. It may even stock the *Bird of Grace* for a trip or two coastwise, come spring. But, brother, why should that turn us a profit? We have made ten, twelve such trips last year with nothing to show. Look.' She banged open the ledger. 'I have cast it up three times, and I cannot make it anything other than a working loss of more than four hundred dollars on the year. And that is leaving aside old debts, and the need for repairs, and – look, here!' She slid her hand down the damning column of figures and slapped the page.

But he looked away, mouth set in a down-turned line. 'May the Lord forgive you for an ungrateful girl. Friend Richard has given us the money. He has come to our aid in time of trouble. And you –'

She bit back the response that rose to her lips. There was no point in angering him further. A silence fell; and a bitter wind off the sea rattled the little windowpanes.

Even ever-patient Dorcas was moved to gentle reproach, though she waited until she and Rebecca were alone in the kitchen, before she spoke. It was the warmest room in the house, with its big old fireplace and warm brick floor, and they spent much of their winter days there, whether there was kitchen work to do or not.

'Surely, sister, you should bow to your brothers' better judgement in this?' Bent over the bread trough, her arms sticky with dough, she did not have to meet Rebecca's eye. 'Though you are named in the will, it is for men to judge what is meant by it, and for us to be guided by their wisdom.' She straightened up, red-faced, easing her back, and shot a hopeful glance at her silent sister-in-law. 'So Providence ordains, and so we work best,' she added, timidly.

To argue with her would be unkind, as well as pointless. Rebecca forced a small smile, then muttered her excuses and retreated to the counting house to find her customary refuge in work.

But there was no escape. It seemed that every mortal soul in the town had heard the news and found some excuse to call. They came to look at her, as if she might have changed in the night, she thought bitterly. The daily traffic of the Wistons' shipping office was subtly changed. Of recent months, their few unexpected callers had come in because they had some bad news or other to tell – a reliable seaman run away to join another captain, or one of the family's two remaining ships returned with half her cargo unsold. Otherwise, most days, they were accustomed to seeing only harassed creditors looking for payment, or, worse, dark-jowled men demanding it on their behalf. But in those icy weeks of February, after the law office had spread its gossip of legacies through the town, unexpected people found their way down to the end of the quay and, smiling through the foggy window glass at Rebecca perched on her tall stool in the back of the counting-house, found occasion to step inside.

To have become, overnight, an object of interest and of envy was a novelty Rebecca would gladly have forgone. A motherless girl without dowry or prospects, she had learned early that she could not expect to be much sought after either by friends or by wooers. Her wildness had been tamed long since; what the world saw was a young woman given to seriousness and privacy, not one who looked for suitors. She had grown accustomed to the quiet life which made use of her talents and put a neat fence of formality between her and other people. Now suddenly those people were pushing at the fence, trying to grasp her, and it made her edgy and afraid.

The worst of them was Abraham Brewer, ship's chandler and Samuel's close friend, who had a warehouse three doors away. Usually too conscious of his own importance to call at the counting-house in person, the old man had taken to dropping by unexpectedly. He clearly sought to catch her when she was alone, and her flesh shrank when she saw his eager, whiskery face at the window. The third Mrs Brewer had died last spring, and it was generally known that Abraham was in the market for another wife. Rebecca was not vain enough to suppose that he really fancied either her face or her modest fortune but, until he found better pickings, he was clearly not averse to amusing himself with the new game in town. She schooled herself to be pleasant, telling herself that he must be lonely. In any case, she could not cut him off sharply, for he was their biggest creditor. They depended on credit for their survival now, and Friend Brewer held a substantial mortgage on the business that they could ill afford to repay. So she endured his endless self-congratulations, and his increasingly familiar stares, praying fervently that the next ship would bring some buxom, ambitious widow to take his attention elsewhere.

However trying these visitors were, her brothers' behaviour galled her more. They were small men, Samuel and Barnabas. Their father, bless him, had been likewise short in inches, but a man of big ideas, vital and strong. Whatever he did, little Rebecca's had not been the only admiring eyes that followed him. He had come from the Old Country, and spoke wistfully sometimes of the place of his birth, but she knew he could have been a leader in the new world, a fighter for their right to conduct their own lives and build new ways, new trades. After the war with England, her brothers' failure to seize the moment had driven her almost to distraction. Merchantmen went forth from the Bay to the China seas, silks and other precious cargoes and ton upon ton of choice tea flowed in, and Boston men were suddenly as rich as London or Liverpool merchants. She remembered how the town had buzzed with excitement when, on a lovely day last May, Elias Derby's *Grand Turk* had been sighted off Baker Island. The cannon had sounded and everyone stopped what they were doing to run down to the harbour and cheer as the battered old *Turk* hove to at Derby's wharf, two long years since she'd set sail, but loaded now with tea and all the wonders of the Orient.

After nearly a year of repairs to her hull and rigging, Rebecca knew that Elias Derby was already trading for cargo for the *Grand Turk*'s next voyage. Everything some folk touched turned to gold – but Samuel was cautious, and Barnabas just plain dumb. Alistair Wiston would not have hesitated to join in when their neighbours set out to trade for themselves in the Indies, the Azores, all over the known world; but his sons did not venture; their ships went no further than Maryland. During the war years, the young firebrand Rebecca had been despairingly convinced that her brothers wished the British would take or sink their paltry little boats, to relieve them of the responsibilities of a failing trade. Of course, she knew better now. They were simply small men. It had all come too late for them: they were a little too old, a little too set in their ways; and they were timid.

So unwilling was she to provoke yet another argument with Samuel that she felt unable to ask the questions teeming in her mind. Where was the money, exactly, and how was it to be paid? If it were to be handed over to her brothers, she had little chance of laying hands on it or determining its use. And what form was it in? Was Barnabas right when he said it was in 'good sound coin'? Or might Richard have been so patriotic as to put his savings into worthless paper dollars? The extent to which she worried about these things, perched on her office stool, forced her finally to admit to herself that she did after all care very much to be an heiress. It occurred to her that John Fell, the lawyer, would know; and he would tell her, too.

Without letting herself think any further, she flung on her cloak and strode out of the office. By the time she reached the lawyer's door, she was regretting her haste. Perhaps she had been wrong to come? But the solemn little maidservant who let her in looked interested rather than surprised, and her old friend John, bursting into the hall with loud exclamations of pleasure, seemed almost to be expecting her. He seized her arm and carried her into his business room, shutting the door in the face of the little maid. Rebecca smiled as he landed her in a comfortable chair and sat himself down beside her.

'Well – Friend Rebecca! How are you finding your change of fortune? You are the talk of the town, as I'm sure you know.'

His directness was a relief. 'It's quite dreadful!' she replied. 'As if I had suddenly become public property.'

'As indeed you have.' He rolled his eyes comically. 'The intended property, at least, of every doting mother and hopeful son in Salem County – at least until you make one of them happy and dash the hopes of all the rest.'

'Don't speak of it! I feel like a heifer at market! But, John, am I really so rich? My brothers talk of two thousand dollars, which is a great fortune indeed, if it is secure, but is that the true estimate of the sum?'

He smiled and rose to his feet. 'You had ever a shrewd brain, Rebecca. And it is prudent to make sure for yourself where you stand.' He looked down at her, his dark brows drawn together. 'But have your brothers not told you all?'

Anxiety clenched her stomach so that she could not speak but stared at him, waiting.

The lawyer turned and walked to a tall oak cupboard. When he opened it, she could see that all the shelves were stuffed tight with papers and parchments, some old and yellow, the tape that tied them faded with age. The document he laid on the table was new, the seal and ribbon still bright. The will. It was in Richard's own neat lawyer's hand; somehow, she had not expected that, and felt the unexpected sting of tears at the sight of the familiar writing.

John smoothed the sheet flat, and his eyes moved across it. 'You know that our friend left his house and garden, and all his household goods and chattels, to his housekeeper, Tabitha Gates?'

'Yes, I was glad. It was like him, was it not?'

He looked up. 'He was a good man. The world is poorer for his passing.' His finger continued tracing the lines of the will, then stopped. 'Here we are. *To my Friend Rebecca Judith Wiston, daughter of Alistair Wiston merchant of Salem, for her sole use, at her Discretion and no other's, I bequeath all the residue of my Estate, namely five hundred English guineas in gold coin of that realm.* That is, as you say, about two thousand American dollars at the present rate. However, without being unpatriotic, I would say it was in a safer shape than dollars. Would you not agree?'

But Rebecca stared at him, stunned. *For her sole use... at her discretion and no other's...* Richard had known how it would be. And still her brothers had not told her. Fury pushed her to her feet, as if she must confront them now, while anger made her brave.

John Fell looked up, surprised. 'Rebecca? There is one thing more, friend. Pray sit; it will not take long.'

She sat, only half attentive as his finger moved again over the dark, even strokes of Richard's writing.

'*And also all those messuages or tenements known as Farley's Rents, together with the gardens, yards and orchards adjacent thereto, situate at Madeley in the County of Salop in England.*' He looked up. 'A slightly more tricky prospect, given the current situation. You may have to send someone to London to make sure of the property. But the rents – or the profit from selling them, wisely invested – will be an income worth having.' He smiled. 'I should congratulate you on your good fortune, friend.'

3

Rebecca Judith Wiston allowed herself the luxury of anger. How *dare* they? she repeated to herself. She would not, could not tolerate it. She was a grown woman, twenty-eight years old and her own mistress. Striding home through the wintry streets, she ranted inwardly at Samuel and Barnabas, plotted fine phrases and heroic resistance. But when she reached home, her face numb with cold and her skirts soaked to the knee, she found only Dorcas sewing quietly by the parlour fire, and her brothers gone out on Friends' business. So she was forced to swallow her anger and to bide her time. It would not be long until Barnabas raised the subject again. Even more than their elder brother, he was convinced that Richard's legacy was the hand of Providence saving them from their debts. Two thousand dollars? Enough to put all right! Rebecca set her teeth at the picture of him fluttering his soft white hands. But when the moment did come, only two days later, it was Samuel who precipitated the row.

It began at the Meeting House. The Wistons were prominent members of the Society of Friends in Salem. Their father, though born into a very different church, had become a Quaker soon after he met their mother. That was long ago, in England, before they and Richard Farley took ship together to make a new life in the colonies. Richard's tales had made Rebecca understand that religion was a more challenging matter in those days, to which they had all borne daily witness. Her mother's strict and simple faith, her father's honest dealings and Richard's restless questing after truth had all shaped her own fiercely held personal beliefs. It was a recurring test of her humility that her brothers seemed to have imbibed only the outward habits of piety.

The household were regular attenders at First Day Meeting, but it was all too clear to Rebecca that Samuel and Barnabas, circulating affably as the meeting dispersed, were there as an extension of their business activities. She was not sure what went on in Dorcas' head; sometimes she thought that sitting quietly at Meeting was the only way God could find to give her sister-in-law an hour's rest when she was not at the beck and call of others. But for that blessed time of silence Rebecca herself sought to set aside such judgements, to tame her fretfulness, and to school herself to patience for the trials of the week to come. She had never, like some of the women there, felt moved to speak in the meeting; she listened, and thought her own thoughts, and promised herself she would try harder to be good, by which she meant contented with her lot. This particular week, the third First Day since the will was read, she prayed a new prayer, for guidance over the vexatious matter of the money, and wisdom to act rightly in it; but she rose from her seat as angry and confused as before.

As they joined the departing crowd, she was aware yet again of her new visibility. People smiled and nodded at her; they made some excuse to say a word. As she talked to one friend after another, she was aware of Abraham Brewer's eyes on her. He was heading her way. She took a firm hold of Dorcas's arm, urging her towards the door. They made their escape, but without the men; and Rebecca saw the chandler change tack, to engage her brothers in earnest conversation.

Dorcas said nothing of the little scene, and they hurried home. They sat a few moments in the parlour while Matty, their maid, laid the table. Eventually their brothers arrived, and they went in to eat. Dinner was always cold on Meeting days. It was usually a silent meal, and today Rebecca was so wrapped in her own thoughts that she noticed nothing amiss until the family rose from table. Then Samuel turned to her.

'Sister.' He turned his back importantly to the empty grate, coughed again, and announced, 'Rebecca, I have joyful news.'

She blinked – joy was nowhere apparent in his manner – and waited warily for him to proceed.

Samuel walked to the window and looked out at the cold street. He spoke to the frosty glass. 'You need to know, Rebecca, that our good Friend Abraham Brewer has approached me… that is to say, he has done us the honour…' He turned to face her. 'To put no finer point on it, sister, he has asked for your hand. May the Lord be praised who watches over his faithful servants.' He took two steps, sank into a chair and allowed his features to break into a satisfied smile.

The sickening lurch of panic which gripped Rebecca at the idea of belonging to such a man as Abraham Brewer was quickly replaced by fury. For a full minute she struggled to compose herself, while her brother looked on, apparently well pleased with what he must have mistaken for maidenly confusion.

Finally, she said coldly, 'I hope you told him at once that it was out of the question?'

He stared, then reddened. 'No false modesty, Miss! He knows as well as we do that you cannot have expected such a good offer, and at your age can hardly afford to be nice about your choice. And as you would no doubt hasten to point out yourself, it will be the saving of the business.' He rubbed his hands. 'Accept my congratulations, sister. I will send to Friend Abraham straight away, and you can agree with him this very afternoon.'

'*I will do nothing of the kind!*' She had not meant to shout; but her words came out louder than she intended and surprised them both. 'I will not accept his offer, and you will do no such thing, brother. If you think it best, I will write to him and say so myself.'

Now he saw she was in earnest, it was Samuel's turn to raise his voice, in a tone of some bewilderment. 'Don't be a fool! Do you mean to ruin us? Have you forgotten what we owe him? What he could do to us if you displease him? Do you want to ruin us all?'

'What we *owe* him?' said Rebecca furiously. 'Do you intend then, brother, to sell me, in order to clear our debts? Is Abraham Brewer the highest bidder? Perhaps you should put me to market, and see if you can make a better speculation?'

Her brother's flush deepened to a dull brick red; he took a hastily cut-off step towards her before he swallowed and calmed. She clearly saw the conviction of his own power reassert itself behind his eyes as he spoke more gently. 'I see that you are distressed by the suddenness of all this. It is not surprising in a young woman of modest sensibility. Go and talk to your sister Dorcas, and when you are more composed we will talk again.'

Rebecca stood still. She spoke clearly and slowly. 'Samuel, I will not marry Abraham Brewer, either to please him or to mend your debts. Listen to me, for I mean this from my heart. I beseech you never to mention the matter to me again.'

With great care she opened the door of the library and went out into the hall. Then she turned back. He was still standing, gaping, on the rug before the empty fireplace. 'You should know, Brother, that I called upon John Fell on Wednesday last, and I read Cousin Richard's will – including those words which you had not seen fit to share with me. The money is, as I now understand, entirely at my own disposal. And dispose of it I will.'

Having delivered the line just as she had rehearsed it, she climbed the stairs to the top of the house, went into the small white-painted room where she slept, and shut and locked the door behind her. She was shaking, whether from fear or anger she could not tell. She lay on her bed and stared at the ceiling. After a few minutes, she heard the front door slam.

A kind of strangled suspense settled upon the whole household. Samuel came home, Rebecca went downstairs, they drank tea; they retired. Three days passed, with scarcely as many words spoken. The cheerful droppers-in continued to call at the counting-house; Barnabas feared he had caught a chill, and retired to his room; Dorcas fluttered apologetically round Rebecca trying to find courage to speak, until Rebecca thought she would be driven mad. She fled to her desk.

She began to read the shipping news with a new eye, and she pondered the market reports; she decided she must find means to speak to Simon Forrester, who was fitting a small venture for the China seas. It was exciting to be able at last to make such plans; but she must begin prudently, with a small cargo of tested commodities for that market; she knew several men who might gather it for her, on commission. She began to plan, putting the uneasy silence in the house out of her mind. She was devouring the new *Intelligencer*, when a boy ran in with a note for Samuel. She scarcely looked up; she heard him send the child away, and clear his throat. She kept her eyes on the newspaper, and he rose to take his letter upstairs. She had forgotten him when she heard his voice suddenly speak her name from the doorway.

His face was flushed. He clutched the letter open in his hand and held it out wordlessly towards her.

'What is it? Is somebody ill?' she asked, rising.

'Indeed, you may say so. Very ill. He writes – perhaps now you will see...' Alarmingly, he choked and coughed, and the letter dropped from his hand.

Rebecca rushed to his side, but he shook her off and picked up the fallen page. He thrust it into her hand. 'Look! Read! You have ruined us with your selfishness,' he said. 'Abraham Brewer has called in the mortgage.'

As she lay in bed that night, the knowledge of what she had to do pressed down on her like a great stifling weight. At last she rose and knelt, wrestling with her conscience; but she was scarcely submitting to the Lord's will – rather, struggling to find another way. In her heart she knew there was none. When light began to seep into the room she rose, rubbing hands and feet back to painful life, and opened the little writing desk that stood on her toilet table. First, she wrote to John Fell, instructing him that Richard's money should be used to discharge in full the debt to Abraham Brewer. Then, because she wanted no more argument or shouting, and because she felt too bitter and disappointed to speak to him about it, she wrote to Samuel. There were two things she needed him to know. One was that she had cleared the mortgage. The other was that she had decided, with the handful of dollars that remained of her money, to take ship for England.

4

On a March day of rare fine weather, Rebecca stood on the shore and looked towards England. The three-thousand-mile-wide chest of the monster Atlantic rose and fell, breathing calmly. Rebecca breathed harder, trying to imagine the land of her odd inheritance. She had only the haziest picture of the Old Country. The stories she had heard as a child had left her with a confused impression that it was green and beautiful, but also full of mines, forges and foundries for making iron pots. She put a hand to the neck of her gown and drew out the locket Richard had given her, the only thing she owned that had come from England.

It was old: the heavy gold case was elaborately figured, the chain fine but strong. She sprang the catch open, and the young woman inside gazed out at her: a pale face framed by dark ringlets, an old-fashioned brocade gown cut low and edged around with points of fine French lace. Aunt Isabella, painted when she was very young, before war and politics fractured the family in England and left Rebecca's father and his only sister on opposite sides of the world. Rebecca had supposed that the locket must originally have belonged to her father; but perhaps it had always been Richard's? There had been a kind of wistfulness in Richard's voice when he talked about Isabella that had made Rebecca wonder if her beautiful aunt had been his reason for leaving England. Whatever the truth of it, it was all in the past now, and all the people in the story were dead. Richard had been as old as the century, nearing ninety when he died, an extraordinary age. The lovely girl in the portrait had grown old too, and died long ago. Rebecca stared for a moment into the dark brown eyes before she clasped the locket shut.

She wondered idly, as she tucked it away, whether English women still dressed in brocade and lace. She had no idea, though people in Salem said the English were both rich and haughty. As for London, Rebecca had a vague but forbidding notion of street upon street of tall dark houses, all alike. She shivered. But she would go there, all the same, and perhaps to 'Madeley in the county of Salop,' too – wherever that was – if it proved necessary. John Fell had tried to tell her that it could all be done by proxy, the inheritance claimed, the houses sold, all brought home in ready money; but even he had not looked quite convinced, and she knew that whatever the truth of it, she wanted to go.

It had proved remarkably easy to arrange, she thought. Few ships went from Salem to the port of London or to Bristol these days, what with the tariffs and the tolls and the frozen post-war British faces; but the *Valiant* was bound for Liverpool, with a cargo of furs and room for a handful of paying passengers. It would sail soon – as soon as spring smoothed out the ocean. Rebecca found herself anxiously scanning the sky every morning, and walking out to see what was stirring whenever the temperature rose. It would not be long now, she was sure. Most of her packing was done already. Her two best gowns and a good supply of petticoats and linen lay folded into a stout trunk that had been her father's, just right for a sea voyage; her warmest clothes were mended and ready for the long weeks at sea.

By good fortune, a respectable neighbour and Friend, Isaiah Salcombe, would be travelling with her. He was a follower of that staunch abolitionist John Woolman, and had resolved to speak on the situation of slaves at London Yearly Meeting, as Woolman had done before him. So Rebecca could travel with Friend Salcombe and his wife, which silenced at least some of her brothers' objections. Her passage would take a good bite out of the remaining ready money, but with prudence there would be enough for her to seek out the lawyers, deal with her business, and claim her remaining inheritance. And then she would be rich once more. She smiled a little ruefully – riches had not so far proved to be too pleasant. Maybe next time she would make a better hand of it. A mouthful of wind pushed at the side of her hat, and she turned to walk back to the office, bracing herself for the looks of suffering reproach which were now her daily cross.

But today as she opened the street door Barnabas looked up from his desk with a smirk. 'Ah – Rebecca.'

Her heart turned over at his gloating tone.

'You have had a visitor. No,' as she moved towards the parlour, 'no, he could not wait. It was Friend Salcombe. He came to tell you that *Valiant* is not now to sail until the summer.'

Rebecca froze in the act of taking off her hat. Let it not be true, she thought desperately. I must go, I must! He *must* be wrong.

Ignoring his sister's expression of shock, Barnabas continued, 'Whittier has sold on some of his furs, and needs to wait on the trappers for more. He's a careful merchant, of course; he will not buy less than the best. He may not be suited with goods for the British market again for many months.'

There was no mistaking his satisfaction. Rebecca felt her attempt at a smile pull tightly at her cheeks as she turned to go into the house. 'In that case, brother,' she said, 'I must make other arrangements.' She went into the hall, slamming the door behind her.

This time it was less easy. After three weeks haunting the shipping offices, and calling in vain upon all the Friends to hear of travellers from anywhere along the coast who were bound for England, she was almost in despair. Life at home had become unbearable, yet she feared that the longer she waited the more likely she was to succumb to the pressure to stay.

She had taken to calling regularly on Tabitha, whose friendship was a comfort after the frozen disapproval at home. She was sitting one afternoon at the big table in Richard's kitchen, where already the touches of Tabitha's new trade showed up in hampers of vegetables, a great soup vat on the stove, and more washing-up than one elderly bachelor had made in the space of a week. Tabitha finished boiling a basketful of lobster, poured coffee for them both and eased herself into a chair across from Rebecca. She blew steam from her cup, then asked, 'You have any idea, friend, where Jamaica is?'

'Yes,' said Rebecca, 'it's about two weeks south of here. It's an island. Hot. Why?'

''Cause you could go there, next Tuesday.'

'*What?*'

Tabitha smiled widely, pleased with her surprise. 'You see that worm-eaten old tub in the little harbour? Loading cask-staves – been there two, three weeks? Gentleman in my front room says she's bound for Jamaica. Casks for sugar plantations.' Tabitha's face said all she needed to say about sugar plantations, but she went on, 'She's Captain Singleton's vessel, him who married Betsy Roper, you recall? And I just heard Mr and Miz Roper is sailing with him this time, to go see their daughter in Kingston and her new little one.'

Rebecca's mind's eye scanned the charts on the counting-house wall. Jamaica was a short winter voyage south on the prevailing wind. Why had she not thought of it? 'Thank you, Tabitha,' she said. 'Thank you very much! Jamaica is still a colony. There will be no end of ships crossing to England from there.'

Tabitha embraced her as she left, and held her a little tighter than usual. Rebecca was aware of her old friend's struggle. She would miss Tabitha too; but she did want, very much, to go.

5

A fierce squall shook Lotta awake. The wind screamed like
a horse in heat; the roof shingles rattled under its hooves.
She wriggled across the bed and squinted through the slats of the
shutter. Mother of God, barely first light! And she had not got
rid of the man until two or three. She groaned and pulled the
bedcover over her head.

But the sea crashed so loudly below her window that there
was no chance of more sleep. She called out groggily to Maria,
then remembered that her sister had gone home to tend their
mama. She pushed the thin stuff of the bedcover into her ears, but
the wind joined in the racket; and soon she realised there were
other noises, too. She rolled out of bed and opened the shutter
cautiously, holding tight against the snatching gusts, blinking
to make her eyes work. Sure enough, in the green light of the
false dawn, there was a craft banging murderously upon the reef,
losing spars and, even as she looked, heaving its keel upwards.
She reached for her dress, pulling it on as she ran.

Lotta's house was the first off the cliff steps; no one reached
the back beach before her, but Franco and his donkey were soon
at her heels. The wet sand under their feet had been swept clean
of its usual filth by the strength of the outgoing tide; and, sure
enough, huge waves were already dumping the shattered ship
ashore. Broken spars, sodden lumps of sailcloth and all the other
rubbish of a wreck were already flung along the beach. Lotta
leaned into the wind, heading for a wooden chest that was driven
into the sand by its edge. Skirting a spouting rock, she found
the first body, face down in a new-formed pool tinged pink. She

heaved him over. His head was a mush of bone and brains, and she could tell nothing about his face. Crossing herself, she turned away. She did not need to rob the dead, though of course there would be those who would.

She reached the chest. A good, strong box and still shut, even though it was not roped together. It was either locked or stuck. With a quick thanks to San Antonio, who looks after things that are lost, Lotta called out to Franco. He rose from his knees beside the corpse, where she hoped he had been praying, and helped her pull the box out and rope it onto the beast. Lotta picked her way over a clutter of new white planks. Someone with a cart could fire a baker's oven all next year. She shrugged. And then she saw the boy.

He lay awkwardly on his front, one white arm thrown forward, long legs splayed, his bloody shirt rucked up to show their full extent. His pigtail had come free so that his long pale hair clung to his face and fanned across his bare shoulder; a golden chain gleamed through it at his neck. He lay as if asleep; but of course, he must be dead. He was handsome, in a stern northern way that Lotta had seen before: strong brow, high straight nose, a perfect mouth, smooth cheek. No sign of a beard, though he must be taller than she was herself. She reached out to touch – and he was warm. Urgently, she tipped him onto his back, pulling the ripped shirt away, and put her cheek to his throat to feel for a pulse. There were two surprises: he was alive; and he was a girl.

It was bright day by the time they got the limp body up to the house, and the storm was wearing itself out. Lotta could not tell how badly hurt the stranger was, nor whether the donkey's slow, jolting climb might make the harm much worse. But there was no leaving that beautiful body on the beach, and now the girl was lying in Maria's bed, deathly pale but still alive. Lotta bent her head and listened to the low breathing. She put her fingers in the mouth. No blood. Holy Mary be praised, then, the broken ribs – there must be broken ribs – had not pierced the lung. There was nothing more Lotta could do, except wait. So after she had taken the gold locket and put it into her dress for safekeeping, she placed a bucket by the bed in case the stranger woke and then, leaving the shutters closed against the sun, went out to buy food just as if it was an ordinary day. But all the time she was at the market, she thought about the stranger with the beautiful pale face, lying in her sister's bed.

When she returned, the young woman was still unconscious, her breathing shallow but regular. American, they had said in the town – a merchantman out of Salem (wherever that was) bound for Jamaica and lost with all hands. Lotta didn't intend to lose this one, however. She touched the pale face. It would not hurt to wash away the blood, and perhaps then she would be able to see how bad the wounds were. She fetched water and a sponge, and gently wiped the girl's cheek, combing back the fine, light hair with her fingers. Then, very carefully, she pulled off the stained shift and began to wash away the blood and dirt. The cuts that had made all this blood were not, after all, too deep; the worst hurt was the purple bruising all along the left side, and almost certainly there were broken ribs there, as she had thought. But perhaps not too bad. She smiled and continued her work. It was a grown woman's body, she realised, not a young girl's as she had supposed from its thinness. She could not tell how old: no childish roundness in the face or neck, but no sign of childbearing either – the small breasts and flat belly were firm and unstretched. Lotta could see why she had mistaken this long, straight-limbed body for a boy's. She smiled. The bodies she knew best were men's, but she took pleasure in women, too. She bent and kissed the lips of the boy-girl from the sea, then covered her tenderly with the bright cotton coverlet.

It was fortunate that Maria was gone to look after their mama, for it meant there was a room for this stranger and Lotta did not have to put off the men who came. She had found nothing on the beach worth selling, taken up as she was with her rescue and with the sea chest – and that she was saving for later. So her little curio shop by the harbour stayed closed, and she would be relying upon her other income, from the sailors. There were two that afternoon, and it was not until the second one had gone that she went again to look at her American, and found her awake.

The young woman did little that day but doze and mutter – in English, of which Lotta knew almost nothing – but the next day, when she could sit up and eat a little, they began the difficult work of trying to talk. It was hard indeed, when they had so little language between them. Lotta had lived in Havana since she was a tiny girl; Spanish and the local patois both came as easily to her as her native French. Beyond that she knew a few curses and the words for what men wanted, in a dozen languages including English, but none of it was useful now. This woman, like the few other Americans Lotta had come across, understood no language but her own.

So Lotta simply talked all the time, in her own mixture of Spanish and French, with dumbshow to help explain her meaning. This worked quite well when she wanted to find out where the woman had pain, or whether she felt hot or cold, or needed the chamber pot, or if she was hungry or thirsty. On the second morning, Lotta tried to ask her guest's name, pointing to herself, saying 'Lotta!' then tapping her friend's chest.

For a moment the American woman looked so blank that Lotta was worried she might have lost her memory in the wreck. But then she looked straight at Lotta and said firmly, 'Judith.' At which, to Lotta's horror, the grey eyes filled with tears, and the tears spilled over and rolled down Judith's face, and she lay there not even trying to wipe them away.

And of course Lotta reached out and held her, kissing the wet face and holding it against her own, but that was wrong, too, for Judith reddened and flinched away, and pulled the thin sheet up under her arms as if she did not like to be looked at, let alone touched.

For the first few days Judith dozed or gazed blankly through the window at the hot blue sky, and seemed too weak, or stunned, to talk much. But as the days went by and she returned to herself, she began to talk much more, and grew distressed when she could not make herself understood. Lotta did understand, quite quickly, that the woman wanted to speak to the Governor. But he was dead of the yellow fever, like most white folks who came fresh from Europe. As this Judith would very soon be also, Lotta feared; but she could not tell her any of this. Slowly she made her understand that no others had come from the wreck alive, and that the seaman's box she and Franco had brought up from the beach was the only chest that had come ashore whole. She went and fetched the locket, and put it round Judith's neck, so she would know something of her own had been saved.

She smiled at that, and opened it, showing Lotta the beautiful old picture inside – which Lotta admired afresh, asking her guest whether the picture was her mother, or her grandmother, or some fine lady who had been patron of the family? She had such splendid jewels, such a haughty turn of the head, it was hard to imagine she belonged in the New World. Judith said something, urgently; but Lotta could not make it out. She finally got her guest to understand that the locket was all that had survived the shipwreck. Then Judith gazed out of the window for a long time without speaking, as if she thought, or prayed. When she turned back, she looked so lonely that Lotta took her in her arms and this time she did not resist, laying her head on Lotta's breasts like a child. This time she did not cry.

So, what with cooking and washing and bandages, and trying to learn English words and teach Judith Spanish ones, Lotta did not find much time for her clients. Sometimes men came banging on the door, and she shouted to them to go away and come back next week, she was busy; and they went off cursing her for a faithless whore, or laughed and said the man she had in there with her must be a fine one, to last so many days. Sometimes when Judith was asleep, Lotta had time for one of her regular clients, so there was at least money for food.

She wondered what food they ate in the north, in New England. Judith clearly did not recognise most of the things that Lotta put in front of her, poking at her plate uncertainly, as if the food would burn her. After a while, though, she ate more heartily and Lotta, who prided herself on her cooking, took trouble to make tasty dishes to tempt her. In particular, Judith had clearly never seen a tomato before, and looked quite shocked the first time she was asked to put one in her mouth, but soon she got quite a taste for them, watching hungrily from her window as Lotta tended the vines in the yard where the big red and green fruit grew. She only tried once to help, but bending made her cry out with pain. Lotta tried to comfort her, counting on her fingers the weeks that would mend the broken ribs, and then pretending to be Judith marching about with a watering pot for the tomatoes. It made her new friend laugh, though whether she understood the meaning of it was hard to tell. Judith was always very brave about the pain, and made Lotta strap the bandages tightly so she could be up and moving round the house. The weather was hot, and no one could see her, so she did not need more than her shift and sometimes, at night, a shawl. But the problem of her clothes – and indeed all her other lost possessions – would have to be faced soon.

6

The days passed and Judith mended quickly. She moved more easily and smiled more often; her fair skin flushed gold in the sun. They did not talk much – at least, Judith did not. Lotta told her every thought that came into her head, but it did not matter, since she could not understand. Sometimes, though, Lotta felt they were very aware of each other, moving carefully, alert, like two stranger cats in the same room. She would catch Judith's eyes on her and preen a little to show she knew she was being watched, and Judith would look down – but not for long. They drank wine, ate and slept and laughed, tidied the house, sat on the terrace; and all the while Judith's body mended and Lotta fell more in love with it, and with her.

Lotta began to dread the moment when her friend would be well, would go away. But she also knew that she would soon run out of money. She had few hours now to give to the clients, and was worried Judith would say something about them. But most of all, as she grew more and more fond of her handsome new friend, she was more and more afraid about the yellow fever. Few incomers lasted much more than a month in Cuba before they succumbed to the shakes and the vile black vomiting; you had to have been born here to have much chance of surviving, or at least to have had the fever as a child. Lotta remembered her dose well, soon after she arrived from France with her parents, when she was seven, and they had set up their little shop. The fever had killed her father; her mother had survived. Mama had always been a strong woman, and was today, even now she was old. Her fall last month and the broken leg had still not killed her. Lotta wondered briefly how Mama and Maria were getting on, out in the country. Perhaps Maria would have to stay there for good now. Then Judith would not have to go away, but live here always and they would be lovers. She smiled wistfully, knowing it for the dream it was; Judith must go, before the fever came. So Lotta pushed aside a pleasing picture of kissing Judith, very slowly, all over, and started to look around for an answer to her problem.

It came much sooner than she cared for. They had only had two weeks together after Judith began to move about, when the *Belle Héloïse* was sighted beyond the harbour bar. The cannon boomed out, and people began to flow down to the harbour to see her come in. A French ship meant old friends as well as customers. Lotta oiled her hair, put on her red dress and went downtown. She took her keys, and checked the shop was secure and all was well there, before she joined the expectant crowd of traders, rooming-house keepers and whores on the quayside. The ship was only a few days out of San Domingue, they said, on the voyage home to France, and had stopped to add good Cuban tobacco to its cargo. That done, and more water and fresh fruit taken on board, it would sail again in a few days.

She was in luck. The *Héloïse* carried many of the same crew as the last time it had put in at Havana, and she found a dozen old friends at their accustomed inn. The night was a profitable one. She bought a bargain walrus tusk, with neat pictures of harpooning, from a sailor who'd gambled away his advance pay already. Even more usefully, talking to old acquaintances gave her an idea about what she could do for Judith. She went home in the early morning feeling hopeful. Over the next few days she did brisk home business. She knew Judith did not like it when the men came. But Judith would soon be gone; and next week there was the rent to pay. She sighed. Her new friend would have to go. But not before she had taught her some useful things. Lotta smiled to herself.

The next afternoon, she looked out and saw what she had been waiting for: a brown-skinned man with a great belly and blue tattoos on his forearms, sweating up the steps from the beach. Armand. She ran out, smiling and waving. She had known him since she first started working here, when she was scarcely more than a pretty child and he a thin, lonely young man far from home. Now he was fat and bald and had friends everywhere. For the last three years he had been ship's cook on board the *Belle Héloïse,* but still he never failed to come to visit whenever they were in port.

'Armand! You are welcome, *cheri,* as always,' she told him, and took his arm to lead him indoors. 'Now I will do something nice for you. And then, *mon vieux,* you will do a little something for me.'

He laughed and pulled her close. '*Bien sûr* I will do that,' he said.

In the end, he did agree to what she asked. Judith, not surprisingly, took longer to convince. But, as Lotta pointed out, she had no money, and no way of earning any. There was clearly no point in Lotta offering to take her into the trade, and there was no honest work here for a woman who had neither French nor Spanish. Judith had no friends – except Lotta – and no clothes. And soon she would take the yellow fever, and then she would die.

Judith agreed, with whitening face, to each elaborately acted-out argument. And finally Lotta, triumphant, produced the things she had found in the seaman's chest. Shirt, breeches, waistcoat, all washed and aired and mended; knife, tinderbox, tobacco box. Then she told Judith, with much miming of pot-stirring, tasting, swaying on her feet and looking out to sea, about Armand, and about their plan. Judith was outraged, incredulous, scandalised. If there had been any other possibility at all, she would never have agreed. But what choice did she have? So finally she calmed down, and let Lotta help her to put the clothes on.

Lotta, who had helped numberless men get in and out of their breeches, was an expert. She showed Judith how to wrap the long tails of her shirt between her legs, as men did to protect their soft parts. In a moment of inspiration, she took the ends of the shirt-tails and twisted then into a knot in front. When Judith had pulled on the breeks and buttoned them up, the effect was truly impressive. Lotta laughed out loud, and Judith blushed.

When Judith was completely dressed, her hair bound into a sailor's pigtail and a red handkerchief knotted at her throat, Lotta fetched the piece of looking-glass from the bedroom and Judith looked at herself. She did this for several minutes, frowning and holding the glass at different angles. Then she put it down slowly and, with a wistful little smile, lifted a pretend spy-glass to her eye and gazed out to sea. Then she turned back to Lotta and gave a little bow.

'*Buenas noches, Señora,*' she said. 'My name is Jude.'

Lotta, surprised, put out her hand, and her friend grasped it formally, raising it to her lips, as she had seen a French sailor do.

Lotta giggled.

So they had two days to alter the clothes to fit, and to teach Jude to be a boy. She swaggered up and down the little yard, or sat astride her chair, or lounged against a wall, while Lotta looked judiciously on and told her what to do differently. Judith's stiff shyness had vanished. In her new clothes, she was not *playing* the boy: quickly, quickly she became one. Her chin tilted up, and her eyes flashed; she laughed; she filled the room. Lotta was more than delighted, indeed overwhelmed. The second evening, they went out and walked in the street, with Lotta holding her new client's arm, and no one looked at them twice.

That night Lotta said, 'One more lesson only.' And she pulled Judith's face down to hers and kissed her. Then she led her into her own room, where the big bed was.

Judith sat down warily on the edge of the bed. She looked like any awkward boy sent by his shipmates to learn the first lesson of manhood. Lotta had taught that lesson to more lads than she could remember – though none quite like this one. The boy that Judith had become sat with legs apart, elbows resting on his knees, and looked at Lotta with a questioning frown.

For reply, Lotta smiled again and began to unlace her gown. The moon shone through the narrow window onto her as she slipped off her bodice and stepped out of her petticoats. Except on Sundays, when she went to mass, she did not bother with stays; in the humid night her shift clung damply to her skin.

Judith said nothing. But neither, Lotta noted, did she make any attempt to leave. And she had not taken her eyes from Lotta for the space of a single heartbeat. Still smiling reassuringly, Lotta went to stand before her. 'You are ready for this, my fine fellow, I think?' She stroked Judith's face and tugged gently at the red handkerchief.

Judith unknotted it.

'That's right! And now –' Lotta slipped her own hands down, swiftly unbuttoning to the waist, and caught at Judith's retreating fists, guiding them to her own shoulders. The shift slipped easily away. 'Good!' she leant forward and kissed Judith on the lips, gently parting the shirt; then she sat back on her heels, considering. 'The broken ribs are better, aren't they? And you don't need the bandages in bed, anyway…' Quickly she unwrapped them, and pushed Judith gently back on to the bed, stroking her face.

'No need to fear, little one,' she said. 'I expect you are thinking, "What have I got, to satisfy a woman? They will soon find me out – and Lotta, she knows already!" But I will tell you something about men.' She knew that Judith didn't understand what she was saying, but that a gentle voice would calm and soothe her. Still talking, Lotta unlaced the borrowed breeches. 'There are many men who have not much more equipment than you,' she confided, pushing away Judith's feebly protesting hands, then slipping her own hands under her and pulling the breeches away, down, off.

Judith lay there, naked and startled. Lotta felt a great surge of affection – and something more. She shook her head. 'It's true, though, what I tell you. I have known men with such little ones, they are hidden in their hair. But it doesn't matter!' She leaned down, whispering in her friend's uncomprehending ear. 'They are good lovers, all the same. Some of the best! Because everyone' – she sat up, and swung herself astride Judith's thighs, holding up her hands – 'everyone has a mouth, yes? And fingers? You shall see.' She was stroking Judith's sides and belly now, kneeling over her, her nipples trailing across Judith's face.

Judith made a small noise, turning her head into the pillows, trying ineffectually to fold up, away from the touch of hands, breasts, passion. Then her head fell back, and she looked into Lotta's eyes. She reached up and pulled Lotta down.

After the first shock of surprise, Lotta began to laugh. She had judged this Judith to be quite innocent of the body's pleasures – but clearly, she had been wrong! And she quickly guessed that Judith had shared those pleasures with a woman. And after that it ceased to matter whether they spoke English, Spanish or French, as Lotta, with great care and thoroughness, showed Judith new ways in which her body could be loved. Judith's laughter turned to ragged gasps, then whimpers, and finally swelled into a shout of joyful release.

For a while they lay gazing foolishly at each other, pleased with themselves. Then Lotta drew Judith's hand towards her, as if to say, now show me what you have learned. And Judith smiled, and repeated her lesson perfectly, like a good student, until Lotta in her turn cried out with a pleasure she had more often pretended than known.

All this while, the pale light from the window moved steadily across the tangle of their bodies on the bed, until the moon went down over the headland beyond the harbour. In the darkness before dawn, they kissed for the last time, and fell asleep. And when the sun rose out of the sea, Lotta's newest lover got up, put on her breeches, picked up her bundle, and was gone.

7

Annette's chamber was at the top of one of the towers flanking the entrance to the château. From the window, she could see across the courtyard to the chapel and the stables, and beyond them to the wide plain where the river flowed in slow curves between the vineyards. All the land she could see belonged to her father, and all of it was planted with vines. The gnarled black stems stood row on row, like black characters on a whitey-brown page, telling the story of her family's wealth and her own inheritance.

Below her, the château was already awake and busy. A woman crossed the cobbles slowly with two pails on a yoke; a girl scattered crumbs for a flurry of doves and a screw-necked peacock. Annette watched as a young man emerged from the stable block, his hair straw-gold in the morning sun. It was a moment before she recognised Father Lamontaine, the chaplain. Pierre. She stared. His hair was beautiful. She had hardly ever seen him without his neat little clerical wig. She watched as he set his slender shoulders and started off towards the chapel. He would say his morning Office while waiting for her father. Annette suppressed a sigh at the thought of her stern and so predictable papa. Philippe Lavigne-Brillac was a devout man; he would not breakfast before he had heard mass. But neither would he hear mass until he had taken his morning ride.

A groom came out from the stable – slight, very young, in high boots of which he seemed rather proud. Annette did not know him; he must be new. She must find out his name and something about him, so that she could show a kindly interest if she had cause to speak to him. The lad was listening, head cocked; and, sure enough, there was her father on his big chestnut stallion, breaking out of the oak wood at the bend of the road, two hounds trotting at his side. He entered the yard and the boy ran to his stirrup, tugging his forelock and averting his eyes in the proper manner, reaching up for the bridle. But of course, her father ignored him. He jerked Hector's head aside so sharply that the stallion reared and the boy almost fell in his anxiety to get clear. He followed his master at a safe distance until Monseigneur deigned to drop the bridle, then dived for it and missed. Annette did not hear what her father said as he dismounted, but the cut across the face with his crop spoke clearly enough. The boy stood like a statue, holding the horse, until his master disappeared into the house.

There was the noise of wooden shoes on the stairs. Annette turned from the window and climbed quickly back into bed, drawing the heavy brocaded hangings close. It was Jacqueline's job to wake her mistress, and she took it as a personal failing if Annette was up before she arrived. Annette dived across the wide mattress and snuggled back into the warm hollow in the feather bed. Soon the door creaked open and she heard the click of pattens on bare oak boards. There was the rattle of the tray being put down, then the ring of the fire-irons and the wheeze of the bellows as Jacqueline blew life into the embers of last night's fire. The routine never varied. Sometimes Annette longed for her to drop the fire tongs or knock over the chocolate pot, just for the sake of variety.

At last the bed hangings were twitched aside and the maid's pale face appeared, almost on a level with Annette's own, since the bed was high and Jacqueline rather short.

'Bonjour, Mademoiselle! You are awake?'

'Bonjour, Jacqueline. All's well?'

'Very well, Mademoiselle, thank you. It is a fine day. The sun is shining. You are ready for your chocolate?'

'Thank you, I am.' Annette propped herself up on her pillows and took the tall porcelain cup with its delicate pattern of flowers. While she sipped, Jacqueline fastened back the bed curtains and laid out her mistress's silk *robe de chambre* at the foot of the bed. Then, dropping a low curtsey which caused her almost to disappear from sight, she picked up the slop pail and departed to fetch hot water.

With a sigh, Annette contemplated her day. She would dearly have liked to ride out herself this morning; the brisk weather with its hint of spring to come called to her to be out of doors. But there would be visitors for dinner: relations, therefore boring as well as demanding. That would mean at least two hours' dressing; with her lessons and her daily devotions, and writing to her godmother in England, there would be no time left for riding. She hoped one of the boys would exercise Aurore; the little grey was frisky enough already and had not been ridden yesterday either. Annette sighed again. It promised to be a tedious day, apart from the hour she would spend this morning in her thrice-weekly lesson with the chaplain. The thought made her smile. Thank heaven for Father Lamontaine. Far more than tutor or confessor, he was her friend and ally, the only other person in the house anywhere near her own age, and the only one with whom she could have any conversation about things that mattered. She felt under her pillow for the book they were discussing: the *Social Contract* of Jean-Jacques Rousseau. She could not imagine exactly what her father would say or do if he knew his daughter was reading such revolutionary writing, but she certainly did not want to find out. She pushed the book back under the pillow as Jacqueline clattered in to help her rise and dress.

Madame Desmoulins, the aged lady-in-waiting who chaperoned Annette's lessons, was not, it must be said, very effective. Of course, no one seriously thought Mademoiselle Annette at all likely to commence an indiscretion with the wizened little creature who supervised her failure to play the harpsichord, nor the fierce old fop of a dancing master. Pierre Lamontaine was the only young man amongst her teachers, but he was a priest, and therefore above suspicion. So the old lady always sat at a discreet distance from her mistress and the confessor; after half an hour her needlework would slip to her lap and her head would drop forward. Even then, Annette and Pierre always spoke quietly, and laid several impeccable works of devotion beside them and opened a volume of sermons, while they discussed quite other texts.

They had reached the chapter about aristocracy.

'He is quite clear about it,' Pierre said. 'Hereditary aristocracy is the worst of all governments. And he praises democracy – though he says it is impossible to be truly achieved on earth.'

'*Were there a people of gods, their government would be democratic,*' Annette quoted wistfully. 'But yes, after that he says, *So perfect a government is not for men.*'

'Whereas he says that in a republic, the people raise the best and most capable to power. But he does not say *how* all this is to be changed.' The priest looked out of the window, across the park. He seemed restless – as he often did, Annette thought; as if his quiet, easy life in her father's house irked him somewhere, deep down.

'But what do *you* think, Pierre?' she asked. 'Would a republic really be the best form of government?'

He didn't answer. Annoying. She pushed on. 'The Americans have made a republic, have they not?'

She'd thought he would enjoy telling her that tale again, about the glorious defeat of the bloody British army, and the brave new American Constitution. But his eyes were far away, down the ride where the cold March wind whipped the still bare branches to and fro, and a crowd of black crows flapped in the tree-tops.

He turned to face her again. 'Do you actually *know* what is happening *here*, in France, at this very moment?' His voice caught in his throat, and he glanced briefly at Madame Desmoulins, before turning the intensity of his gaze back to Annette.

'Yes, of course I do,' she said.

He said nothing, but raised a questioning eyebrow.

She was flustered but determined. 'The King has called the *parlement* to meet. To discuss the financial crisis. And the failed harvest. And... and the Future of the Nation?' she managed.

'Yes. And how long has the *parlement* been meeting, so far, up there at Versailles?' he asked.

'Since last summer? We have talked about this before, haven't we?' she said, slightly bewildered.

'Indeed. And what have they done, so far? What has the King done, about *anything*?'

She shook her head, but he rushed on.

'Nothing. Worse than nothing! And meanwhile, the people, the Third Estate, as we still call them – *third*, third-rate, also-ran, the Third Estate – cannot even *speak* with the King, while he waits upon the grandees and the damned hypocrites of the Church.' He spat the words across the table, spattering the sermons laid out before them, 'And all this while, the people *starve*.'

'I don't understand!' she burst out. 'How can these politics, or this philosophy we are reading – how can any of it make any difference to a ruined harvest or a late spring? *That* is why the people go hungry, isn't it?'

He slumped back in his chair. There was a silence. 'No, of course philosophy will solve nothing,' he said at last, pushing the little book away from him. 'And of course, it is in no way the fault of our families and elders, of my papa, or your exalted relatives, that the common people *starve*.'

'Oh Pierre!' She was hurt by the bitterness of his tone. 'I didn't mean we should not take our responsibilities to the poor seriously. My aunt, the Abbess, might be a disgrace to her cloth – but Cousin Henri has some progressive ideas.'

Pierre looked straight at her again. 'Really?' he said, 'What are they?'

At least he was calming down, she thought. He was really very handsome when he was excited, but rather frightening, too.

'Henri thinks feudal dues should be abolished, and that the nobility should pay taxes like everyone else,' she said earnestly. 'He says that France must become an open and efficient society, if we are to thrive in the modern world of free trade and competition.'

Pierre bounced to his feet, as if unable to contain himself sitting at the library table. '*That*,' he whispered furiously, 'is exactly what is most dangerous to the cause of freedom! These aristocratic modernisers are the real enemy of the people! Much worse than the poor old traditionalists like your esteemed papa and mine. It is your cousin Henri's creed – efficiency, free trade, competition – that is the *real* danger to the poor man who has nothing.' He pounced back to the table and started to scrabble among the papers. The pile of sermons tottered dangerously, and they both grabbed at it.

'Sorry, sorry,' he hissed, sitting down with exaggerated gentleness. He smiled again, reaching across the table and patting her hand before he sat back and picked up a pen to make his points. 'Look. Let me lay it out for you. The Count your cousin proposes to give up the 'ancient privileges' of his rank – but he will keep all his lands, his houses, his dockyards, his ships, and all his rights! All the unfair advantages to himself, like the right to export the wine of this estate through the great port to rich markets in England, while the little man over the next hill has to sell his at home for next to nothing.'

'But Henri does want reform,' Anette argued. 'I have heard him tell Papa that there should be a free trade in bread, so that poor people can afford to eat.'

'Of course!' said Pierre scornfully. 'The poor man will be quiet then, and docile; because he will need less pay in order to eat. And who pays him? Cousin Henri and his like, *they* pay him, for his labour in the dock or at the loom or on the building site; so, the real benefit goes to them, the employers. They get grateful workers, stronger arms and longer hours for half the price! The poor man just labours on, with nothing to show but a cheaper loaf. Yet he still pays taxes – unlike the rich – and has no money to clothe his children.' He seized the volume of Rousseau and turned back to the beginning.

Annette reached out and put her hand on the page. 'I know, I know!' she said, 'You don't need to read it to me. *Man was born free, but everywhere he is in chains.*'

Pierre smiled then and held her hand for a moment. Just then the stable clock chimed faintly across the yard. He picked up *Meditations upon the Holy Spirit* and cocked his head towards Madame Desmoulins.

Annette smiled back. 'Yes,' she said, 'I'd better go and dress.'

They grinned like conspirators, and he banged the book down on the table, raising a cloud of leathery dust. Madame Desmoulins twitched, and woke in time to see Mademoiselle Annette bow her head gravely for the priest's farewell blessing.

More than two hours later, Annette picked her way down the winding stone stairs from her turret chamber. She held herself stiffly upright, both to balance the extravagant mass of her hair and because the bones of her best stays were less painful that way. She gazed ahead, feeling for the edge of each invisible step with the back of her foot.

Dressing Annette for a formal dinner was work for several people. Jacqueline was very strict about who should do what. Only she herself touched Mademoiselle's body, but she could not be said to be shy or respectful about it. Lacing body-length stays involved hauling with all her strength, with a foot in Annette's back, and she tucked and tugged and stroked at many layers of underclothes before she wrapped her charge in a silk *peignoir* for the attentions of the hairdresser. He came coughing up the stairs, white with the hair-powder ingrained in his clothes and skin, carrying the tools of his trade in a leather-clad box. It was her own choice, really, Annette told herself as he began his first slow combing-out of her long and heavy hair. She could simply have had it all pinned up and netted to take a ready-dressed wig. She had sometimes done that in the past, and her father liked to see it – he had been known to pay her one of his rare compliments at the sight of the fifteen-inch pile of identically formed white curls. But since Pierre had explained to her, some time last year, that the hair came from peasant girls forced by poverty to sell it in order to eat, she had felt justified in refusing to put up with the abominable thing, its scratchy heat and the way it drove the hairpins into her scalp. So today she submitted to the attentions of the *coiffeur* as he teased, coated and powdered her springing dark curls into a silvery cloud. The Queen herself was reported to be wearing her own hair, these days – though that was not an argument that would have weighed with Annette's father. He would have been less than pleased to think that his daughter copied the light-minded Marie-Antoinette, in this way or any other.

Once her hair was arranged, she could do even less for herself. A girl brought her newest satin slippers, whose stacked heels gave her backache in minutes. Jacqueline worked for half an hour on the gown, before they could send for the final touch – the family jewellery, which must be brought up from the vaults. One of the ways in which Annette was most definitely not allowed to emulate the Court was in the matter of face paint; so once the last bracelet was clasped in place, she was ready for family dinner.

She reached the foot of the stairs without tripping. Moving carefully by long practice, she managed to keep the pins in her tight silk bodice from pricking her too much as she paraded down the stone-flagged corridors to the *grande salle*. On either side, portraits of her ancestors leaned out from the walls. Generations of great-great-greats stared down their noses into the everlasting dimness of the corridor. They were mostly her father's relations, since his was the noble line; and they shared his hawk-like piercing eye. Annette always looked out for the picture of her paternal grandmother and namesake, which hung in the darkest corner by the turn to the kitchen stair. The first Annette had been painted when she was no older than her granddaughter was now. Her eyes were dark pools, her expression quite unlike the rest. She had been unlike them in other ways too: her story was quite a romance. She had married, against her family's wishes, a young man who had arrived in France in the court of the banished English king, James Stuart. Annette wasn't sure what had happened next, nor what had become of that gallant cavalier, but his young wife had died in childbed, and her baby son – Annette's own father – had been swiftly returned to Brillac, to the safety of her good Catholic family.

As Annette approached the end of the long corridor, two footmen in their best deep-blue livery appeared to open the double doors of the *grande salle*. Usually there was only old Anton, but her father was always on his mettle when Cousin Henri paid him a visit. She entered the room, and became the focus of three more pairs of Lavigne eyes. Her father and his two visitors, standing by the tall windows a dozen yards away, stopped talking and watched her walk the length of the carpet towards them. It felt like an eternity before she was near enough to sink in her finest curtsey before the Abbess Honorine. Her great-aunt extended a plump white hand, on which the nun's plain wedding-band was extinguished by a huge showy ruby set in a cross of diamonds. Obediently, Annette kissed this insignia of high office, before turning to greet Cousin Henri.

'Charming,' murmured the Abbess, 'Quite charming. And her mother's emeralds sit well with that simple gown. You are right, Philippe, she is a most acceptable young woman.'

They had been talking about her, then. Annette extended her own hand to the Count, who bowed stiffly over it. Released, she turned to her father. He seemed a little uncomfortable, she thought. Almost at once he signalled to his ever-vigilant personal servant Edouard to open the doors into the dining room. He offered his arm to the Abbess, and Cousin Henri stepped forward to escort Annette to the table.

8

Her place, since her mother's death, was at the foot of her father's table; the long and laden board separated her from him and from his guests, who sat to his left and right at the head of the table. The many dishes of the first course, all rapidly cooling, lay between them, so that her family appeared to her like a picture in a soft-sheened silver frame of tableware. Her father faced down the table towards her, his scowling face resting on the bleached folds of his neckcloth like a pig's mask on a platter. Footmen began to hand the dishes about. Poor Anton laboured up and down from the Count to herself, offering her salvers bearing a series of ever more ingenious variations upon the lamprey, though he knew perfectly well she never ate them; she settled for a helping of oyster pie and watched her elders return to conversation, casting about for a topic they could discuss in her hearing.

Her father's voice was still a little strained. 'How is your house building, Monseigneur?' he asked. 'When do you move to the Boulevards?'

'Not this summer, cousin,' Henri answered. 'The masons are done, at last, and I have some kind of roof. But I seem to have been cursed with the most drunken set of men who ever straddled a ridge. I will not bore you with the details, but no fewer than three of them have fallen off over the last two months. After the last one, the rest tried to blame the job, or indeed me, and walked away for two days, while the rain poured in on my new chestnut floors! But yes, now they have finished. I shall not pay them, you may be sure.' He paused to bite the head off a sardine.

Annette could hear the crunch of its tiny bones as he went on, 'The carpenters are in at last; the *salons* should be panelled and wainscoted by the autumn.'

'That will be pleasing,' the Abbess said. She too was crunching, though more delicately, through a plate of little fishes. She flicked her silver forks expertly to and fro. 'And will you let out your present house? One of those upstart Parliamentarians would be delighted to take it, I imagine – so convenient for the Château Trompette.'

Both men brayed with laughter at this sally. Annette knew that the Château Trompette was where the local *parlement* were meeting now, to send their recommendations to the great meeting at Versailles. Their leader, the Duke of Artois, had the task of gathering local opinions – and also the petitions of the common people – and presenting them to the King. No doubt it was because people below their own rank were being allowed to have a say that her aunt was being so poisonous about it. Annette sat very still, in the hope they would forget she was there and move into a political conversation.

Henri said, 'I shall be glad to be out of the shadow of the crumbling turrets of the Ombrière, at any rate. The Duke's architecture is positively savage. And my new house will still be convenient for the Grand Théâtre – Annette, you will come and visit me, I trust.'

She smiled as convincingly as she could manage, and he lifted his glass. Edouard rushed to fill hers so that she could respond. She quite liked the old Ducal palace of the Ombrière, herself – it was most romantically provided with ivy-covered retreats where you could get away for a moment to sit and dream. Admittedly the sparkling new streets of tall modern houses, where Henri was building, were much better furnished with coffee-houses and fashionable shops. But she didn't want him to think she was keen to go and visit him there, and be sneered at by all his fashionable friends. She pushed the idea away, politely setting her glass to her lips. She looked at her father, wondering what he would have noticed. She was sure Papa's unease this evening had something to do with family deliberations about herself, and that might mean Monseigneur wanted her to move to town and meet some frightful old man who... she dragged her mind back to the table, and the safer ground of politics.

Fortunately, her father ignored Henri's gallantry, and followed the familiar hare started by her aunt Honorine – the threat posed by the newly-made-up representatives of the lesser gentry who were being included in the local deliberations. 'As you say, Madame, there will undoubtedly be no shortage of jumped-up sons of fishermen eager to assert their new nobility by renting our cousin's house. They can have no notion of how to conduct such a household, however.'

He glanced up, and Anton nodded towards the door. Six footmen glided swiftly into the room and swept all the dishes, eaten and uneaten, from the table, replacing them with a second course equally extensive. Annette counted three lobsters and five more fishy things, and a sweet tart. She would manage with that – she did so hate Lenten fare.

Henri put down his glass as a clean plate appeared before him, and leaned back to speak to her father. 'The work is endless. Writing these summaries of our views for the Estates to consider when they meet – never-ending! Even now we have not done. It is astonishing to me how slowly men come to understand the obvious. The inevitable. Narrow views can hamper progress to such a degree! Artois was beside himself with frustration last week, poor man. If I were him, I might simply refuse to go to Versailles with a document so hung about with timid reservations.'

'But the Duke is obliged to safeguard us,' the Abbess cut in. 'Heads of old families – like yourself, Henri – must make sure there is no threat to our ancient rights.' She fixed him with a glance that must have intimidated generations of novice nuns.

The Count was entirely unperturbed. 'You are right, of course, Madame.' He tucked his napkin under his chin and resumed his dinner. 'We will take care of our first duty, have no fear.' He looked up, and spoke like someone making an announcement. 'But change is on the way – and it is necessary.' He stared at each of his cousins in turn; they knew better than to interrupt.

Annette wondered what was coming next; she must remember it all, to report it exactly to Pierre. The Count went on, 'The King is entirely penniless; before long the unpaid soldiers will march back to Prussia, and our peasants will starve in their cottages – or else they will come raging about our gates with fire and sword. Something must be done, and that soon. But it can be managed.' He picked up a lobster claw. 'We have simply to ensure that power is devolved into the right hands, as it was in England a hundred years ago.'

'Oh, I do hope so!' said Annette. 'And that all will be well for the poor peasants!'

Her elders turned their pale faces towards her. The Abbess made a slight gesture, silencing the men before they could speak.

'My dear,' she said, 'I had no notion you were such an... enthusiast. We must have a little talk about God's design for the poor. It is a great concern for the Church, as I am sure you know.' She bowed to the Count, then raised a finger to Anton, who filled her plate with lobster.

Annette, silenced, finished her almond tart.

After an interval in which no one spoke at all, the Abbess put down her fork and turned to Annette. 'These *grandes affaires* are, after all, matters for men, and we should leave the gentlemen to them,' she said.

Annette rose obediently and made her curtsey to her father and cousin.

'You may show me your skills in the art of the drawing room,' said the Abbess. 'A dish of coffee would be most agreeable.'

A small fire was burning in the *petit salon*, Annette's favourite sitting room, three floors down from her own bedroom in the southwest tower. The curious old decoration – a bright blue ground with a rambling frieze of vines – was so antique that it came into her father's category of ancient things not to be disturbed, so it had been regularly repainted. In front of the fire the table stood ready laid with fragile cups and saucers, tea pot, coffee pot and urn, and a set of Venetian glass decanters. The waiting footman proffered the keys of the tea-caddy and coffee box and then retired.

'Alas, I cannot take tea,' said the Abbess. 'It is not good for my health. Coffee, on the other hand, suits my constitution well.'

Annette spooned grounds into the little pot. The Abbess watched her every move with cups, spoons, and urn, until she cocked her wrist and poured out the coffee.

'Charming,' her great-aunt said then. 'And you sing and play? Paint a little?'

Annette nodded, concentrating on the coffee.

'And languages?'

'I have learned a little Latin with Father Lamontaine, and I correspond in English with my godmother Lady Waldon, in London. But you know my father disapproves of too much learning in a woman.'

'Moderation in all things,' the Abbess agreed smoothly as she sat forward to take the cup. 'St Paul teaches us well in that. Oh, no, my dear, I must not take cream. Far too rich for those of us who know the simplicity of the cloister.' Leaning forward, she unstopped one of the decanters and poured a generous dose of brandy into her coffee. Then, with a rustle of dark brown silk, she sat back and looked at Annette. 'It is time to talk about your future, my dear.'

'Madame?'

'You are – how old now? Nineteen? Then in only two years' time you will come into your fortune. You may be aware that it is, happily for you, considerable. The money you inherit from your mother and grandmother, and which your father has used wisely on your behalf, will be yours to use as you wish. When you marry, this personal fortune will go with you. Out of the family.' She put down her cup and looked at Annette, as if to check that she was following. 'There will be, of course, a dowry to find also, and other moneys to be promised, if not immediately paid, as part of your marriage settlement.'

None of this was actually new to Annette; but she wondered where it was leading.

'These are not matters for a young woman to worry about,' the Abbess continued. 'Your father will, of course, dispose of your future in the way he thinks best. However, there are things you should understand.' The sharp black eyes in the soft face watched Annette closely. 'Your father is lord of this château, and of his quite extensive lands, but he has little else. He is, as you might say, the farmer of the family. Henri has the title, the seat in the *parlement*, the licence to export the wines your father produces for us. He also has the family money. Your father's connection to the Lavigne line is only through his mother. And as I am sure you are aware, his father left him nothing.'

Here was something Annette did want to hear about. 'Madam, no one ever speaks of my grandfather,' she said, trying to sound cool and judicious. 'Will you tell me more?'

'A love match,' said the Abbess dismissively. 'Always a bad idea. An unsuitable alliance with an English refugee. A gentleman of sorts, yes, but penniless and landless – a younger son. With a price on his head. And not a Catholic. When it was over, your father was brought home to Brillac and the whole matter was forgotten, as far as such things can be. But this is a digression.' She poured more brandy into her now-empty cup. 'The story is of no importance, and I advise you to think no more about it, except as it explains your father's circumstances. Your mother's dowry, though good, hardly changed anything; and you are, of course, the only child – and a girl. So you will understand, my dear, that it would be best for everyone if your fortune could be kept in the family.'

There was a pause. The bones of Annette's stays poked into her breasts excruciatingly. She sat up straighter. Meeting her aunt's gaze, and keeping her voice as steady as she could, she asked, 'How, Madam, could that be achieved?'

'Good girl. There are two ways. The first, and simplest, would be for you to marry within the family. Your father and the Count are, I believe, discussing that at the moment. However, your cousin François is only six, and not robust, so that I think will be decisive.'

Annette stared in disbelief. The old woman might have been discussing a choice of gloves.

'The alternative,' she continued, 'and to my mind the obvious choice, is for you to take the veil. You are a sensible girl and would soon adapt to the religious life. And as my cousin, you would have golden prospects at Our Lady of the Little Angels. Your dowry would come to us, therefore, but only during your lifetime. The promise of its safe return in the future would provide a surety against which your father could raise other moneys, should the need arise.' She sat back in her chair. 'Excellent coffee. I'll take a little of the cherry brandy now, if you will kindly pass it.'

9

Annette put Aurore at the hedge by the water meadow and the little mare shied again. She was quite impossible this morning. After six days in the stable – and clearly no one had bothered so much as to talk to her, let alone take her out – she was completely out of control. Annette was not having this. She cut the mare sharply, several times, and finally pulled her up snorting and stamping on a short rein.

She looked round for the groom, who was still hesitating on the far side of the ditch. 'Come on, man, keep up!' she called. There were two grooms whose task it was to accompany their mistress when it pleased her to go out riding – this was the dull one, Luc. Irritated, Annette kicked the mare and set off, leaving him to follow as he might.

This was what Aurore had wanted. They flew along at a smart gallop, kicking up divots from the wet meadow, creating their own fresh breeze. They ran and ran, reaching the end of the low meadows and coming back flawlessly over the high fence into the rows of vines. They slowed to a canter uphill along the hard-pruned rows almost ready to break into leaf. Both horse and rider were beginning to feel better. At a gap in the planting, marked by a rose bush already showing red buds, Annette pulled up to wait for Luc. Her father liked her to stay in sight of the manservant, even though she was safe enough here at the heart of the estate. Aurore snorted, shook her head and did a little sideways dance.

Annette patted her neck. 'I'm sorry I was cross.' She had been edgy all week, she knew, ever since the conversation with Cousin Honorine. Pierre had been less help on the subject than she expected. He seemed to assume that whether one was married or not, or even shut up in a convent, was immaterial to the real life, the life of the mind and the heart. She felt he was being uncharacteristically obtuse – but perhaps he meant to comfort her, for he knew whatever happened would not be by her choice. This morning, however, had been the last straw. Putting aside the volume they had been reading – one of Rousseau's less fascinating works, Annette could not help but feel – he had leant back and regarded her with a teasing smile. 'Do you know what I've just heard?' he began. 'In a letter this morning from my friend in Paris? He says the *daughter* of Minister Necker has published a book about Rousseau. Imagine!'

Annette frowned. 'What?' she said. 'Imagine what?'

Pierre sat up slightly. 'Well,' he said, 'imagine a slip of a girl writing about the master! And then publishing what she writes!'

He could not know, of course. She had not shown him any of her writing. But it was, secretly in her heart, Annette's dearest wish to write, and to be published. She knew she could write well – she practised every day, in her private journal. One day she would write for the world. And publish. Why not? 'How old is Mademoiselle Necker?' she asked.

'Oh, she's not Mademoiselle. She's married – she's Madame de Staël. But still very young.' He smiled provokingly.

'Then why should she not publish?' Annette asked, in her iciest voice. 'It would not be improper. She has her husband's permission, I suppose?'

'I don't question that – of course, everyone should have freedom to speak. But to write about Rousseau – about philosophy! And she so young – not much older than you, my lady.' He stopped and looked at her. 'But we should be getting on.'

Annette had not answered. She stood, dropped him a curtsey, and left the room.

Well, she would try hard not to think about any of it. She gazed out across the ranks of vines to the little hill, a budding copse where her father's pheasants would be sitting now. It was the middle of Lent, when birds and beasts could raise their young, safe from hungry hunters. She smiled rather grimly. It was Pierre, the man of God, who had pointed out to her that the real need for those forty days and forty nights was the body's, not the soul's. If Christians were forbidden to eat meat or eggs in the burgeoning spring it was, quite practically, so that there would be meat and eggs to eat in the coming seasons. After all, he had said reasonably, who needed to practise self-denial for the good of their soul at a time of year when food was running short anyway, and most people were already hungrier than they wanted to be? And they had agreed that this understanding was another way in which Feeling had helped the mind to rise above Superstition: a nurturing love for God's teeming world being far healthier than mere ritual observance. And it helped to make six weeks dominated by lamprey a little more bearable.

Luc was still half a mile behind. Annette clicked her tongue, pressed her heel gently to the mare's flank and they began to walk quietly along the edge of the covert, looking for primroses. Yet again the conversation with the Abbess thrust itself into her mind. Every day since, she had waited for her father to speak, to make it real, even if it was to tell her that he had not yet made the final decision; but he had said nothing. Would he really send her to spend the rest of her life in the convent of Our Lady of the Little Angels? A lump of dread had settled in her stomach at the thought, and now it rose sickeningly in her throat. She tried to imagine living without morning rides, without the green of the vines in the spring and the gold of the walnut trees in the autumn; a life behind stone walls in the great dark city of Bordeaux. The thought of that obedient, passionless life quickened her heart with fear. To spend one's days in reading and study – Pierre's 'life of the mind' – that was bearable, perhaps. But what of the heart? What of love? Annette was not childish enough to suppose that she would fall in love with her husband – though some people did. But whether or no, she had assumed that somewhere, someday, there would be the *possibility* of love, of the thrilling, passionate 'language of the heart' that Rousseau spoke of.

A large buck rabbit bounced across her path. Aurore whinnied, and Annette brought her attention back to the ride. They had come to the end of the little wood, and the sandy bank of her father's warrens opened up to their left hand, its grassy surface pocked with hundreds of rabbit holes. Annette rode slowly, and Aurore trod delicately, both looking out for the fresh burrows that often opened in the grassy path. It was quite likely they would come upon one unfilled, at the moment, since the warrener was away. There was no trapping to be done in Lent, and each year her father gave the man and his wife leave to pay a week's visit to their elder daughter, who was married, Annette now recalled, to a baker in Bergerac.

So she was startled to round a bend and see a man, well up the hillside, crouching at the mouth of a burrow. He held a long net in place, and a short cosh was balanced in his other hand. A little white dog quivered at his side. It saw the horse and rider, and gave a short yap and a growl. The man looked up and his eyes met Annette's.

She knew him – she knew all her father's workers by sight. When she met them in the fields and lanes, she would greet them and they would take off their hats and smile. The man with the dog worked in the vineyards, she thought. But today he did not speak, or smile, or take off his hat. And he was not alone. There were other men, half a dozen or more, strung out along the hill ahead of her, all with nets. Not expecting to find anyone here, she had not seen them, their faded breeks and ragged shirts and their brown skin merging with the sandy hill. A child's voice suddenly sang out – in greeting to her, or in panic, she could not tell – and she saw that there were women and children squatting in the ride, skinning rabbits. They had obviously been there for a while. Time stopped. The breeze brushed Annette's hot face.

Then the people all stood up, one by one, and faced her; one woman held a skinned rabbit dangling from her left hand, and with the other she held on to her little girl – as thin as the rabbit, and scarcely better covered. No one spoke. Annette was confused, then furious. Poaching? And in Lent? What on earth were they thinking of? She was about to speak, to remind them of the need to let the creatures breed in peace, when she thought: In broad day? And all these people, all together? A cold feather of fear brushed her skin, standing all the hairs on her arms on end.

Then two things happened. Three of the nets exploded with bolt-eyed rabbits, as the underground dogs drove them into the open, while instinctively the men beside them dropped onto their knees and began to club the creatures to death; and Luc came round the hill at a clumsy trot. His jaw dropped with astonishment, and then his face filled with panic as he took in the scene. He reached for Annette's bridle.

'Mademoiselle! Come. Come away. Come now.' He was turning Aurore's head, sawing at the mouth of his own mount. 'Come quickly, Mademoiselle, for the love of God!'

She could not explain why she had let him lead her away. 'I suppose I was afraid,' she said to Pierre, 'or too startled to think. But I should not have run from them. They were not showing any signs of attacking me, after all. I should have talked to them, asked them why they were doing it.'

He looked at her sharply. 'You needed to ask?'

'Surely one should ask questions, and so learn,' she replied lightly, 'as you have always taught me?'

He did not smile, but stood up and walked to the window. 'Come,' he said, 'and tell me what you see.'

Annette went to stand beside him. 'I see the garden beginning to flower,' she said obediently, 'and the vines budding; and the sun on the river – I see spring coming.'

'A late and hungry spring,' said Pierre angrily, 'after a bad harvest and a hungry winter.'

Was he angry with her again? 'Yes, of course I know about the harvest,' she said. 'We talked about it yesterday, and anyway my father and the steward spoke of nothing else last autumn, and I also know that the *parlement* in Bordeaux has been debating the price we are to charge for our flour these last two months or more. And there was a bad harvest the year before, too. I do understand, Pierre.' She could not bear it if he went back to blaming her and calling her ignorant, as he had seemed to yesterday morning.

'And now the grass and the corn spring up again and hope is renewed?' he said in a flat voice.

'Well, yes, of course.'

'For everyone?'

'What do you mean?' she asked irritably. He treated her like a child sometimes, even though he was only four years older than she was.

'The plants grow, and the little boys run about to scare away the birds, for men must eat before birds do. On your father's fields, these little boys must run about from dawn to dusk to protect his crops. Good. But his game must also be protected, as we know, or there will be no roast pheasant next winter. So where shall Monseigneur's pheasants and hares – oh, and his rabbits, let us not forget the rabbits – where will *they* feed, when they have been chased out of his fields? Ah. I see you take my point. They must browse on crops that are not my lord's.'

Now Annette saw exactly where the conversation was going. 'In the people's gardens,' she said quietly, 'and in their poor little fields.'

'Indeed. And they are not to be trapped or shot there,' said Pierre. He turned from the window and looked at her. 'On pain of death.'

There was a pause before she said, 'I did not know that part. Oh, Pierre! I am surprised they have not acted before.'

'No surprise,' he said wearily. 'It is never easy to change the prevailing order of things. But it seems now that the people are pressed so hard that they will do anything. I will show you something.' He picked up a book from the table and slid a paper from inside the cover.

It was some kind of printed handbill, Annette saw. Across the top in large letters it said, 'Attention, the people of France!' It called upon the people to unite against the violation of God's will that was called the Law of the Chase; to go out on March 11th and on every subsequent day until justice had been done, and to partake freely of the bounty of heaven in the shape of those creatures He had put on earth to feed every one of his children. It was a call to trespass; a call to revolt. Annette put the paper down and looked at her friend. 'And you think this is what roused our people to do what they did?'

Pierre shrugged. 'That, and news on the road. The 11th of March is two weeks ago now, and word travels fast. They say that in Chantilly and Oisy whole herds of deer were slaughtered, as well as rabbits and poultry. Your father may take some comfort from the fact that he is not alone.' He stood up. 'We haven't read all of Rousseau,' he said, 'but you should look at his *Discourse on the Origin of Inequality*. That's where he says, *the fruits of the earth belong to all, and the earth to no one.*'

10

As Annette sipped her chocolate next morning, still thinking about a very thin little girl and a skinned rabbit, Jacqueline burst into the room, scarlet-faced.

'Mademoiselle!' she gasped. 'Such doings!'

Annette looked up with a frown; but a second glance at the woman's face brought her to her feet. 'What?'

'They are breaking in!' Her excitement tipped over into fear, and she began to cry.

'Who? Where?' Annette dashed to the window, but nothing was happening in the courtyard. She pushed her feet into slippers and began to pull on a loose gown. 'Show me!'

Ignoring Jacqueline's wail of protest, she hurried downstairs. In the hall, Edouard was mustering a group of footmen. None of them seemed very enthusiastic about going out. Slipping past them while the steward's back was turned, Annette ran outside. Nothing seemed to be happening here either, until she saw two gardeners run by, carrying picks. If she hesitated, Annette knew she would be called back, so she followed them towards whatever the disturbance was. They ran along the front of the west wing and round the corner, away from the stable block towards the gardens.

By the time Annette came through the garden gate she had lost them, but now she could hear voices from down the slope beyond the terrace. Running along the gravel path, she reached one of the gazebos that flanked the lower edge of the formal parterres, and climbed the steps into the little stone pavilion. Trying to slow her breath, she pressed herself against the folded shutter beside the unglazed window, so she would not be seen from the wide lawn below.

A band of peasants, maybe ten or a dozen, stood in a tight knot, a dark, uncouth outline against the spring green of the grass. Some of them held weapons, a thick stick or a spade or hoe, which was strange, because they were all women. Or at least, they all wore skirts, though some of them were tall and wide-shouldered; and today there were no children. And this time Annette could not recognise any of them: she stared in horror at the faces of painted devils. Red, glaring eyes stood out against black masks. Then she realised, with a little rush of relief, that they were disguised, painted with black stain or soot: one man's brow was streaked with white where he had wiped away his sweat.

Confronting this grim band were the outdoor servants – five of them, now that the gardeners had arrived. Annette could hear the voices, but could not make out the words. The head groom shrugged and turned towards his fellows. They conferred for a moment then, to her surprise, turned and walked away.

A cheer went up from the trespassers, who immediately started to run, hoisting their cumbersome skirts over their knees and charging up the slope toward the terrace. Annette drew back from the window, but they were not heading for the gazebo. Shouting, they rushed past her hiding place, making for the little stone dove-house that stood at the western corner of the garden. Their leader, yelling and brandishing his stick, ran straight in at the door. There was a flurry of white wings as the whole flock took to the air in panic; then, as Annette watched, half the peasants stopped, pulled catapults and started to shoot the doves out of the air. The rest ran on, following their leader. Soon a terrible squawking, shouting and sounds of smashing wood came from inside the house. It only lasted a few minutes. Then the men were out again, in a cloud of feathers, scattering dead birds and broken perches as they ran away. They were heading downhill now towards the home farm, where the big dovecote stood that kept the family in pigeon casserole and squab pies all year round.

It wasn't difficult, in the uproar that was going on, to get back indoors without being seen. She sat alone in her room, still seeing the fluttering of wounded birds, the blackened faces smeared with blood and stuck with feathers, the hatred in their eyes. She understood, since yesterday, that pigeons were much the same as rabbits, really: if you were forbidden to stop them, even when they ate every miserable lettuce in your garden and your children were crying with hunger, you would naturally be desperate. But at least it had looked as if the rabbits would be eaten. This carnage felt so pointless. She very much wanted to talk to Pierre about it. She hadn't seen him at all this morning, she realised – the raid on the dovecotes had completely upset the iron routine of the household. She would find him later.

When she was dressed, Annette sent for Madame Desmoulins – it was the day for her dancing lesson – and went down to the *petit salon* to wait for her. Monsieur Perrault would not be here for another half hour. The little room was full of spring sunshine; Annette found her embroidery and sat in the window, looking out over the now quiet gardens. A bumble bee blundered about in the blossom outside; everything in the world seemed at peace again. But it wasn't: something was very wrong, she knew – not just here, but in all of France. For the first time she could feel, on her pulses, exactly what the great meeting of the Estates General at Versailles might mean, beyond the realm of philosophy and books. She wondered if the King knew about all the things that were happening, and if he really would be able to find an answer for everyone.

Then an odd thing happened. A figure darkened the window and a hand banged on the glass. To her astonishment she saw it was Pierre, his face white and desperate. He was gesturing to her to open the casement. He looked as if he had seen a ghost. She was still struggling with the stiff catches when a footman ran up, grabbed the chaplain unceremoniously by the arm and started to drag him away. Annette wrenched at the latch and finally managed to wrest the window open, but by now her friend was held between two men and they were disappearing round the corner of the tower. One of the footmen was holding a black travelling bag. Annette's throat closed in panic; she could not even call out after him. Just before they vanished, Pierre waved one arm in a kind of farewell. And then he was gone.

It didn't take long to find out what had happened. Annette didn't even have to ask; everyone in the château was talking about it. Father Lamontaine had been caught, in Jacqueline's words, 'doing it' with the new stable-boy. The disruption of everyone's routine by the trespassers had brought about his downfall, for Monseigneur had sent unexpectedly for a horse, to ride out yet again to check his coverts and speak to the gamekeeper in the Big Wood; Edouard, rushing into the lower stable on this errand, had caught the two of them in the straw.

Jacqueline went into no further detail about what they were actually doing at the moment of Edouard's arrival, and Annette did not feel able to ask – but she did wonder why it had caused quite such an enormous fuss. She remembered quite clearly the last occasion on which anything remotely similar had happened: Edouard's predecessor, a poor relation of her father's who had acted as his private secretary and steward, had got one of the maids with child. Annette had been about ten at the time, all the more agog to know about it because no one wanted to tell her; but she was sure that Cousin Georges had not been unceremoniously bundled out of the house. The girl had been turned away, of course – but Georges had stayed; he had only died last year. Annette could not see why anything these two young men might have been doing was worse than fathering a bastard on a servant. But Jacqueline just sucked her teeth and shook her head when Annette tried to re-open the conversation.

The house was in complete disorder. Annette dined alone in her room, and was trying in vain to order her thoughts by recording the events of the morning in her journal, when Jacqueline reappeared, looking agitated.

'Your noble father, Mademoiselle. He requests the pleasure of your company at once. He is in the *grande salle,* Mademoiselle. Please go quickly!'

Monseigneur Lavigne-Brillac was standing at the end of the always-chilly room, his back to the huge carved fireplace. He did not acknowledge her or ask her to sit. As soon as she rose from her curtsey, he said 'Father Lamontaine has left this house this afternoon, Mademoiselle. You will oblige me by not attempting to contact him or communicate with him in any way.'

She had often seen her father angry, but this cold fury was something new. He was white; his hand shook as he spoke. 'Is that understood, Mademoiselle?'

'Yes, yes, of course, father,' she stammered. 'But –'

'You will not ask, and we will speak no more of it. It is not a thing for a young girl to think of. And you will, of course, not encourage the servants in any gossip on the subject.'

As if they needed encouragement! Annette held her tongue.

Her father spoke again, his voice strained. 'However, *I* must ask *you* a question – a painful one. It has been brought to my attention that Père Lamontaine was in possession of more than one immoral and irreligious book.'

Annette froze. She pictured the tiny blue book even now hidden under her pillow, and the two companion volumes resting under a pile of handkerchiefs in her dressing table drawer. She swallowed.

'He was your tutor. Can you assure me that he never, at any time, put this wicked filth in your way? Never offered you anything to read that was not of the purest piety?'

Annette met his eye. 'No – I mean yes, father,' she lied. 'I cannot think what you could mean.'

His face cleared a little, but he did not take his eyes from hers. She willed herself not to blush but then, realising that maidenly confusion would be an appropriate enough reaction, she looked down, and up again at him with big round eyes.

He strode two paces across the wide hearth while she held her breath, then turned back to her abruptly.

It had not worked.

'Nonetheless,' he said, 'one cannot be sure what paths corruption takes to an innocent mind. You must be put beyond further harm at once. Tell your woman to pack your immediate necessaries tonight. You must go in the morning to the sisters at Bordeaux.'

11

Jude Wiston, ship's cook's boy on the stately French merchantman *La Belle Héloïse*, slung his hammock in the galley, so he could keep the stove alight through the night and protect the provisions from hungry sailors. He rose at first light, like any housemaid, to set water to boil for the cook; he padded barefoot along the heaving planks of the deck to collect eggs from the hen coop amidships, and milked the two goats for the captain's and passengers' breakfasts. He watered all the animals and mucked them out, stoked the galley stove, laid the mess trays, collected, stacked and washed them, and made and ate his own bait on the run between these tasks. He cleaned the galley, washed the officers' tableware – less their plates and glasses, which the mess steward did with the hot water Jude provided – and made all ready for the men's dinner time. After that he cleaned and washed the pans, peeled and soaked and laid out once again for the passengers' dinner. Then he washed and cleaned more completely, including mopping the stained, frayed planks of the galley floor, and stowed everything away so that the constant tug of the ocean would not roll the pots and pans about in the night.

Jude learned all this fast, and well, and unresentfully. In the first few days there was no time to pause, and checking back to Armand at every turn's end was exhausting; but the routine made itself and was, in its way, a thing of beauty. Rebecca Wiston's skills were useful to some extent: she had known how to judge weight and measure, how to boil, stew and fry and – more abstractly – how to overlap tasks and how to keep everyone happy, or at least to stop them from too much complaining. A smile, a rueful gesture at the language problem and an extra ladleful of stew worked wonders when mistakes were made. Certainly, Rebecca had never slept in the grip of a tight and swaying canvas cocoon, but once you were actually inside a hammock it was not unpleasant. The ship's rats could not walk on your face; and, alone in the galley, you were not troubled by men's smells or snores, nor their prying eyes.

But while the cook's new boy had a measure of privacy for himself, his own eyes and ears were ever on the alert, watching the men. He studied the way they walked and stood, leaned and sat; he collected their looks and gestures, their manner of eating, spitting, and laughing. And out of these scraps he constructed his new self. It was an absorbing business, and full of surprises. Lotta had given Jude her first lessons and she had learned well; passing through the bustling market with Lotta on her arm, it had been enough. But here, on board ship, with no woman beside her to make her look the man, she had to work harder at her transformation. Rebecca, who had lived all her life among men, had never needed to notice how much they performed even the smallest of actions quite differently from women. Now, with urgent concentration, she noticed everything. She might throw underhand, as if to a child; a man threw overhead, with a stinging flick of the wrist. As a woman, she had unfastened her dress and let it slip down from her shoulders; a man dragged his shirt off over his head. A knife in a woman's hands, from girlhood on, makes the small, deft downward movements of chopping and slicing; a knife in a boy's hand hacks and whittles and sharpens with outward strokes. A woman peels an apple or a turnip with the blade towards her; a man peels the bark from a branch with the blade sweeping away. The most important observation of all was the hardest to act on: that a woman's movements are a way of hiding, and a man's are a way of being seen. It would have been easier to hide; but Jude's whole existence now depended on bracing back her shoulders, lengthening her stride and learning to be larger, louder – to take up more space in the new and dangerous world of the ship.

Doing the endless scrubbing, carrying casks of water or salt meat along a swaying deck, running up and down companionways with trays and pretending never to spill anything, Jude developed aches, and then muscles, that Rebecca had never had. But putting on a little bulk and much new strength was not a problem – rather the reverse. On the other hand, her lack of more than a handful of French words – and most of those suitable only for the boudoir – soon turned from a good excuse to a nuisance and a barrier, and had to be remedied as soon as could be, in Jude's leisure hours.

These fell in the afternoons, when all the cooked food had been served and nothing remained in the galley but the supper trays for the passengers and the bottle service for the officers' mess. At this point Armand slept, his brandy bottle to hand; the boy's time was his own. At first Jude sat alone in their doorway, watching the endless shifts and curls of the wake and the running patterns of blue and green that crossed the face of the ocean. She did not think much. Somewhere in the back of her head, she was aware that there were things that must be thought on: such as who she was, and where she was going. But since the night she became a sailor, that night in Lotta's bed, the first question had lost all meaning; and the second was not, at least just now, in her control. Time enough for thinking when they reached Bordeaux.

Off duty, the rest of the crew came to lounge or play on the deck just aft of where she sat, for the few passenger cabins were for'ard, well away from their laughter. After a while Jude grew brave enough to join them, squatting at the edge of the group with the other boys. You did not need to understand their French to see who were the leaders among the crew. The chief topman, Jean-Baptiste, a mighty fellow with a tarred pigtail to his waist and huge shoulders the colour of ripening oak, was clearly one of them. He was a keen dancer and had the fiddler playing for him most afternoons he was off watch. The boys, Jude realised, were supposed to learn and admire. She quickly learned to sing out 'Bravo' with the others.

Then came the day when Jean-Baptiste formed a five-boy line, gesturing like a lord to Jude to come out too; and Jude had no choice but to stand up. The steps were easy, even on the slowly rolling deck – a short stride right, left and to the back, change of feet, a stamp, begin again. Then they linked in a leaning line, arms round shoulders, and the beat of it kept them together – until someone stamped too soon and barged his neighbour, and the little pack fell together in a laughing tangle. Jude was fast on her feet, bouncing away from too much contact; but, to her consternation, this agility brought Jean-Baptiste down on her with cries of encouragement. The big man held the reluctant cook's boy firmly to his side, counting and nodding and showing him more steps. Jude, quelling panic, learned swiftly, till she could shake the man off as if keen to show her paces. Jean-Baptiste laughed at her success and led the clapping to the end of the tune.

Every time the topman stood up, after that, Jude was called out to join him. Jean-Baptiste had taken a liking and, after the dancing, would talk knowingly to Jude about the names of the dances and their tunes and which parts of France they came from. From this he progressed to the voyage, and the ship, and the passengers, and what he would do when he came home to his mother's house in Bordeaux. Quite soon Jude began to understand what he was saying and, in this way, learned not only dancing and French, but also knotting and splicing and lots of (she suspected, very rude) words with which to describe rich people and their ways.

Jean-Baptiste's hatred of the rich was shared by most of the crew. The half-dozen or so passengers aboard were especially despised, as first-hand examples of the arrogant and stupid nobility. As evidence of the unbelievable extravagance of their betters, Jean-Baptiste introduced her to a little man whom Jude had noticed already amongst the non-sailors of the ship. He was dressed more like a clerk than a seaman, in a decent coat only a little stained about the cuffs, and he spent his time strolling or sitting on deck, watching the weather. He cocked his head as they shook hands.

'Pleased to meet you, young man,' he said. 'Are you a wine drinker yourself?'

Jude shook her head, puzzled, and both Frenchmen smiled.

'Come, Jude,' said Jean-Baptiste, 'Our friend will show you his charges.'

They climbed down and down, below the level of the mess deck, into the black hold, where the stink of the bilges and the constant dropping of slime as the *Héloïse* rolled had Jude dodging and weaving along in the wake of the little man's lantern. At last he opened a kind of vertical hatch, a shuttered rabbit-hole in a creaking bulkhead, and they stepped through. He lifted his arm, so that the light fell on a row of wooden circles – barrel ends, she realised, belonging to big vats cradled in wooden footings, swaying in time to the ship's motion.

Above them was a stretched canvas, a kind of canopy strung out to protect them from the ooze of the ship's side. Hanging his lantern, their guide patted the first round flank as if it were alive, a huge cow that he was about to milk. Taking a little hammer from a hook, he tapped up and down the concavity, listening, and finally clambered to ride on top, feet sticking out each side. He leant forward, his ear to something protruding from the top – the bung, presumably. Shaking her head in amazement, Jude turned to Jean-Baptiste.

'This is wine, my friend,' he said. 'In each cask, nine hundred litres of the finest Bordeaux. And is it for us, the crew? Of course not. Have you been serving it up to the officers, the captain, even the passengers? No. It is not here to be drunk; it has come with us for the good of its health.' He slapped the resounding wood. 'The *Héloïse* took it out to the Indies – and she is bringing it back, much improved by the journey. These beauties will not be unshipped until they are back on the *quais* at home, after many months away, five thousand miles of heaving ocean behind them, and their friend here – their servant, their vintner – along all the way, just to keep them fresh and safe and sound.'

As Jude gaped uncomprehendingly, the vintner threw his leg over, as if he were dismounting a horse, and slid down, looking slightly put out.

'So, Jean-Baptiste, why should that trouble you? If this is what it takes, to make the very best, then this is what I will do. I am proud of my craft, me.' He turned to Jude. '*Retour des Isles* – the finest Bordeaux anywhere; the drink of kings.'

Jean-Baptiste struck his fist, this time, against the nearest barrel. The vintner jumped.

'Kings?' the topman roared. 'There is but one king in France, and I have no quarrel with him – let him drink ambrosia, if it pleases him. He is the father of his people, and we do not grudge him the best. But this? This is not the food of the gods. It is made, and bought and sold, and always its price comes out of the blood and sweat of the poor. Ten *livres* a bottle, they will sell this for – and the men who pruned the vines, and picked the grapes, and made the must, and racked it, and fined it, and those who made the barrels and the bottles and carried them so carefully – will they see as many *sous*, between them? And then the lord who buys it, to grace his table when he entertains – who wastes it, perhaps, with his fancy women or his gambling friends – where did each coin come from, that Milord spends by the handful? From the sweat of the man who digs or ploughs or builds for him – or pays taxes to him on each pitiful loaf of bread.' He wagged a rhetorical finger at the vintner. 'But the Third Estate will have their day, my friend – like the Americans. Then we shall see who drinks the wine that comes back from the Isles!'

12

The *Belle Héloïse*, like all ships from the Caribbean bound on the North Atlantic easterly crossing, had to beat up the American coast on the prevailing south-westerlies, but against headwinds inshore. The same coastal winds had carried the *Robin* to her untimely end on the rocks – though Armand told Jude that those northerlies were chiefly a winter gale, and they had slacked off now it was April. Now the ship had reached quite northerly latitudes, off New France, and the crew, especially the thinly clad boys, had to be chided and chased from crowding too much round the galley stove, the only heat on board. But after this the *Héloïse* turned east and struck out into the Atlantic to begin the long glide home to France on the prevailing Trades. The sails were set, the course unchanged for days together; and Jude had time to draw breath, and to watch some more, and think.

She watched the sailors, now, to note their moods, their whispered conferences, the glances they turned on their officers: the old sea-bitten captain, whom they seemed to like, and the trio of younger men under him. These officers they trusted less, especially the harassed third officer, Durand, who had not long been at sea but sported a fine blue coat and a fashionable wig. There was a level of excitement on the ship that easily built into blows and shouting. On the mess deck, papers were passing from hand to hand: cartoons, often, whose subjects Jude could not understand, but also written pamphlets that only a few of the men could read unaided. The crew were deeply divided over them. Jean-Baptiste showed one to her. They were sitting together on the after-deck in the strengthening sun, and she had just achieved a deft running bowline in the piece of tarry twine on which he was teaching her knots. He slapped her back in congratulation.

'Well done! Tomorrow, the Turk's head.' He laid back, tipping his hat forward against the brightness.

Jude suddenly remembered something she had been meaning to ask, ever since they had visited the wine casks. 'Jean-Baptiste,' she said, 'what is the Third Estate?'

'Aha! A good question.' He sat up, pocketing his string, and glanced around like a conspirator. 'You are an American – a democrat. But in France we are not as far behind as you might think.' Satisfied that they were alone, he squirmed sideways and delved deep in his breeches pocket. He brought out a folded pamphlet and smoothed it on the whitened boards between them. 'This is from Paris – only a few months ago. At Christmas the good doctor who wrote it was brought up before the judges, so they tell me, but the people saw to it that he was set free. It is very learned.' He patted it and sat back. Jude looked, but of course it was in French.

'But I am not learned,' she said in her best accent. 'I cannot read it.'

'Ah! I am sorry – No doubt you will learn, when we get home. I will interpret.'

The paper disappeared into his fist. But after a moment he put it down again – obviously she was not going to get a reading. 'It says,' he began, 'that there is to be a great meeting of all the representatives of the people of France, to advise the King. It will be this Spring, at the royal palace at Versailles. And they are the representatives of the three Estates. The Church is the first; then the Nobility' – he spat swiftly into the scuppers – 'and the Third Estate is all the rest – the common people. They will come together, and all will be sorted out. I believe it, though many do not think the great ones will let it happen. But he says here, the good doctor, that the will of the Third Estate *can* be done – it is all a matter of voting. There must be twice as many votes for the people as there are for the nobility. The Patriots, he says, not the Privileged, shall decide. I have not had news from home for months now – I got this from a man who had sailed in January. But I make no doubt, they will be voting this way, when it comes to the day of reckoning. He is a very learned doctor – see how many words!'

Jude looked down at the far-travelled pamphlet. The author's name, at least, she could read. Joseph-Ignace Guillotin; obviously an ingenious and optimistic man. 'Thank you,' she said, getting to her feet, 'I learn the most interesting things from you, my friend!'

It seemed to Jude that Jean-Baptiste, who so hated the nobility, was actually some sort of natural lord himself: lord of the masthead, lord of the dance, bigger, swifter, stronger, more alive than the rest. Could I be falling in love with this Frenchman? she asked herself one night, as she swung in her snug cocoon. But she could find nothing in her admiration of his mastery that came from anywhere near her passion for Lizzie or her intimate, startling responses to Lotta, unless it was the huge revelation of the beauty of the human body. Perhaps I simply envy him, she thought. He was so easy, so assured. She had watched him that very day swarm up the mainmast, racing the three other Gascon hands who were his best friends. The wind was so stiff that the *Héloïse* creamed through the water at a steep angle, her spars dipping towards the curling waves to port, white water whispering all along her sides. At midday the wind had strengthened yet more, and the mainstays hummed. The officer of the watch finally sang out an order to shorten sail, and the crew threw themselves aloft, climbing the wind, hanging nonchalantly outboard, sixty feet above the towering waves. Magnificent. She would have liked to be up there with them, in the tearing sunshine, alive, sure of themselves, of their bodies.

That was the point, of course. She was very unsure about this new thing – her body. She turned in her hammock, rubbing her hands down her thighs, and unbidden the memory of her night with Lotta came warmly to the pit of her stomach. Once more she revisited the shock of Lotta's fingers plunging into her, a surge of pleasure such as she had never imagined. She understood, now, that her passion for Lizzie, which had seemed so complete a thing, had only ever been one way; at least, in terms of the body. It had seemed enough, in those far-off days back home, to give her darling pleasure, to feel the thrill of touching; but Lotta had taught her that she might delight in being touched, herself. She wriggled her right hand free and grasped the rope from which she hung suspended. Think! she told herself sternly. But she had no idea, really, what to make of it. All she was sure of was that she would never be the same again, never be able, whatever came to pass, to revert to her former self, to being Rebecca, to fall back into that suppressed, disembodied place. She could not summon chapter and verse on the subject, but she supposed she was in a state of sin. She smiled to herself; she had certainly eaten of the tree of knowledge. And the fruit in this particular garden of Eden was quite remarkable, certainly worth leaving the confines of Salem for. All she now had to do was work out what to do with her new information, how to conduct her transformed life. At the moment she had no idea, beyond the need to be up and feeding the stove before first light.

The next afternoon Jean-Baptiste's tall shadow darkened the galley door. He had come to speak to Armand about Jude. The lad would make a seaman, he said, so would the cook let him out of this little hot hell for an hour, to learn to climb the rigging? Jude, taken aback at the sudden offer to realise her dreams of yesterday, was relieved at Armand's stream of possessive excuses; but afterwards, thinking about it, was regretful. As she went about her errands, she stared up into the shrouds. Why should she not venture up there, into the streaming, ever-changing sky? So, when there came a morning of lighter wind, and then no wind at all, and the hands lay sunning themselves on deck while the ship moved less than a cork in a puddle, Jude flopped down beside Jean-Baptiste and cocked her head towards the shrouds.

The young Frenchman grinned. 'The old man sleeps?'

Jude nodded, and they stood up.

The first part was easy. She made the spring from the deck

out to the ratlines as she had seen the sailors do a thousand times, and began to climb, each thick rope comforting under her bare instep. Jean-Baptiste came behind, shouting instructions. They reached a landing at the first yard-arm – Jude did not catch the word for it, but there was a firm standing-place. She looked down to the deck below, already far away, as her new friend swung casually round her, hooked by one hand, and raced away along the head of the slack sail to stand up tall, out on the tip of it, right over the ocean.

'Don't follow!' he called, unnecessarily.

Jude had not dreamed of it, but nodded anyway.

'Go on up, *mon brave!*' cried Jean-Baptiste, swarming back towards her.

Jude turned her eyes to the mast, swaying gently above them: a mere twig, a quill, dwindling up into the sky. She laid hold of the ropes.

As they climbed it got harder. The air seemed sharp in her lungs as she sucked it in. Shoulders and hands sang with pain, but there was no easing up, no letting go. There was no wind, but up here the air sighed and shifted, whispering about its power. She kept her eyes firmly turned upwards, away from the shifting gulf beneath her feet, until she saw that she was coming up beneath planks, a kind of ceiling – the cross trees, where the lookout was posted. The ladder of rope – thin now and sticky with salt, harder to hold – tilted back over her head, running outwards from near the mast to the edge of this platform. To climb further meant hanging from your hands and feet.

'Stop!' shouted Jean-Baptiste against the whispering breeze. 'Use the hatch!'

Jude pulled her eyes back to the inner edge of the planking, against the mast, and sure enough there was a gap through which one might crawl, hand over hand amongst the ivy-stems of rope. She climbed cautiously around to the back of the ratlines, reached for the slack loops, and wriggled upwards.

Above, the open sky swept by in blue triumph to the distant golden line of the horizon. Jude gasped at the sudden deluge of beauty, feeling an impulse to praise a God she had left a thousand miles away.

Then Jean-Baptiste's grin appeared over the edge of the platform, and he leapt up to slap his pupil on the back.

Jude grinned back, punching him on the shoulder in triumph. Even while she did it, she was thinking, next time I shall come up here on my own. I could be alone here, and think more clearly, in the open air.

So she climbed again, and again. As the winds got up once more, she learned to roll with the sway of the ship, to spring upwards when it helped her onwards and not to let go when she would be torn away. The little platform aloft, only needed by the mariners when there were other ships in view or a landfall to look out for, became Jude's private place on the long eastward passage. Bracing her back against the rope-wrapped mast, jamming bare heels into a crack, she let the rise and fall of the ocean rock her like a child in a giant's arms. Staring out at the brilliant line of the horizon, past her bare brown knees, she finally allowed the strange stream of events that had changed her life to trickle back into her mind, running like the fine grains of silver sand in an hourglass – soft, separate, their conjunction unplanned and unstoppable. She thought coldly of her brothers' home, and their lie that had finally allowed her to break away, and of the moments aboard the *Robin*, on her own at last, when she began to see the bonds that had held her in her place. Thoughts of the *Robin* led to thoughts of the wreck, and what followed... she drew back from that indulgence. It would be best to begin to make sense of things right from the beginning.

She dwelt and dawdled in her childhood, remembering slowly, piecemeal, moments when she had felt, and then hidden from herself, the painful grip of duty and self-repression. She reached back for the memories she had lost, the glimpses of something richer, stronger, more active than the slowly contracting life of a dutiful daughter. She remembered the men in her father's office who smelt of distant places, and Richard's recognition of Judith as well as Rebecca. And she came back to the beach in Havana, and the little rooms above it where she had left Rebecca behind. But she could not yet, she thought, decide between her two selves. So much of her life had been spent as Rebecca – and much remained unresolved. She could not yet imagine Jude, all alone for the rest of his life. She rubbed her eyes and looked down to the tiny world of the deck, knowing she would have to plunge back into real life, some time.

13

As the shadows of the new-leaved lime avenue flickered across the blue plush interior of the family coach, Annette found she was trying hard not to cry – impotent tears of frustration at her inability to change what was happening. She feared, somewhere deep inside, that it was not morality but politics that mattered so much: it was the discovery of Pierre's books that had driven her father to expel him from the house. She glanced uneasily at her smallest box – she had brought the Rousseau with her, of course, for she could not risk the books being found after she had gone. Pierre had had one of the offending blue volumes in his jacket when they found him, and then they searched his rooms, and that was that. Immorality and impiety were one thing, but this was treason; and so it meant disgrace. The boy, who she had now learned was called Jean-Marie, had lost his place, of course, with a good whipping to remind him of his station.

'Mademoiselle is sad to leave her home – I am sorry.' Jacqueline, sitting opposite her mistress in a great nest of bags and packages, was doing her very best to look sympathetic, but Annette had noticed that she seemed unexpectedly pleased at the idea of going into Bordeaux. Now she half-remembered that the girl had come from the city – perhaps her family were still there. It occurred to her for the first time that perhaps Jacqueline had missed city life. It was a strange idea, but she could not quite think how to ask about it, after all this time. She stared at the dark-eyed, animated, elfin face. Her maid was pretty in a citified sort of way, quite unlike the plump slowness of the village girls. How had she come to serve at the château? It struck Annette that she knew almost nothing about this young woman with whom she had been – in some ways – on the most intimate terms for nearly six years. There was nothing odd about that, of course; one did not think about one's servants. She put the idea away and concentrated on the view from the carriage window.

The coach shook as they passed the great gates and the driver turned the horses into the Bordeaux road. All along the way the woods and hedges were bright with new green: the world was starting into life while she, Annette, was going to prison. She bit her lip.

A mile or two further on they passed through a small village. The cottages along the muddy road showed no sign of life at all; many of the windows were shuttered or curtained with rags. Somewhere out of sight a dog howled. As they left the clutch of dwellings behind, they saw a single scrawny cow, bony and bloated, being led along a straggling hedge by a silent, big-eyed child. Annette watched as the little girl reached out a thin arm to claw the tiny new leaves of hawthorn from the hedge and cram them into her mouth.

A lesson, she thought. There are always those in a worse case than your own. She turned back to Jacqueline. 'I do not know how long we shall be at the convent,' she said, as brightly as she could. 'I hope you had time to pack your own things?'

'Oh, yes, Mademoiselle! There was not much,' replied the maid, smiling. 'And I packed some extra things of yours, too, if you please – just in case.'

'In case of what?' Annette asked, mystified. 'What sort of things?'

'Your jewels, Mademoiselle. Not the family ones, of course, just those little bits that are your own. You never know when they will come in useful.'

'That was very kind of you,' said Annette, 'though I can't imagine that I shall be wearing very much jewellery, among the nuns.'

It was another hour before they came down to the estuary. The brown, slow-moving water lay like a great lake beside the road; every so often a loaded barge slipped smoothly downstream. A handful of small rowing boats lay up-ended on the grassy bank. Then they came to a place where the bank widened into a gravelly beach. A big sailing barge lay slewed on its side, hatches yawning open in the midst of a churned patch of mud. There was no one in sight. Neither of them had any idea what could have happened, but it somehow seemed to be another thing out of order, a threat, a reminder of the fragility of normal life. They sat without speaking as the coach rolled on to the cobbles of the city streets.

'Annette – my dear.'

Her aunt's voice had slightly more than its usual edge. She was rising slowly from her *prie-dieu* as the attendant nun ushered Annette into the pretty sitting room. The Abbess stood for a moment, plump white hands lightly clasped before her. In the sharp spring sunshine that spilled in from the tall window and flooded the room with shifting light off the sea, she looked the picture of devotion.

Annette glanced across to the little table between her aunt's comfortable chair and the fire, where a glass of something amber stood half-full beside a sweetmeat box. She smiled to herself. The image of God's sunlight blessing the Mother Superior's fair and pious face was so much more appropriate to the occasion than if she were found quaffing brandy and munching sugared almonds by an extravagantly unseasonal fire. The picture was only spoiled by the fact that this life of self-denial had made the old woman so fat. Annette dropped her curtsey with as much lithe youthful grace as she could muster.

News must have raced ahead of her from the château; her aunt's dark eyes probed keenly into hers, but the Abbess was careful to offer no opening to any kind of discussion. She bade her great-niece welcome and was sure she would have a fruitful stay. Then she rang a little bell.

'Sister Josephine will look after you today – you will enjoy seeing into all the quiet places that are our retreat from the common, bustling world. She is our novice mistress,' she added, with a small smile.

There was a tap on the door and, before Annette could respond, a substantial woman stepped into the room, bobbed to the Mother Superior, and fixed Annette with a stern grey eye.

Determined as she was not to show weakness before her aunt, Annette could not stop the protest that rose to her lips. 'But I am not to be a novice,' she squeaked.

'No, no, my dear,' said Mother Honorine smoothly. 'You are our guest.' She smiled graciously and patted her niece's arm. 'Sister Josephine knows that you are not seeking admission to the Order. At any rate, not yet.' Then she turned back quite conclusively to her prayers. The interview was over.

Leaving the light and comfortable salon, Annette followed the silent nun into the depths of the ancient building, along tight, bleak corridors where no sunlight had penetrated for three hundred years. It was only then that she really understood that she was being imprisoned, as surely as any errant young lord sent to the dread Bastille under his father's *lettres de cachet*. More surely, indeed, since she was merely a girl and no one would think she was hard done by, to be locked away in dank darkness simply at her father's will. It had all been so sudden, so astonishing, that until now she had not been able to think about it. It had been easier to sympathise with the peasants they had seen on the way, suffering, as she told herself, the agonies of poverty and near-starvation. These things, rather than her own plight, had bitten into her mind. Now reality hit her with a shock. She felt as if the earth had opened and swallowed her up. The imposing Sister Josephine was not to be her friend, but her gaoler.

Sister Josephine led her up and down worn stone stairs, opening doors onto the sewing room, the laundry, the sanatorium. The heavy doors opened into gloom: Annette realised that, apart from those in the Abbess's salon, there were few windows that faced out to the sea. All these rooms looked inwards, onto the dim little courtyard at the centre of the old building. As the nun opened each door, faces turned towards them – eager faces, seeking diversion from whatever they were doing. Only in the hot and dripping laundry, where the shapes of women seemed to loom misshapen out of the fug of steam, were the faces lacking in curiosity or, indeed, any expression at all.

'The lay sisters,' said Sister Josephine, briskly. 'Ruined girls, mostly, cast out from honest society. They are taken in by the Order as an act of charity. Their work is a penance for their sins.' And she hurried her visitor onwards.

At a tiny staircase window, Annette caught a glimpse down into the green depths of the courtyard and saw that the whole convent sat on squat round arches, built out from the city walls unimaginably long ago. She followed the nun down a twisting stair and through a door which led out into this yard. Looking up, she saw that they were walking under the arches she had glimpsed from above. She had scarcely had time for a good deep breath of outside air before she was swept on into a huge, echoing hall where the smell of damp stone and beeswax was overlaid with the tired ghosts of generations of soup. Two long lines of polished tables stretched away into the distance.

'The refectory,' said Sister Josephine unnecessarily. 'You will eat here with the other lady guests and the rest of the community.' She rapidly led the way to a different door, and plunged them into a maze of even narrower corridors with, this time, rattling wooden flights of stairs. They came to a row of dark doors.

'This is the guest wing, where you will be staying,' said the novice mistress. 'We have five other lady guests at the moment; you will be the sixth.' She pushed open the second door along, and ushered Annette into a small, plainly furnished chamber.

Annette tried not to let her dismay show on her face. She had not expected luxury, of course – had not even desired it, here; but the bleak ugliness of the room shocked her. The sludge-grey walls of mildewed plaster framed a narrow bed with limp, plain curtains, and beside it a washstand with prominent slop-bucket. In the corner was a *prie-dieu* of splintery plain deal, not at all like the carved oak of Lady Honorine's; it confronted a large crucifix. Kneeling there, you would have the dying Christ's ivory-coloured toes three inches from your nose. Annette immediately resolved never to do so, come what may. She turned her eyes to her own trunk, standing at the foot of the bed.

'You may leave your outdoor clothes here,' said the novice mistress briskly. 'There is a peg behind the door for your cloak. Then, if there is time before chapel, I will show you the rest of the house.'

Annette took off her cloak and hat, conscious of the sharp, assessing eyes of the nun. Even in her hasty departure she had chosen her plainest gowns and caps but, now that she was here, the oyster satin felt ridiculously frivolous.

'While you are here, you should wear a veil,' said the nun, picking up a square-folded white cloth from the bed. 'Bend your head.'

And before Annette knew what was happening, Sister Josephine had plucked off her little lace cap and tied on the veil, pulling the white linen firmly down on her forehead and knotting the tapes at the back of her head. With a practised hand she pulled the ends of the veil forward over Annette's shoulders, drew a pin from the front of her habit and clamped the thing under Annette's chin.

Astonished, Annette cast around for a looking-glass; but of course, there was none. Just as well, she thought grimly, I must look hideous. She wondered what Jacqueline would think – and, indeed, where she was. Presumably there were servants' quarters for the lady guests' maids? But what would they do all day here? It was perfectly ridiculous. A wave of misery hit her; it was all she could do not to slide onto her bed and howl like a child. She could not look at Sister Josephine.

A clanging bell suddenly, blessedly, broke in upon them.

'Noon – the hour of Sext,' said the sister, in the voice of one who is accustomed to instruct others. 'It is one of the hours when we must sing our Office in chapel. Come!' As she led the way from the room, folding her hands into her sleeves, she added, 'You will like the chapel.'

Annette did not like the chapel. The chapel was perfectly hideous. They came in among the last of those hurrying to their places;

even so, Sister Josephine led her a long way down an empty and echoing nave before they reached a mere handful of benches at the front, where sat the lay sisters (some still drippy from the laundry) and the 'lady guests'. Annette took her seat on the end of a row of five kneeling ladies. Three had their faces shaded by delicate hands, showing only the fall of their rather pretty (and obviously expensive) veils; the other two turned to her in undisguised curiosity. One was a woman so like Madame Desmoulins that Annette blinked, and was about to say something silly, when the Office began with a high nasal bleat from the old priest at the altar. They all faced front, but not before Annette had registered that the other face that had looked into hers, with a slight smile, was black.

The shadowy figures of the nuns, gathered like a crowd of starlings in the front pews of the choir, seemed equally dwarfed by their surroundings. The order of Our Lady of the Little Angels must once have had many more members than it had now. Annette tried in vain to attend to the high, thin chanting of the nuns and the baas of the priest, but very quickly gave up and turned her attention to the hateful room they were in. Words and music seemed to evaporate in the echoing, over-decorated space. At home, the tiny chapel had been at the ancient core of the château, a feeling, intimate space surrounded by simple arches and massive stone walls. It held Annette's prayers and hopes as a mother's arms might do; it was full of magic. This place was huge and cold, with high gothic vaulting and elaborate tracery; it was full only of furniture.

Behind the edgy, pointed arches, narrow side-chapels crowded upwards, each with its twinkling chandelier of crystal drops and its alcove bulging with jewelled reliquaries and silver-gilt altar lamps. In the shadows between the chapels lurked heavily carved confessionals, polished – no doubt by the lay sisters – to a dull gleam. The fat, round pillars of the Brillac chapel had been topped by crudely carved, out-of-proportion stone pictures of birds and leaves and even little beasts and people, immensely ancient; here every teetering column ended in a pair of perfect whirls like a modern wig. Carved between the pillars were gruesome bas-reliefs of the stations of the cross, alternating with paintings of saints on pink backgrounds. The three examples of these blessed ones that she could make out from her seat were all female, two in the advanced stages of martyrdom – one with her cut-off breasts in a dish at her feet – and the third in the throes of a religious ecstasy that looked almost as painful.

As the priest stopped speaking and the voices of the nuns rose again in a shapeless plainsong, Annette decided that the only thing really worth looking at was the painting over the altar. She had been shown it before, when she had visited here as a child – it was the Madonna of the Little Angels, the treasure from which the convent took its name. Gratefully, she fixed her mind on the rich, dark colours, the living paint that spoke to her of the painter, working in Italy two hundred years ago. His Madonna was young and solemn, her expression as she looked down at the child rather sad. The infant Jesus – a stiff and unhealthy-looking baby with a pale square face – was comical, in danger of falling off his mother's pink silk lap as he stretched out one pudgy hand to the little angel with the basket of apples in the lower left-hand corner of the picture. When she had first seen it, Annette had decided that the little angels were the real subject of the painting – a whole family of beautiful children with golden hair and dark eyes attendant on the Madonna and child. They were too old to be cherubs, and too young to be real, grown-up angels, though they had soft wings in all the colours of the rainbow. They were clearly enjoying the sunshine in this Italian garden: two were making music on a mandolin and a flute and one picking grapes from a vine on the wall; the littlest angel was playing with a small white dog.

Two years ago, she had adored the little angels. But now her eye was more taken by the figure of the Madonna. She thought that the sad-faced model who had sat for the portrait of Christ's mother bore a resemblance to her grandmother in the portrait at home. Somewhere, behind the pretty image, there was a real woman, a real life shaped and confined by others' wills, as women's lives must be in all ages. Annette sighed. Even the great Jean-Jacques held that women's role in the order of things was to be subject without question to their fathers and husbands – it had been the section of *Emile* that had caused her and Pierre to argue most fiercely. Liberty and equality, yes – but for whom?

Mentally she shook herself. There was no point in giving in to despair. Better to concentrate on these real women. She had need of friends, of allies, and for once there would be a number of people, even girls her own age, around her. She stole another glance at her fellow guests. At the far end of the row were two pretty girls, dressed so alike that they might be sisters; then the dark-skinned young woman who had smiled at her when she came in. Next there kneeled the much older lady who had reminded Annette of her chaperone – though Madame Desmoulins would never have worn her gown so *décolleté*. And was that rouge on her cheeks? Annette blinked. The fifth guest, just beside her, was a bold-faced girl who was making no attempt to take any interest in the proceedings, and who, as Annette turned to look at her, yawned widely and then grinned.

Annette smiled back. Clearly not everyone in this gloomy place was overwhelmed by it. Perhaps her stay here would be more pleasant than she had feared. She quite looked forward to getting to know her fellow prisoners.

14

As the *Belle Héloïse* swept eastwards towards Europe, there was less and less for the crew to do, and nothing at all to entertain the passengers. That was what led to Jean-Baptiste's spot of trouble.

Jude was busy with a burnt porridge pot that she had put aside soaking after crew breakfast and come back to at the end of the mess. It was hard to clean it well with salt water, and the main wash was not hot enough. She was scouring at it with a rope's end, while Armand nodded at the galley table, when there were sudden shouts of command along the deck. Armand woke with a grunt. They looked at each other.

The cook raised an eyebrow. 'What now?'

Jude shrugged – she had taken to the shrug during her conversations with Jean-Baptiste, as a useful delaying tactic while she summoned enough French for an answer – and stepped to the doorway, hands dripping.

A knot of men had gathered at the rail that separated the crew from the politer parts of the ship. Facing them across it were two of the passengers and Durand, the young third officer. Durand was bowing and gesticulating; the lady passenger clutched her escort's arm. The other side of the rail stood Jean-Baptiste, his fists clenched, while his topmast mates loomed behind and muttered in his ears. He wore no shirt, and the mermaid tattooed on his broad brown chest was rippling ominously.

'Those are the English passengers,' Jude said. She had noted, on errands to the cabins, that there were a couple of fine folk from Britain on board. Their ability to look straight through her while drawling minute orders into the air had confirmed all she had ever heard about British insolence.

Armand shrugged in his turn. 'Perhaps the lady does not like your friend's *décor*,' he said, not very interested.

As Jude watched, the Englishman began to speak. He looked like thunder, and he was pointing at Jean-Baptiste.

A thought struck Jude. 'Durand speaks no English,' she said.

'Ah, you are needed, my little friend. Go, interpret for Milord,' Armand said expansively, and he tipped his hat over his eyes, sinking back in his chair.

Jean-Baptiste saw Jude coming and tilted up his head.

Jude went up to the rail and addressed the officer with careful respect. 'Your pardon, sir. May I be of assistance? I speak English.'

Durand stared wildly at her for a moment. 'Who are you? Good God, the scullion. American, aren't you? Yes, boy, I hope you can help.' He indicated Jean-Baptiste. 'See if you can find out from Milord what this sailor is supposed to have done amiss, will you? Otherwise, I shall find myself stringing him up for a flogging just to keep the peace.' He turned to the passengers, bowing again, but still speaking French. 'A thousand pardons, Monsieur – you will tell it once more?'

The English Milord did not deign to reply. He stood with his arm around his wife like some noble but ridiculous statue, breathing heavily down his aristocratic nose.

Jude remembered to bow. 'My Lord, please be so good as to allow me to be your interpreter. What is amiss?'

Milord lowered his eyes slowly to examine the barefoot lad before him, and said faintly to his wife, 'A colonial, my dear. We are in luck at last.' He turned back to Jude. 'Listen, boy. This...' He pointed at Jean-Baptiste. 'This low fellow has insulted Lady Belling. He approached her in an indelicate manner, and made a... beastly attempt on her person. She has told me about it. He denies it. He should be flogged – the maximum sentence. Tell that to this jackanapes of an officer, will you? And be quick about it.'

Jude nodded seriously, and glanced across to Jean-Baptiste, who rolled his eyes heavenwards. His expression was anything but helpful. Suppressing a sigh, she turned back to Durand. 'Sir will permit me to speak to the sailor?'

'Quickly,' said the lieutenant nervously. 'The Captain will get wind of this any moment.'

Now Jude understood his agitation: it would obviously not do for an officer to be seen to be unable to sort this out without the aid of the galley. She spoke rapidly to the fuming Jean-Baptiste. 'What's going on? What did she think you did?'

'By God, I did nothing! I swear it on my mother's life! This bitch' – he indicated the Englishwoman with a toss of the head – 'was passing by. She came to watch, I make no doubt, to watch young men, huh? And to be watched. Why else does she dress like this, with her neck all bare, I ask you? We were coiling the forebraces. I had taken off my shirt, I saw her cut her eyes at me. I say to myself, aha! Baptiste, she has a passion for you! Then the ship rolls, and she totters towards me. Of course, I put out a hand, in case she falls – and *pouf!* she is screaming. She is hot for me, this one, I tell you. This milksop' – he indicated the English Milord – 'is no good for her.'

There was a rumble of amusement from the gathered sailors.

Jude spoke more urgently. 'Whether he is or no, my friend, he wants to see you bleed. He is demanding a hundred lashes for your politeness to his lady – is that sensible? Come, make your bow to Milady.' She smiled. 'You can take a closer look at her pretty little feet.'

To Jude's surprise, several of the men agreed. 'The boy's right, Baptiste,' said one of them. 'Why suffer a lashing for an English whore?' Two or three other voices joined in.

Before Jean-Baptiste could argue, Jude turned back to the Englishman, explaining the desolation of the simple sailor at his genuine mistake, his lack of any intention to be insulting, his wish to abase himself, to apologise most humbly, to throw himself on Milady's mercy. She wondered if this was going a bit far, but the Englishwoman, blushing prettily, seemed to be enjoying her moment of power.

Jude met her eye. 'My lady would surely not wish such a

creature to suffer on her account, when he had meant her no harm?'

Milady coloured more deeply and looked away, turning her face into her husband's coat, whispering something Jude did not hear.

Milord finally looked Jude in the eye. 'Let him make his apology,' he said gruffly.

It was only then that Jude realised what she had done. She had asked Jean-Baptiste, hero of the after-deck, to humble himself in front of his mates. For a sickening moment, she thought he wouldn't do it. Then, with an exaggerated, almost insulting flourish, Jean-Baptiste bowed low in front of the lady. She and her husband turned quickly away, and did not hear Jean-Baptiste's comment as he straightened up and faced his mates.

'Fat legs,' he said, 'and she smells of sick.'

The men roared appreciatively, and Jean-Baptiste's reputation was saved.

Jude's own standing with the men was affected by the incident too, she found. There were a tense couple of days during which the rumour flew about that the cook's boy was English, but Jean-Baptiste soon scotched that one. The boy spoke English, of course, but how could these dolts mistake a brave American colonist for a miserable *anglais*? Had not they seen how coolly the boy took on Milord, just as America had taken on their English oppressors, when they shook off the yoke of servitude? Jean-Baptiste's voice became rich with emotion. America, he said, was the land of freedom and brotherhood – and could not France herself take a lesson from these noble sons of nature, who had fought and died for Liberty, rather than cower under the heel of a tyrant?

Jude didn't know whether she was glad or sorry to meet with this public approval; humble obscurity had had its advantages. But it was pleasant to be liked. Her friendship with Jean-Baptiste survived, too – though, as he was careful to explain to her on more than one occasion, a flogging was nothing. For himself, he could have borne it; but yes, Jude had been right, for it would have been a disgrace to his whole mess that his unblemished shoulders should bear such scars. He must think also of the honour of his family: how would his dear widowed mother have borne the pain of his disgrace? He talked a good deal about his honour, for a few days, and they remained friends.

It was much warmer now; May was advancing, and the days had lengthened. Soon they might sight land, the coastal islands of Europe, so Jude could no longer seek solitude at the masthead – one or other of the sailor boys squatted there for hours every day, staring out to the east. When the first sighting came it was something of an anti-climax – a mere bump on the northern horizon that they bypassed without making contact; but then came the shout of 'Land ho! Land dead ahead!' and everyone crowded to the rails. It still took more than an hour before the coast was visible from the deck; but eventually Jude could make out a low, blurred outline that did not change or break. All hands were called to wear ship, turning, according to Armand, to run up the coast a little to find the Gironde estuary.

'Go catch the last of the fowls,' he said. 'The officers will want a good dinner this afternoon.'

While the officers consumed the two scraggy chickens and several decanters of the best cabin-wine, Jude hung over the port rail watching the shoreline, a fine spray in her face. It seemed a dull sort of coast, low dunes sifting into the sea with here and there a small stand of pines. The coastal traffic was busy, little fishing craft with patched sails and painted hulls, mostly heading for home at the end of the day.

'They are called *pinassayres*,' said Jean-Baptiste's voice behind her. 'After herring. That green one with the blue sail would be my cousin's.'

'How can you tell?'

'His house is that colour,' said Jean-Baptiste mysteriously. He leant beside her on the rail, pointing ahead. 'We are coming up to the estuary – the oak forest is on the headland, the Pointe de Grave.' He straightened up. 'I have been out almost a year. I shall be glad to be home – with my pockets full.' He turned to look at her. 'Whatever has happened up in Versailles, money will be needed!'

The rounding of the point took until sunset. To avoid sailing into the narrow mouth in the darkness they dropped anchor, with much cursing, rusty creaking of the anchor chain and scampering of rats that had nested in its coils all the way across the Atlantic. As dawn came up, Jude heard the thump and running feet of the watch and quickly rolled out to make breakfast. The banks were visible either side, and ahead a tall tower, glaring white on the top.

'Lighthouse,' explained Armand, and indeed one was clearly needed, for it stood on a headland that divided the river mouth in two. Soon they were navigating the slender, winding southerly channel that led between shelving banks into a river mouth. Jude gazed hungrily at the oak trees, decked in the blazing bronze of springtime. It was amazing how the sight of growing things refreshed the spirit. They sailed cautiously for an hour, heaving the lead all the time, as the treed islets and sand dune banks gave way to scrubby working beaches littered with tackle and small boats. And then, astonishingly, they came up on the starboard tack and saw the city.

It looked at first view not to be a city built by man at all, but a sea-cliff, or one face of a canyon – a golden, dazzling rock-face, neatly sliced by a mighty river. But it was too regular for that. Glittering in the sunshine, the cliff-face described a slight but perfect curve. It was all one height, cut off as neatly above as below, and on its face were seams, or lines, or some such regular marks. It was all made by the hand of man: a row of golden buildings. Jude gasped. Jean-Baptiste appeared grinning at her shoulder.

'The *grande façade*, they call it,' he said, 'and very grand it is, no? The masons of the Bordelais are the best in the world. No doubt they have been just as busy since I left. Tomorrow we shall see.'

'Tomorrow? But we are nearly in port, surely? I saw the passengers taken off in the long boat, ten minutes ago.'

Jean-Baptiste spat over the rail. 'Indeed. The rats left the ship – but we go no further, until more rats have been aboard. In France, *mon ami*, the rats are unusual. Most of them – the two-legged ones – don't bother to go to sea with the ships. They wait till we return to take their share, before we can go into harbour.'

'The excise?' Jude said in English. 'Customs?' She did not know the French word.

But Jean-Baptiste recognised the English ones. He nodded, and spat again. Then he shrugged. 'But we will have other visitors first – look! I must seek out Nicolas.'

He ran off to find his tail-mate. Whoever these first-comers were, Jude realised, they were worth the compliment of a freshly tied and tarred pigtail. She stared upstream. Among the distant bustle on the shore, at the foot of the amazing cliff of buildings, several small boats were indeed filling with a mill of tiny figures, as if to come out to meet the ship. She strained her eyes, wishing for the thousandth time on the voyage that she had her old telescope.

The ant-like figures were hardly embarked, and only the first of the boats had actually put off into the channel, when half an hour later a drum rolled on the quarter-deck. Immediately, as if they had been waiting, sailors turned out from all over the ship, pushing past her to assemble in the waist, all in high good humour. From the galley came Armand, dressed in his coat and even carrying his hat. He slapped her back.

'Come, little one – payday. Get your hat and stand in line with me.'

15

Pay. She had money in her hand once again – a good sum in gold, enough to take her on to England. Why did she not feel more pleased? Walking away, scooping the coins from her hat, Jude glanced up to the mainmast, but there was for some reason already a crowd of men up there, all laughing and waving towards the shore. Not her retreat today, then; she would have to find some other quiet place to think. She glanced into the galley. Armand had apparently gone elsewhere. She sat down at the table.

It was not as if she had not thought this through already. Her plans were laid: to find a second-hand clothes shop and to buy something suitably quiet, but reasonably new and fine – she did not want to give an impression of poverty. It would include a particularly good, lady-like pair of gloves, to cover the ravages of salt-water skivvying. Then she would seek out a ferry office – she had already learnt the name of two likely ones from Jean-Baptiste – and book herself a passage to London. And from then on, she would be once more Miss Rebecca Wiston, come to claim her inheritance. She shifted, and rattled the coins in her pocket. Then she became aware of herself, sitting – elbows on the table, legs splayed, one foot tucked behind the chair leg, her hand thrust into the front of her hair. Miss? She straightened up: ankles together, hands folded in lap, chin up, and gazed out of the doorway. Could she do this?

What other choice did she have? She shook her head.

Armand appeared suddenly. He was grinning, but his expression changed when he saw Jude.

'Ah. Yes. Little one…' He was clearly embarrassed.

'*Maître?*' Jude stood up.

'You stay in here, I think.' He gathered two unopened bottles from his private store under the bread-hutch. Jude watched, puzzled, as he dipped to look at himself in the largest copper pan, stroking back his hair. Then he looked at her again. 'Or – perhaps you want to come to the party? You like to dance, no? But there will be... girls.'

As he spoke, an unmistakably female voice rang out from over the ship's side.

'Ahoy, *Héloïse!*' it cried.

There was a deep answering roar. Jude jumped up to see. Every man on board, washed, shaved and dressed in his best, was lined up along the port rail waving, cheering, whistling.

Now many shrill voices could be heard from below, calling out greetings to the sailors. Over the heads of the men, just beside Jude as she stood watching at the galley door, there rose a nodding plume of feathers, at least a foot high and dyed in garish pinks and greens. Below this headdress appeared a face almost as unnatural: huge black-rimmed eyes, skin painted white as a wall with two red discs high on the cheekbones and a splatter of black dots, stars and crescents, stuck to the quivering jowls. Embedded in the ample flesh of her nose, a diamond caught the sun.

With cries of delight the men lifted this creature aboard. She shook out her brightly coloured skirts like an old parrot settling its feathers, then looked sharply around. Her glance travelled so coldly over Jude that it made her shiver; but the woman greeted Armand with a familiar nod.

'Madame!' cried Armand, bending over her hand with a flourish.

Extricating herself with a professional smile, the keeper turned back to marshal her girls.

Jude had rarely seen anything as ghastly, or as sad, as the women who now appeared, simpering and shrieking as they affected to need the support of manly arms to clamber aboard. There were only about a dozen of them, of all ages or none, but all wore the same air of desperate gaiety. And the clothes! Jude – or rather Rebecca – had seen nothing like them on the God-fearing streets of Salem. Bedraggled skirts in violent shades of pink and purple; petticoats of figured silk and brocade, heavily embossed but threadbare at seat and hem and marked with unnameable stains; torn silver lace and holed silk stockings. Two of the youngest girls wore nothing but smocks of once-white muslin, now butter-yellow and looped to disguise their tatters, though not in any way to cover their thin shoulders and hard little breasts. They all lined up along the ship's rail in what they had obviously been taught were fetching poses, while Madame thrust a pack of eager mariners into a queue behind her, tapping them smartly into line with her silver-topped cane. She hauled a cloth money-bag from her cleavage; at the sight of it the men started to dig in their pockets.

Armand appeared at Jude's side. 'Come,' he said, taking her firmly by the elbow, 'we will get a good place for the dancing.' And he steered her forward along the deck.

During the afternoon three more boats arrived, bearing more girls but also gin-sellers and a quartet of two fiddles, oboe and horn. The girls on the final boat had no one in charge of them, Jude noticed. They made their own bargains with the remaining men before disappearing down the hatches to the mess deck where the hammocks were still slung side by side.

The day wore on and some of the men and girls reappeared, drifting towards the sound of the fiddle. By the time the moon came up, both dancers and players were growing tired. Jude, who had enjoyed the new music enough to show off her best hornpipe several times, sat with her back against a stanchion, the only person listening alone as the little band played a last languorous tune. She felt melancholy, and not very well. Over the course of the voyage she had learned to take a little grog, but the suspicion of nausea in her stomach told her that the tankard of wine Armand had bought her from the hawker had been stronger than she was used to. She stood up cautiously and, stepping with care on the unfamiliar stability of the deck, headed back towards the galley. Presumably the officers were somewhere aboard still, and might call for service?

As she leaned on the door, a row broke out under her feet: shouting and shrieking, and the thumping of bodies against bulkheads. A fight. As Jude turned back, a girl shot out of the aft companion-way and careered along the deck, clutching a bundle of clothes, naked except for a little straw hat still skewered to her curls. Three men came lumbering after her, yelling and swinging blows at each other as they ran. Only one of them had on more than a shirt. None of them saw the legs of the couple tucked in under the jolly-boat: the first man fell over them and they all went down like skittles, fists flying. The howls of the girl behind the boat and the curses of her young man added to the mayhem; the musicians stopped abruptly and tucked their instruments protectively under their arms.

The naked girl, evading grabbing hands and attempts to trip her, fled forward, then doubled back, heading straight for Jude, who saw the terror in her eyes. Without thinking, she opened the galley door, stepped inside and bolted it firmly behind them both.

The girl swayed on her feet for a few seconds, rallied with an effort, and stepped towards Jude. '*Salut*, sailor,' she slurred. Then she collapsed into Jude's arms.

With some difficulty Jude got her into Armand's chair. Taking the blanket from her hammock, she tried to rouse the girl enough to wrap her in it, but without success. She was unconscious; the smell of gin was overwhelming. Jude lifted the elaborately coiffed head and gazed into the little painted face. The young whore was no more than a child; eleven or twelve at most. Another wave of nausea rose in Jude's throat. She listened for a moment to the strained and noisy breathing, then laid the blanket over the child and went to listen at the door. The men had gone; the only noise of voices was at a distance. Jude slid back the bolt and looked cautiously out.

The party was over. Here and there a sailor lay spreadeagled on the deck; the musicians and hawkers were already pushing off in one of the shore boats. Armand was nowhere in sight.

Jude, swaying and nauseous but determined to do her duty to the end, went to see if any of the officers needed the services of the galley before she turned in. On the way back, she was very sick over the starboard rail. Falling in through the galley door, she automatically pulled off her breeches and scrambled into her hammock. She had no time to miss her blanket before she fell into a deep pit of sleep.

Next morning, the girl had gone. And so had Jude's breeches. She still had her shirt, since she slept in it, but the wretched child had made away with her patched and grubby breeks. Her anger soon turned to a sheepish amusement – they hadn't been much of a prize. Unlike her mates, she had not dressed in her best for the previous evening, so she still had a clean shirt and her shore-going breeches in the bundle which doubled as her pillow. She turned out on deck as the ship slid into its moorings, feeling that she had escaped quite lightly from her first – no, her second – brush with a whore.

It was only as she stepped from the ladder into the rocking boat that she realised her pay had still been in her lost breeches pocket. The world spun; the man next to her caught her arm to stop her from going overboard.

'Too much grog or too much whoring?' he chuckled. 'You should leave all that to us old 'uns.'

Frozen with shock, Jude saw nothing as they rowed ashore. The boat grounded and her mates leapt out, splashing through the shallow waters to the waiting crowd. Blindly, she followed them and stood helpless at the water's edge, trying to contain rising panic. She was in a foreign country. She had no friends, no money, nothing but the clothes she stood up in. Her hand went to her throat. The locket was still there. She drew a long breath. It was ridiculous to be so relieved, for she would never sell it, but it felt as if the golden token somehow held her life.

Still clutching the locket with its tiny image of Aunt Isabella, she raised her head. Not more than thirty yards away, across an empty stretch of shingle and timber decking, Isabella herself was looking out of a window – a window in an upright box, standing on the quay, suspended on poles between two uniformed men. Jude blinked and shook her head. The window framed the pale face, the lace-trimmed gown, the dark ringlets, just as the locket framed the portrait. But she was alive, breathing. At that moment her dark eyes turned on Jude, and for an instant they looked at each other across space and time.

Then the crowd shifted, the men stepped forward, and the apparition was gone.

PART TWO

1789

Spring into Summer

16

In the dreary weeks that followed her arrival at the convent, Annette had more than enough time to get to know her fellow prisoners; but her hope of finding friends and allies was short-lived. The lady guests were expected to spend most of their time in a crowded little parlour, which had a view, of a sidelong kind, out into the square before the convent gates. They were constantly under the eye of the antique beauty Madame Grimaud. Annette was not sure why they were supposed to stay together in this way, but it was probably because most of the girls were there for their sins, and must be guarded to stop them from committing more. Their parents had given up trying to keep them in order and sent them to the custody of the convent until they could be safely married off.

This was certainly the case with Michèle, the young woman who had sat next to Annette in chapel that first day. She had eloped one moonlit night from her family's mansion here in the city, and had been caught and brought back, her reputation entirely ruined. Now she must stay with the sisters until the scandal had died down and her parents could find someone to marry her in spite of it.

'She'll be all right, though – her fortune's *huge*. Her dowry includes most of the ugliest houses in the city, as well as half the Guyenne, doesn't it, Michèle?' Thus Sophie, eating grapes on the only sofa, with her head in Thérèse's lap. This pretty pair were the ones Annette had assumed to be sisters; they were in fact old schoolfriends, but shrieked with childish delight when she told them. They always wore identical gowns, spent much of their time dressing each other's hair to match, and loved having a new audience for telling everyone's stories, especially their own. Giggling, they took turns at describing how they had met at school and been inseparable until, at sixteen, they were returned to their two families to be married. This sudden idleness had gone to their heads.

'I was so lonely!' Thérèse exclaimed, clasping her hands and rolling her eyes in the best tragedy mode.

'We had to find something to fill the empty hours.' Sophie licked sugar from her fingers.

The upshot was that she had been caught exchanging love tokens with an officer; while Thérèse had outclassed her by planning an elopement with a penniless marquis in the same regiment, before being betrayed (as she climbed out of her chamber window) by a jealous little sister.

Only Charlotte, the young black woman with the friendly smile, seemed to have done nothing to deserve her imprisonment, except to look distressingly unlike the rest of her aristocratic French relations. Michèle told Annette that Charlotte's family owned big plantations in the West Indies and had lived for many years in Guadeloupe.

'Her father has any amount of blackamoor bastards, of course, but Charlotte was the only girl – a pretty baby, apparently. The sentimental old fool insisted on her being brought up in the family, but now she's grown they don't know what to do with her. She's never been to school, and she's always lived abroad, so she has no proper accomplishments. I suppose they could settle an enormous fortune on her, but who would want a black wife?' She shrugged and popped another sugar plum into her mouth.

Annette, horrified by the girl's unthinking cruelty, instinctively crossed the room to stand beside Charlotte, who was looking out of the window, pretending not to hear.

Michèle was cruel, Sophie-and-Thérèse silly and slightly pathetic, Charlotte silent and sad. Annette found it all tedious, empty-headed, unbearably childish. Almost the worst of them was the determinedly youthful Madame Grimaud. In spite of her lady-like manners and apparently intimate acquaintance with all the noble families of Bordeaux, she came, as Michèle whispered to Annette, of a *bourgeois* family, and had no real breeding.

'Otherwise, she would know better than to wear those tawdry jewels, wouldn't she? And the paint! What a fright! If one is going to assist nature, one should do it with style, don't you think?'

Annette gazed curiously at Madame Grimaud. It had not occurred to her that cosmetics could aim at an impression of nature. These certainly didn't, unless one naturally went around in a high blush and grew eyebrows arched halfway to one's hair.

'She's a widow,' Michèle continued, 'and poor as a rat. The nuns give her board and lodging in exchange for chaperoning us.' She snorted with laughter. 'And wouldn't they have a fit if they knew how she does it!'

In that respect at least, Michèle was right. The widow Grimaud exercised very little control over her charges; indeed, she seemed to be of as flighty a turn of mind as any of them.

Conversation in the little salon was entirely mindless. They discussed their embroidery and exchanged patterns for it; they admired each other's ribbons, and passed comment on the personal appearance and family backgrounds of the novices who occasionally passed the window in a gaggle behind Sister Josephine. They were endlessly curious about each other's families, fortunes and connections, and chattered for hours about the royal family, about whom they appeared to know every intimate detail, from how much the King drank and how many new lovers the Queen had taken, to the latest bulletin on the health of the Dauphin. The only news from outside the walls that interested them was gossip and scandal. In a few days Annette learned more about the private lives of the great than she cared to hear, including several highly dubious stories about the local magnates, even the Duke of Artois; but nothing at all about the riots or the all-important progress of the Estates General.

She scored social points in the salon because the Abbess was her great-aunt, though the other girls did not envy Annette her weekly summons to take coffee with her important relation. She was glad of anything that got her out of the parlour even for an hour, but the conversation in her great-aunt's room, while very different, was hardly an improvement. She laboured to keep up her end of polite and pious exchanges about absolutely nothing, all the while struggling to work out what her relative was really thinking. No more had been said about Annette's future, either in the short or the long term, and she feared to ask lest she should provoke some unwelcome decision. But she looked forward with pleasure to being in the light and beautiful room itself. She always made a point of getting up from her chair to fetch some little thing for the Abbess, so as to be able to gaze briefly out of the window, where the red-brown sails of barges skimmed the murky waters of the estuary, and the clouds moved against the blue of the sky. Once there was a big ship under sail, like a great swan among ducks, and she watched it, entranced, until her great-aunt called her sharply back to the table. She was a prisoner here and must not look with too much longing at the world outside the bars.

One of the things that surprised her, however, was that the lady guests had so much contact with the outside world. All kinds of comforts were regularly imported into the salon – silk cushions, footstools, inlaid workboxes, dishes of sweetmeats, bottles and flasks of 'cordials'. The servants seemed to come and go freely on errands for their mistresses, who teased each other constantly about little notes and *billets-doux* and the admirers who had sent them. Annette did not actually see many notes, and suspected that most of the admirers were figments of idle imagination. Perhaps that was why Madame Grimaud did not feel she must stop the coming and going, and in fact took advantage of other people's errands to send for little things of her own, since, she said, she did not care to keep a servant with her. As soon as Annette had asked, of course, Jacqueline had smiled and gone off to fetch things for her, too. This morning Annette had asked for news, and the dear girl found her the latest report from Paris, which she hid under her pillow, saving it for bedtime.

The bleak bed-chamber which had so repelled her on the first day had become her only refuge. As early in the evening as she could do so without causing comment, she would retire to her room, ostensibly to sleep but in truth simply to be alone and to write. That was the worst thing: that she had so little time to herself, to be alone, to think. Back at Brillac, in her lonely childhood, she had often longed for the company of sisters or brothers – now she had company, it was driving her to distraction. All meals were communal, though blessedly silent except for a sing-song reading from the lives of the saints, which was intrusive and incredible without being in the least interesting. Most of the rest of the time she was confined to the salon with nothing to do except listen to the endless inanities. The only daily change was the interminable time they spent in chapel. Here the nuns at least had the occupation of singing the Office, but Annette and the other lady guests had nothing to do but sit on the hard, wooden pews and listen to the repetition of the services; any thoughts she might have there were only of how she might escape. But escape from chapel meant only to be shut up again in the dreadful parlour with its futile conversation and childish games.

She had not expected life in the convent to be pleasant. She knew the house would be dark, the garden small and overshadowed by high walls, the food plain. She had foreseen the absence of physical pleasure – but not this terrible starvation of the mind. The library was one of the biggest disappointments. When Sister Josephine had thrown open the door of the oak-panelled room with its two great bookcases and wide leather-topped table, Annette had promised herself an hour or two each day in that exciting space. It did not take her long to realise that the library contained only the dullest of religious books, many of which were not even in French. Clearly, reading was not expected. They did not know that she would die without it. But, since no one in this benighted house ever read anything except prayer-books or love-letters, it occurred to her that this might be a place where she could sometimes take refuge.

One afternoon, a particularly witless argument about the exact sequence of the Duke of Artois' mistresses drove Annette from the parlour in search of somewhere to be alone. Pushing open the heavy door of the library, she was surprised to see Charlotte seated at the table by the window.

'Forgive me,' said Annette hastily, 'I did not know you were here...'

'It's not a private place,' said Charlotte. 'And I was about to go. One should not keep Sister Josephine waiting.' But she did not move, only turned back to looking out of the window. 'Don't you sometimes long to get away from them all?'

'Oh, I do!' cried Annette fervently. 'Sometimes I think I shall go mad for lack of a reasonable conversation!'

'Or just a blessed silence,' said Charlotte. 'How they chatter!' She rose from her chair and made for the door. 'Don't worry, I shan't tell them where you are,' she said with a smile. 'But perhaps I shall see you here again?'

Sometime after Vespers on the evening of the Wednesday before Easter, Annette was lying on her narrow bed staring at the ceiling. She knew she should not be here, but she could not have stayed another minute in the parlour, where an extended argument about whether one should lace one's stays at the front or at the back in order to be truly fashionable had reduced her almost to tears. She felt as if she was going mad. Pleading a headache, she had escaped to her room.

Listlessly, she picked up the book she had been attempting to read. It was the *Social Contract*. She tried hard for a few minutes to concentrate on the revolutionary thoughts of the great Rousseau, but it was not the same without Pierre to argue with, and she put it down again. Recently she had taken to simply reading the parts of the writings that were most like stories: Emile's wooing of the virtuous Sophie, or the first half of the *Nouvelle Héloïse* with its tale of passionate love. Part of her knew that this giving in to romance reduced her to the level of her silly companions in the parlour, and she despised herself for it, but could not stop. She opened the book again, but the words danced before her eyes, making no sense. She was seized with panic. Her mind was rotting away. What if she forgot how to read philosophy, how to think – forgot all she had ever learned? Who would she be, then?

She felt tears starting. Somewhere outside these walls, not just in stories, people were living and working, arguing and falling in love – *living*. Even the peasants on her father's estate, who had so little – whose lives her father owned, as surely as he owned hers – were free to walk out into the air, to come and go, while she was penned up here, like a dumb beast in a cage. And what was the alternative? Soon her father would negotiate a suitable match for her, and she would find herself in a different kind of cage; or he would decide to leave her here forever.

'No! No!' She realised she had spoken aloud.

In that moment she knew, come what may, she simply could not stay here. Another week would drive her mad; a whole lifetime was beyond imagination. Something had to be done. She had to escape. It was really no more than she had thought before – had thought every moment since the first day she had arrived – but the idea was almost as terrifying as the idea of staying here. Where would she go? How could she live? She tried to breathe more slowly, willing herself to be calm. She had the jewels that Jacqueline had thought to bring – but not the first idea about how to turn them into money, or how to spend the money if she had it. She was old enough to be married, but she had as much idea of how to survive in the world as a new-born baby. She had never so much as dressed herself without help; had never had to do a single practical thing for herself. She thought of Jacqueline, labouring up the stairs every morning with a heavy can of hot water; of Jacqueline drawing the curtains and carrying away the breakfast things. Annette had never cooked a meal for herself, let alone washed the pots after it. She had been brought up to be helpless. How could she think that she could save herself? She was seized with terror again.

Just at that moment, she heard the distant jangle of the street doorbell. She got to her feet, though there was no point in going to her window, which gave no view of the street. She stood listening but, as she already knew, no further sound would reach her here.

She could not guess who had called. She heard the bell most days; another reminder that some people could come and go.

Eventually, as she listened, the city clocks began chiming nine and the chapel bell started to ring for Compline. The lady guests, having attended Vespers, were excused the final service of the day, and for them the bell was the signal that the tea-urn had arrived in the salon. Annette gritted her teeth. One last hour of her fellow guests' company was the price she had to pay if she wanted tea before bedtime. With an effort, she stood up, tied on the hated veil and headed downstairs.

17

Her entry into the salon caused more stir than usual. They must have been talking about her.

'Here she is, the sly little minx,' cried Madame Grimaud. 'What a close one you are!' She patted Annette's cheek with a powdery hand. 'And may we know the name of your admirer, my dear?'

Annette simply stared. Her look of total mystification drew delighted giggles from Sophie-and-Thérèse, who clearly thought she was acting. Then she saw that the chaperone was waving a letter enticingly.

'Is it for me?' Annette asked. 'If so, may I please have it?' She held out her hand.

But Madame Grimaud wanted more return than that. 'It is indeed for you, my dear!' she trilled, 'And sealed! Which is, of course, against all the rules.' She turned it over. 'No impression upon the wax – *someone* does not want us to know who he is, I can tell!'

Now Annette was growing angry. 'I assure you, Madame, I have no more idea who has sent it than you do,' she said. 'If you would allow me to look?'

Curiosity overcame the old lady's sham scruples. She handed the letter over; all eyes rested expectantly on Annette.

With a pretty curtsey, Annette took the letter and tucked it quickly into her bodice. 'Thank you,' she said. 'I shall attend to it later.' The disappointment in the room was palpable. Only Charlotte's eyes twinkled with amusement as Annette continued, 'Is the tea made yet? I thirst exceedingly!'

*

It was from Pierre. It must have been Pierre at the door, that very evening – he who had rung the bell! How had he persuaded the porter to accept his letter? But he had – she had it in her hand, as she sat upon her hard little bed. She could hear her own heartbeat as she broke the seal and unfolded the paper.

It was very like him, the letter. He was living in Bordeaux now, he said. He had seen Jacqueline more than once going and coming from the convent, and guessed that Annette was there. He was devastated to think that his own misfortune had cost her her liberty; he hoped fervently that she would be able to forgive him his indiscretion and the consequences it had had for her. Then he ran on rapidly to the really important matters: whether she still felt as he did, that the greater cause was the suffering of a whole People deprived of freedom? Would she signify as much to him in a note by return, to the bakery under the sign of the Windmill in the Rue des Cordeliers?

She closed her eyes, the better to imagine the street where Pierre was – where things, life, still happened, where thought was free. Then she opened them again. All very well, she said to the letter. You, my friend, are at liberty in the Rue des Cordeliers, and I am incarcerated here. But still the image of him, writing, thinking, being, in the world outside, was a breath of life. She did of course forgive him, in a magnanimous note which she hoped made clear that she was suffering a great deal more than he seemed to be. After much puzzling over how to send it, she took Jacqueline into her confidence and gave it to her to deliver.

'Did you see him?' she asked eagerly when the girl returned. 'How was he? Well? What is the place like, where he is lodging?'

Jacqueline hesitated. She looked down, and up, and aside, before she said finally, 'Madame Marsan, the baker, is a respectable person.' She turned away, pretending to settle the coverlet on Annette's bed. 'But she seems to have a whole crowd of lodgers over her shop, and not all of them gentlemen like Father Lamontaine.'

Annette laughed. 'Pierre always felt a sympathy with the

common people,' she said, 'so now he can sympathise with them at close quarters! Did he send any answer?'

'I am to go for it tomorrow afternoon, Mademoiselle.'

Tomorrow was Good Friday, and only the inner thrill of waiting for Pierre's letter sustained Annette through the gruelling gloom which marked that most solemn of days in the convent of Our Lady of the Little Angels. Up to now, life in the convent had been mind-numbingly uneventful: it was Lent, and the dreary round of self-denying observances prevailed, except in the private salon, where there seemed to be some mysterious exception in favour of sugar-plums. But, as Annette had discovered in the past week, Easter was even worse.

At home, the spring festival had always been a time for rejoicing: sunshine, servants in new clothes, all two hundred windows scrubbed and shining, and celebration food on all the tables of the household, after the rigours of Lent. Easter marked the real end of winter and the hope of a plenteous year. After mass on Easter morning, a great vat of broth was distributed among her father's workers, and the family sat down to roast suckling pig and lamb cutlets.

In the convent, Easter was about Christ's sufferings. The whole of Holy Week so far had been given over to the litany of the Passion: all the statues and ornaments and crucifixes in the building were draped in purple and black as a sign of mourning; the whole community trailed round the Stations of the Cross every afternoon; and the poor nuns seemed never to sleep at all. So on this Good Friday Annette, along with everyone else, spent almost all day in chapel, tracing in every detail the story of Christ's suffering. After nine hours, she was stiff, bored and very hungry; but even while she knelt on the stone floor, she knew that Jacqueline was on her way to the baker's shop to fetch her letter.

He had sent two whole sheets, overflowing with his bold, dashing hand, the old Pierre in full spate – as his life was, now. He was no longer talking politics, but living them. He was part of a company, he said, a group of the like-minded who were preparing for the great days, making themselves ready by meetings and discussions for the time that was about to break upon them when France would throw off her chains, and all unjust exactions, all taxes and impositions would be cast aside and the Patriot King would remake the nation according to the advice of his people – the Estates General, about to meet in Versailles. Meanwhile Pierre and his friends – a growing, gathering multitude – met almost daily to speak and convert others to the cause, in the Jardin Public in Bordeaux, just as others were meeting all over the country. Soon now the good King would hear their voices. Meanwhile he, Pierre, was speaking about the future of France the next day, at the gardens, when a holiday crowd would be gathered; he intended to share the message of hope with hundreds of those who needed it most.

Annette felt tears sting in her eyes. Tomorrow! If only she could hear him! She had always thought Pierre should be a writer, or a preacher – he had the glow of the ideal about him that could move multitudes.

How could she get out?

In fact, it was quite disgracefully easy. She marched into the salon in the morning with an air of mystery, her letter clutched in her hand, and the most monstrous story of romance, love and destiny ready to tell. Michèle looked up from her plate and smiled; Sophie nudged Thérèse. Charlotte looked quizzical, but said nothing.

'My dears, I need your help so much,' Annette began. Five chocolate cups were lowered as she sat down. By the end, she had almost convinced herself that there really was a handsome Prussian hussar serving in the King's forces, whom she had known and loved and lost to his duties in Paris; that he had just been posted unexpectedly south and was stopping over in Bordeaux for only a few days. Her audience were practically in tears of sympathy.

'*Amor vincit omnia*,' sighed Madame Grimaud dramatically, hand on heart. 'Something must be done. Now, where is my reticule…?' Reaching under a nearby cushion, she pulled out a beaded netting purse, from which she took a key. 'Sophie, you must lend Mademoiselle Annette your black domino and your mask.' She held out the key. 'Michèle, show her how to open the back gate.'

18

Annette had visited Bordeaux before, on visits to Cousin Henri's town-house; but she had never been out in the streets alone. Even when she was safe in the chair, she still felt nervous, putting up her mask and pulling the silk folds of Sophie's hooded cloak close round her. But the chairmen had hardly glanced at her and seemed not to have the slightest interest in whom they might be carrying. They trundled steadily along, jouncing her stolidly up and down at each step. Annette's tension gradually subsided. She would get there; she had no idea how big the park was, exactly where or even at what time Pierre might be going to speak. But it was scarcely noon; she would be in time.

Once they had emerged from the little dark streets of the old town, everything was bright and modern. The chair carried her across the wide cobbled square, past the huge pillared facade of the Grand Théâtre. She had been there, twice, to the opera. She remembered the gold and crimson of the interior, and the wonderful sweep of the wide stairs as she floated down them after the performance, dressed in a gown of gold tissue. It had seemed like heaven, at the time. Today all she saw from her little window were the hawkers and beggars of the daylight hours, sheltering between the pillars of the great portico. As the chair jogged by, she saw them in turn like a puppet show: a man with six tiny dogs on strings; a sherbet seller; a woman with bunches of lavender. But the largest number, it seemed, were *colporteurs*, hung about with trays of printed pamphlets and dangling news sheets.

The chairmen jogged imperturbably on, out into the mêlée of horses and coaches at the bottom of the Allées de Tourny, whose elegant vistas down tall terraces of stone houses she'd once admired from Cousin Henri's carriage. Now the chair took her along the right-hand *allée*, past the rows of fashionable shops under the crumbling back walls of the old Château de Trompette. Two years ago, this had seemed to her the very height of sophistication; today she felt something hectic and hard-hearted in it – a street for Sophie and Thérèse to waste their time in. Remembering to keep her mask before her face, Annette leaned out and looked ahead. Yes, there were the splendid gates of the Jardin Public. Her heart started to thump again as she took in the crowds of people around the gates. She stopped the chair and got out.

It was quite extraordinary. Walking alone across the wide, thronged space, she might have been invisible. She had never been in a crowd that moved like this, going all ways at once, but all surging forwards – jumping, shouting children, mothers holding a little one up in arms and another by the hand, babies on their fathers' backs, couples together, hurrying groups of youths – common people, talking, laughing, arm in arm, dressed in their best but still smelling strongly of massed humanity. Annette's heart was in her throat as she walked along, trying with all her might not to stumble. Through her thin slippers she felt every tussock of the dry grass; her skirts were already sweeping dust into their inner folds.

The common goal was clear – the trampled pathways and lawns sloped up towards a row of shops and cafés, with little latticed wooden balconies just above ground level, crowded with people. To her left, tables spilled out from other cafés onto the ride – but only a few straggling groups had stopped to sit down. The main mass swept forward, past a platform on which a band of six men were playing an overture in march time, with a vulgar farting bass beat that made Annette smile. She prayed her right slipper wouldn't fall to pieces; she already felt blisters coming on both her heels.

Halfway to the thronged cafés, she began to hear applause and shouts, and then the voice of a speaker, straining above the hubbub. She wished the band behind her would stop – perhaps it was Pierre, already, and she was missing him? She ran a few steps, but her shoe came off and she had to squat down, in imminent danger of being kicked in the back as she wrestled it on beneath her skirts. When she stood up she caught a louder cheer, and the crowds ahead swirled and stopped as people began to move away. A speech had come to an end – Annette pushed on, tense with frustration and anxiety. Moving forwards, now, against the flow, she struggled towards the middle balcony, where the crowd was still thickest, and began to walk along the line of cafés.

It was then she saw Pierre. He was not on the balcony, but nearer, only a few feet away, sitting at a table with a group of men around him. He looked wonderful. His straw-coloured hair hung loose, so that it fell over the open collar of his shirt; it made him look very young. She had only ever seen him in clerical black; but now he wore a blue jacket, and instead of a gentleman's breeches he had on white trousers, rather tight and thin, and heavy, flat-soled shoes, like a workman. He was leaning forward in his chair, one hand hammering his knee, and looking up and talking to a dark, curly-haired man. Annette was relieved to see they were not all men: there was a young woman among them, standing hand in hand with the dark-haired man.

'Pierre!' she cried, and ran towards them.

For a moment he did not recognise her. When he did, he looked so totally dumbfounded that Annette was seized with a terrible certainty that she should not have come. But he sprang to his feet and seized her hand.

'Annette! Let me present my friend Jacques, my friend Eugénie. Friends, you must excuse me: this young lady and I have much to talk of.'

And he strode forward, out of the crowd of his friends, to take her firmly by the arm.

'But Pierre – Have I missed your speech?' she said, all out of breath.

He smiled and shook his head, half-laughing. 'Yes – but also no, because I shall speak again by and by. The debate rages, today and every day. But I can walk with you for a while. Come.'

She clung to his arm to keep up as he set off along the outer edge of the crowd, back towards the gate.

When he realised she was struggling, he slowed down. 'Is all well?' he asked. Reading her face for an answer, he swept her in through a gateway into one of the drinking booths. Taking her by the elbows, he plumped her down in a little basket-work chair. A waiter appeared instantly, and Pierre ordered coffee. Then he sat down, across the table from her, as they had always sat together, at Brillac; and he really looked at her, for the first time. 'Annette – bless you for coming. I am moved to the heart. But what will happen? Can you go back safely? You won't be caught?'

'Oh yes, Pierre,' she said. 'All's well. I will go soon, and I can creep back into the cloister. But this morning, this is where I want to be.' She raised an arm, taking in the whole brilliant day and all its people. 'Here – with you.'

He did not speak for a moment. The waiter brought two thick little cups of muddy coffee. Then Pierre squeezed her hand and grinned like a delighted little boy.

'Now tell me about all this,' she said.

'This?' He sat back, expanding visibly before her eyes. 'This is the most important thing that has ever happened – certainly in France, and possibly in the whole world.' Pierre rapped the table, an old gesture of excitement that went straight to Annette's heart. 'In America, they rebelled against the English, and their Republic was set up in reaction and blood; here, in France, it will be peacefully – by the assent of the people and the King – that the marvellous change comes about.' He nodded. 'I am a Patriot,' he said.

He talked for an hour, almost non-stop. She had missed his speech – or maybe he was rehearsing it now; she had no chance to stop him and ask. It hardly mattered; she was getting it all to herself. It was like watching a huge firework display – breath-taking, beautiful and frightening at the same time. He was like a man possessed, a man illuminated by a passion which had eclipsed all others. This was the Hour of the People in their struggle for freedom, for a new constitution of rights under the King. For

Pierre and for the People, the meeting of the Estates, at the Palace of Versailles, had become a matter of life and death, the one great hope for their beloved France. His friend Martin wrote daily to keep him informed of what was happening there.

She struggled to understand the substance behind his exhilaration. Despite her best will, it seemed to her that very little had actually happened. The great moment was to be the first grand meeting of the Estates General, on the fifth of May – next week. But Pierre's friend Martin suspected that the nobility would refuse to share their views with the people, and that the Church would be divided between the two – and then, once the processions and speeches were over, and they had started to talk to each other, and to the King, they had to work out how to vote on what was to be done. Annette shook her head: how could he be so wildly enthusiastic about the prospect of a lot of old men standing on their dignity? While the people – the women and children she saw all round them, laughing and on holiday today, but thin and tired and worn away as they so clearly were – waited for bread?

Pierre was unabashed. 'Don't worry,' he said. 'The cause of the People will win out in the end: change will come slowly at first, but then an avalanche – you'll see. That is one good reason for us to meet here, to be ready, when the day comes.' His face shone with conviction.

'But what day? How will it come?'

Something crossed his face – a moment of decision not to speak. She frowned. Was he afraid to tell her of the future he saw? Before she could challenge him, he suddenly sat back and raised his coffee cup to her. 'In the end,' he said, 'France will be free, and the world will be quite different. To the future, Annette!'

She looked down into her empty cup.

He reached out and patted her hand. 'I knew you would come,' he said, somewhat to her surprise. He had certainly not looked as if he had expected her.

She smiled at him. 'I could not bear to be left out,' she said.

'You are too brave to hide behind your maid. Or behind this.' He picked up the mask that lay on the table between them. 'But she is a good woman, Jacqueline. Her brother is one of our friends.'

He clearly had many friends – ever since he and Annette had sat down, there had been men stopping to speak to him, or just clapping him on the shoulder as they passed. There was an excitement about all of them, not just Pierre, as if they shared some wonderful secret.

Pierre was leaning back in his chair, hands behind his head, beaming at her. She noticed for the first time that the soft-collared shirt, while very romantic, was not especially clean.

'Pierre,' she said hesitantly, 'is all well with you? No, of course it is, more so than I have ever seen you, but – well – do you have somewhere to live? People to look after you?'

'Of course he does!' cried a man passing behind Pierre's chair. 'He is loved and tended by the delicious Marie, are you not, you rascal?' He gave Pierre a great smack on the shoulder and passed on, grinning.

Pierre looked uncomfortable for a moment. 'I am in lodgings with a band of good friends,' he said. 'We look after each other. Jeanne Marsan is a good landlady and a Patriot; we live like one big family.'

'Oh,' Annette said. 'I see.'

19

It was not difficult to creep back into the convent. The chairmen stopped at her request on the deserted stretch of the waterside below the old walls and the leader handed her out onto the cobbles without so much as a raised eyebrow. While she fumbled for the coins to pay him, he stared politely out to sea, as if absolute discretion was part of his regular service. Nonetheless, she made sure to tip both men generously before ducking through the little postern gate she had left unlocked three hours before.

She arrived, as she had hoped, just in time for chapel, where she would be free for an hour from the curiosity and comment of the other girls. Fixedly ignoring their nudges and mimed questions directed towards her, she closed her eyes and relived in every detail her visit to the gardens and her meeting with Pierre, trying to hold on to the excitement of the afternoon. Now that she had been outside once, she knew that she must go again. She started to sketch in the details of her fictional tryst with the gallant hussar, angling the story to make another meeting essential.

In the end, she found that the girls were less interested in her adventure, real or imagined, than she had expected. They had more immediate and engrossing news. That very afternoon, while Annette had been at the gardens, Charlotte had stunned them all by announcing that she had decided to enter the Order.

Sophie and Thérèse were round-eyed with horror as they told her. 'Imagine! She will have all her hair cut off, and have to give away all her things!' said Sophie, shuddering.

'Everything?' Thérèse interrupted. 'Even her blue silk work-box with the silver scissors? Who will she give that to, do you think?'

'And she will have to wear a veil right down to *here*,' Sophie continued dramatically, clamping a hand over her eyebrows, 'and a horrid scratchy brown habit, right up to *here*.' She gripped her throat with the other hand and then paused, considering. 'Do nuns wear stays, do you think?'

No one was able to answer this important question.

'At any rate,' Sophie continued, 'her family will have to pay all her marriage portion to the convent, exactly as if she were getting married. But now she never will,' she finished sadly.

Michèle looked up from the cap she was trimming with yards of expensive lace. 'You *are* a ninny, Sophie,' she said scornfully. 'No one would have married her anyway, so what's the difference?'

Madame Grimaud shook her head mournfully. 'Poor, poor child,' she said - in much the same tone of voice, Annette thought, as if Charlotte had died.

Annette did not know what to think. What would make someone choose that? Had something dreadful happened? Had Charlotte been forced by her parents? Surely the bleak, narrow life of a nun could not be one that she would embrace of her own free will? Annette tried to imagine how bad life must have to be, to make the veil seem the better alternative. Of all the girls, Charlotte was the one she had been most drawn to, had enjoyed talking to on the rare occasions they found themselves alone together. But now she realised that she knew almost nothing about her, really, beyond the bare facts of her life as conveyed by the spiteful Michèle. Sitting always on the edge of the group, Charlotte had rarely joined in their chatter, though whenever Annette caught her eye she had smiled slightly before dropping her head again to her sewing, as if she saw Annette's thoughts about the others, and shared them. Annette felt a twinge of regret that her conversations with Charlotte had been so few. If she hadn't been so caught up in her own misery and frustration, she could have made a greater effort to befriend someone who must have felt even lonelier than she did.

On an instinct, she made for the library. Sure enough, Charlotte was there, standing by the window. She turned as Annette came in.

Annette hesitated. Now she was here, she had no idea what to say. 'Are you – is everything – well?' she stuttered finally. She felt clumsy, as if she might break something without meaning to.

There was a short silence before Charlotte said, 'I see you have heard my news. Yes. Thank you. I am well. You are kind to ask, but you need not worry about me. I think I am better now that I have accepted my vocation.' Her smile did not reach her eyes.

Good manners required Annette to accept the answer at face value, but she could not. 'Charlotte, I don't understand!' she shook her head. 'How can you do it? How can you shut yourself up in this place? Away from the light, away from everything that's alive? How can you give up all you have?'

Charlotte frowned, as if weighing up how to explain. Then she said slowly, 'I am fortunate, I think, in having lived once before without "all that I have" now. When I was a small child, I lived with my mother, who had nothing.' She looked up at Annette. 'I did not think myself unhappy then.'

Annette's mind raced. Her *mother*? A black slave. She gazed helplessly at the other girl.

'I was six when my father took me to live in his house, to make me a lady. Before that I lived with my mother.' Her dark eyes held Annette's as she continued, 'The poverty of the sisters is no poverty compared to hers. The obedience of the sisters is at least their own choice. As mine will be.'

Annette had no words.

'My father meant well, I think, but he made me fit for nothing except to stay at home with him. Now he has a new wife, and my stepmother does not relish a family of grown daughters. The others she can marry off quite quickly, but no one will offer for me, and she certainly doesn't want me at home, reminding her of something she would rather not know.'

'And this is the only…?'

'I have thought about it for a long time. It must be what God meant for me all along. I listened as hard as I could, to hear if He would speak to me about it.' Her voice was calm and kind, as if she was speaking to a child and did not want her to be upset. 'He was "despised and rejected of men", you know? So I thought that He might understand, and could help me. I prayed to Him, and came to understand that I was called to serve Him.'

She smiled again, and this time it seemed more real. 'I shall be safe here,' she said.

Annette backed out of the room. Charlotte's choice seemed to her the bleakest thing she had ever heard.

There was no one she could talk to. Even Jacqueline was behaving rather oddly. She came and went far more than she used to; often Annette did not see her all day. On the fifth of May, the magic day when the Estates General were to meet for the first time, she disappeared for most of the morning; but when she came back, Annette, hungry for news, could get nothing out of her.

'No Mademoiselle, there's no news,' she said, 'Nothing from Versailles, anyway.' She stood with her eyes down, demurely hiding her hands under her apron.

'Have you been at the gardens?' Annette asked.

'No Mademoiselle.' She did not raise her eyes.

'Well – why –' Annette bit back her impatience. Clearly the girl did not want to say where she had been. 'Please take that veil and wash it,' she said, and turned away.

By the end of the week Annette was desperate to know what was going on; but Jacqueline was still unhelpful. Annette would sit apart, imagining the crowds in the streets, straining for any sound: shouting, a horse at the gallop, even more traffic than usual; anything, any clue.

'Annette – Annette! *Please* close the window! My hair is blowing everywhere! Whatever are you thinking of?'

'I'm sorry, Michèle.' She jerked back into the dark little parlour and drew the casement to; the convent closed her in again. She could not bear it. 'I have a headache,' she announced. 'I'm going to lie down until Vespers. If Jacqueline comes back, please send her up to me.'

She was surprised when her maid appeared almost as soon as she had reached her room.

'Mademoiselle – are you ill? What can I get for you?' She looked flustered; her face was red, as if she had been out in the sun.

'I'm dying – of not knowing what's going on! Surely there is news from Versailles by now? Have you heard nothing in the streets – are there no newspapers? Tell me, Jacqueline!' She wanted to shake the girl out of her silence.

Jacqueline stood still, looking at her. Then she said, 'They are all out in the gardens today, Madame – there is news, and great anger because of it.'

'What news?'

'Well – it is news of nothing, so to say – nothing has happened at the Palace. The Third Estate has met, in some stately apartment, but the others, the great lords, will not go there to join them.' Her tone said more clearly than her words what she thought of these great lords. 'They are meeting elsewhere, or maybe not meeting at all, I don't know. The great ones are all a-buzz, like bees round an overturned hive – but their King Bee does not come to their call.' Jacqueline tilted her chin, rather pleased with this image, which she had no doubt heard from some politician in the street. She folded her hands provokingly. 'So you see, Mademoiselle, there is nothing of interest to you – nothing that concerns a lady.'

'Of course it concerns me! What do you mean?' But Annette could get no more out of her. She came to a sudden decision. 'They are meeting in the gardens, you say – who? Is Father Lamontaine there?'

Jacqueline closed her lips. 'I do not know, Mademoiselle,' she said.

'Go, then.' Annette kept her voice down with an effort. 'I have a headache. I will lie down – do not disturb me until supper.'

She had to leave on foot. She had brazenly filched the garden gate key from Madame Grimaud's reticule. She took care to wear her riding boots, this time. No one was watching, but her heart was racing by the time she got clear of the convent and could hail a chair. Even then she could not rest, but sat with the window wound down, gripping the sill in both hands and staring up and down the streets. Everything seemed surprisingly normal. The only notices she saw were for the Grand Théâtre: heavy black letters announcing that *The Marriage of Figaro* was to be played there this night. She wondered in a feverish kind of way why they were bothering with vaudevilles about weddings on such a day as this; then remembered that Pierre had mentioned this play, once upon a time. She searched her memory. Was it a banned play? She could not remember. But soon she would get to see him again. She would ask.

She almost gave up. The gardens were no longer in holiday mood; the grass was trampled away, and a gritty dust hung in the air between the knots of the crowd. No one looked at her or spoke to her; the cheerful eagerness seemed to have given way to arguments and sullen stares. At one of the cafés a man in rusty black was standing on a chair, shouting at no one; the biggest gathering was round a man reading aloud from a paper, but when she stopped, she found he was speaking a broad Gascon and she could scarcely understand him. The café where she had sat with Pierre was closed; she turned away in despair.

As she walked slowly back towards the gate, she saw a face she thought she knew. She stared at the boy, trying to call him to mind. He was young; his long black hair hung loose around his face and he wore a flashy red coat with too much braid. Their eyes met, and she saw the same puzzled recognition in his. Then it came to her – he was the stable lad her father had turned away. The boy whom Pierre… She saw the shock as he, in turn, recognised her. His whole body froze in panic; and then he dived into the crowd and she lost him.

As she stood, not knowing what to do, Pierre came bursting through the press of people, holding out his hands to her.

'Annette! How marvellous! Come in out of the crowd.' He hurried her into the back of the little *cabaret* – a dirtier place, this time, smelling strongly of sour wine. He swept a chair clear for her, and stood over her, holding her hands.

A figure in a red coat appeared at Pierre's shoulder. Annette dared not meet his eyes.

'You know Mademoiselle Annette, Jean-Marie,' said Pierre reassuringly. 'She is one of our friends now, a Patriot. Go and fetch her a glass of wine.'

The two men locked eyes in a conversation without words, while Annette studiously examined the rush-strewn floor. Then Jean-Marie shrugged and turned away, threading a path between the furniture.

An empty wine-jug stood in a puddle on the table. The other chairs had all been turned to surround the next table, where the conversation was low and urgent; the men there ignored her. She felt no more comfortable when the former stable boy returned, with wine in a thick tumbler. A look of reproach and another shrug passed rapidly between him and Pierre, before Pierre turned back to Annette.

'You have come to hear what is happening,' he said, 'and I can tell you it's worth hearing! The Third is in conclave, and the bravest men of the other two Estates are with them. The great Mirabeau is their leader. Jean-Marie, where's that paper? The man is a tiger! Listen to this!' He grabbed the dog-eared sheet and spread it eagerly on the table in front of her.

She read the heading: *Journal of the Estates General*. Then there was a motto in Latin, above tight columns of print peppered with points of exclamation.

'*Novus rerum nascitur ordo!*' Pierre proclaimed, jabbing his finger under the words. 'Translate, Jean-Marie.'

'A new order of things is born,' said the boy promptly. He still did not look at Annette, but he preened a little in the warmth of Pierre's smile of approval.

Annette struggled to gather her wits. 'So – have they told the King their grievances? When will the taxes be repealed?'

'Oh, soon – that is, other things have to be arranged first. The King cannot come to them until all three Estates are met in the same place. Mirabeau has demanded that the Church and the Nobles come to the Salle and register their credentials alongside the Third. They are taking a roll-call there, every day, and every day more have joined them. Especially of the First Estate! Martin says the *curés* who come across are humble, pious men, no different from the peasants who are their flocks – countrymen, and from the weaving towns – Oh! I'm sorry!' He fell forward, catching hold of her shoulder to avoid falling into her lap, as a big man in workman's clothes pushed by.

Jean-Marie giggled, then quickly put his hands over his mouth.

Annette struggled to her feet. 'I'm sorry – I should not have come again without an invitation. I must go now, in any case, before I'm missed.'

As the two of them made a way to the door for her, shouldering through the press of backs, Annette came face to face with Jacques, the man Pierre had introduced to her on her first visit.

He stared at her; and then, slowly, he turned his head away and spat upon the floor.

Pierre had not seen. She opened her mouth to speak, to ask him why, but no words came to her. In the open air again, she tried to listen to Pierre's uninterrupted flow of excited information; but she had had enough, for the moment, of the Patriots.

'Could you walk with me to the gates, do you think?' she asked Pierre.

'Of course,' said her friend. He turned back to the young man who had once been her father's servant and smiled into his eyes. 'I'll see you at home, Marie,' he said, before taking Annette's arm.

20

Annette could not rest. Her mind was in turmoil. Her latest venture outside the walls had been rather frightening, not to say incomprehensible; but inside the convent was quite deadly. She burned to know, even if the news from Versailles was frustratingly slow, and she might have found it difficult to maintain the enthusiasm Pierre did in the face of the petty squabbles that were all the Estates General had yet produced. Any news at all would have been better than the mental stagnation of the house of the Little Angels. Annette took to walking every morning round and round the tiny cloister, like a captive animal circling in its cage, because it was so hard to sit still and do nothing. If only something – anything – would happen!

Then, without warning, two things happened on the same day, neither of which she would have wished for. It was Jacqueline who delivered the first shock. She had just finished dressing Annette's hair and was tidying away the brush and comb when she said, 'Mademoiselle, I must give my notice.'

It was so unexpected that Annette did not at first take it in.

'I am to be married, Mademoiselle. He is a good man, Matthieu, a carpenter like my father. We have had an understanding since he finished his apprenticeship, that he would ask for me once he was settled in his trade. Now he has work and could support a wife.' Jacqueline's voice was warm with pride. 'He spoke to my father last night.'

Annette frowned. 'I see.' Was this why Jacqueline had been away so much? Dutifully, she rallied and produced a smile. 'I congratulate you. But I should like you to stay with me a little longer, at least while I am here in Bordeaux.'

The maid looked embarrassed. 'Matthieu would prefer not, Mademoiselle.'

Annette frowned. What was the girl talking about? Did the man not realise how fortunate his fiancée was? Did he think such positions were there for the asking?

'He is a Patriot,' said Jacqueline, as if it were an explanation. Then, seeing that Annette had not understood, 'With respect, Mademoiselle, one who would not wish his wife to serve in a noble house.'

After Jacqueline had gone downstairs, Annette remained in her room, thinking furiously. She must do something about a wedding present, of course – Jacqueline had been with her as long as she could remember. It was hard to think of life without her. Annette supposed she must send to her father for one of the other girls from the château. Or maybe she should hire a maid here in Bordeaux? Madame Grimaud would no doubt be full of advice on the subject. Jacqueline's parting words had upset her more than she cared to admit. The man was a Patriot, and so he did not wish his wife to serve her any more? Annette felt a mixture of anger and shame. Was she the enemy, now?

There was a soft knock at the door. It was one of the nuns – Annette did not know her – with a message from the Abbess. 'Reverend Mother requests the pleasure of your company in her salon, Mademoiselle,' she said.

It went without saying that a request, however polite, from Great-aunt Honorine was to be obeyed as an immediate order. Annette hurried after the nun, wondering a little anxiously what news from home could be too pressing to wait for their weekly meeting. Was her father ill? She could think of nothing else that would require such urgency.

The Abbess was standing by the window. She acknowledged Annette's curtsey with only the slightest of nods, and waited until the messenger had withdrawn before speaking. Her voice was like ice as she said, 'I am surprised that you can face me, Mademoiselle.'

Annette stared.

Her great-aunt's gaze did not waver. Her tone was heavily sarcastic as she went on. 'Perhaps you thought that you could disgrace your family and bring shame on this house without my hearing of it? I gave you credit for more intelligence.'

The diffused anxiety she had felt coming up the stairs shrank to a tight ball of fear in the pit of Annette's stomach. 'Madame?' she croaked. But she knew already what her aunt was talking about.

It was Cousin Henri who had seen her. Standing on the steps of the Grand Théâtre, he had been shocked to the core by the sight of his young cousin staring boldly from the window of a sedan chair for all the world to see. Too late, now, for Annette to wish that she had kept the window of the chair pulled up, had taken Sophie's gilded mask with her as she had the first time. Henri had followed her as far as the gardens, where he had lost her in the crowd, though not before he had seen her greeted by the man he supposed to be her lover.

'And that,' her aunt spat, 'was how you repaid my hospitality! Parading the streets unchaperoned, accosting men in a public park like any prostitute! Thank Our Lord and His Blessed Mother that Henri saw you when he did, before the whole world learned of your scandalous behaviour.' Sinking into the armchair by the fire, the Abbess poured herself a restorative brandy. She did not ask her niece to sit down.

There was no point in trying to explain. Nothing Annette could say would make any difference. She listened dumbly as her great-aunt continued the story. Henri had sent word to Annette's father; a family conference had already taken place and decisions had been made.

'As I recall,' said the Abbess icily, 'there was some measure of uncertainty about your future. That uncertainty is now at an end. Your father has agreed to your joining the order of Our Lady and the Little Angels without delay. Discussion about your dowry has already begun and the necessary papers will be drawn up as soon as the details are agreed.'

For a moment the room swam and Annette thought she was going to faint. Breathing hard, she managed to stay on her feet, facing the Abbess.

'I understand, Madame,' she said carefully, 'why my father would wish me to be confined here. But I do not understand why he – you – feel that I should enter the order. I do not have a calling for the religious life.'

Mother Honorine's expression did not soften. 'Vocation is like marriage,' she said calmly. 'Personal commitment, like conjugal affection, usually develops after the ceremonial joining, rather than before it.'

'But, Aunt –' Annette pleaded desperately.

The Abbess held up a hand to stop her. 'To put it bluntly, Mademoiselle, it is your own actions that have resolved the family's dilemma about your future. You have only yourself to blame. It is for the sake of the family's honour that you should now accept a life of seclusion and repentance. You will spend a short time as a postulant, as our dear Charlotte is doing, while your dowry and settlement are negotiated and your father signs the necessary papers. When that is done, you will be admitted to the novitiate and begin the course of instruction that will lead to your final vows as a bride of Christ. A day which your poor father will do his best to hasten forward. Poor Philippe! If the shame of this kills him, as well it might, you may add murder to the sins for which you will spend the rest of your life seeking absolution. God will forgive you, if you are penitent; we can only pray that your father can.'

Annette had never felt so afraid, or so alone. Jacqueline was to leave in a month; there was no longer any safe way of sending a message to Pierre; and, since the news of her disgrace had flown round the convent, she could not bring herself even to talk to the other lady guests. For two days she lay on her bed in the depths of despair, neither eating nor drinking, and rising only to go to chapel simply because, if she didn't, one of the nuns was sent to fetch her.

On the third day she stood up and felt so dizzy that she almost fell, so after Sext she followed the other ladies to the refectory and tried to make herself eat. It appeared that today was the feast of a particularly obscure Roman martyr called St Pancratius, and the reading during the meal, as was the custom of the convent, was the story of his short and miserable life. Annette attempted to swallow bread and soup while the fourteen-year-old orphan became a follower of Jesus, was joyfully baptised and, although scarcely more than a child, promptly arrested for being a Christian. Predictably, Pancratius refused to give up his faith, was sentenced to death and beheaded. His reward, apart from celestial bliss, was to have had a very large church built over his grave. His story was horrible and pointless. By the end of it Annette found she was crying helplessly and could not stop.

'Annette?' It was Sophie. 'Are you ill?'

Tears slid down Annette's nose and wetted the greyish bread still lying on her plate. She could not answer. The girls were looking at her with expressions ranging from sympathy to embarrassment. Sobbing uncontrollably, Annette fled.

After that, she knew there were only two paths. She must escape or go mad. She forced herself to think, to plan. Where could she go? She knew no one in Bordeaux except Cousin Henri. She shuddered at the thought of how he had been watching her that day when she went to find Pierre. Then she remembered the baker's shop where Pierre lived. A respectable woman with many lodgers, Jacqueline had said. Pierre had spoken of a group of friends like a family, all Patriots together. Could she go there? In truth, it was most unlikely that she would be able to escape a third time from the convent but, even if she were caught, what worse could they do to her than was already happening?

Over three nights, in the relatively safe hours when the lady guests were asleep and the nuns in chapel, Annette sewed her small store of money and the jewellery Jacqueline had so providently brought from the château into the padding of her stays and the hems of her petticoats. Using a piece cut from her bedspread, she made a strong cotton pocket to tie round her waist under her skirt:

she could carry few possessions, but she could not leave behind her journal or her little blue volumes of Rousseau. She selected her two plainest gowns, leaving the others, and anything else she couldn't take with her, for Jacqueline. What the girl couldn't use, she could sell, and since everyone thought that Annette was about to become a nun, it seemed the expected thing to do. She would have preferred not to take the risk of telling anyone at all about her plan, but Madame Grimaud held on to her reticule with the key to the back gate more securely now, so that, in the end, Annette had to risk asking for her help. Judging that the idea of aiding her permanent escape would be too much for the old lady to risk, but that a last despairing farewell to the handsome hussar might touch her sentimental heart, Annette threw herself on the chaperone's mercy.

'Ah, love! Love!' exclaimed the old woman, damp-eyed, as she gripped Annette's hand. 'Be very careful, my dear!'

Annette did not need to be told.

And so it was that, on the afternoon of the fifteenth of May, when she had made sure to be seen in chapel at the noon service and everyone else was safely occupied in the refectory, Annette, her heart hammering so that she could hardly breathe, slipped out of the convent and hailed a chair to take her to the Rue des Cordeliers, at the other end of the long quay. She leaned back in the seat, shaking, and wondered whether she was going to be sick. The chair swayed along in its usual rhythm to the steady plod of the chairmen's feet, and gradually her heart resumed something like its normal pace. Outside, the noisy life of the waterfront went on, impervious to her wild adventure: men shouted, pulleys creaked, carts trundled over cobbles. After a while the voices came closer, and Annette felt the chair slow to a halt. It seemed they were in an agitated crowd; but she could not tell what the excitement was about. Finally, curiosity got the better of her caution. Surely they were a good way from the convent now, and she could not have been missed yet? She drew back the curtain and looked out.

'There's a ship in, Mademoiselle,' said the first chairman.

'Crew coming ashore. Better wait a bit, if you don't want to be overturned. It won't be long.'

And indeed, all around them people were waving and shouting to men who clambered from boats at the water's edge. The home-coming sailors were welcomed and embraced; tears flowed freely as the watchers discovered whether their long wait was to end in good or bad news. Annette watched, excluded from their happiness and sorrow, until the crowd had thinned and the chair was hoisted up once more to set off.

It was at that moment that she saw the young sailor. He stood alone at the edge of the quay with no one, apparently, to welcome him home. He was the only one among the men from the ship who did not look happy. He seemed sad and frightened, as alone as she was herself; Annette's heart went out to him. The young man gazed helplessly about and, as she watched, looked straight at her. His expression changed to something like shocked recognition, though Annette was certain she had never seen him before, and she thought he opened his mouth to speak. Of course, he was too far away for her to hear him, even if he had. For a moment, they looked at each other across everything that separated them, and then the chair lurched forward and Annette could not see him any more.

21

Jude sat down on her sea chest and closed her eyes, steadying herself. When she stood up, the ghost of her aunt Isabella was gone.

A great surge of loneliness engulfed her. She felt as if she had just scrambled to her feet in the shallows of a stony beach only to be toppled again by the next wave. It took all her willpower to hold back the tears that burned in her throat. She forced herself to think. There must be things she could do. In such a major port as this, there must be an American agent of some kind? But when she tried to imagine the conversation she might have with such a person, she realised how hopeless that would be. First, he would need to be persuaded that the pigtailed ragamuffin before him was really a respectable merchant's daughter from Massachusetts. Jude looked down hopelessly at her salt-stiffened shirt, cracked hands and grimy feet. And then, she would have to convince him that, although this hapless wretch had just been robbed of his – no, her – last *sou* by a common prostitute, she had a promising fortune in England. And the proof of her story lay at the bottom of the sea, somewhere off the island of Cuba.

No. Any approach to the authorities must wait until she had the means to present herself in a different light. She racked her brains. Armand? Surely, he might take pity on his boy? He must come ashore eventually. Jude looked about. A hull grated on the shingle, men splashed ashore and dispersed into the crowd on the quay, slipping away on their own business. Beside her, one of Jean-Baptiste's messmates shouted with delight as he seized hold of a man so like him that they must be brothers. Jude tried not to stare as they embraced, kissing each other on both cheeks as she had already seen others do here on meeting, both men and women alike.

A second boat scraped onto the sand only a few feet from where she stood, and there was more scrambling and shouting. This time Jude saw Jean-Baptiste leap ashore. He dropped his sea chest on the sand, then waded back, grabbed two more bundles from the bottom of the boat and piled them beside the chest. Straightening up, he saw Jude and waved. At that moment a girl of about sixteen pushed through the onlookers and ran towards him, her thin face alight with excitement. 'Jean-Baptiste!' she screamed. 'Here! I'm here! Jean-Baptiste!'

For an instant the young sailor looked blank, then his face broke into a huge grin and he swept the girl into his arms. 'Eugénie! my little one!' He held her out at arm's length. 'Look how tall you have grown! Come, don't cry. All's well, I am safe. And you? And my mother? She is well?'

The girl nodded wordlessly, clinging to him and laughing, tears running down her face.

Jude, more alone than ever, watched their reunion.

Then Jean-Baptiste came splashing through the puddles towards her, pulling the girl along at his side. 'Eugénie, let me present to you my American friend, Jude Wiston. The Americans are true democrats – your Jacques will like to meet him, huh? See, Jude, this is my little sister Eugénie, come to welcome me home. Isn't she beautiful? Eugénie, bid my good friend welcome.'

Eugénie blushed and curtsied and tilted up her face. Jude, seeing it was expected, kissed her first on one cheek and then the other, as she had seen her shipmates do.

Jean-Baptiste looked pleased. 'Now you shall meet my baby sister also, and my dear *maman*.' He picked up Jude's sea chest, banged it down beside his own heap of luggage and shouted something Jude didn't understand. At once a ragged boy with a one-wheeled barrow appeared beside them and started to heave the boxes and bundles into it.

'Rue de la Fusterie,' said Jean-Baptiste. 'Follow me!'

The street of the barrel-makers was no more than a crack, a tall black fissure in the pale stone cliff of the waterfront. The three of them hurried along, arm in arm to avoid losing each other in the crowd. Jean-Baptiste looked back to make sure their little porter had not made off with their luggage and then, beckoning the boy to follow, turned in through the tall arch of a great stone gateway. To Jude it looked huge and golden as the Gate of Heaven: it led, apparently, to Hell. The bright-walled houses that faced the harbour were thin, perhaps only a room deep; and behind them dark streets and alleys ran away at crazy angles like rat-holes behind wainscot. Walls of wood and plaster as well as grimy stone squeezed in on them as they walked along, skipping to and fro over the wide and evil-smelling gutter that ran down the middle of the street.

Brother and sister talked non-stop. Jude could understand scarcely anything of their rapid, urgent conversation. Her French was meagre, and the words she did know were those that had been useful onboard ship: the names of ropes and sails, the words for food and cooking. She did think once or twice that she caught the words 'bread' and 'flour' but decided she must be wrong, and concentrated instead on looking around her. As her eyes adjusted to the shadows, she saw that the buildings were far older here than on the quayside, dark, solid and substantial. At ground level the street was a series of open arcades, supported on great stone arches or massive wooden lintels, squared baulks of timber a yard thick. Within these cavernous openings Jude glimpsed high stacks of wooden staves, great festoons of hoops hanging under ceilings and – everywhere – clean new barrels of every size. She saw one cask so large it could only have been moved by horses; dozens of little kegs such as might hold spirits, all neatly stacked; and every size in between, from butter barrels to ale casks.

Both talking at once, Jean-Baptiste and Eugénie plunged without warning under one of the great arches, and Jude followed. There was good smooth stone underfoot as they threaded a dim passageway, lined with yet more barrels, and came into a courtyard. A small girl in wooden shoes appeared in a doorway.

Jean-Baptiste stared, then turned to Eugénie. 'Is this the baby? This is little Françoise? But she was a mere infant when I...'

Overcome with shyness at the sight of two strangers, the child looked ready to run away, but encouraged by Eugénie she was soon shrieking with delight as her brother swung her off her feet. The noise brought out the rest of the family, and a babble of welcome broke out, reverberating off the stone walls of the little yard. Then another doorway opened and a woman of about forty, dressed entirely in black, appeared. She stood quite still for a moment, one hand to her mouth, before she opened her arms and Jean-Baptiste walked into them. Jude needed no French to understand Madame Bonnat's welcome of her son after so long at sea. Tears prickled in her own eyes as she watched them.

More people swarmed into the yard; Jude lost track of who they all were. Soon she was swept by the laughing and weeping crowd into a dark, low-ceilinged kitchen, to be embraced and patted and generally admired as something Jean-Baptiste had brought back from the New World. She was giddy with tiredness, and confused by the noisy conversation which she could not understand; but eventually Madame Bonnat said something about food, and the members of the crowd who were neighbours rather than family melted politely away. Little Françoise was sent out with coins from her brother's pocket, and came back with a big loaf which formed the main part of their meal.

Jude accepted a slice: it was gritty and sour-tasting, but like manna after the maggoty crunch of ship's biscuit. She watched as the remainder of the loaf, a good four pounds of bread, disappeared with astonishing speed. This was clearly a hungry household. She politely refused the last slice, and watched Madame Bonnat divide it between Jean-Baptiste and Françoise.

Jean-Baptiste, who had not eaten much either, caught her eye. 'It has been a bad year in Bordeaux,' he said.

'Is that what your sister was telling you this morning? About flour? And bread?'

'You may well ask!' he exclaimed, leaning earnestly toward her across the table. 'The harvest was bad enough last year, they say, but this year it has been worse. Grain is scarce, so the price of flour goes up. And anything to do with flour deals us two blows in this family, you understand?'

Jude frowned, not understanding at all.

Jean-Baptiste poured himself more wine and settled into his exposition. 'You see that my mother is in the coopering trade? It was my father's *métier*, and she carries it on. Barrels are for many things, obviously. The house of Bonnat makes kegs for butter and candles and herring,' he stretched his hands wide, to cover the rest, and added, 'and also for the wine of Bordeaux, like everyone else. But here, chiefly, we have made barrels for flour, the good wheat-flour of Gascony. The Ministry, God rot them, always have much to say on the subject of flour – who has it, who sells it, where and for how much – but wherever it goes, beyond the village mill, it goes in Bonnat's barrels. And if there is no flour, there is no call for barrels, and the coopers lack work.'

Eugénie interrupted him impatiently. 'It is worse than that. There *is* flour, we know it, but it is kept under lock and key by those who would make the cost higher still. Last year, just after Jean-Baptiste sailed, the ministry decided that there was not enough flour in the cities, in Bordeaux or in Paris, and –'

'Paris!' said her brother darkly. 'Of course, they must have their *brioche* in Paris, even if we starve for it!'

'So they took off the restrictions on trading it,' Eugénie continued. 'They said it would ease the movement of the stocks, but it simply meant that the merchants could charge what they wished.'

Jude, concentrating hard, nodded to show she was following.

'And what is the proper price of flour?' Jean-Baptiste demanded of the company at large. 'Four *sous* a pound? Six? Eight? There is no proper price – the ministry has abolished it! So, when I went away, a loaf cost eighteen *sous*. And today, little one?' He turned to Françoise.

'Fifty,' the child whispered.

'Exactly!' Jean-Baptiste sat back. 'How can a poor man put bread on his table at such a price? It is a scandal.'

'Indeed,' said his mother quietly, speaking for the first time. 'And has Eugénie told you the latest thing? Now they have said, if the people are hungry, there must be no more storing of flour to force up prices. No more carrying it about to be sold for a fortune in Paris! A good thing, yes? But how will they make it happen?' She turned to her son, and the exasperation in her tone had a desperate edge. 'They say, no one shall transport flour from one region to another!' She gazed intensely into his face, and came to her point. 'So. No more need for flour casks, then – stop making them!' She looked at Jude, and her voice shook. 'My son comes home at a sad time.'

'A mad time, you should say!' said Jean-Baptiste, striking the table. 'These ministers are insane.' Seeing Jude's frown of incomprehension, he screwed his fingers into his temples. 'Mad in the head,' he explained. 'The flour is in the mills, yes? The mills are in the fields. But see, Jude, my friend. There are to be no barrels. So the flour cannot come to the city. Bread is as valuable as gold, the bakers ask more and more for filthy loaves like this one we have just eaten – full of acorns, would you not say?'

Jude nodded again, wordlessly. It seemed Jean-Baptiste had come home in the nick of time, and his pay would put bread on the table for a while. But she was an extra mouth to feed, with no way of paying for her lodging. She could not stay in this house.

When they had finished eating and had drunk the rest of the jug of wine, Jean-Baptiste unlocked his sea chest and unrolled the canvas bundles. Jude was not his only trophy from overseas. He produced one marvel after another. The carved tusk of the narwhal was particularly admired, before Madame Bonnat put it carefully away in her cabinet. The little girls squeaked and squabbled delightedly over coloured beads and woven leather purses; Eugénie, speechless but with shining eyes, paraded in the silver necklace her brother had bought for her in Saint Domingue. By the time everyone had sampled the Islands rum, it was more than time for bed.

Jude found herself stowed in an empty store-room, on a truckle bed that neither rolled up around her nor swayed with the wind and tide. She lay fingering the quilt and listening to the unfamiliar noises of the street, thinking of another household, halfway across the world. She was homeless and penniless, and she did not know what to do; but even so, she could not wish herself back in Salem.

22

The people of Bordeaux were not only hungry, but also very angry. Jude had not felt this sense of danger, this expectation in the air, since she was a small child listening in corners to her elders discussing the war with Britain. The people here did not yet know what it was that they were roused to do; but the same excitement hung in the air, a sense that anything might happen. On the first morning, Jean-Baptiste and Eugénie had introduced Jude to their friend Jacques, who, as far as Jude could understand, was a tiler laid off in the great stoppage of building work in the city. He was a handsome fellow with dark curly hair; Eugénie's adoring eyes never left him. He was, as Jean-Baptiste had predicted, impressed to meet a real American, and keen to enrol Jude in what was going on.

'Will you come with us to the gardens? There may be news from Versailles by midday. If the King has responded to the prayers of his people, we shall hear it there. And if not,' he smiled, self-mocking, 'I can at least introduce our friends to a countryman of the great Benjamin Franklin!'

Long before they reached the gardens, Jude's head was reeling with new and extraordinary sights. She had expected Bordeaux to contain more people than she'd ever seen in one place before, and she was not disappointed: they swarmed everywhere, busy and various and strangely clad, in everything from sky-blue shot satin to near-nakedness. In Salem there had been both masters and servants, richer and poorer, but none so flamboyantly rich or so wastingly poor as she saw here. The contrast was mind-numbing. She did not see very many of the hated nobility, except for glimpses of pale faces in the carriages and the strange chairs on poles that men carried by; but she did see, and wonder at, the many people who wore the uniforms of their religion. The women with bonnets like great white candle-snuffers were nuns, Eugénie said. There were flocks of them, not only in demure black but also in brown and in black and white, walking alone or in silent groups. There were priests, too, in red and purple; and even barefoot monks. Monks were something out of a warning tract, to Jude, an idea to frighten children with. She tried not to stare.

The priests and nuns scurried in and out of the towering churches that loomed up at every hand. Jude had seen a fine stone church once before, in Havana. That had made the meeting-houses of Salem look like store-sheds on a wharf, but these were like palaces – fantastic, elaborate, with soaring towers and elaborately carved doorways. The first church they passed, a massive structure squatting like a dragon in the middle of the square of St Michel, had its spire on the ground beside it, a white plume swaggering up to the sky, a riot of turrets with lacy top-work like paper cut-outs crazily done in stone. She could not imagine what God thought of it all. But then, she reflected – as another young girl smiled shyly at her, and she stepped aside like a gallant letting a woman pass – I'm not at all sure what He can be making of me, in this shirt and breeches.

When they got to the gardens, no news was to be had. It was very bright and hot, and very foreign – not a garden at all, to Jude's way of thinking, but a wide, open space surrounded by rows of drinking dens. There were only workers here – no gentry in their silks and high wigs, and certainly no monks or nuns. Knots of men, and some women, stood or scurried about, and there was much animated talk, but Jacques did not find the people he was looking for. While he went to enquire, he left Jude for a moment standing in front of a closed café, whose covered windows were being used as a noticeboard. Jude gazed at the papers nailed there, realising with a shock that, although she now understood a good part of what was said to her, she could not read French at all. The pictures spoke clearly enough, though. In the cartoons of fat men bursting out of their fine clothes, and farmers crushed under the heels of tax-gatherers' carriages, she read the same angry rebellion that she saw on the faces of Jacques and his friends. One drawing held her eye with its savage, disturbing detail. At its centre a peasant in rags, her face a grimace of pain, leaned heavily on a staff. Her back was bowed under the weight of two other women, who rode her like a mule. One was dressed in what Jude now recognised as a nun's habit, the other in the finery of a great lady.

Eugénie appeared at her elbow as Jude was studying this picture. 'It is the Three Estates,' she said bitterly. 'You have heard us talk of them? The Church is the First, and the nobles the Second. Do you see,' she pointed a thin finger, 'how the Third Estate is crushed almost to death by their greed?' And she spat on the dusty ground.

On her third morning in the Rue de la Fusterie, Jude woke determined either to find work or to seek a ship at once. Jean-Baptiste could afford to haunt the park and listen to the orators, for he had brought home his sailor's pay and need not look for another job yet; but Jude must do something to relieve Madame Bonnat of the burden of an uninvited extra mouth. But what? She was not skilled in making anything except ship's biscuit pudding, and anyway some of the best tradesmen of Bordeaux were out of work; what could she do? She recalled the tantalising notices in the park: perhaps a good first step would be to learn to read. She asked Madame Bonnat if there was a book in the house which she might borrow.

'Or anything in print,' she added, 'that I might try to read.'

Madame Bonnat raised an ironic eyebrow. 'Has Eugénie not given you enough pamphlets?' she asked. 'Then you shall have something better.'

She opened a door on the far side of the kitchen. Jude followed her along a passageway, through the now silent workshop where only two men sat in the vaulted gloom, languidly shaping staves for a small order of cider barrels. The older woman opened another door at the end of the passage, which led into a slip of a room lit by a dirty window high in the stone wall. Dusty light fell on piles of papers, so stacked and thrust together that it was a moment before Jude saw the tall desk buried under them. She looked round curiously. An office? For a moment she had a vivid memory of the draughty wooden counting-house, with its orderly ledgers and jar of mended quills at the ready, where Rebecca Wiston had worked for so many years. She shook her head to drive the picture away.

With only the sketchiest effort to keep the heaps of paper from cascading to the floor, Madame Bonnat reached into the desk and drew out a thick brown book. 'It is a bible,' she said. 'If you know your scripture in your own tongue, here you will understand what you read.'

Jude took the book from her and began to turn the pages. It looked and felt familiar, and she could see at once that Madame Bonnat was right: the translation was already there, in her own head.

The Frenchwoman smiled. 'You thought, perhaps, because we are French, and Catholics, we do not read the word of God for ourselves, but listen only to the priests? It is partly true. But there are many here in Bordeaux who follow the teachings of Calvin and like to read the Scripture in good black Geneva print. That book belonged to one of them.'

Jude sat with the Bible for the daylight hours of each day in a shady corner of the courtyard and began, haltingly, to read the gospel of Matthew in French. It was comparatively easy to match the printed verses to the texts she had known since childhood. Whenever she came across a French word she already knew, she thought about the way that the sounds and the letters matched. Or, very often, didn't match – for French words seemed to be full of letters that were never pronounced. But after a few days she found that the names painted over doorways, and the words chalked up on the shutters of shops, began to take on meaning.

Meanwhile, she was not allowed to opt out of the politics of the city. Eugénie brought each day's paper and often a new pamphlet into the house, and Jean-Baptiste read them aloud over the evening glasses of wine. As best they could, they followed the unintelligible doings at Versailles, and imagined a new world. One hot evening in late May, Eugénie came home with Jacques in tow and skidded up to the room she shared with her sisters to put on her best dress. Jacques sat at the outside table to wait for her, watching Jude as she read.

'You are a believing man, Jude?' he asked, after a few moments. Like all Jude's new friends, he pronounced her name as if it had an extra syllable on the end.

She looked up warily. The family did not go in for personal questions, and she could not quite see what was behind this one. But the man gestured at the bible in an explanatory way, without seeming to mean anything more by it, so she said, 'Indeed, yes. But I am a Protestant, Monsieur – I was raised in the Society of Friends, if you have heard of that?'

Jacques shrugged. 'I have not,' he said, 'but it is all one to me. Catholic, Protestant, Huguenot, Cathar – it means nothing, or worse than nothing. For me, you may believe what you will, it makes little difference. In the new France, thought will be free.' Before Jude could rise to this, he went on, 'Are you coming to the lecture? There is a man speaking tonight – he is a priest, I think, or he was once, but he is now a Patriot. He is lecturing on the great thinker and atheist, Jean-Jacques Rousseau.'

'Thank you,' said Jude, 'I should like to hear that.'

23

The lecture was taking place in a workshop behind a bakery in the Rue des Cordeliers, in the Faubourg des Chartrons. Jude followed her friends as they made their way there through the old streets of the quarter, full of raffish, faded-elegant shops with names and notices in many tongues. The bakery was in a huge old house – a paper tacked to the doorpost listed more than a dozen occupants. The evening was cool, which was just as well, since so many people were flocking in. Jacques pushed his way forward, towing the others behind, and took one of two free chairs in the front row, with Eugénie on his knee and Jean-Baptiste next to them. Jude was left to perch on the ledge of an arch in the wall. She realised these arches were the backs of the baker's ovens – and hoped the business of the evening would be done before they were fired for the night's bread-making.

Sitting there, she was slightly higher than the rest of the audience. As they crowded in, she was curious to see who would come to such a talk. Mostly they seemed to be tradesmen, members of the *bourgeoisie* like her friends the Bonnats, all dressed up for the occasion; and some poor folk who had not had time to change, or maybe had nothing else to put on. She saw three porters with their woven head-pads on their knees and all the filth of the fish market still on their shoulders. Many of the men had no coats, and a few had coats but no shirts. There were almost as many girls as men, and they were mostly neater, spruced-up like Eugénie for an occasion, with clean white neckerchiefs over their everyday gowns, and feathers in their hats. Jude marvelled that the working people of the city had acquired the taste for philosophical lectures;

she wondered how much she would understand herself.

It all took a long time. Every now and then someone would start a song, which the audience would take up with gusto. When the room could hold no more, and the singing of these jaunty and sometimes blood-thirsty songs had begun to flag, there was a stir at a door to Jude's right and the platform party appeared. Two of the men wore rusty black suits – the black of the junior clergy, perhaps; the third wore a workman's coat over a ruffled shirt. A gentleman in disguise, Jude thought. Behind him came a young woman with a pile of books and papers in her arms; she sat at the end of the table, only a few feet from Jude. Her dress was unremarkable: a wool jacket and plain worsted petticoat short enough to show serviceable shoes and stockings – the clothes of a respectable *bourgeoise*. But there was something in the way she held herself, her confidence and directness when she spoke to the young man, that was at odds with her appearance. A lady? Here? Perhaps she was the gentleman's sister, or his wife.

One of the men in black, apparently well known to the audience, introduced the speaker as Pierre Lamontaine – he was a Patriot, and a new philosopher of the people, and was to talk to them this evening about the great and good Jean-Jacques Rousseau, especially that author's prescription for a new social contract between the people and the King. When the cheers had died down, the young man in ruffles stepped forward. His intense enthusiasm was immediately infectious: here was the kind of conviction Jude had felt herself years ago, as the war for independence had transformed the lives of the American colonists. His passionate speech transfixed the whole audience. As he warmed to his subject, his language grew more abstract and difficult, and Jude began to struggle with the words. When he started to read rather fast from a little blue volume of the thinker's own writing, she was lost. Her attention wavered, and was caught again by the young woman sitting only a few feet from her on the platform.

The girl was intent upon Lamontaine – nodding, agreeing, her own lips mouthing the words of the text that he read out. She was lovely – not just young and eager, but really beautiful. Her shining dark hair, piled high under the modest cap, contrasted with her perfect pale skin and sparkling eyes. A single escaped curl lay on her neck. At that moment Jean-Baptiste turned his head and, noticing where Jude's eyes were fixed, grinned conspiratorially. Jude felt herself redden and forced her eyes back to the speaker. But a moment later she found herself watching the girl again. She had a lady's delicate complexion; her hands were small and white. No shopkeeper's daughter had hands like that. And there was something else; she seemed vaguely familiar, as if Jude had seen her before, but could not think where. Jude studied her profile, trying to place her. Then, at an outburst of applause, the girl sat back for a moment, turning her face Jude's way, and Jude knew her. It was the face that had looked out of the sedan chair on the quay – the girl she had taken for her aunt Isabella.

She was staring at Jude, too. Then she blushed, and turned her eyes back to the speaker.

Jude found she had given up all attempts to understand any more of the philosophy of Rousseau; besides, Jean-Baptiste and his sister would be rehearsing it in summary for days. She settled back against the bricks of the baker's oven and went on watching the dark-haired girl.

Encouraged by the extent to which she had understood the lecture, and more eager than ever to read well in French, Jude went back to her biblical studies with new energy next morning. She decided she could progress to the Epistles of St Paul; but after an hour in the fig-tree shade all that stern advice seemed less than appealing. She thought she might just find Jean-Baptiste's mother and thank her again for the loan of the bible.

Madame Bonnat was not in the kitchen. Jude opened the door to the passage and found her own way to the room with the desk. There was no one there, either. Jude looked around curiously. It seemed even more strange, this room, the second time she saw it: so unlike her friend's energetic and organised mother to leave such a mess shut away anywhere in her house. Jude picked up a piece of paper from one of the heaps. It looked like an invoice. So did the next one, and the next. They were not in exactly the same form as the ones she was familiar with at home, but without doubt these were bills for goods and services, and from several different creditors. Two had elaborate crests stamped into them – requests for taxes, perhaps? The words were unfamiliar so she couldn't tell. She put them down again, thoughtfully.

Back in the kitchen, Eugénie had just arrived with a pail of water. Jude asked her about the little room full of papers, and she sighed.

'It's just the office,' she said. 'No one has really seen to it, since Papa died. My mother is good at business, she is good with the men, and knows the trade – but she does not like papers and accounts.' She shrugged. 'So she pretends they are not there, I think.'

And so it came about that Rebecca Judith Wiston found herself at an office desk once more, a world away from the counting-house in Salem, painstakingly bringing order to the affairs of another struggling business. One of the first things she did, now pen and paper were before her, was to write a letter of her own. She felt slightly guilty that she had not thought to let her brothers know, before this, that she was alive. She needed someone to write on her behalf to the lawyers in London, since, should she ever get there, she would have no proof to show them of either her identity or her business. At least if she were expected, there would be some chance that they would accept she was Miss Rebecca Wiston, even without the papers that went down off Havana. The more she thought about her brothers' anger, however, the less convinced she became that they would help her. Or even that they would regard her survival as good news. She certainly could not trust them to write to the lawyers for her. In the end, she wrote also to John Fell, the attorney who had shown her Richard's will, asking *him* to tell the lawyers she was on her way and attest to her inheritance. She could put no address on the letter, for who knew where she would be, months from now, when (or if) a reply might come?

After the letter was done and entrusted to a former shipmate of Jean-Baptiste who was sailing to New England, Jude settled down to mastering the Bonnats' accounts. Every so often she would emerge to demand of one or other member of the family how many *sous* were in a *livre*, or what a certain word meant, but slowly and steadily she got control of the first batches of papers. It was a relief to her to find that many of the older invoices had in fact been paid, and just needed to be entered into the ledgers and put away in the right bundle; but there were new debts which she knew it would be hard for the Bonnats to meet. Nevertheless, Madame Bonnat was extravagantly grateful. She was overheard one morning telling a neighbour that Jean-Baptiste's friend was surely not from the American colonies at all, but an angel straight from heaven. This caused great merriment among her children and their friends, and much teasing of Jude, but Madame Bonnat was unabashed. She had lit candles, she said, before the Virgin in the nearby church of St Michel, in thanks for the miracle that was Jude Wiston.

The prayers were answered, too. When Jude had reduced the spilling loose papers to order, she decided one morning that it was time to open the desk and investigate the drawers within. Inside, she found a row of spikes, bristling with documents. Carefully easing them off, she began to read. They were copies – all in the same hand – not of incoming bills, but of invoices headed with the name of Bonnat. Outgoing bills for the barrels! She leafed through them until she found one, and then a second, scribbled across: endorsed as paid. So the others were – not paid?

When she had made a list, she took it to Jean-Baptiste. He was sitting reading a newspaper, which he was keen to tell her had come from Versailles, from the meeting of Estates; but she waved it away and handed over her penmanship instead.

'Look,' she said. 'Read. Tell me who all these people are.'

He picked it up and cocked his head. 'Grèves, Rustin, Marat... They are – were – my father's customers.' He looked at her over the paper. 'You are a deep one, Jude. Where did you find such an inventory? Look here – the Duke! Never been known to pay within the year, but he orders on a grand scale, all the same. And old Faustinier – I'm sure he's dead! But they are good customers, on the whole. Most of the people we sell to are here. Half of them are millers, of course – so, hardly customers any more. But what of it, eh?'

'Look at the last column,' she said. 'The figures.'

Jean-Baptiste ran his finger over the paper, and blinked.

'Unless I am much mistaken,' said Jude, 'that is what each of them owes to your mother.'

24

Annette glared into the spotty little mirror, pulling the soft kerchief against the back of her neck and pushing one end into the top of her stays. However carefully she did it, the thing always popped out the minute she lifted her arms. And how could she do her hair without lifting her arms?

'Louise,' she asked, 'can you help me with this, do you think?'

The baker's daughter laughed. 'You want to stuff it right down between your bosoms – like this.' She plunged a hard hand down Annette's front.

Annette tried not to flinch. She was perfectly able to dress herself now; only the details kept escaping her control. Taking on the short petticoats and woollen jacket of a *bourgeoise* had helped a lot – her satin had become hem-fallen and muddy from walking in the street, in only a couple of days. She had worn this new dress for more than three weeks now and felt she was almost used to looking like an artisan, a Patriot. She tried not to think too much about what others saw when they looked at her.

'Did you notice the young man at the meeting last night, sitting in the back of your mother's brioche oven?' she asked now. She was careful not to sound too eager. 'In the blue coat – with a pigtail?'

'Bit of all right, that one, isn't he? A bit refined-looking, but *gorgeous*. Did you see his eyelashes? Long as a girl's. He's that friend of Eugénie Bonnat's brother, that came in on the *Belle Héloïse*.'

'Mm. I thought he looked like a sailor.' Annette tried to sound casual. Of course, she had known him at once. The lonely sailor she had seen on her flight from the convent. It seemed strangely romantic, that he should turn up again in this very house.

'He's an American,' Louise said. Louise always knew everything. 'He's very clever – he's working in the Bonnats' office. Just till he sorts himself out, you know. Seems a bit serious, though. Eugénie says he reads the bible all the time he's not working! Just fancy.'

'Oh.' Annette was not at all sure she liked the sound of that. A pious American; no doubt a Puritan of some kind. She turned away from the mirror. 'Do you happen to know where Pierre is?' she asked.

Louise shrugged. 'His little Marie went out a while ago. Getting them breakfast in bed, I expect.'

'Surely not! There is so much to do today – we must have the handbill for the big meeting ready for the printer before noon.'

'That never stopped those two, did it? At it like randy goats, they are, day and night. What a waste! I could show that handsome Jean-Marie a different way to do it, I can tell you.' Then, seeing Annette's expression, 'Begging your pardon, Miss.' She pulled another length of rag out of a ratty brown ringlet. 'Have you finished with the looking-glass?'

Annette clattered down the twisting attic stair, remembering to avoid contact with the wall under the little skylight where the leaky roof had loosened the plaster. She would not let Pierre's extraordinary friendship with the stables get under her skin; nor would she criticise her room-mate's manners. It was very kind of Louise's ferocious mother to have taken her in like a stray cat, asking no questions; Annette tried always to remember that she was an inconvenience to Madame Marsan, even if she was, as it happened, probably the only one of Madame's guests who actually paid her rent on time. And Louise had been a friend, too. Louise was a Woman of the People; they were what the patriotic struggle was all about. With every day that passed, Annette's affection and respect for the working people she now lived among grew; but at the same time she saw more and more clearly that she would always be different from them. She might have left the life of an aristocrat behind, but she would always carry it with her; she would always be, as Louise would put it, 'refined'. She smiled to herself. Like the American. As soon as she walked into the room, she had seen him, perched casually in the whitened alcove, smiling to himself and looking out over the packed room. Her sailor. She might be able to ask Eugénie Bonnat more about him – if she could ever get hold of her without Jacques.

She skidded past Pierre's second-floor room in a hurry, making lots of noise, and passed three men carrying a bundle of something mysterious into the store-room next to the shop. They stopped until she had passed by, but did not speak.

She hurried down the corridor, past the morning heat-blast of the ovens and into the back room. She was relieved to find it was empty: she could get on with her writing task in peace. She sat down at the table on the platform and uncapped the inkwell. She loved this, this sense that she was doing something, taking part, having an effect – working for the cause. She was thrilled every day by the sense that she was at the centre of things, in this buzzing, ramshackle old house – the Nest of Patriots, Pierre called it, the Nursery of New Bordeaux. She had loved it ever since the chair set her down outside, almost a month ago, and she had just walked in, along with the crowd come to buy their evening loaves, and asked for Monsieur Lamontaine. They had taken her in; and they had all been wonderful.

Well – maybe not quite all. If she was honest, Jacques had been a problem all along. He had looked at her oddly, right from that first day, back in the gardens. He never spoke to her unless he had to; and yesterday, when she had come in as the men were setting up the room for the meeting, she had heard his voice raised as if in a speech of his own, denouncing all the nobility as enemies of the people. The rotten-hearted aristocrats, he had called them, who treated honest workmen worse than animals, starving them of their wages, insensible to their pain. The other men had nodded and agreed, egging him on. He had noticed Annette come in, but he had not stopped. He was telling a story about a fellow who had been killed when he fell from a roof. 'Because Count Lavigne, damn him to hell, insisted we work in the rain.'

Annette had stopped in her tracks. Cousin Henri. She had stood very still, trying to make herself invisible. She need not have feared, for Jacques had pointedly ignored her presence as he went on. 'Now Guillaume's family are near to starving – and the Count has not even paid him what he earned, let alone a gift in compensation. But what would one expect from the nobility of France?' And he spat on the floor. Then he spun round to face Annette as he went on: 'The time will come, my friends, when all their money and their airs and graces, their sneers and their big houses will not protect them; when Justice will walk the streets. The time will come. And I shall be there!' and he had struck at the air with the hammer he held in his hand.

Pierre had not been in the room at the time; but when Annette had mentioned it to him, just before the meeting, he only frowned and said something about a strong speech by Mirabeau reported in the paper. Sometimes, she thought, men seemed unable to distinguish between fine political speeches and what was really going on. She began to draft the notice they had agreed on, late last night, to advertise the second lecture on philosophy.

Later she would take it to the printing shop along the road; she had been there several times. That was how she had noticed the jeweller's next door. She felt the comforting weight of gold *livres* in the pocket under her skirt; the goldsmith had given her a good price for her smallest pair of earrings, and asked no questions. But the printer's workshop was far more exciting than the dark little cave of the jeweller's: a cluttered space, brightly lit by tall windows to the north; paper everywhere, and in the centre three presses gleaming with wet ink. Two men in paper caps and worn linen aprons worked the machines, their nimble fingers stained with their trade. Last time Annette had been there, they had been pulling a big placard off the press; wet copies hung from the ceiling like a forest canopy, every leaf shouting 'Liberty!' in thick black type.

She made some final alterations to the wording of the handbill, then mended her pen and pulled a fresh sheet of paper towards her. As she started on her fair copy, the three men she had seen in the passage came in, talking hard, and sat with their heads together at the other end of the room. A few minutes later the shop bell rang and she heard Madame Marsan shouting up the stairs from the bakery for Louise to come and serve a customer. It was never quiet in the Rue des Cordeliers, but that was one of the exciting things. Annette thought of the long mornings she had spent alone at the château, the hours of boredom in the convent chapel, and knew that, however frightening her freedom sometimes felt, this was a better place to be.

She had just finished writing when there was the thud of running footsteps outside and the noise of the street door opening, then an explosion of shouting in the passageway. Pierre burst into the room, followed by Jacques and a man she had not seen before.

Pierre was red-faced and panting, though whether from running or from excitement Annette could not tell. 'Such news!' he gasped. 'This good fellow has just ridden post from Limoges, overnight, to bring it. No more talk of the Estates General, my friends – we have a National Assembly now! An end to unfair taxation! It will be the birth of a new France.'

'A fairer France, you should say. The end to oppression!' agreed Jacques. He looked as excited as Pierre.

'National Assembly?' Annette was struggling to grasp what he meant.

Pierre looked at her. 'Come with us!' he said, catching her arm. 'We are going to tell all of Bordeaux about it. Jacques, you go to the Bonnats – Eugénie won't have heard yet. I'll call on Henri Pinot, and we'll meet at St Michel.'

Pinot was the printer. 'I was just going there,' said Annette, picking up the handbill. 'If you will look this over –'

Pierre focussed on it briefly, then pushed it aside. 'No point in that now,' he said. 'We have more important things to do.'

25

Jude's discovery of the list of creditors had been more timely than she had realised. Rent day, the dreaded *terme,* which for some of their neighbours would be a final and disastrous reckoning with the noble lord who owned the row of houses and workshops, was only a couple of weeks off now. Not all those who owed the Bonnats money were willing and able to pay but, by the time Jean-Baptiste had made a dozen visits, he had enough cash in hand to give the men in the coopering shop some part of the pay they were owed, and to put away three-quarters of the rent for the house and works in the iron chest behind the desk in the office. They were almost safe.

He wrung Jude's hand. 'You are a true friend,' he said.

Even so, there was still little or no money to spend day by day, and Jude had to admire the skill with which Madame Bonnat kept food on the family table, even if it meant lentil porridge three times a week. Meanwhile, Jude had her own financial problems; or rather, she had no money at all. She looked on her hours in the office as payment for her keep, and had steadily refused all offers of a salary, which she knew the Bonnats could not afford. Madame Bonnat had pressed her to accept a coat – old, but a striking sky blue – a formidable cocked hat, some good linen shirts and several pairs of stockings; they were all her late husband's, and had been too small for Jean-Baptiste to take to. But Jude was still in real need of a pair of boots, and she had not a single *sou* in the pocket of her well-worn breeches. The only thing of value she owned was the locket, and the thought of parting with that was more than she could bear. But then came a neighbour from across the road, where they made wine barrels, with a letter from England.

'I know what he says – I've had trade with the English, down the years. He wants seasoned barrels for his spirits from the Indies. But I need to make terms with him, you know? And that needs a good business style. Will you write for me, Monsieur Wiston? I will make it worth your time, of course.'

As soon as she had done that, others came. There was quite a flurry of English letters. Jude thought she could well set up as translator to the Bordeaux business community. She bought her boots, and a lighter coat, only a little worn.

The twenty-fourth of June was Jean-Baptiste's fête day. Not, as Jude at first thought, the anniversary of his own birth, but the feast day of the saint for whom he was named. This was the first time in three years that he had been at home for this auspicious day, and a celebration dinner must be made, come what may. Eugénie and her mother plotted and scavenged for days to produce the feast, while the family lived on a *pot au feu* that was little more than cabbage water, helped down by the increasingly gritty bread. The neighbours helped, with such contributions as they could spare – a couple of eggs, a head of curled lettuce, some goose fat. One of the workmen even went out early one morning with a slingshot and brought down a pigeon that had been foolish enough to land on the spire at St Michel, but it was as starved and thin as every other inhabitant of the quarter, and only good for soup. At least there was no problem about wine for, as Madame Bonnat said to Jude, a good vintage will keep until Judgement Day, and her husband had stocked the cellar well.

On the great day, Eugénie and Françoise brought in flowers and vine leaves to decorate the salon; the table was laid with Madame Bonnat's best Sèvres plates on a good linen cloth, and at four o'clock the family sat down to a dinner of three triumphant courses. A salad with boiled eggs and artichokes soon disappeared; then Madame Bonnat, flushed with success, placed a rich-smelling casserole on the table and began to serve each person with meat and gravy. Cries of admiration greeted her achievement. It was a long time since they had seen meat.

'It is cooked *à la bordelaise*,' she said to Jude as she handed her a steaming plate, 'with red wine, garlic and herbs.'

The stew had a strong taste, which neither wine nor herbs had managed to disguise. Jude found she was taking more of Monsieur Bonnat's good vintage than she would normally do, to wash the food down. The room was hot, and the unaccustomed quantity of food made her hotter.

Jean-Baptiste sat back in his chair. 'I am a lucky fellow,' he said. 'Here I sit with my family around me and my good friend by my side, with food on my table and a glass of wine in my hand. How many men are so fortunate?' He turned to Jude. 'How many men have such a mother, eh? Let us drink a toast to her, my friend.' He filled Jude's glass again.

After that more toasts were drunk: to Jean-Baptiste's health, to his mother's cooking, to Jude, and to France. Jude's head began to swim. She put down her fork.

'You do not like your dinner?' Eugénie asked solicitously.

Her mother looked anxious.

'On the contrary,' said Jude hurriedly, with a smile for Madame Bonnat. 'It is… delicious.'

Her hostess looked relieved and patted Jude's hand. 'Of course,' she said, 'one would not eat rat by choice, that goes without saying. But a good sauce does work wonders, I believe.'

Jude was saved from the need to reply – and the impulse to throw up – by a violent knocking on the yard door. A man's voice shouted something unintelligible.

'Jacques!' cried Eugénie, as she ran to let him in.

The tiler's dark face was flushed. 'A thousand pardons for disturbing your dinner, Madame, but this is too important to miss. There's big news from Versailles – what a gift for your fête day, Jean-Baptiste! We're just going down to St Michel to hear all about it. Come now, or we'll miss the beginning!'

Her brain still fogged with wine, Jude followed the others. The street was full, the people all hurrying one way. When they reached the open space around the church and its strange detached spire, it was already crammed, the white arrow of masonry rising from a sea of jostling bodies. Jude recognised some of the faces from meetings she had attended in the park and from the lecture at the baker's shop. She found she was looking out for the girl with dark hair, whom she'd not seen since that night.

There was shouting for quiet, but it was drowned in the general hubbub. Then Jude saw someone climbing on to the spire itself, finding footholds among the carvings, pulling himself up till he could be seen all across the square. His fair hair shone like a beacon: it was the man who had lectured on Rousseau. She craned her neck to see if the girl was with him, but the crowd was too thick to be sure.

Now he began to speak; the crowd fell silent. 'People of Bordeaux! I have news – news of the most important kind!'

The crowd cheered.

He went on, 'The Third Estate is no more!'

Another roar, louder, but less confident – what did he mean? The crowd turned audience, and its pulse began to beat to the orator's drum.

'Nor is the First Estate – nor, my friends, the Second!'

The excitement was wild now, but it choked off like a single strangled cry when he tore off his hat, flung out an arm, and cried, 'We have no Estates General, summoned by the King – we have, instead, a National Assembly!' They tore off their hats too, and flung them in the air; clogs thundered like a spring tide on a rocky coast.

Jude felt the surge of excitement, though she knew no more than they did what a National Assembly might be.

The speaker was getting into his stride now, the crowd intent on every word. 'The representatives of the people have declared two things – two magnificent, incontrovertible things! First –' He paused, holding both hands out, asking for silence. 'First, my friends, they have declared that all taxes – everything we pay now, *all* current taxes – *are to be abolished*!'

Jude was almost thrown down by the wild surge of people, shouting, struggling forward, attempting to get to Lamontaine and lift him from his perch. But he stopped them, stabbing his arm skywards in a theatrical gesture of appeal to the gods. They fell back a little in front of him, and suddenly Jude saw the girl. She was half hidden behind the buttress of the tower on which the man stood; her face was turned up to the speaker and shone with delight. Her kerchief had come out of her dress on one side; her flush of excitement ran all the way down to her breasts.

'There will be taxes, of course!' the orator continued, speeding up now, 'but they will be *fair* taxes. Everyone will pay, my friends, not just the poor! And the nobility, who have the most money, will pay the most!' Riding the surge of their exultation, he went on, 'They have tried to stop us, but they cannot! The King is on our side! The National Assembly has taken a great oath, never to be parted, nor sent away, until the constitution of the kingdom is established and consolidated upon firm foundations!'

It was hot in the square; the sunlight striking off pale stone was blinding. Something – the wine, or the stewed rat – had given Jude a headache. He's lost me, she thought. I don't know what all that might mean. Nor, apparently, did everyone in the crowd. There were some shouted questions – Jude caught the word 'nobility' thrown back at him, with some curse she had not heard before. Other voices cried down the hecklers and there was a swirl of fists, somewhere over to the left. She looked back anxiously to the speaker, but he was climbing down to talk to someone else at the foot of the column. The girl had disappeared behind the intervening crush of arguing faces and waving arms.

Jude pushed through the crowd to lean against a shaded doorway on the edge of the square, where she could go on watching without being shoved and elbowed. A few feet away, two serving men in a deep blue livery were doing the same. Snatches of their conversation reached her between the bursts of applause and shouting.

'It's him, I'd lay money on it. Talks like a priest, doesn't he?'

The other looked doubtful. 'Did you ever see him before, then?'

'When would I have seen him? Stuck out in the country, wasn't he, on some vineyard. But that was the name. Lamontaine. I'm sure that's what they said. And if the girl's anywhere, it's odds on she'll be with him.'

His fellow shrugged, non-committal. 'Well, if you're right, Monseigneur the Count will be glad to hear of it, I reckon.' He rubbed his thumb and finger together, smiling. 'Buy me a drink on the strength of it?'

26

The rejoicing in the square lasted well into the night, in a cacophony of dancing and argument; but Jude went to her bed quite soon, nursing her head. It was not until next morning that she remembered the two footmen.

Jean-Baptiste shook his head. 'If he's a priest, he must be red hot in the pulpit,' he said. 'Maybe the nobs really are after him – he's not exactly their best friend, is he? But never fear, hundreds of good *bordelais* will be standing between him and danger.'

'Whose men would those two be, though?' Jude persisted.

Jean-Baptiste shrugged. 'No idea – ask Jacques, he's had more to do with the rich than I have.'

Even then she would not have pursued it further, had not Jacques appeared in the kitchen ten minutes later, on his way to take Eugénie to yet another meeting.

He slapped Jude's shoulder in greeting. 'Good morning, my bible-reading friend!'

'Jacques! Maybe you would explain something to me?'

'If I can.' Jacques dumped himself down astride a chair. 'But you're the big reader, not me.'

'In the crowd yesterday, I overheard two men – footmen, in livery – saying that the speaker was a runaway priest, and that the Count would be glad to hear of him. I felt worried for – for him – you know? What is his story? Would he be needing to avoid someone who was looking for him, do you think?'

Jacques was interested. 'What was the livery like?' he said.

'Plain – dark blue – very rich – with something embroidered on the collar, I think, but in the same colour.'

Jacques stood up abruptly. 'Lavigne!' he exclaimed. 'That's the swine who refused to pay us!' He shook Jude's hand and made for the door. 'I don't know what he's after, but it's sure to be nothing good. I'd better warn Lamontaine.'

Jude was glad she had not mentioned what the two men had said about the girl. She could imagine what Jacques and his friends would think about a runaway lady putting their best speaker in danger from her irate family. But she was still worried about her; and later in the morning she went round to the baker's.

It was a warren of a place, she discovered. The paper of names on the doorpost had gone – ripped off in last night's celebrations, perhaps. She stood back, squinting up the peeling plasterwork at the tall narrow windows above. Many of them were standing open on this hot day, though not a breath of wind stirred to cool the air within. A tune played on a fiddle came from somewhere at the back; high above the street a boy, wedged sideways in a window, was reading a pamphlet. A peal of laughter – girlish, or at least on a high note – floated out.

The heavy door was ajar, but Jude decided not to wander in unannounced; she went into the shop. The baker was stacking new loaves on the shelf behind the counter. Was it Jude's imagination, or were loaves getting smaller, as well as grittier? Baking must be a hard trade, these days.

Jude stammered out her errand, and Madame elbowed open the door behind her. 'Louise!' she called. A pasty-faced girl appeared from the back room. 'Take Monsieur to see Mademoiselle Annette.'

Annette? Annette. Jude followed the girl down a dark passage as hot as hell, and came out into a sunny courtyard. Annette was sitting on a bench in the shade of a dusty olive tree. She rose to meet them with the same assurance Jude had noticed before, and an expression of expectant curiosity.

Jude made a little bow. They both looked at Louise, but the girl sat down on the bench, grinning. Jude concentrated on keeping her voice deep as she introduced herself.

'Ah, yes!' said Annette, 'I thought it might be you, when Jacques said "our American". Thank you again for sending word about the Count's men. I'm sure Pierre is perfectly safe, but I –' She paused, as if reconsidering whether to go on. 'I will need to take more care myself, I think.'

Jude, conscious of Louise listening with deep interest to every word, said only, 'Yes, I think you must.' She hoped her tone would convey more than her words.

Annette frowned slightly, then said, 'Louise, would you fetch us a drink of water? Monsieur Jude has walked here through the heat.' As soon as the girl had disappeared, Annette turned to Jude. 'Is there more?'

'Yes. I could not be sure, but I believe the danger was indeed to you as well as to him. I'm sure I heard them say something about a girl...' What more could she say? She couldn't ask directly about her past – or her present, for that matter.

Annette took a deep breath – her kerchief was better anchored today, Jude noticed, watching it rise and fall – and said, 'You are right, Monsieur. I am a runaway, you see, even more than Pierre is. I have left my family, and moreover the cloister, for the sake of my country. And that Count, Henri Lavigne, is my cousin, and lives here in Bordeaux. Even so, I thought myself safe enough – I do not think he has ever set foot in this quarter of the city!' She smiled ruefully. 'But I did not think of his servants.'

'Then I'm glad I was able to warn you.' Jude smiled into her eyes, and was rewarded with a pretty blush. What should she say next? Framing her French very carefully, she added, 'If I can be of any further service to you – or to "your country" – you have only to command me.'

Annette looked at her with a slight frown. 'Are you mocking me, Monsieur Jude?'

Jude shook her head once and bowed. 'A thousand pardons, Milady,' she said. She raised her eyes slowly and looked at the girl. The girl looked straight back. They both smiled.

Louise, arriving with a pitcher and two beakers, sniggered.

Later, Jude thought she should probably have been more careful. Flirting was fun, but dangerous. Whatever would she do if a girl

– if this girl – took her seriously? She was safer in the role of the pious and lonely American in which Jacques had cast her.

Normal life was, in any case, coming to a halt. The city was no longer simply hungry; it was starving. Deaths had been reported, in the depths of the little streets behind the harbour. When Jude walked out to look at the sea, as she liked to do from time to time, there were fewer ships; hardly more was going on here than on the docks at Salem. She had the sense that more ships were sailing out than she ever saw return. But the strange feeling in the air was not only the heat, and the dearth, and the lack of employment: the city seemed suspended by expectation, as if it held its breath. Word from the north, from the National Assembly, was brought by an excited and exhausted rider who galloped in at mid-afternoon most days, with his packet of smudgily printed, sensational news; men gathered at the northern gate to receive him.

For a week, the news-sheets reported chaos. The King had agreed to recognise the Assembly; then he had not agreed, because Queen Marie-Antoinette had stopped him. The finance minister, Necker, had been recalled; had been dismissed; had endorsed the Assembly; had cancelled all taxes. In Lyons, a mob had seized on all the grain stores in the name of the King, and given food to the starving. Madame Bonnat pursed her lips over this one, and prayed that the good people of Bordeaux would do nothing so foolish. In fact, they did nothing at all that week. The streets became like the public gardens, full of arguing people – and they were all thirstily hot, and very hungry.

Finally, the news that came from Paris made no sense at all: the people had gone to Versailles to insist their king came to the capital to live with them, instead of with his court. The papers began to report the massing of troops, and confrontations between the foreign squadrons of the King's guard and the French units of the army. Old men shook their heads; the Bordeaux *parlement* gave up all its powers to a military council, commanded by the Duke. Only a few miles out of town, Jean-Baptiste said, there had been rioting over the price of food, and three men had been killed.

In this strange atmosphere, Jude's resolution to avoid the

bakery did not last long. Just a week later, Eugénie brought a message. 'Pierre would like to meet you, Jude,' she said. 'He was grateful for your concern for his safety, and he'd like to invite you to come to a small meeting of friends, to discuss what goes forth at Versailles. He's a great admirer of Americans, and particularly of your Constitution. I think he would value your opinions of the grand designs afoot at the National Assembly.'

'Our Constitution?' thought Jude. 'What now?' She was, in truth, deeply puzzled about what the French thought they were doing, though she could hardly say so. They were apparently trying to set up a new system of government – a democracy – but without losing the king to whom they were unstintingly loyal. To Jude this was a contradiction in terms. As far as she could make out, the National Assembly, having invented itself and agreed to do away with the powers of the rich, would only do so if the King agreed. But that was ridiculous! Perhaps it was just that her French wasn't good enough to grasp the subtleties.

'Of course I should like to come,' she heard herself say to Eugénie. 'Thank you – I'll be there by seven.'

She dressed with what care she could, given that her wardrobe was so meagre, flattening her hair with water and brushing the blue coat as thoroughly as possible. She tapped Monsieur Bonnat's old cocked hat firmly in place. Swinging down the street towards the quay, she told herself that all this effort was in the good cause of keeping up the honour of her country before Pierre Lamontaine and his patriotic friends; but she didn't fool herself. Catching sight of her reflection in a window, she grinned and adjusted the hat to a dashing angle. A passing girl with a basket of fish on her arm gave her an approving wink, and Jude passed on feeling rather pleased with herself.

To reach the bakery, her way lay either through or round the park; to avoid the crush, she decided on the streets. She had passed through Sainte-Eulalie, the grid of streets beside the gardens, only once before. It was not old, like the Faubourg des Chartrons where the bakery stood, but a place for the smart and the rich: newly built houses, all clean dressed stone with gleaming shutters and steps. The main street, Rue Moreau, had an ostentatious air of wealth and importance: the facades were broad, the steps swept clean, the twin brass dolphin door-handles shining. And it was quiet there. Jude turned off the busy main road with some relief.

Only a step or two along, she realised that something was amiss here too. The steps of the grand house on the end of the row were splattered with red paint; someone had tried to clean it up, and spread a pink stain everywhere. Her eyes travelled up to the house and she saw that the door was daubed with red too. No, not just daubed: it was a painted capital P. She looked down the street; the paint trailed ahead of her. As she walked along – rather briskly, with a rising sense that this was not a good place to be – she found three more doors clearly marked with the same letter P. They were the two central doors in the row, and the one at the far end of the block – the biggest and richest houses in the street. She was glad to turn the corner, and head for the Chartrons.

27

It seemed to Annette that Louise was never silent. They were sitting sewing in the room they shared, and Louise had not stopped talking for two hours. Her prattle reminded Annette all too vividly of the deadly afternoons in the salon at the convent; her choice of subject matter was, in spite of the differences in their circumstances, alarmingly like that of Sophie and Thérèse.

'It's the Queen I feel sorry for,' she said now.

Annette looked up sharply. 'You do?'

'Well, it's no time at all since the poor little Dauphin died, and she must be grieving dreadfully, mustn't she?' Louise put down her needle and looked tragic. 'But she still has to dress up and go to do all her royal duties, just as if nothing was happening. You know that man who came with the news yesterday? He says his friend saw her at Versailles. Dressed all in cloth of silver, he said, and the King in cloth of gold, but Marie-Antoinette looked really thin and ill, poor thing. Her bosom was all sunken, he said, and her face full of lines.' Louise sighed sympathetically. 'A mother's grief.'

'It hasn't stopped her trying to wreck the new National Assembly,' said Annette unkindly. 'Believe me, Louise, the Queen is certainly not so prostrated with grief that she can't plot with the Duke of Artois against the people. Pierre is afraid that between them they will persuade the King not to endorse the new Assembly, and that would be dreadful, after we've come so far.'

'I'm sure you know best,' said Louise peaceably. 'I don't understand all those matters. But I still think it's unfair to say such disgusting things about her – all those stories about her lovers and that. If I was rich and beautiful, and married to a boring old sot like King Louis, I'd have *hundreds* of lovers!' She paused briefly, thinking. 'Not women, though. Ugh! I couldn't do that. You don't think it's really true, do you, about the Queen and the Princesse de Lamballe?'

Annette looked out of the window. She had never had a lover, of either sex. Not even an admirer. She wondered restlessly what it would be like. Then she wondered – again – if the American Jude Wiston was coming to the meeting this evening. She had overheard Pierre telling Eugénie Bonnat to invite him. Would it be worth going to the meeting after all, to see him? In the last few days Annette had, though she was loath to admit it even to herself, grown just a little impatient of the endless debates and wrangles over what was – or was not – happening in Paris and Versailles. The shining ideals of Liberty and Justice were becoming clouded in confusion as each new victory seemed to fizzle out in waiting for the next, and nothing really changed. Even the declaration that all taxes had been abolished had turned out to be a promise for the future rather than a fact. Meanwhile Madame Marsan was paying more and more for her flour, while her customers were less and less able to pay for her bread; the men idling on street corners grew more angry day by day, their wives and children more emaciated. Could the National Assembly really put an end to all that? And what if Pierre's fears were realised and, instead, the King put an end to the National Assembly?

'You shouldn't listen to such gossip,' she said absently. 'Look, there's Jacques coming down the street. Go and open the door – it must be nearly time for the meeting.'

Louise clattered downstairs. Annette stayed by the window, watching for the other visitors to arrive; waiting to see if the slight figure of the young American would appear at the end of the street. Jude. He was not like any of the men she knew. He was interesting. And very polite. And kind, she felt sure. But so was Pierre – all those things – so that wasn't exactly it. There was something... *different* about the young American. And when he had looked at her in the courtyard that day Annette had felt...

Well, she had no words for how it had made her feel, but very much hoped it might happen again.

In the end she almost missed him, looking down from her window, because his large hat obscured his face. Her heart jumped. Should she go down and join the meeting? No, she looked a fright. She must do something to her hair. Perhaps it would be better to bump into him accidentally afterwards? She heard Louise open the door and then Jude's voice in the passage: the light, boyish voice with the delicious foreign accent that had captivated her when she talked to him last week. She imagined his smile of thanks to Louise for opening the door, and a little shiver of pleasure ran down her back. Then she heard Pierre's characteristic tones, enthusiastically welcoming his visitor. Would he and Jude become friends? She would like that. And of course, it would mean that she would see Jude more often. Perhaps she would go to the meeting after all? Frantic with indecision, Annette hesitated until the door of the back room closed and the house was quiet again.

No matter. She would wait until they had finished their endless arguments and explanations, and talk to them – to him – afterwards. She picked up her sewing, but immediately put it down again. She looked at herself in the dressing glass, and despaired. This was no good. She could simply not stay here waiting; she would burst. She must do something. Picking up her hat, she went quietly downstairs and let herself out into the street. She would walk as far as the printer's and see if there was any news in from Paris; if there was, she could bring it back to Pierre and the others and they could argue all over again about what it meant. And if there was no news, then at least the walk might calm her restlessness.

It was a warm evening and there were still plenty of people in the streets; Annette knew some of them by sight as customers at the bakery. As she turned the corner into the alley where the printer's shop was, she came face to face with a young woman. For a moment she did not recognise the familiar face in an unexpected place.

'Bonjour, Mademoiselle. You are well?'

It was Jacqueline: paint-smart and pale-faced, but otherwise exactly as Annette had last seen her – except that now she wore the buff bodice and skirt of a citizen, instead of Lavigne blue, and she was visibly pregnant. Annette felt a rush of affection for her, and realised how much she had missed her company. 'I am well, thank you. And I see that you are! How long now, until the baby is born?'

'Another four months,' said Jacqueline. 'The middle of November, God willing.'

There was a pause. Neither of them wanted to walk on, but neither could think of the right thing to say.

'You know I am a Patriot now?' Annette said at last. 'That I live at the bakery in the Rue des Cordeliers and work alongside Father Lamontaine for the new France?'

'Yes,' said Jacqueline. 'I do know. I hear about you. Everyone knows there is a handsome lady living at Madame Marsan's.' She avoided Annette's eye, staring at two boys who were scuffling in the dust on the other side of the street. It was difficult to tell what she was thinking. 'My husband is a leader among the Patriots in our *faubourg*,' she explained, 'so I hear all the news, you see.' She glanced at Annette. 'Matthieu Boucher – perhaps you have heard of him?'

Annette shook her head. 'I don't think so.'

'He is a leader,' Jacqueline repeated, her voice tinged with pride. 'Men listen to Matthieu who would heed no one else. Only last week he stopped them from killing a man who they took for a spy because he had pen and paper about him; it is hard, sometimes, to keep people calm. But he is strong for the people, Matthieu – that is why they listen. They know he is one of them and will never put himself above the next man.' Then, as if she had made her mind up about something, she looked Annette in the eye. 'You will take great care, Mademoiselle?'

'Of course,' said Annette, touched. 'You must not worry about me, Jacqueline.'

'No, Mademoiselle,' said her former maid politely. 'It is just that, well... Do you know Jacques Dupré? Eugénie Bonnat's man?'

'Oh yes,' said Annette. 'He is often at the bakery. He is something of a leader among the people, too.'

Jacqueline looked round quickly and lowered her voice. 'But did you know how much he despises Father Lamontaine, and seeks to turn others against him? It is because Father Lamontaine is of noble birth, for you must know how Jacques hates the great ones – oh, your pardon, Mademoiselle!'

Annette tried to smile reassuringly. 'It's not difficult to tell that he doesn't care for me, either.'

Jacqueline did not smile. She seemed determined to have her say now, in spite of her embarrassment. 'Jacques says that he should not be puffing himself up into a leader of the people, he can never be one of us and he should be put in his place,' she said. 'Then two or three days ago, Jacques came to see my Matthieu, and they were drinking, and Jacques started cursing Father Lamontaine, and he said he had just found out, that day –' she dropped her voice to a whisper – 'that Father Lamontaine had been employed at Brillac. And he had discovered that you are one of them too, not a servant, but a Lavigne! I kicked Matthieu, under the table, and kept very quiet, you may be sure, else I swear Jacques would have been at my throat upon the spot! He was full of hate, Mademoiselle, and used the most filthy language – I have rarely heard such profanity.'

'But why?' Annette broke in 'He must know how tirelessly Pierre has worked for the cause! They call him the philosopher of the people, did you know that? And he is not the only one – many of the First Estate have sided with the commons against the lords!'

'It is partly that Jacques cannot abide aristocrats, my lady, having worked on the buildings of Bordeaux all his life, and so been at their beck and call, as you might say – but it is more than that. His best friend, the man married to his sister, worked on the roof at my lord the Count's new house, and fell to his death because they were forced to work in the rain. Since then the name of Lavigne has been like a curse to him. So, you will do nothing to enrage him, Mademoiselle? For your own sake?'

Annette assured her that keeping out of Jacques' way would be no trouble at all and, after an exchange of good wishes, they parted. As she walked on, Annette wondered what Jacqueline's own opinion of the nobility was; better not to ask, perhaps. At least Jacqueline had given her an explanation for Jacques' inability to be even commonly polite. Well, his friendship was no loss; and personal likes and dislikes must be buried now in the shared struggle for freedom.

The doors of the printer's shop stood open to the air. Inside Annette could see Monsieur Pinot, sweating and black-handed, hard at work. He did not see her come in; she stood and watched for a while as he heaved on the great lever of the press, then deftly peeled each wet sheet from the bed of type and pegged it up to dry. This piece must only just have begun printing, for there were no more than half a dozen sheets hanging from the racks. She did not need to pick out the words 'Necker', 'Majesty' and 'Estates' from the gently swaying broadsides to know that it was the day's news from Versailles.

The printer paused to wipe an inky forearm across his brow and noticed his customer. 'Good evening, Mademoiselle. You are eager for the news today?' His long face looked even more lugubrious than usual.

'It's a pleasant evening for a walk.' She smiled. 'But I don't suppose the news is very different from yesterday or the day before.'

'Perhaps,' he said. 'And perhaps not.'

His expression did not change, but Annette caught the gleam in his eyes before he turned away to pull down a page and fold it deftly for her to carry. How extraordinary to be in his trade, she thought, to be able to give out joy and sorrow, truth and lies, on bits of paper that might change people's lives! Hurriedly, she paid him and took her news into the street where it was still light enough to see. When she had read the whole page through, standing outside the shop, she sat down hard on the edge of a horse trough and read it all over again to make sure it was true.

And then she was running, as a lady should not, through the streets to the baker's shop, to share the amazing news.

By the time she pushed open the door to the meeting room she was too breathless to speak. There was a ludicrous moment when a dozen expectant faces were turned to her – she saw Pierre, Jacques, Jude – as she waved the crumpled paper and gasped for air. At last, struggling to control her voice, she said, 'It has happened! It says here that the King has ordered the First and Second Estates to join the Assembly! He has forced the nobility and the princes of the church to take part in the great project. They are to make a new constitution, based on liberty and equality for all. France is to be united at last!' And then she burst into tears, because she was so happy.

28

Jude, swept into the park with Pierre and his supporters, simply let herself swim in the excitement. Ten or twelve strong, they burst into their usual café and crashed onto the terrace, taking over all the tables; the noise was overwhelming, the people drunk with excitement and visions of a new future. Jude felt herself embraced by the crowd – by the new nation of France. Vivid faces flashed before her as she sat in a corner of the café's terrace, back to the wall, and watched them surge and return. As the heat of the day subsided into sticky darkness, the racket and the crush of bodies grew greater; lamps flared, and bottles of wine appeared from the dark back regions of the house.

Last week's rejoicing was nothing compared to this. She felt the city stretch out and vibrate with triumph – it ran through Bordeaux like wildfire. Printers all over the city had seized on the few sheets that had come from Paris; in an hour, men were coming back to the park with armfuls of the broadside Annette had seen, telling that the King had ordered the nobles to the Assembly, and proclaiming the victory of the people. After the news-vendors came waves of running youths, screaming, jumping, and carrying banners – any banners – the flag of the city, hand-lettered sheets shouting '*Liberté!*' and even the arms of noble families – whatever could be held up to snap in the breeze as they ran through the streets, rejoicing.

Pierre, transfigured by joy, held court outside the café. Two bands were playing nearby, more or less together; when Eugénie improvised a simple set of new words to an old tune, Jude sang along. She toasted the King with dozens of people who came and went alongside their platform. Fireworks burst out from the top of the town almost before it was dark; thousands of people danced and sang and toasted the new world. And when Annette tilted her head and smiled an invitation, Jude stood up and danced with her in the trodden grass and dust. She had never danced, except on shipboard; it would have been unthinkable, where she had grown up. But here, with Annette's hand warm in her own and the beat of the music shaking the ground under her feet and a dozen other couples to follow, she capered with the best of them.

They were still dancing at midnight, when Jean-Baptiste came pushing through the crowd and grabbed her by the arm.

'There you are! I've found you, my little dancer! That's a piece of luck – they said at the baker's that you were all gone to the park, but in the dark and with this mad crowd it could have taken me an hour to find you.'

'What's wrong?' Jude handed Annette back to her seat and turned to her friend.

'Nothing, nothing – but Maman was concerned to know where you had got to. She thinks there will be bloodshed before dawn.'

'What? Why should there be?'

Jean-Baptiste took her by the elbow and turned their backs to the party. 'You have not been down the town for a while? The city grandees have decided to show their love for the people in their usual way. At sunset, the fountains at the doors of the Ombrière began to run with wine. It was thin and sour, to be sure, but it was strong enough. The mob are crazy drunk. They are happy so far, and the worst of them are already lying in the gutters like so many swine in muck, but soon they will be running and roaring.' He spat. 'Maman is right – their temper will not last. You passed through Rue Moreau on your way here? Or along the Allées? Did you see what happened to the most hated houses last night?'

'What? Oh, the Ps on the doors?' Jude recalled the shiver of the deserted streets she had passed through, their threatening silence, the hint of… witch-hunting.

Jean-Baptiste nodded. 'P for *proscrit*.' He paused, seeing Jude's

puzzled frown. 'You don't know that French word? It means…
condemned – denounced?'

Jude nodded, and Jean-Baptiste went on, 'Yesterday's papers
said the Patriots in Paris were marking out the nobility for
slaughter, and so our fine hotheads must needs do it here, eh? And
with this much wine in them, who knows? They might begin upon
the cull, regardless of the King and his Assembly.'

Jude thought fast. 'Tell your mother I'll come home, but I must
see Annette to her place first.'

'Oh ho! It's Annette, is it?' Jean-Baptiste peered over Jude's
shoulder at the party at the tables.

'No – well, yes. We have been dancing, that's all,' Jude said
lamely.

'And any woman would love you, on your nimble feet, my
little monkey! But it seems a pity to drag you away, eh? Do you
think, tonight –?' He flexed his arm.

'No, no! She's a lady,' Jude said, before she could stop to think.

Jean-Baptiste roared with laughter and slapped her on the
back. 'Then she's bound to be hot for you, my friend! I'll see you
tomorrow!' And he merged into the darkness outside the lamps.

Jude turned back towards the light and the noise and stood
for a moment, watching. Annette was talking to the pretty boy
they called Marie, but she looked up at once and caught Jude's
eye, as if she had felt her gaze. Annette's cheeks were flushed
with excitement, or wine; her dark eyes shone. She did not look
like a lady in an old portrait any more, and certainly not like
anyone's aunt. Jude swallowed. Jean-Baptiste had sobered her a
little, but that had only served to bring her down to earth enough
to understand her own feelings. She looked at Annette and knew
how much she wanted her. Panic rose in her throat – how had she
allowed this to happen?

Then Annette turned away to say something to Jean-Marie.
She lived in the same house as the priest and his boy – what had
she thought about those two, Jude wondered? What did she make
of such an idea – two men together? Or two women? Jude shook
her head – whatever Annette thought about that, she would have

no reason to apply it to herself and Jude. With a sigh, she made for the table where Annette was sitting.

Annette was having a wonderful evening. The King had answered the call of his people, the people had risen up rejoicing and united, and she had danced all evening with Jude Wiston. She could still feel the warmth of his hand in hers as he led her down the impromptu dance. The breathless pace of the fiddle player, the darkness, the uproar of voices, the giddiness of having drunk cheap wine all evening without eating – it had all been a million miles away from the dancing lessons of her youth, back in the château of Brillac. Here was a different way of being: rich and poor, high and low together, building the new order of things in France. Tears of happiness pricked her eyelids.

She looked up and saw Jude pushing between the tables. She pointed to the chair beside her and he sat down, smiling his thanks. Something was troubling him, Annette thought. He looked worried. She found she was having some difficulty focussing. This wine must be very strong.

Jude said, 'Jean-Baptiste thinks there may be trouble in the streets later. You should perhaps go home.'

He looked so handsome when he was serious. 'I don't think I should go on my own, without an escort, do you?' she teased.

'Then please allow me to escort you,' Jude replied courteously.

'I should like that,' said Annette. Then before she could stop herself she added, 'I'll tell you what else I should like,' and she leaned forward and kissed him.

For a moment the whole world seemed to hold its breath. Then Annette buried her face in her hands, overcome with confusion. When she looked up, no one else was taking any notice, and Jude was on his feet with his hand stretched towards her. His face was a blank mask as he said, 'I will take you back to Madame Marsan's now.'

But he had kissed her back. He had; she was sure of it. Without hesitation, she put her hand in his and allowed him to lead her away.

The thick crowds still in the park gave her an excuse to cling to her escort's arm. Jude was slight but wiry; Annette could feel the warmth of him through the sleeve of the blue coat. She felt giddy, and happier than she had ever been in her life. As they came to the north gate of the gardens, the lights faded away and only the moon showed them where to go. Then her foot slipped suddenly on something spilled on the grass, and she felt Jude's arm go round her waist to catch her. Without hesitation, she turned into his embrace. His breath was sweet, his cheek quite smooth as she found his lips. For a moment he held her fiercely and she felt her body melt with delight.

Then he took her firmly by the shoulders and put her away from him, staring at her with an expression she could not read. 'Come now,' was all he said as he took her arm again.

It was too short a distance. They were turning into the Rue des Cordeliers before Annette had time to come down to earth or think what she might do when they arrived. As they skirted a group of ten or a dozen neighbours still drinking and singing outside the wine shop, she tried to find the words that would keep this wonderful night from ending. The rest of the street was quiet and dark. Beyond the baker's shop a closed carriage stood at the kerb, but its lamps were not lit, and the only light came from the baker's window, where Madame Marsan had left a lantern burning to guide her lodgers home. Its soft glow lit the planes of Jude's face as he bade Annette goodnight. She gazed at him and could not speak.

Taking her silence for dismissal, Jude bowed and turned away, settling his hat as he walked slowly back towards the late party on the corner.

Annette opened her mouth to call after him, if only to say goodnight – and the sky fell in upon her head. A hard hand clamped across her open mouth and a filthy, stinking darkness came down over her eyes. She tried to scream, but choked; instinctively she kicked backwards with all her strength and bit down on the hand, fighting the nightmare darkness. With a curse the man loosened his grip and she fell to the cobbles. She curled up, screaming and sobbing, as hands grasped her. He was pulling and kicking at her, still cursing, trying to lift her up. Desperately she tried to squirm out of his grasp.

There was the noise of running feet and shouting; her attacker's curses took on a note of alarm and he grabbed her roughly round the waist. She clung to his leg, fighting to stop him picking her up. He fumbled and staggered, then he found her hair. This time she screamed in earnest, striking out at any part of him she could reach.

The thudding feet were nearer.

'Come away!' a more distant voice shouted. 'Bring her or leave her, but come on, for God's sake!'

'Be still, bitch!' The hand in her hair wrenched her head sideways and a fist smashed into her face. For a moment the pain was so great that she stopped struggling. She was dragged along the pavement, but not far. Then he dropped her and she fell flat out, as all the running feet pelted past and away after him.

Then she knew that Jude was there, his hands gentle as he lifted her up, and she looked past his shoulder at the departing carriage with half Madame Marsan's neighbours hanging on its tail screaming rape and murder. But after that there was a blank, until she woke up as they were lifting her on to the counter in the shop. It hurt a lot, and she had time only to make sure that Jude was still there before she fainted again.

When she opened her eyes, Madame Marsan was talking to Jude.

'I've three pans of dough trying to run over the floor by now; I'll have to leave you to watch her. No doubt you saw worse on-board ship. Let her rest a while. Don't try to talk to her. I'll send Louise to help her upstairs.' She picked up a bowl of murky pink water and a handful of bloodstained rags, then paused and looked carefully at Jude. 'I'll leave you the brandy,' she added, 'but don't give too much of it to my patient.'

The door closed. There was a silence for a long time. Then Annette whispered, 'I'm sorry. I should have taken more notice of what you said about Henri's men. I didn't mean to get you involved in all this dreadful…'

Jude took her hands. 'Nonsense. He was useless, an amateur – he hardly waited until my back was turned. He wore the Lavigne coat, I'm pretty sure. Then he scrambled off in a carriage – not your average footpad.' He was making light of it to reassure her, Annette thought. 'You were right to think you needed an escort home,' Jude went on. 'But one sailor was clearly not enough. Next time you had better recruit the whole boat.'

29

It would have been polite – at least, by Salem standards – for Jude to call at the bakery next day and enquire after Annette. Miss Rebecca Wiston would not have hesitated. Jude stared out of the window. See what a tangle comes of such vile pretences as this disguise, she told herself. What are you going to do about it? She picked up her pen and put it down again, shaking her head. We'll see, she thought. These are changing times. She tried not to listen to the yammer of anxiety that was beginning in the back of her head – nor to attend to the warm glow that persisted deep in her insides.

There were plenty of other things to think about, that morning. Jean-Baptiste had come home in the dawn and roused her to help close the big gates to the yard. Left open except on rare occasions such as this when they were needed to defend the tunnel entrance to the house and workshops, they had sunk into the cobbles and needed two pairs of arms to shift them.

'The mob is out,' Jean-Baptiste said, 'thousands of them in the square. They are breaking in everywhere.' He put his shoulder under the rusty old bar that secured the massive oak barrier.

But his sister did not return that morning, nor the next. A street boy came banging on the gates with the message that she was well and safe, and Madame Bonnat had to be satisfied with that, until Eugénie appeared on the following Sunday to collect her things.

'I'm working for the People,' she said, 'We are collecting food for the poor, down at the Rue des Cordeliers.' She looked at Jude. 'We could do with more help, if anyone cares to come.'

Her mother was furious – how could it be Eugénie's business to work for the poor? Was she being paid? And if so, by whom? Some city father, parliamentarian, noble lord? Jean-Baptiste shook his head – it was not safe. Who knew how such people might behave, given the idea that food was to be had for free? And the bakery – was it secured at night? How could they be sure the mob would not simply pour over their threshold and help themselves?

But Eugénie tossed her head and picked up her bag. 'Are you coming?' she asked. But Jude shook her head.

Over the next few weeks, there were some at the bakery in the Rue des Cordeliers, too, who came to share Jean-Baptiste's misgivings.

'We could all be raped in our beds,' Jean-Marie said, stretching his eyes wide as he stirred the everlasting vat of soup.

'Not if I am in that bed with you!' Pierre laughed, coming in from the street with a basket of muddy swedes. 'I'll protect you, sweetheart.' He turned to Annette. 'Did you finish that new banner this morning? We could hang it up over the door, I thought.'

Annette took the basket and turned to the shallow wooden sink. 'Pump for me, Marie.'

The boy sighed elaborately and went to lick the spoon before he put it down, but thought better of it, wrinkling his nose. 'What's in this muck, Pierre?' he asked.

By way of an answer, his lover took him by the back of the neck and kissed him. Annette looked away. 'I hung it on the banisters to dry,' she said. 'But are you sure we want to make ourselves that obvious? Marie may be right – there were some ugly moments yesterday, when that mob came in and started pushing their way through the women.'

'You're all faint-hearted!' Nothing seemed to dint Pierre's joyous self-confidence. In the three weeks that had passed since the night of the great jubilation, he had been everywhere in the city, speaking to crowds, haranguing such members of the Bordeaux *parlement* as were still in the city, writing and printing news sheets whenever word came from Paris, and then also joining his friends knocking on doors to ask for alms – they had so far picked up three children and an old man who were actually starving on the streets, and hundreds came to the soup kitchen they had set up in the bakery yard. Pierre had patiently argued away everyone's fears about the rumoured foreign mercenaries being sent from Versailles to stamp out rebellion in the provincial cities, and he had laughed outright when broadsheets appeared peddling a foreign-invasion panic, saying that the Spanish were massing troops and ships to invade the city because the garrison had lost control.

But today the news was real and momentous – even Pierre had stopped dead when he heard that the people of Paris, thousands strong, had stormed the royal prison of the Bastille. 'The King will not stand for that,' he had said, in the end. 'This will be a trial of wills, my friends – and more than will – of armed strength: the forces of the royal guard against the people. But the French troops, bless them, will not fire on us. All will be well.'

Nonetheless Annette had noticed that he had gone to his room and come back smelling of oil and gunpowder. Now he was back on course, bustling and organising; but she could not get him to talk about anything but the banner for the door, and the soup. Eventually, pleading another headache – these were her only remaining hurts from the attack – she went to her room to think.

What she thought about, of course, was mainly Jude Wiston, and why he had never returned.

Back at the Bonnats', the news of the fall of the Bastille was received as the final proof that France had descended into chaos.

'Of course, the old prison was an evil thing,' Jean-Baptiste said. 'Who knows how many poor souls were shut up there, for no fault of their own? And the King will be sure to listen to his people first – now that they are in arms.' For the news was that countless muskets, and cannon even, had been seized by the people of Paris, and would be opposed to any foreign troops who stood against them. 'But,' he said, 'who has these guns, eh? How are they led, commanded?'

'And how are they fed – how are we all to be fed?' his mother interjected. 'No one can eat gunpowder. Children do not thrive on bullets, mark my word.'

Jean-Baptiste shook his head. 'And what will happen here when our own *sans-culottes* hear of the triumph of the Paris mob? Will they go for the Château Trompette, where I suppose they could get guns, or the Ombrière? You know what that would mean.'

Jude looked at Madame Bonnat; the older woman's face was grim. 'The filth that would pour out of those dungeons would overwhelm the city,' she said.

It was the talk of starvation, as much as the whiff of gunpowder in the air, that drove Jude to commune with herself seriously that night, as she lay in her little truckle bed in the store-room. She had paid her way so far with the Bonnats, and had made herself enough pocket money to live on, before this apocalypse had broken upon the city; but now there was little chance of collecting any more debts, and all business was at a standstill. She was still eating with the family – when they ate – *and* no longer turned up her nose at the odd rat brought in fat from the vineyards. But it could not go on. She brought out the locket and the old gold glinted in the pale light of the summer moon. These last weeks she had half forgotten that she had come here on her way to somewhere else: that she had been on her way to England, to find her way to 'Madeley in the County of Salop' – wherever that was – and to collect her inheritance. It was time to take the road again. Once the London lawyers had heard from John Fell, they would be able to acknowledge her – at least, they would when she had changed back into Rebecca. Then Jude would be no more; Annette would forget him.

In the morning, Jude made her way out of the Porte des Salinières, back to the quay of international shipping. She had walked here, from time to time, ever since she came to the city – she needed to recall the sound of the sea, even if the estuary lacked the roar of the Atlantic breakers off Naugus Head. This morning she was again struck by how few ships could be seen. Nothing was loading or unloading at the Quai de la Douane; no one was by the water except a few mudlarks fishing listlessly for bottles with their toes. The lamprey fishermen did not sail from here, and the small French coastal vessels tended to moor further upstream; there was only one barque in the offing. Jude sat on a bollard until it put off a boat and she could speak to the officer who came ashore.

She was in luck – he was English. It was warming to hear her native tongue again, even spoken in the clipped British way. The man seemed in a great hurry, however, and would not stay to hear the story she had made up to get herself a berth. The ship was bound for London, yes, was about to sail in a day or two at most, but no, it did not need a ship's cook, nor any hands of any kind; and even if they did, he seemed to imply, they would not think of hiring a damned colonial.

'Passengers, then?' Jude heard herself say. 'Do you carry any passengers?'

The officer paused then, and looked her up and down. Finally he answered with a sneer that the state cabin was vacant, if five gold *louis* in passage money happened to be at your disposal. He flicked a dismissive finger at the peak of his hat and strode away.

30

It was late July now and the city, already jumpy with hunger and suspicion, began to crackle with the first of the summer thunderstorms. In the Rue des Cordeliers they were still busy, even though the bakery no longer had any decent flour at all. Madame Marsan experimented more and more desperately with acorns and other substitutes, trying out each recipe on her long-suffering family. In return for their forbearance, she had begun helping with the People's Soup, which improved its taste and quality no end although, as far as Annette could see, the ingredients were just as meagre as before.

Annette, Jean-Marie and Louise were labouring over the vats in the yard under a sky the colour of a bruise, when Pierre suddenly appeared at the street gate. He scarcely glanced at them, throwing a word of greeting over his shoulder as he raced upstairs, his satchel, bulging with papers, bouncing at his back.

Louise raised her eyebrows. 'He seems happy,' she said.

Annette was not so sure. She followed him and found the door to the room he shared with Jean-Marie standing open. Pierre was face down on the bed, the satchel flung on the floor and papers spilling everywhere.

'Pierre?' When he did not answer, she sank to her knees and began to collect up the handbills. After a few moments he turned over and sat up.

'I'm sorry – you don't need to do that.' His face was puffy, as if he had been crying.

She sat back on her heels. 'Tell me?' she said.

He was silent for a moment, then tucked up his feet and sat

cross-legged like a little boy, rocking slightly. 'I shouldn't be surprised,' he said. 'How could they behave otherwise? What training have they had in governing themselves? Plato tells us –' He stopped, swallowing hard.

'Pierre, who? What has happened?'

He looked at her and tried a smile. 'I was down by the docks – the old grain warehouse. I heard the racket, and I ran, and – they are looting and smashing and scattering everything to the wind, and – I couldn't stop them.' He passed his hands wearily over his face. 'Hundreds of them. Mostly women, oddly enough. Real women, not men in skirts this time. Women with children at the breast, hungry, angry women, calling for bread. And for blood. I tried. I spoke, but they did not want to hear me. I was – afraid.' He flung himself full-length and turned his face to the wall.

Annette put out a hand and tried to think what it was Plato might have said. Then she stood up. 'I'll fetch Jean-Marie,' she said.

Jude went to the quay again in the afternoon, but of course no other London ships had put in; it was not safe. It seemed there had been some kind of riot, half a mile away along the dock, and an old warehouse was in smoking ruins. No one was out of doors. She understood at the wharfingers' bar that almost all the British had cleared off smartish, weeks ago; the local crews were doing nothing but drinking and discussing news from Paris; and the wine shippers would not be active until after the vintage, when, please God, things would have quietened down enough for there to be some trade. But that would be two months away. The solitary British ship still lay at anchor. Five *louis*! She had scarcely as many *sous*.

By the evening, she was almost determined to leave the Bonnats anyway, and take her chance on the road. For dinner they ate the worst bread yet, and little enough of that; Madame was pretending she did not want any. As soon as was polite, Jude went to bed. But she could not sleep. Visions of Salem haunted her, and when she expelled those she was in Havana, in Lotta's bed. She shook herself awake from a dream in which she made love to Lotta but found that it was Annette's body beneath hers. She got up and stepped into the yard. The summer night was hot and heavy – there was rain on the way, which would at least clean some of the stink from the streets. She thought she would like to smell the sea. Fetching her hat and boots, she let herself out of the postern in the heavy oak gates.

Almost at once, she heard footsteps – running footsteps, their clatter bouncing off the high buildings. She turned, bracing her back to the gates for defence; but staring into the darkness she made out that the running figure was a woman, skirts clutched high, hair flying, tearing down the street as if pursued by heaven and earth.

'Jude!' she shouted, down the length of the street. 'Is that you? Help!'

It was Eugénie. Panting and sobbing, she fell into Jude's arms.

'What is it?' Jude could not imagine what panic could have brought Eugénie flying home all on her own. 'Is something the matter with Annette?'

'No – yes! Where is Jean-Baptiste? They are attacking the bakery!'

As they ran, the story came out in fragments. 'There's a dozen or more of them,' Eugénie gasped, 'with sticks and shovels. They are shouting that Madame Marsan has hidden flour there and is giving it to the *aristos* – they mean Pierre, and Annette.'

'Save your breath for running, little one,' her brother grunted, hefting the massive crowbar he carried in both hands.

But Eugénie, breathless as she was, could not stop. 'And my Jacques – he is one of them!' She stopped in her tracks, tears streaming. 'He told me not to go out tonight, not to go there, but I didn't know where he was, and when I got there, he... They were breaking down the door!'

Jude, who badly needed to know that Annette was safe, grabbed Eugénie's hand, pulling her along with them. They collected five more men as they ran – three journeymen coopers and two of

Jean-Baptiste's shipmates; they all thundered down the Allées in a block, scaring passers-by out of their way. This time, thought Jude, we really have brought the whole boat. Strangely, she was not frightened for herself. Annette took up all her thoughts.

They could hear the crowd from several streets away. Jean-Baptiste panted out that the racket was a good sign. 'If they were in and looting, they'd be quiet about it.' Then he added, 'But it sounds like more than a dozen men to me.'

They rounded the corner into the Rue des Cordeliers. Jean-Baptiste was both right and wrong. There were many more than twelve men, but they were inside as well as out; the whole street was in chaos. Men armed with cutlasses and pick-axes and all kinds of weapons had staved in the shutters of the bakery and smashed the window and door. They were tossing fixtures and fittings about in the shop and out into the street, screaming for bread and cursing the aristocrats – Jude could hear a kind of throbbing, mad chant of '*À bas les aristos*!' Their efforts to destroy the place were being hindered, to some extent, by Madame Marsan's guests and her neighbours, who had turned out in force with kitchen spits and shovels and even cooking pans to defend the bakery; they were not succeeding, but they were making an amazing amount of noise.

The rescue party flung themselves into the fray. Jean-Baptiste hit a looter such a blow with his iron crow that the man fell flat on the pavement, his head split open, blood gushing underfoot. A howl of fury went up from the rest, who turned at bay. The neighbours, seeing reinforcements at hand, rallied behind the sailors, waving their pots and pans in triumph. Jude, scanning the crowd for Annette, sidestepped the fight – which was clearly going to be a very short one – and clambered through the broken door into the house.

The looters had been through here already. The banisters were dangling from the landing above, and all the doors downstairs were wrenched open or off. They must have been searching for some imaginary hidden store of grain or flour. They had pulled the place apart. Jude thought they had gone – were all outside, or in the shop – until she heard, from above, a woman's voice. It was a low, terrified wail, mounting – as Jude sprang up the wrecked staircase – to a scream.

Transported with rage, Jude flung herself with a yell on the man whose body covered Annette's. It was Jacques, the tiler: Eugénie had been right about him being with the attackers. Jude wrenched his head back by the hair and clamped her arm across his throat, squeezing with all her strength. Taken by surprise, Jacques collapsed into her arms, choking and retching; they fell to the floor by the bed. Keeping herself on top, Jude kicked at him, forcing him face down into the heap of bedclothes. But of course, he was too strong for her. He heaved himself upright and she crashed off his back into the wall.

Annette screamed again... and then the man screamed too, as Annette swung a brass candlestick at his head. He fell, clutching his face, and lay writhing on the floor.

Jude was on her feet, panting, grabbing Annette. 'Leave him. We must get out of here – Jean-Baptiste and the crew are in the street – safe there...'

They flung themselves in giant strides down the attic stair. Jacques did not follow.

Outside, the fight was still going on. Jean-Baptiste stood in the shop door, bellowing challenges to whoever was left inside. Back-to-back with him was one of his shipmates – Jude recognised him from the *Belle Héloïse*, though now he looked thin and wild – and the rest were still struggling all up and down the street with what seemed to be a bigger mob than they had found when they arrived.

She held Annette tight in her arms. 'This is not good,' she said in the girl's ear, quietly. 'There seem to be more coming to join in. Where is your friend Pierre?'

'I don't know,' said Annette. She pushed herself free to look up and down the street. 'I had not seen what was going on – Jacques trapped me –' She turned her face up to Jude's. 'He brought them here – he set them on. He was looking for Pierre – and for me.'

A ragged roar went up from the street around them, cat-calls and boos and another cry of '*À bas les aristos!*' They looked up.

It was Pierre. He stood, in his open-necked white shirt, without coat or waistcoat, arms outstretched like an actor on a stage balcony, framed in the high window of his room. Incredibly, he was holding a book. 'Listen!' he cried. 'Listen, my friends, my compatriots, listen to me!'

'*À bas! À bas! À bas les aristos!*' The chant sprang up and strengthened, sweeping down the street.

Pierre shook his head, opened his arms, appealing for a hearing – and then, suddenly, Jacques appeared behind him. They saw Pierre lurch forward; his body jerked as his knees hit the windowsill, then he plunged head first to the street.

There was a moment of utter silence.

Jacques had taken Pierre's place at the window, his bloodied face a mask of fury. 'Now see how you like to eat the pavement, *aristo* priest!' he screamed. 'That is for my friend who fell from the roof, and for all the other good men killed by evil lords!'

The rioters, suddenly shocked at what they had done, began to melt away into the night. Jean-Baptiste had seized hold of Jacques, but they had no idea what to do with him, other than string him up from the nearest tree, and they could not bring themselves to do that; so when he kicked out and ran off into the darkness, no one followed. They were, in any case, too intent upon tending their own hurts; and upon the tableau on the pavement, where Jean-Marie sat with ashen face, holding Pierre's body in his lap.

He would not let anyone near and, since it was obvious to all that Pierre was dead, they did not insist. The boy sat, silent, for a long time. Then he began to sing, at first under his breath and then out loud, a little country song of springtime and love that Annette remembered from Brillac.

'He used to sing as he worked, sometimes,' she said to Jude. 'They all did. When my father was away, particularly.'

There was a clap of thunder in the distance. In a few moments more, the rain began – heavy spots, faster and thicker until everyone ran indoors. But Jean-Marie still sat, water streaming down his face. At last, Annette and Jude went out to him, and he allowed them to lift Pierre and carry him into the dry. He walked behind them, as if at a funeral.

The people had gone home now. Jean-Baptiste had disappeared into the house to help Madame Marsan restore some kind of order, and the shop was empty. Rain pelted in through the broken window. They laid the priest on the table, where Annette had lain when Henri's man attacked her. The three of them stood round the body, and Jean-Marie held Pierre's hand.

Annette was still numb, struggling to take in what had happened: Pierre looked asleep, as if he might wake at any moment and rally them with a passionate quotation from Rousseau. The little tune ran in her head, taking her home to Brillac and to the excitement of their secret conversations. How simple it had all seemed then, that promise of a better world.

Jean-Marie looked up. 'This is how it will be, now,' he said simply. 'So you must go. You must get away. Now. Together.'

'But – we can't just leave you... or Pierre,' said Annette. 'What will you do? Where will you go?'

'I don't know. It doesn't matter. But you must go! You are in more danger than I am. Jude, you must take her somewhere safe.' He looked from one to the other. 'You will stay together, won't you?'

There was a moment's silence. Then Annette moved round the table and put her arms round him. They clung together for a moment, before Jean-Marie pushed her away.

'Go *now*,' he repeated. Then, as if he had been back in the chapel at Brillac, rather than in the ruins of their new world, he went down on his knees beside Pierre, and made the sign of the cross.

Annette put her hand in Jude's and allowed herself to be led away.

They walked up the stairs, but on the first landing Annette turned to Jude.

'I don't want to sleep here... in that room, where... not ever again,' she said.

'No, that's all right,' Jude said, 'but we can sit up together for a little, and talk. When the rain stops, we'll go to the Rue de la Fusterie.'

'Thank you,' Annette said.

Jude took the candlestick away and came back with a lighted taper that she stuck in the bracket on the wall, though light was already coming up in the east, behind the storm-clouds.

Annette looked up. 'I think Louise must be with her mother,' she said. She sat on the pillows, leaning against the white wall, her hair falling over her face and shoulders, drooping with tiredness. 'He's right,' she said. 'We must go away.'

There was a silence.

Jude sat down on the foot of the bed, not looking at her. 'I was going to go,' she said. 'To England.'

'Without telling me?' asked Annette, in a very small voice.

'Yes, I'm afraid so.'

'But now – will you take me too?'

Jude stared at her; it was too much to bear. She cast around desperately for an answer. 'I would. I promise you, I would,' she said, 'but I cannot. I have no money. There is a ship in the harbour – well, it was still there last night – bound for London, and I enquired about a passage. But they will not take me on as a hand, and they want a huge sum for a cabin. I had begun to think I might try to stow away – but you could not do that.'

Annette sat up straight. 'I could pay!' she said, and strength and colour flooded back into her voice. 'Jude, I can pay for us both. I have jewels, and gold.' She smiled a small ironic smile. 'I was going to buy more food for the poor, but –' She shrugged. 'And I have friends in England. I could go to my godmother in London. Let me buy our passage. Please?'

Jude looked at her, long and hard, and shook her head. 'No,' she said. 'No. It is not possible. You don't know me – you know nothing about me. I'm sorry, but –'

There was a pause before Annette spoke again.

'I know the most important thing about you,' she said. 'I know that you're a woman.'

31

And that, in spite of anything Jude could say, was that.

Of course, there was no denying that they would both be wise to leave France; and it would be impossible for Annette to go alone. Jude's disguise would help them to travel, if not entirely unnoticed then at least without much danger. They would take ship together, keep each other's courage up on the voyage and, whatever a bunch of English sailors might say behind their hands about a young Frenchwoman with no wedding ring sharing a cabin with a male companion, the two of them would know the truth, and the world at large would be none the wiser.

Jude could find no acceptable argument against the plan. Her reason for not wanting to get further involved with the beautiful French girl was not one she could explain aloud. Her heart leapt with excitement at the idea of two days alone together; her reason warned against any such thing. Annette might have kissed Jude, the sailor boy, when they were both drunk, but she was hardly likely to kiss Rebecca – to pursue a romance with a woman. When the house was finally quiet, she helped Annette pack her few possessions into a bag and they hurried together through the empty dawn streets to the Rue de la Fusterie. Jude's sea chest took no time at all to pack and tie up. Among all her other emotions, she was deeply distressed at having to leave the Bonnats in this way, but having her plans known would help no one; she must write to them from England to explain. And so, as the next frantic and uncertain day in Bordeaux began, she handed Annette aboard the *Man of Kent,* ready to sail on the afternoon tide.

The ship was a disgrace. Compared to the *Belle Héloïse,* it was a floating shambles. The hostile and silent officer stuffed Annette's gold into his pocket, giving her change in British coins, and handed his passengers over to the slovenly steward. Jude was still holding their luggage, and had to force it upon a passing barefoot boy. The deck was filthy; clearly the crew chewed tobacco and spat it anywhere the fancy took them. Ropes were tumbled all around in ankle-breaking coils; and the lad sniggered when Jude took Annette's arm to guide her round the iridescent puddles in the scuppers.

'I thought British ships were supposed to be shipshape and Bristol fashion,' Jude muttered. 'No discipline, no cleanliness. I don't like to think about the galley.'

Annette, who had never been nearer to a ship than the quayside, smiled and squeezed Jude's arm. 'We shan't be here long. And it will take us to England. That's all that matters, isn't it?' Then she staggered and lost her balance as the motion of the waves heaved the deck up under her feet. She fell heavily against Jude.

The steward, turning back at that moment, winked at Jude and laid a conspiratorial finger alongside his nose. 'I do love a wench that can't stay upright,' he remarked. 'I'd get a good grip on her if I was you, cully.'

Jude scowled. She was glad that Annette's English was limited; if it would not save her from insults, it might at least save her from understanding them. The events of the last few days had taken their toll and Annette looked drawn and pale. 'Come below now,' Jude said, as shouted orders began to rattle down on them from the quarterdeck, and a rope's end slithered dangerously past their feet. 'We shall only be in the way here.'

At least in the 'state cabin' they could be private. It turned out to be a mere hutch, no cleaner than the rest of the ship and with only a shuttered pop-hole for a window, but with a real bed, big enough for two – and it gave them some respite from the shouting and running and curious glances.

Annette looked round and then sat down suddenly on the side of the bed. 'I feel a little unwell,' she said. 'A little giddy.'

'From tiredness, I expect,' said Jude. 'And if you've never been to sea before you may feel sick at first. Perhaps we should have stayed on deck – they always say it helps to look at the horizon.'

'Oh, no,' said Annette, closing her eyes. 'I think I will just lie down for a moment here…'

Jude lifted her feet on to the bed and, gently placing a hand behind her shoulders, guided her head down onto the bolster. She loosened the ties of the hat that Annette had hastily thrust on her head that morning, lifting her gently to pull it away, and stifled a gasp of delight at the sight of Annette's hair tumbling onto the pillow. Troubled by the force of her own thoughts she moved to the foot of the bed to remove Annette's beautiful – but very battered – riding boots. Having recovered herself a little, she looked up; but Annette was already asleep.

Jude smiled as she placed the boots neatly at the foot of the bed. Not surprising really, given the events of the last twelve hours; she was pretty much exhausted herself. She looked around the cabin and tested the door: it opened inwards. As quietly as she could, she jammed her sea chest across it, securing it behind a bulkhead. Annette did not wake. Gently, Jude lowered herself on to the bed next to her and lay on her back, staring at the knots in the planking four feet above her head, trying to think. She must fix her mind on her business in England and delivering Annette to her English friends, and suppress all dreams about a girl to whom she could offer nothing. She began to feel once more under her shoulders the familiar press and fall of the sea; it was deeply comforting. She had come a long way since she first stepped into her role as a ship's boy. From many of those steps there was no going back. She knew, now, that she was one who loved women, rather than men; and that for her, happiness would come in the shape of a woman – a wife. There was much to do, if she was to make that good, and much of it would have to be in the guise of Rebecca, rather than Jude. She had no idea which of her outward selves she would wear in the end, but perhaps, one day, on the other side of the world, when she had possession of her inheritance and a house of her own, she would find another girl to love, one to whom she could offer a home and a future.

Trying to believe it, she too closed her eyes; but her mind and body resisted sleep. She listened to the rise and fall of Annette's breathing beside her and turned, as silently as she could, raising herself onto her elbow and looking down on Annette's sleeping face. She wanted to drink in each moment, and began to let herself savour their closeness. Before she was really aware of it, she was tracing the shape of Annette's body. Her hand hovered a few inches away from actual contact as she moved down the curve of her breasts, dipped to the slender waist, swept up to the rise of her hips and marked the long line of her legs. She moved her hand down these contours and then up again, each sweep taking her hand closer to Annette's sleeping body but always just short of touching her. Jude felt the warmth of desire rise in her as she paused, letting her hand hover just a little longer above Annette's breast. She closed her eyes, breathing in the moment to seal it in her memory.

Annette's hand grabbed frantically at her wrist as a sudden noise like a thousand iron pots and pans being dragged along the cabin wall filled the small space. It took Jude several seconds to realise that it was the noise of the anchor being hauled up: she had never been below decks on the *Héloïse* when that happened. She was stunned by the din.

Annette was wide-eyed as she clung to Jude's wrist.

Jude raised herself up to look out of the porthole. 'They are hauling up the anchor, that's all,' she explained. 'We shall soon be on our way to England.' She turned back to Annette, looking for any sign that it had been more than the movement of the anchor that had disturbed her sleep, but Annette's panicky breath settled down again as they lay back side by side, listening to the banging and creaking, the thumping feet and distant shouts as the *Man of Kent* left its mooring and headed for the open sea. Jude pictured the long channel of the estuary, the wooded slopes and great lighthouse she had seen as the *Héloïse* had nosed her way in to her home port. How long ago? It seemed a lifetime.

She turned her head softly towards Annette. 'How are you now?'

'Sick.' Annette made a rueful face. 'And very cross!' she added, unexpectedly.

Startled, Jude once again turned onto her side and propped herself up on her elbow. 'With me?' she asked nervously, desperately thinking of ways she might excuse her rash behaviour.

Annette looked away. After a while she said in a small voice, 'You can't imagine how I was longing for this voyage, for this time alone with you. I thought it would be so romantic, you know? So... exciting. But it's not. It's hot and smelly and full of frightening noises, and I think I'm going to be sick!'

For a giddy moment Jude wondered if her French had let her down, or if she had imagined what Annette had just said. 'You were longing – for what?' she stammered.

Annette still wasn't looking at her. 'You see, I had begun to think I would never find the great passion of the heart that Rousseau writes of, never know love, and I might just as well go back to the convent. And then I met you, and...'

Jude fought inwardly to stay afloat. As Annette turned towards her, she tried desperately to think what she could say. 'Tell me something, then,' she asked at length. 'When you kissed me, that night in the park – did you know then that I was a woman?'

Annette frowned a little and Jude's heart began to beat so hard that she thought Annette must hear it.

'No, I don't think so,' Annette said finally. 'I worked it out afterwards.' She looked up, into Jude's eyes. 'And I found I still loved you just as much. Isn't that strange?' She smiled, and reaching up, she ran one finger gently round the contours of Jude's face. 'On that day, I did know something, straight away,' she said. 'I was so glad that your lips were soft,' she touched the corner of Jude's mouth, 'and your skin – your face. So soft.' She smiled again. 'Kiss me again now?'

Jude sat up a little, preparing herself for a moment she had rehearsed in her mind again and again but which she had thought would never happen. She cupped Annette's face gently in her hands and, closing her eyes, sought her lips. As she moved from the kiss she was immediately seized with doubt. This was not, after all, a wild and rejoicing night in the park, there were no dances beneath the stars, and everyone knew that kisses fuelled with wine were doubly intoxicating. She looked into Annette's face. Her eyes were still closed but there was a little frown that prompted Jude to ask quietly, 'Was that not good?'

Annette kept her eyes closed as she quietly answered, 'Again… please?'

Jude looked for a moment into the sweet upturned face before her. 'This isn't happening,' she thought. 'I must not do this.'

Then she stopped thinking. She took Annette in her arms and kissed her again, meeting the open warmth of her mouth, sweeping her tongue sideways until they melted together and slid down full length upon the hard and rolling bed. Once more she began to trace the outline of Annette's body but now she could feel the curve of her breast beneath her hand, the rise of her hips beneath the rough weave of her dress and she knew that they both wanted more. Jude began to undo the many fastenings of the bodice. This took some time, because Annette was not going to let her stop the delightful activity of tongue and lips that had made her flush with pleasure. Jude finally wrestled the bodice into submission and turned away, folded it neatly, and moved to place it at the end of the bed. But before she could turn back, Annette's arms were round her waist and, to Jude's surprise, her jacket was quickly off and dispatched unceremoniously to the floor.

'So that's how you fine ladies treat your clothes, is it?' She smiled and Annette laughed as first her skirt and then her petticoat were cast into the air to fall wherever they chose. Then she pushed Jude off and knelt up on the bed in front of her, flicking the strings of her corset apart with an expert hand.

'I am a Patriot now, you know – I can dress and undress myself,' she said, grinning wickedly as she pulled away the tall case of whalebone and linen and dropped it to the dirty deck.

'My turn now,' said Jude. Her shirt and breeches quickly followed the rest in an unceremonious heap. They paused, laughing, and then fell together gasping and giggling as Annette seized hold of Jude and whipped around her, unwinding the tight-bound strips of linen that perfected her disguise. Annette raised her eyes to return her lover's look as she cupped Jude's breasts in her hands. Jude slid her hands beneath Annette's flimsy smock and slipped it over her head. They paused again, taking in the sight of each other, delighting in their nakedness and, at first tentatively, touching lightly, seeking the sensation of each other's skin as they melted into another kiss. Annette lay quite still as Jude gently laid her head on the pillow. Jude thought – what does she know? Has she imagined this – or more than this? But as she met her gaze, she knew that here, now, Annette was looking at her with desire and something like understanding.

Annette quivered with anticipation as Jude's hands made the almost familiar journey down her body. She heard Annette gasp as she took a nipple first between her fingers, then with her mouth, running her tongue round and over the nipple, feeling its eager response. Jude gently raised herself up and let her hand slide over Annette's hips and round her thigh. She heard the moan of pleasure as she parted the soft, wet lips and felt the familiar rise within herself as they came together, quickly but gently. Jude, sitting back on her heels, watched Annette's face, and saw a look almost of surprise as she entered her. Annette gasped with pleasure as Jude leant down and forward and moved further and further into her, taking her with an insistent and irresistible force to a place that neither of them had dared to imagine. Jude threw her head back exultantly and as they moved together she felt a sharp new wave of pleasure surge through her body. Annette's touch was as sure and certain as her own; they cried out together as their loving joined them in a complete fusion of their senses. This new dance, rehearsed in the park just a few weeks ago, took on a fresh urgency in its sweet and complete fulfilment. Finally, exhausted for the moment, they lay in each other's arms, lips still touching, fingers entwined, limbs wrapped round each other.

Jude swept the damp tendrils of hair from Annette's face. 'How are you feeling now?'

Annette smiled. 'Wonderful,' she said, 'but very thirsty.'

Jude remembered a flask of good Bordeaux in her chest that Jean-Baptiste had given her. She sat up.

'Don't go,' Annette said as she slipped away from the heaving mattress.

'Drink,' Jude said as she brought the flask back to her.

Annette put the flask to her lips and held out her other hand. 'Come,' she said, 'come back.'

Jude settled back into her lover's arms as naturally as if she had always been there. Annette licked her lips and lifted the flask to Jude's mouth. 'Drink even with me – isn't that what they say, in the bars?' she said. 'I have learnt so much, since I left the convent!'

They laughed in their new-found intimacy. 'Better things than drinking toasts, I hope,' Jude said, accepting the flask. Annette's hand was cool, but it sent sparks through Jude as they touched. She took a mouthful; it burnt sweetly in the throat. 'I've learnt, too,' she said. 'Young women did not drink wine, where I came from – and certainly not from the bottle.'

Annette stretched a hand to touch the locket that still hung from Jude's neck. 'You always wear this, do you not?' she said. 'It is beautiful. Is it old? A family piece?'

Jude slipped the chain over her head and opened the locket to show Annette the portrait. 'My English aunt, Isabella Wiston,' she said. 'I never knew her. But do you not think she resembles you? The first time I saw you, I thought you were her ghost!'

Annette studied the picture. 'A little, perhaps. Or is it just because she is so young, and looks like a lady? The gown is old-fashioned – she must have been of the generation of my grandmother, the one who married an Englishman. Did I tell you about her?'

Jude shook her head.

'Oh, it was romantic! He was a follower of King James, so I was told. But she died young, so there is only one portrait of her – it shows her in a dress like this one...' She looked up at Jude. 'But I am a lady like this no longer.' She smiled mischievously. 'I wonder what Milady your aunt would say if she could see us now? But come, put it on again.'

She reached to clasp the chain round Jude's neck, and then they were locked in another embrace, fiercer and more urgent than before. Jude felt the ship lean into the wind as they swayed deeply to port; the rise and fall of the sea merged with their loving. When the ship righted into a long, racing drive that swept it from end to end, she felt the sweet hum inside her echoed by the sea, and the rush of pleasure matching the wind as it sang in the rigging overhead.

The day wore on and no one came to disturb them. They lay together, watching through the porthole as the sun began to dip behind the horizon. Jude cradled her love in her arms and thought no further back, nor forward, than the time they had together. She could feel Annette's warmth all down the length of her body. She closed her eyes and luxuriated in a combined sense of pleasure and protectiveness as they sailed inexorably toward England.

PART THREE

1789

Summer into Autumn

32

The ancient tabby was still curled in the folds of the quilt at the bed's foot. It wasn't really asleep: it opened one eye just a crack to watch Lucy as she blew up the fire. The morning sticks laid over last night's embers caught quickly, crackling and spitting as the flames shot a scatter of sparks up the chimney. Lucy laid down the bellows and straightened up, one hand on the small of her back, shaking her head to send away the dream that still clung to her. 'Off there now, you old slug-a-bed,' she said.

The cat cocked an ear, but chose pointedly to ignore her.

Lucy swung out the heavy iron pot on its bracket until it hung directly over the strengthening flames. Then she turned towards the bed. 'I said off, varmint!'

The cat stood up stiffly, arched its back, looked at her. Then it settled down again.

Its mistress emitted a low menacing growl, a perfect imitation of the bull mastiff at the Two Crosses Inn, and reached for the broom. The cat, judging the battle not worth fighting further, slipped off the side of the bed and took refuge on the windowsill, bristling with wounded dignity.

Lucy pulled up the quilt, smoothing the faded patchwork and tucking the ends of the fabric carefully inside the wooden frame. Then she bent down, got a grip on the bed at its foot and pulled upwards. This was always the hardest part, lifting the whole weight of the bed to the point where it would support itself and begin to swing into place.

She staggered but held on. 'One morning,' she grunted, 'I shall let go halfway and that'll be the end of me. Flat as a griddle cake.

Then who'll be your servant, eh?'

The bed clunked into place. Breathing hard, Lucy dropped the catches that held it in its box and leant against the wall until her heart had slowed to its normal pace. A good piece of carpentry: Sal Hamer's second son had made it for her when she came here from the farm, after Bron died. How long ago? Fifteen years? Twenty?

'That's better,' she said to the cat. 'Can't have our visitors finding the house full of unmade bed.' She knew, and the cat knew, that no visitors were expected. Those who did come up the hill to the cottage – a child sent for a cough cure, a servant girl from one of the farms looking for a drench for a scouring calf – rarely crossed the threshold. The bed could lie out all day, and Lucy in it, for all the world would care.

And that, of course, is what would happen, one day in the not-too-distant future. Lucy was not afraid of death; it was not knowing exactly when it would come that annoyed her. But that was what the dreams were for, she thought – to warn her it would not be much longer now. She must remember, come market day, to ask one of the Jones girls to take in the cat after she died. 'That's if you don't go first, Parsley, you old scarecrow,' she told it heartlessly. 'Come down off there and let's break our fast while we're still able to eat.'

The afternoon was hot, in spite of the showers; it was high summer. The wild roses had long since dropped their petals and the scent of honeysuckle was made stronger by the rain, falling just now in unrelenting sheets. Lucy was walking down a green lane in that part of England which was almost Wales and which had been her home now for over half a century. Water dripped from her hat-brim and soaked into the sack she had pulled over her shoulders like a cape. She walked slowly, leaning on a strong ash staff, cocking her head to listen, her sharp black eyes missing nothing. She knew every tree and flower on this path, every nest and burrow, for she had walked it more times than she cared to remember. She had come three miles already, and would go back again, up the hill, tonight. No mere shower was going to stop her making her weekly visit to the Two Crosses.

At the bottom of the path was a stile into the road. She climbed over it slowly, for she knew how easily old bones break, and there was no one left at home now to care for her should she fall. She stood a moment by the stile to catch her breath. It had stopped raining again and the road was clean and stony. She let down the petticoats she had kilted up to save them from the worst of the wet, smoothing them with her hand. Then she unwrapped the wet sack and rolled it into a bundle, before walking the last few yards to the door of the inn. She still had her pride.

A youth in a long apron, fists bristling with empty mugs, paused to smile a welcome as she came in. 'Good day to you, Mother Lucy – Grandfather has been looking for you this half hour.'

She raised a sardonic eyebrow. 'Old fool he is, then,' she replied briskly, making for the parlour door. 'He was ever a poor timekeeper. Where is the miserable blackguard?'

'Not here,' came a voice from the parlour, heavy with sarcasm. 'Over the hills and far away. Gone for a soldier. Where would I be but by my own fireside, you witless crone?'

The boy, grinning, pushed the door open for her.

'Can't see me? Losing your eyesight now, as well as your hearing, is it?' The speaker was a stout, florid man of about her own age, wedged comfortably into an armed chair by the great hearth.

Lucy sniffed dismissively. 'Better than losing my wits, like some I could call to mind.' She lowered herself gently onto the settle on the other side of the fireplace and surveyed him critically. 'So how do 'ee, Joey? Still alive, I see, to plague your acquaintance and be a burden to your family.'

The boy reappeared with a second mug and a pitcher.

Joseph chuckled. 'You were always a sweet-spoken woman, Lucy Weaver. Have a drink.'

He heated the poker to mull the ale and they settled on either side of the fire, for all the world like an old married couple, though they had never been that. Long, long ago, when Lucy was a girl and worked here in the inn, the boy Joey had made sheep's eyes at her in vain, for she was Bron's, then and always. In due course he married Margery Price, and when his father took to sitting by the parlour fire as Joseph did now, he and Margery had kept the Two Crosses in their turn. Now time had brought him and Lucy, the survivors, together again, to keep those memories alive in their tales of the old days.

Lucy sipped the hot spicy ale. Her wet skirts steamed gently in the heat from the fire. 'I saw our Dame last night,' she said.

Joseph frowned. 'You saw Bell? Her ghost?'

'It was a dream, codshead,' Lucy replied scornfully. 'She came to me in my dream.' She gazed into the flames. 'Young and proud and kind, just as she was when I first saw her that day in Shrewsbury town.' She paused, then said, with rare seriousness, 'She came to call me away, Joey. I know it.'

The old man stirred uncomfortably. 'No, no, our Luce. It might not be so. I've seen my Margery, time after time. Those who have left us do come sometimes in dreams, and no harm in it.'

Lucy stared into the fire, thinking, and said nothing.

33

Annette gripped the side of the little boat and tried not to think about how close she was to the water. She had already decided that she hated ships; now she knew she hated boats of every kind. The voyage on the *Man of Kent* had taken three days and two nights, parts of it a nightmare of panic and nausea, during which she had hardly slept at all. She and Jude had talked and kissed, and made love and talked again, and Annette had not known she could possibly, in her whole life, be so happy – or feel so sick. Love was, apparently, the only cure for seasickness; whenever Jude had reached out for her, her pulse had quickened with excitement and the rhythm of the ship had become one with the rhythm of her desire; but the rest of the time she had felt very ill indeed.

Now, that was over – over forever, both the misery and the bliss – and there was this clumsy, bumping rowing boat, three-quarters full of bales and boxes, propelled upstream against the tide by four men in antique embroidered coats and peculiar hats, whose English she could not begin to understand. She clung to Jude's arm as the vessel lurched, slowed, and lurched again. She would not be sick, she would not.

Jude touched her hand. 'Look at the shore,' she said, 'it will help. See, up ahead – that must be the Tower of London.'

Obediently, Annette tried to fix her eyes on the further bank. Silver light splintered off the rippling sheet of water that was the Thames. It was wider than the mouth of the Gironde: more like a sea, except that it was busier than any sea could be. Multitudes of boats and barges and tenders darkened its glistening surface, sailing seawards or rowing against the flow. She peered forward, through a moving forest of masts. Sure enough, a massive white château loomed on the northerly shore ahead of them: square and turreted, it looked like a giant parody of her home. The Tower dominated a sudden narrowing of the river; from this distance it was impossible to see how all the traffic would get through together. The boat rocked; bile rose in Annette's throat and she heard herself whimper.

Jude squeezed her arm. 'It won't be very long. I asked to be put down at Westminster Bridge – and I think Lady Waldon's house will be quite near there.'

Annette buried her face in Jude's shoulder. She could not bear to think of the parting that must come.

'Don't cry,' Jude said helplessly. 'Please don't cry…'

They sat in miserable silence. After a while – Annette had lost all sense of how long they had been on the river – the wherry moved across the stream, nearer to the northern bank, and seemed to be speeding up. They shot past the Tower and took up a place in a nautical queue, with other rowers close behind and ahead. The motion was smoother now and Annette felt less sick; but that only made room for utter desolation. She closed her eyes.

Jude felt Annette sag against her side, and drew a deep breath. If she could just get through this next couple of hours, it would all be done. Responsibility for Annette, for them both, for being in love, was becoming almost more than she could bear. But it was still clear what she had to do; and she would do it. They had boarded the ship with the understanding that they would part in London. She would despatch Annette to the house of her English godmother, her dead mother's dearest friend who would be her supporter against the demands of her family and would keep her safe until France calmed down and order was restored.

Then Jude would pursue her own plan: first she would write to the lawyers, to make sure that they had heard from John Fell, her lawyer in Salem – and possibly even from her brothers – before she turned up at their doors as a shipwrecked survivor. Annette had lent her money for several days at a modest inn, and even enough for a change of clothes, if she had to play it that way; but for the moment it would be much safer, alone in the great city, to remain Jude Wiston, sailor, and simply write as her former self. Except, of course, that that would mean she could not so much as bow Annette in through her godmother's door. She felt vulnerable enough, just sitting in this damned boat, stared at by four Thames watermen at close quarters and with Annette clinging so intimately to her side. She shifted uncomfortably and peered round the man ahead of her to see where they were going.

'Not long nah, sir,' he said. 'She's turned. Slack under the arches – shoot 'er in no time, nah.'

Jude grunted, which seemed to satisfy him. She had been wrong about Annette having no English, but charmingly accented lesson-book sentences were no preparation for the language of London's docks. It was no wonder Annette did not understand a word these men said; Jude herself had quickly realised there were more British accents than were spoken by the travelling gentry, and most of them quite impenetrable. Negotiating their passage ashore, she had come up against the mysteries of London speech; it was surprising they were sitting in the right boat. Always assuming this was the right boat. They were edging up to towering walls of masonry: London Bridge, she supposed. Suddenly the men leant on their oars and, with a splashing swerve, the wherry shot through the race between two slimy, festooned piers of stone.

Annette, opening her eyes at the unexpected movement, gave a squeak of panic.

'Hold hard – almost there now, I think,' Jude said, taking her hand.

Eventually they beached, with a bone-shaking rattle, on the shingle of the north bank just downstream from another bridge. One of the boatmen leapt out into the shallows and lifted Annette bodily to dry land; Jude splashed after them with the baggage. The man who took their money had ready answers for all Jude's questions – yes, there was a respectable inn where they could find refreshment, just at the top of the stairs. The landlord there would send a boy on an errand, or call a chair, or anything else that strangers to town might want. He tipped his ridiculous hat and they pushed off again.

Jude and Annette stood on the foreshore and looked around them. The air smelled of dead fish and all the other nameless flotsam that lay fermenting in the muddy water at the river's edge on this hot July afternoon. The wharfside buildings seemed ancient as the river; wooden walls leaned out dangerously over jetties of sodden black timber. Jude and Annette picked their way along a causeway bearded with barnacles and weed, to the 'stairs' the boatman had indicated. The steep granite steps led to a cobbled street and quite soon, as the wherryman had promised, to the Bear and Staff, the best hostelry in these parts, and run by his second cousin, a most honest man. By now both Jude and Annette were past judging the quality, or indeed the honesty, of any inn or its keeper. The huge woman who greeted them and brought them pint pots of cloudy ale was friendly enough. Jude charmed her into providing pen and ink, and helped Annette to write a polite note in English, informing her godmother of her arrival in London and begging for the honour of waiting upon her at her earliest convenience. They had no way of judging, either, whether the boy who pocketed tuppence along with the note would actually deliver it. All they could do was wait for him to come back.

Jude could not tell how long they sat in the dark little inn parlour, numb with misery, waiting to be parted. They spoke very little; there seemed nothing to say. At one point, Annette suggested listlessly that Jude might teach her some more English words, and for a few minutes they named the everyday objects they could see, but it felt so futile that they stopped. The sun sank down until it shone through the grimy window and struck warm lights from Annette's dark curls. Jude put her head in her hands and waited for her heart to break.

There was a knock at the door, and the boy was back with a reply from Lady Waldon – a cocked-hat of scented paper. Annette unfolded it.

'She is at home, and will be happy to receive me,' she said blankly.

They gazed into each other's eyes and Jude saw Annette's fill with unshed tears. Wordlessly, she reached out and took her hands and kissed them.

'You'll be wantin' a cab?' The boy was still there, hopping from one bare foot to the other, his eyes darting everywhere between them and their luggage.

'No.' Annette spoke up, her voice surprisingly steady. 'No, a *share*, thank you.'

Jude looked at the boy, daring him to pretend he did not understand.

'Yes, Miss,' he said, and ducked away and out of the door. It seemed only seconds before he was back.

Jude nodded him to Annette's bag. Then she stood and called for the reckoning; when she had settled it, they stepped outside together.

Annette turned towards Jude. 'Thank you, my dear love,' she said in French. 'You have shown me the meaning of life. I am indebted to you forever.' She turned, upright and trembling, and stepped into the chair. 'Goodbye, Jude,' she said. 'Write to me! Goodbye.' She sat back and struck her hand once on the little window in front of her face; the chairmen set off.

Jude stood in the gutter outside the inn until they turned the corner, but Annette did not look back.

34

Annette held her head up and her back straight, all the way through the evening traffic of the London streets to the house, up the steps and into the arms of Lady Waldon. Even so, she must have looked drained, for her godmother asked few questions and soon called for a girl to lead Annette to the little bedroom already prepared for her at the back of the house. 'Monsieur Perrault would have been proud of my deportment,' she thought fuzzily, before dropping into an exhausted sleep. But it was a fearful night. She woke every hour or so as a clock struck, a cat screamed or a carriage rumbled by on the cobbles; and slept again to see Pierre falling to his death, or Jude washed overboard from a boat which left her ever further and further behind. At dawn the other noises were joined by the crowing of a dozen cocks and the creak of carts trundling by. Annette gave up the futile attempt to rest and got up to look out of the window.

Roofs and chimneys stretched away in all directions, punctuated here and there by a mouldering church spire. They were not the silvery leaded turrets of Brillac, nor the red tiles of Bordeaux; these roofs were grim and grey, with many chimneys of sooty yellow brick. A man's voice floated up from below, shouting something unintelligible. Suddenly Annette was afraid. She was alone, in a foreign land where she knew no one; even her godmother, her correspondent of many years, was really a stranger. What on earth had possessed her to come here – apart, of course, from the powerful impulse to go wherever Jude went? She had told herself there was good sense in it. Her mother's old friend had always seemed to her a light in the darkness, a beacon of intelligence: she was, as Annette had understood it, a blue-stocking hostess with a circle of philosophical and literary friends. Such a person, she had thought, would be a welcoming protector against the hard family faces that would confront her if she tried to return to Brillac. Lady Waldon would understand why Annette had had to do what she did.

But now, staring out at a foreign city through a grimy windowpane, she was seized with doubt. Would Lady Waldon really sympathise? She might not think Annette should have stayed in the convent all her life, with no vocation – but still, she would want to know what had brought her goddaughter all the way to England, alone, without servants or luggage; and why she had not simply returned to her father when Bordeaux fell into turmoil. Of course, her godmother might not even know about all that – Annette had no idea whether news of what was happening in France had reached England; or, if it had, what position an English noblewoman would take. But, whatever her politics, Lady Waldon would want to hear Annette's story, and in some detail. Dancing-class deportment was not going to be enough to carry her through the inevitable interrogation which would take place as soon as she appeared downstairs.

There was a knock at the door of her chamber and the girl who had shown her to her room last night came in with a tray.

'My lady says I'm to help you dress, Miss, and do your hair, until you get a maid of your own,' she said, looking at the floor.

Annette, suddenly homesick for Jacqueline's cheerful competence, forced a smile. 'My godmother is very kind,' she said.

Lady Waldon was taking breakfast in the sunny morning room that looked out over the street. She was immaculately coiffed and gowned; clusters of tiny pearls hung from her ears and from the slender chain around her neck. She looked up as her goddaughter entered.

In spite of the maid's endeavours, Annette knew she looked a fright: in her travel-stained *bourgeois* costume with its short, bunched skirts, she felt like an awkward schoolgirl.

Her godmother beckoned her to a chair on the opposite side

of the dainty table and reached for a cup. 'My dear – how are you?' The bright eyes flickered over Annette's clothes, and a small frown appeared between the delicately plucked eyebrows.

'I am well, thank you,' Annette said.

'And slept well, I hope?

Annette smiled politely.

'After all your trials and tribulations. Yes. Coffee? Or chocolate?'

Annette gratefully accepted a cup of chocolate.

Her godmother barely stopped for breath. 'We are hearing such fearful matters from Paris: riots, battles, outright rebellion are talked of – and I can't imagine what can have happened at Bordeaux, to make your poor father feel he had to send you to England!'

This was obviously an invitation to explain, but Annette could not think what to say.

Lady Waldon came at the matter from a different direction. 'London can think of nothing else but these French troubles, as you will soon see for yourself,' she said. 'The reason we are still in town, despite the ending of the season, is because Waldon is involved in a committee – with most of the families who have any connections to France – that is meeting constantly, to deal with petitions and letters. People are beginning to write with such frightful tales – heart-breaking pleas – and even to arrive… As you have, my dear.' She stopped again, with an enquiring smile, and picked up the bread basket.

Annette took a sweet roll and broke it on her plate. She found she was very hungry; she had not eaten since… when? She could not remember.

'I am agog to hear the tale of your adventures,' Lady Waldon went on, 'but I shall not press you until you are completely recovered from your journey. When you are ready, and not before, you must tell me the whole story.'

The undisguised curiosity in her eyes belied her words. She held her head a little on one side and looked at Annette with the sharp gaze of a thrush listening for a worm. In fact, she was altogether rather like a bird, Annette thought, with her shiny plumage and beady eyes and that fast, twittering voice.

'But first, we must get you some more fitting clothes. Whatever course of action we decide on for you, some fresh gowns – something you can be seen in – will make you feel better. I have asked my dressmaker to call this morning and take your measure.'

'You are too kind,' said Annette. A carriage rattled by. Outside their window the great city went about its business; somewhere out there was Jude. Annette's heart ached.

'Not at all!' cried Lady Waldon emphatically. 'What is happening in France is *deeply* shocking to us all, and we can only be glad that you have escaped for the time being. For your dear mother's sake, as well as your own, I am delighted to be able to help.' The bright eyes peered, pierced, pried. When there was no response, she went on, 'I shall write to your father this morning, to assure him of your safety and to insist that you stay here with me until the situation is a little more settled.'

Annette looked at her plate. There was a long, long pause.

When Lady Waldon spoke again, her voice had a harder edge. 'You have not told me, my dear, how it was that you came to be travelling alone? Your father surely did not intend it, when you set out?'

Annette swallowed. 'I had left Brillac some time before I left France, Madam,' she said carefully, hoping her hesitation would be put down to her searching for the right English words. 'My father had sent me to live with the nuns at Bordeaux.'

'With your great-aunt?' cried Lady Waldon. She frowned. '*She* sent you here? But, surely, the convent was safe enough from the mob? However brutish, they would not...'

'I had left the convent by then,' said Annette.

It was no good. She was going to have to tell her godmother the truth – or at least a part of it. She took a deep breath.

'Have you read the works of the philosopher Jean-Jacques Rousseau?' she began.

Afterwards, she wondered if there was any way she could have made Lady Waldon understand. Probably not: her godmother, like the lady guests in the convent, could imagine nothing that would drive a girl to run away other than an affair of the heart. She showed great interest in Pierre, and in Annette's feelings for him. Annette had not told her the full story of Pierre's dismissal, of course, representing it simply as a matter of a political conflict with her father; but when she reached the point in the story where she left the convent for the bakery, she had seen what her godmother was thinking.

'And where,' she asked, fixing Annette with the bird-like stare, 'is this young priest now? Did you travel to England with him?'

'Oh, no. I travelled with… an American lady, who was also sailing for London,' said Annette. 'Father Lamontaine is dead, Madam.' She had to force back the tears that came to her eyes as she said it. 'He died in the riots in Bordeaux.'

That, at least, had given Lady Waldon pause. Her hand had gone to her throat and she had simply said, 'Oh, my dear!'

But, of course, she would not rest until she had the whole story – or thought she had; Annette was sure of that. In the meantime, she insisted on showing her goddaughter the sights of the town. The dressmaker came and went; and in only twenty-four hours two walking gowns arrived, and Lady Waldon was lending her hats, shoes and stockings. Soon Annette was equipped to walk abroad in the sticky, noisy, late-summer city of London.

'You can enjoy at least a week or two of society – such as it is at this time of year, for the season is pretty much over – before we are forced to return to Waldon Hall and rusticate for the winter! That will restore your spirits, child, and bring back your bloom.'

The next day a fashionable gown in embroidered muslin came home and they were ready to entertain.

At first, Annette thought that she must be putting her godmother to a great deal of trouble, but she soon realised that she was merely the latest excuse for her frenetic social activity. Lady Waldon was famous for two things, Annette discovered: her extraordinary fidelity to Sir Charles Waldon, her husband of twenty-five years; and the glittering array of the great and good who attended her parties. The latter was, in fact, a direct result of the former, for Sir Charles was deeply, numbingly dull. He was rarely at home; Annette met him only at dinner, when he treated her with the same distant courtesy he showed towards his wife. After dinner, he disappeared into the library with a pipe and a decanter. Annette could not help but wonder if Lord and Lady Waldon had ever been in love; had ever shared the kind of passion she had known with Jude. It was hard to imagine. But Lady Waldon's old-fashioned religious beliefs did not allow her – unlike most of the ladies of her acquaintance – to find amusement with lovers. Instead, she satisfied her appetite for novelty by seeking out and cultivating the wits, beauties and sprightly blue-stockings of the *beau monde*. So, she and Annette had travelled in the carriage to Hyde Park, to look at all the people of quality and at the Serpentine River with its little boats; to the Summer Exhibition at the Royal Academy, where the pictures hung so thick on the walls that Annette could make nothing of any of them; and, one hot night, to Vauxhall for the fireworks. Whenever they went out, Annette found herself looking for Jude, though she knew it was foolish – and what would she do if she saw her?

In addition, Lady Waldon had thrown herself into arranging parties for Annette to meet people; though, as she said, the town was sadly depleted just now.

'I would not wish to put your ladyship to any trouble,' Annette said in her halting English. 'I do not require to be… amused.'

'La, what a child it is! You are quite a prize, my dear, as you must know. London loves a French beauty – and the Catholic aristocracy has a sad dearth of young women of good family to cheer the hearts of its hopeful young men! Besides, the philosophers and the politicians will be eager to hear about the doings of France – straight, as they say, from the horse's mouth!'

The possibility of talking to people with political understanding, who might be able to bring her news from France, was tempting, but outweighed by the horror of encountering the hopeful young men. She had come here to hide, to be quiet, not to be shown off in the marriage market of London.

Before she could think of anything to say, her godmother went on, 'So you will excuse me, my dear, if I ask you a very personal question. You have no mother to look after your interests, so I must take it upon myself.'

There were no servants in the room. Lady Waldon opened the door and then, satisfied there were no lurking listeners outside either, closed it again and turned to her goddaughter.

'My dear, do you still have your maidenhead?'

Annette was so taken aback that she could not for a moment find any words, either in English or in French.

'I can assure you, Madam,' she said at last, with as much composure as she could muster, 'that no man has ever been near me in that way.'

If her godmother took the flush of anger that rose to her cheeks as the blush of modesty, all well and good.

'Excellent!' cried Lady Waldon, quite unabashed. 'Then I'm sure that, if we can find you a good match among our young men here, your father will soon come round – and reconsider the matter of your dowry into the bargain!'

35

Jude paused on the pavement outside the least grubby of the row of second-hand clothes shops. An iron bar protruded from the beam over the window; garments hung from hooks along its length. Coats and waistcoats of every pattern and colour swayed gently in the breeze. The window was relatively clean, revealing women's clothes on a rail inside. Indecision gripped her: the acquiring of a gown and petticoats was fraught with difficulty, and she still did not know exactly when she would need to change her identity. The letter that had arrived this morning from the Middle Temple was courteous but unhelpful. Messrs Bartram and Speke presented their compliments to Miss Wiston and thanked her for honouring them with her enquiry, but regretted they had so far received no communication from Salem. She bit her lip. She had no assurance that her pleas from Bordeaux had ever reached Salem. Should she wait? Or should she transform herself back into Rebecca Wiston and see whether a face-to-face conversation could persuade the lawyers of her *bona fides*? It seemed her only other option, but it might not work.

'Good morning, sir – may I be of assistance?' The young man was hovering in his shop doorway, hands clasped. A tape measure hung round his neck.

Jude took a step backwards.

'Are you requiring something for yourself? I have several good summer coats I could show you, this season's cut. Step inside, sir?'

'No,' Jude said, 'no.' She took a breath. This was the moment. 'Not for myself – it's for my sister.'

The shopman looked at her once, sharply; then bowed and stepped back, and she found herself walking inside.

He led her to the rail she had seen. 'Did you have anything particular in mind, sir? An everyday gown, or perhaps something for an evening party? I've a lovely silk polonaise just come in, hardly worn, with an embroidered petticoat and sash...'

There was something odd about his smile, Jude thought. Fear gripped her. Had he guessed?

He rummaged along the rail, then turned and looked directly at her. 'Would your sister be about your height and make, sir?'

Jude felt herself blush hotly and nodded, speechless.

The young man smiled again. 'A charming girl, then, I'll make bold to say. Now, here's a satin turban, fit for court dress! A couple of ostrich feathers and a duchess could wear it. Very striking with a large hoop...'

'I'll – no, a day dress,' Jude said, lowering her voice. 'Something sober – for walking out.' She strove to meet his gaze steadily, to look a little imperious – like a man – while suppressing her rising panic. A hoop was only half the problem; what of a smock and stays? Even if she acquired a gown, she would never dare to ask about underlinen.

He was looking at her oddly again. 'Certainly, sir,' he said in the end, and moved away to sort through the rail, turning to look at Jude twice more before he pulled out an open robe in a dark blue woollen cloth that even she could see was old-fashioned. The seams were worn to white, and an air of defeat hung in its many folds.

She shook her head vehemently. 'It's too hot for serge,' she said. 'Have you something in a finer wool?'

'In your size...' the man said, as if to himself, and turned back to the rail.

Jude's courage failed her. 'Never mind,' she said, and bolted for the door.

She strode blindly down the narrow street, swerving past near-naked children and draggled chickens pecking in the gutters. It was only as she reached the end of the alley that she suddenly thought, perhaps he had not seen through her, but had made some other assumption. For the first time in days, she thought of Jean-Marie. She shook her head in fury at her own cowardice. If she'd gone along with his impertinence, the man might have helped her after all.

Though helpfulness was not, in her experience, a quality much found in Londoners. The people of this dark and stinking city tended to narrow their eyes at her as if they were judging how much they could get away with, rather than how they could help. She had been lucky in finding a lodging: the landlady at the Bear and Staff had taken pity on her and sent her potboy to lead the way to a decent house with rooms for rent in the back streets of Westminster. Jude had taken a hot little attic with a rooftop view towards the river for what seemed a fairly reasonable sum in advance. It was up four flights of stairs, but it was all hers. At least, there were no other human inhabitants; there were several families of mice in the sloping roof, sparrows in the broken gutters outside the tiny window and, of course, bugs in the bedding.

After that, however, her luck had run out. She had spent some of her diminishing cash on pen, ink and paper, and written several letters over the course of the next week but, so far, none of them had come to any good. She had failed to find any way of sending her letter to the Bonnats. No one was sailing to Bordeaux; contact with any part of France was fraught with difficulty. The Londoners whose conversations she overheard seemed to think the French had gone fascinatingly mad, and were to be approached at the moment only with a loaded gun in hand. In the little eating-house where she took her frugal dinner each day, opinions were divided about what the French were up to. They were perhaps, according to the most optimistic estimates, about to admit the infinite superiority of the British way of doing things, and institute a proper parliament under a constitutional monarch; on the other hand, there was much talk of riot and disorder, the rule of the mob. There was general agreement on one point only: that it would be best to leave them strictly alone until their king had brought them to heel.

Jude turned down the alley and into the eating-house now, taking a settle in a dark corner. The note she had received from the lawyers that morning was the result of three letters she had written to them in the past week. It was clear they would be hard to convince of her story without letters from home, no matter how she dressed to present herself at the extraordinary warren of buildings that was the Middle Temple. She had been there the previous day and found that it resembled a sprawled, decaying mansion – or the Château Trompette – very old, and swarming with black gowns and little desperate folk with bags of papers.

She was reminded of their hungry eyes as she waited (as always) to be served in the eating-house. When the boy finally deigned to notice her, she ordered a pint of ale and a slice of pie. He looked past her as if he'd never set eyes on her before, though she had eaten here every day since she arrived. In Bordeaux – which was a big city too – victuallers had taken pride in pretending to know their customers, even if they had just blown in for the first time; but here, you obviously needed to have been born two doors away to be recognisable. And even then, Jude thought miserably, they probably would not care.

She was swept by a sense of desolation so sharp that she could have cried. The ache of loneliness was there all the time: as she walked in the town, or sat gazing at the river, she grieved inwardly for Annette. Sometimes, when a sedan chair turned the corner of a street she walked down, she was sure it was the one that had carried Annette away; sometimes the sparrows on the pavement squeaked her name. The never-dark, never-quiet London nights were the worst: as Jude lay in her itchy bed under the tiles, her body remembered the soft warmth of Annette's skin; her hand, stretched on the pillow, reached for the curve of Annette's breast.

This would not do. Jude swallowed a sip of the warm ale and set her jaw. She would not cry out Annette's name, whatever it cost her.

But she could write to her. She banged the ale mug down. The last thing Annette had said was, 'Write to me.' She could do that, surely? That would do no harm? Then Annette might reply – a formal note, no doubt – but Jude would see her handwriting, would know she was still alive and thinking of her. Leaving the pie untouched, she threw twopence on the table and walked briskly back to her room.

36

Annette's knowledge of geography was limited when it came to England. She could recite the lists of all the cities and mountains of France, number the French colonies overseas and name the capitals of Europe – but when Lady Waldon talked of the family seat in the county of Shropshire, no picture formed in Annette's mind. Where was Shropshire? Almost in Wales, apparently; but of that country Annette's ideas were even vaguer. How far away? Two days' travelling would get them to Waldon Hall, said her godmother, always depending on the weather; and there they would stay for the winter.

'We are not entirely without society, in the Marches, as you will see,' Lady Waldon promised. 'There is a good handful of Catholic families up and down the Welsh border. Who knows what may happen before we come back to town next season?' She smiled conspiratorially. 'And if not, why then, all the more time to make peace with your father before we bring you out properly!'

Annette was saved from answering by the entrance of a footman with a silver tray. He sketched a bow, laid a small stack of cards and letters on Lady Waldon's escritoire in the bay window, bobbed his head again and left. Annette's godmother fell on her daily correspondence with characteristic enthusiasm. After a minute she said, 'Goodness, this note is for you, my dear. I thought no one knew of your being in London? How intriguing! Do open it.'

The handwriting was not familiar. Annette broke the blank seal. *Miss Rebecca Wiston presents her compliments to Mademoiselle Lavigne and hopes that she is fully recovered from her voyage.*

That was all, except for an address in Westminster. Annette's heart banged so hard in her throat she thought Lady Waldon must hear it.

'From whom is your note, my dear? I die of curiosity!'

'I – it is the lady I spoke of, Madam – the American lady who travelled to England with me.'

'I don't suppose we know them?' Her godmother took the note and scanned it. 'Wiston…' She stopped, frowning for a moment, then shook her head. 'No. And if American, then not Catholic, we must assume. It was kind of her to write. You should reply of course, but not in any way that would encourage the acquaintance.' She returned to her own correspondence.

Annette thrust the note into her bodice. All through the day she could feel it there, warm against her skin. Jude! She must see her, she must. If she was to be swept away to this Shropshire place, which sounded like an English version of her father's house with the addition of unwelcome English suitors and lots of cold rain, she had to tell Jude what was happening. So that – so that what? She did not know. But the telling her came first. And seeing her just once again.

Next morning, when Peggy – the young woman whom Lady Waldon had now employed as her personal maid – appeared to bring water for washing and open the curtains, Annette was ready. In the few days she had known her, Peggy had become an important person in Annette's mind. Of all those she had left behind in Bordeaux, Annette had found that it was not, after all, Pierre whom she thought of most often. His had been the burning spirit to inspire her, teaching her chapter and verse of the deep transformation needed in France and uprooting her from her complacent life at home; but it was Jacqueline, her erstwhile maid, who occupied her thoughts. She still remembered, with shame, the moment in the coach on the way to the convent, and the many times afterwards, when she had realised how little she knew about the person with whom she had spent more hours of her life than anyone else. As soon as Lady Waldon had mentioned a maid for her here, she had resolved that should not happen again. So, she already knew a good deal about Peggy. She was about thirteen – she was not too sure of the year of it, herself – and had been born in London, though her mother was Irish, and her father French. He was a dancer, in the theatres.

'Not that we see him much now, Miss,' she'd said, 'dancing or otherwise. But he was a kind pa when I was little, and we loved it when he came home with his pockets full of ribbons and bonbons. I learnt the French from him, and that was why Madam thought I'd suit you, so she did.'

Lady Waldon's version had been that Catholic servants who were not wholly Irish (and therefore scarcely trainable) were hard to find; but that this girl seemed quite a good hairdresser for everyday and could sew a straight seam. Today, Annette blessed her stars that she had been inspired to make friends with Peggy. She needed her most urgently now, because she must somehow get a reply to Jude.

And Peggy was amazingly helpful. 'Oh yes, Mademoiselle,' she said promptly. 'You must write two notes. One to Miss the American lady, and one to your beau. Then I can show the first one to Madam when I go down, and get her to send me out with it, and she won't know there's another!'

It was as if she had inbuilt skills as an intriguer and go-between, like a lady's maid in a play. When Annette said as much, Peggy giggled. 'Like Flora, in *A Wonder*? Ooh, I could be! That's a fine play. I've seen it three times, don't you know?'

Annette's surprise at the idea of her little maid as a theatre-goer must have shown in her face, for Peggy went on, 'Well, Miss, I told you my father was on the stage, didn't I? Oh, I've seen all sorts from the top of the house, so I have! Why, I was there the night Mrs Jordan put on the breeches for the first time! Isn't she the greatest actress, now?'

Women in breeches was not a topic Annette wished to pursue. 'I will write the notes as you suggest,' she said hastily.

'That's right, Miss. And if Madam doesn't let me take it, but sends someone else, it won't matter, will it, because they won't take it in at the address, it not being where no American Miss

Wiston lives, and then I could go with the important one whenever I get a chance. You write them now, and then I can do your hair.'

There really was no time to waste, Annette felt, before she was swept away to the far edge of England. So she wrote asking Jude to meet her at noon the very next day at Wetten's in Bruton Street, a confectioner's shop that Peggy told her was very fashionable with young ladies like herself.

Jude turned out of Brewer's Row as the clocks struck eleven. She was wearing a smart green-black satin suit that she had rushed out and hired just an hour ago, from the discreet outfitter on the corner. It fitted rather too tight, but she liked the gleam of it: it had obviously started its life as the fancy of a very rich man, and been discarded, after a promenade or two, as perks to his valet; such amenities the city offered you, to be sure. She was bubbling with glee, a sense that the world was a firework party about to burst into full glory. The note was safely lodged in her waistcoat pocket. She was going to see Annette.

She threaded her way through mean streets and scrubby wasteland, leaving behind the square towers of the great abbey church and heading, according to her landlady's instructions (carefully memorised) for the King's Palace.

'You can't mistake it,' the woman had promised. 'It's big and red and very old.' But everything in London looked very old to Jude.

She came out into a main street with a moving tide of people: mostly ladies and their various appendages, their packages and footmen and small dogs, but also the busy people of the busiest city in the world, crying their wares and running and pushing and wheeling things and shouting and going about their trades. Jude was growing to like London – but it did smell. Ah – no – this smell was not just the city street, she saw as she strode on, but the first landmark she'd been given, the grand stables of the King's horses. It stood back, behind a façade of imposing grey stone arches, through which she glimpsed a wide yard with a pair of beautiful greys being walked about – the cobbles ran with streams of their yellow piss. Could it be that the King's horses were schooled to make water on command, when they were brought out? She grinned inwardly: her crazy exhilaration was colouring the whole world around her.

She turned left, as instructed, and passed along a carriage road which led her to – yes, it must be – the promised King's Residence. St James's Palace. Its street frontage was less imposing than the modern uniformity of the stables, but it certainly looked older – and bigger. Much bigger. A town all to itself, towers and archways and old walls of rosy brick rambling away out of sight, with railings stretching left and right. She followed them for an age, and came upon a large open gate, through which she passed unhindered into an unexpected green space – a park.

It smelled green. The quite different smell of the Jardin Public, of crushed grass and frying food and garlicky sweat and much wine, surged into her memory, overpowering her for a moment. She stopped dead, her hand to her mouth. But this was not really like the Jardin. There were no rows of wine shops; the people following the walks were fewer, and better dressed. The shrubs and flowerbeds were closer together, too, with little paths winding through them. Jude tried in vain to follow a direct route through the artificial maze. She eventually came to a wilder place of rough grass, with the odd sheep grazing. It was as if the city, as it grew, had trapped a bit of countryside inside itself. Her landlady had told her to follow the carriage drive past the big lake, which was presumably that stretch of brown water with ducks on it, over to the left. She pushed on into the carriageway, glad of something more solid underfoot. It led her to a wide street: Piccadilly. She paused to wipe off her boots on the last tussock of green and looked each way at the carriages and the throng.

An old woman sitting by the gate with a wide wicker basket noticed her hesitation and called out: 'Lavender, sir? Lavender for your honour? For your lady? Only three farthings, a nice big bunch?'

'Can you direct me,' Jude said, 'to Bond Street?'

'Third on the left, sir. Sweet lavender, sir?'

Jude gave her a farthing – not three – for a ribbon-tied bunch of perfumed stems. Drunk as she was with anticipation, she was not going to be robbed by a London street-seller. She had brought nothing else for Annette, though. She held them to her nose as she continued her journey along the hot stone pavements.

When she came into Bond Street, shopping for lavender paled into such utter triviality that she almost threw the little bouquet away. Here you could buy anything, anything in the world – as long as you had the money. There were jewellers, confectioners, stationers and tailors all crammed together; drapers, hosiers, glovers, booksellers, purveyors of waters; and tucked up alleys between these smart little shops, she saw a boxing booth, a brass foundry, a timber yard. As if all the wares that came in to the port of London from all over the world ended up here. Jude gazed in upon cups and plates from China, gin from Holland, sugar and rum and tobacco and fruits from the Indies, silks and rugs from the East, tea in drums and bags and sugar-plums in silver paper cases. Her jaw was continually dropping at the extravagance, the magnificence, the sheer plenitude and size of it all. She was truly from the colonies, she thought, the far-flung edges of the world. This was its centre, and it outclassed the biggest place she had seen so far, as completely as a rowboat was dwarfed by a three-masted ship of the line.

She almost forgot to look for Bruton Street. As she turned into it, a clock somewhere chimed for noon and she smiled because that was when Annette had said she would be at the confectioner's shop. Wetten's: Number 33. She straightened her back as she opened the door and stepped inside. Annette was there, sitting at a table with a tiny cup before her, as if it were the most natural thing in the world, and dressed in pink, with a flat veiled hat perched on her curls. Their eyes met… and anything that might have remained of their resolution to separate drained instantly away.

'Mr Wiston,' Annette said, 'how lovely. Won't you be seated?'

They talked. Jude ordered the same tiny cup of chocolate, but could not drink it. They told each other, in minute but incoherent detail, everything they had done since they parted. They stopped speaking for a moment and gazed into each other's faces. The crowds around them seemed to have thickened, and pressed in upon their table.

'Let's go for a walk,' Jude said. 'There might be a park nearby?'

'We could go into the square,' Annette offered. 'It's just at the end of this street.' Hardly speaking, she led Jude along Bruton Street. 'My godmother's house is in Hill Street, on the other side of this square,' she explained. 'So I have a key for the garden.'

Berkeley Square wasn't very large, but it was very quiet; its expanse of grass was traversed by only one path, from which they stepped under a spreading tree heavy with late summer leaves. Jude leaned back on its rough trunk and pulled Annette into her arms. Lost in each other, they did not hear the gate at the other end of the walk click open, nor the footsteps that approached. The first Annette knew of Lady Waldon's arrival was when Jude's arms suddenly tightened round her.

37

As always, the cat accompanied Lucy on her daily walk round her small garden. This afternoon it sat on the stile post and watched her pick a bowl of currants, before they made their way back up the slope of grass to the cottage door. The bench there was in the sun almost all day. Putting her bowl down on the doorstep, Lucy lowered herself onto the seat and pressed her back against the warmth of the stone. The cat, too old to jump straight from the ground to the bench, picked its way gingerly up the log Lucy had propped there for that purpose, and curled up beside her.

It had been a good summer. Even now, Lucy's garden bushes were still heavy with fruit. The year had turned, and an autumn harvest was already preparing in the hedgerows: small green apples and dark green haws, tight little fists of blackberries. Any day now, she knew, there would be mushrooms, a swathe of white dots on the west-facing field beyond the garden. She sighed. Each year the familiar tasks of harvest became a little harder – bending to gather the fruit; heaving the brass pan on to the fire; standing for hours bottling and sealing her syrups and jellies. That was the difference, she thought irritably, between herself and Joey Jones. He had swarms of children and grandchildren to take over the heavy work and to bring him his ale as he sat by the hearth; having none, she must go on fending for herself.

She would see to the currants shortly, but now she closed her eyes and let the afternoon sun soak into her bones. So many summers! She turned them over like the leaves of a book. When she was a girl, a hot day like this had been a blessing. Her mother had kept them both alive by taking in other people's washing; on a fine summer morning, they would hurry to put out the sheets and shirts so that they dried with a freshness they never got from hanging by the fire. Lucy had been fetching home a bag of dirty washing the day she met the travelling players. Such long-ago memories were sharper than recent ones, these days. She could still see, quite clearly, the player folk with their gaudy clothes and loud voices. How strange and wonderful she had thought them – even before she had met Mr Brown. The lover and hero in all their plays, Mr Brown had sported a ruffled shirt, a hat with a feather and a smile to melt a girl's heart. Lucy smiled now at the memory of their first meeting, down by the river, under the willows. Mr Brown! The gallant gentleman who had made her giddy with love – and who had turned out not to be a gentleman at all. Or any kind of man, for that matter. A woman's body in men's clothes; a woman-loving woman, living a man's life. That was the first time Lucy had given her heart – or her body – to anyone. It was a good beginning. She had been more than willing, and Mr Brown had been kind. He'd called her 'the nut-brown maid', which was a great deal pleasanter than the names the villagers called her. She'd laundered his ruffled shirt, tumbled with him in the hayloft, and cried when he went away. A whole long lifetime ago. Before she'd come to these hills; before she'd met Hope or Bell; and long before she had given her heart the final time, to Bron.

Lucy shook her head. How near the past came these days, she thought, as she pushed herself up off the bench and picked up the bowl. It seemed to her sometimes that she spent more time with the dead than with the living; but then, what other company did she have?

'Except for you, you old varmint,' she told the cat.

It opened one eye and, sensing that it might be near dinner time, rose, stretched and followed her inside.

Jude, in deep despair, gazed out at the ragged London skyline from her garret window. She was reminded, suddenly, of the view from her attic at home, the wide sea and the sails that came and went in the round eye of her spyglass. It had all been so –

familiar. Home. A world away, now. Her shoulders slumped. As she twisted away from the window, she caught sight of the letter that had come that morning from the Middle Temple, lying open on the table. From Messrs Bartram and Speke: '*in re: Bequest of Richard Farley, Esq.*' She took it up again, but did not read. She knew what it said. They regretted to inform Miss Wiston that they had as yet still had no instructions from the executor, John Fell. If she would care to call at their chambers at 3, Pump Court, on any day convenient to her, they could discuss the matter further and would be honoured to take her instructions, to be acted upon whenever the letter from Salem should arrive. They remained, etc.

She dropped it again. Another setback; and one too complicated even to consider while she had no means to present herself *as* herself, anywhere at all. The hired suit, still flung over her only chair, winked and grinned its green temptation at her. When was it that I went mad? she wondered. At what point did I slip from the real world of Salem, from my sober dresses and my long cuffs and my ledgers, from the bills of lading and the silent Meeting and my timid, bullying brothers, into this – this fantasy? She shook her head, seized the coat, and settled it on the stick on which it had come, smoothing it down over the breeches. She should take it back. She had hired it for three days, which meant it was due now. She would get her half-guinea deposit, which would be useful for – for something. She dropped the thing on her bed, and sat beside it. For what? What could she do? Nothing. If only she knew what was going on in Hill Street! She returned yet again to the memory of Annette's back, marching stiffly away, dwindling in the distance, held tightly by the shoulder as Lady Waldon propelled her out of the garden. The little bunch of lavender lay on the dusty path where it fell; Jude had not had the heart to pick it up.

There was a tap at the door.

Jude stared incredulously at the flushed and breathless girl who stood on her threshold. The maid – the Irish girl Annette had told her about. Thank God.

'It's Peggy, isn't it? How is she? How is Mademoiselle Lavigne? What has happened?'

The girl nodded vigorously. 'It is indeed myself, sir. I ran all the way, sir.' She drew a panting breath. 'Mr Wiston, my mistress is in great distress. She could not write, sir, but sends me to say –' She stopped for breath again.

'Yes, yes? What does she say?' It was all that Jude could do not to lay hands on the girl and shake the news out of her.

'My lady has her locked up, sir, and is taking her this very day to their house in the country. A post-chaise is ordered already. They go in a few hours. And I'm to tell you that it is to Waldon Hall they are going, in the county of Shropshire.' She looked hopefully at Jude. 'You know of it, perhaps?' Then, seeing the look of hopeless bemusement on Jude's face, she said quickly, 'No doubt there are those who will direct you. Now, I am to give you this –' she dived into a deep pocket under her apron and drew out a black velvet bag – 'and tell you that the contents can be sold for a good price.'

The bag was lumpy and heavy in Jude's hand. Had Annette sent her jewels, to sell? But why?

Seeing that Jude seemed to understand this no more than the location of a family seat in Shropshire, Peggy added, 'My old lady – that's her I served before I came to Lady Waldon, sir – would never go to anyone but Mr Wicks, in Panton Street. They are very respectable, sir, and would give you a fair price, I'm sure. You'll need the money, sir, if you are to pursue her.'

Jude struggled to take in what she was saying. More fantasy. *Pursue?* What fairy tales had the girl been listening to?

'Sure, if you know where your lady is bound, then you can pursue her!' She looked earnestly at Jude. 'As they say, sir, the path of true love never did run smooth. But I'm praying to our Lady and all the saints to guide you, and to bring you both to a safe ending! And I must away now at once, sir, before they miss me.'

Jude looked at the girl – brimming with life and hope and self-assurance and the wonderful romantic story she thought she was part of. Very well, then, she thought. I will go with this fantasy of romance and rescue. Wherever it takes me. What else is there to do?

It was an exhausting afternoon, but she was buoyed up by the idea that there was some action – however lunatic it seemed – that she could take. The jeweller's in Panton Street had a frontage so discreet one might almost miss the door; but the doorman who held it open for her was, she noticed, wearing a pistol in his belt. The transaction was quick and courteous; the shop assistant showed neither surprise nor curiosity as he weighed and assessed Annette's necklaces and counted out a large number of guineas into a saucer on the counter. With the money safely stowed, Jude returned to the second-hand clothes vendor's where she had hired the green suit. The shopkeeper was friendly; from his selection of newish goods for sale she bought a plainer suit and several other items of gentlemen's gear. If she was to have any hope of carrying all this off, Mr Jude Wiston needed to be convincing. On a whim, she bought a leather bag, only slightly scuffed down one side, to hold all these purchases. She reasoned that, if she was to travel any distance, she could hardly appear either on the coach or at an inn without any baggage.

It was a costly afternoon, too, but the guineas from Annette's necklaces went a long way. Jude's final destination was the coaching office: a long walk eastwards, for it was deep in the old city. This was a part of London Jude had scarcely suspected: full of grand offices, no doubt transacting very important business, and an air of moving at quite a different tempo from the rackety west end of the town, where she had been until now.

The all-knowing clerk made it easy for her. 'Shropshire? What part would that be? Ah, Waldon Hall. Yes. That is to the south of the county, so Ludlow rather than Shrewsbury would be your best way. The Ludlow Flyer can be boarded daily at the Bull and Mouth inn, St Martin's. You could go tomorrow morning. Half past six.'

The ticket for an outside seat on the Flyer had not been cheap, but inside would have been still more expensive; and in any case she shrank from the idea of sitting for the best part of two days in a tiny box with five strangers, whether or not in this August heat. Jude arrived back at her lodging exhausted; but for the first time since the meeting at the confectioner's, her despair had been replaced by a sense of expectation. She would set off at dawn to 'pursue her lady'!

They were barely out of London and Annette already felt sick from the jolting, swaying motion. The carriage was insufferably hot; sweat gathered at her hairline. Her godmother was sitting back, opposite, with closed eyes, but not asleep; her fan beat an irregular tattoo upon the silk-gloved hand clenched in her lap. The carriage lurched; Annette let out a kind of whimper. Lady Waldon did not respond.

I will not cry, Annette told herself fiercely. She blinked and tried to swallow. But what can I do? What will become of me? Pushing down her rising panic, she dragged her gaze from the tapping fan, and looked out of the dust-crusted window. They were out of town, almost – there was a hedge, trees, no people. A set of tall gates loomed and passed them by. She drew a deep, ragged breath. It could be worse, she told herself. I could be heading for France, back to Brillac, to my father. Or, worse still, to the convent. Or I could still be locked in my room at Hill Street.

The last twenty-four hours had seemed like an eternity. She had been confined, alone, while Lady Waldon decided what to do with her. Her godmother had heaped furious accusations upon her head – of deceit and concealment, of lying, of a vulgar duplicity that had all but brought social ruin upon her hostess and on her entire family – until Annette almost believed that she really had done something wicked, and began to feel the shame that Lady Waldon insisted she should. It was all her own fault, she knew, for being so foolish as to think that she and Jude could meet without anyone seeing; that their love could have any future. Now she had hurt Jude as well as herself. She was more wretched than she could have imagined. And she still wanted Jude, more than anything in the world.

She had managed to send a message to Jude, but had not been able to speak to Peggy since. And now the poor girl was banished to the outside seats of the carriage, along with the driver and Lady

Waldon's own stern-faced lady's maid. Had Jude ever received her message? And even if she had, what could she do? What would become of them? Annette stared out of the window and tried not to be sick.

Their unrelenting journey paused, as night fell, at the country house of an old friend of Lady Waldon's. The hospitality was as wretched as Annette's mood. They were greeted by a morose old man, Sir Michael something, and at least sixteen dogs; their meagre supper was served on a chipped and stained Sèvres service in a room with crumbling plaster decorations. The blinds were drawn and the house contrived to be cold and dank, despite the heat of the day. Lady Waldon was still not really talking to her, but Annette gathered that this was an eligible stop because it was an old Catholic house. (Two ladies travelling alone could not, after all, put up at a roadside inn.) Annette knew that England was full of Protestants, but she had so far failed to understand the religious exclusivity and resentments displayed by most of the English people she had met. In this case, it seemed to mean they could expect to find hospitality here, however grudging. It was by no means comfortable. Her chamber was huge and grimy, her bed like a musty swamp with damp rocks in its depths: she thought of her pretty little room at Brillac, of Jacqueline bringing her chocolate, and sobbed herself to sleep.

It was a relief to be up and away betimes, rattling through Oxford in the bright early sunshine, bound for Worcester and then for Waldon Hall.

38

It was not yet six o'clock but the inner courtyard of the Bull and Mouth was humming with activity. On three sides of the yard, creaking wooden balconies, piled three deep, towered like cliffs above the heads of the milling people. It was like being at the bottom of a well, Jude thought. The sun was already up, but only a single shaft of light penetrated the enclosed space, lighting up the buildings at the western end and leaving the rest in shadow. The yard was crammed with departing coaches, heaped goods and jostling people. The dust was choking. Flinching from the press of bodies, Jude edged back into the smelly gloom under the first gallery. She soon realised that it, too, was alive with people, close over her head; they seemed to be running up and down, lugging trunks and boxes, so that nameless filth sifted down between the boards of its ancient floor. Jude put on Monsieur Bonnat's old cocked hat. Looking out at the vehicles loading in the yard, watching small men throw huge chests and trunks vertically to be stacked on the roofs of the carriages, she wondered where the outside passengers like herself could be fitted in.

After a surprisingly short time, a team of four cobby horses, short in the leg but broad-shouldered and massy-footed, was led though the arch at the other end of the yard and backed into the traces of the Ludlow Flyer. A door opened behind Jude and a spill of people – the other passengers – hurried out and began to compete madly for the seats inside. The man who had been securing the straps overhead plopped to the ground beside her. Smiling, he bent his knees in what Jude for a moment took to be a bow, but quickly realised was an offer of a leg-up. He laced his hands and she stepped trustingly upon them, shot upwards, grasped for the running handles overhead and twisted aboard, quite snug, into a narrow slot with a board seat, crammed behind the driver's high perch. The man below touched his hat, and Jude had the wit to bend down and drop him a coin. He tossed her bag up to her, tipped his hat again and was gone.

Another body dropped onto the seat beside her. Her fellow passenger was a stocky, red-faced man of middle age, whose ample caped coat padded them both tightly in place. Then the driver snapped his whip and said a word to the horses, and the coach creaked into motion, bumping over the cobbles of the yard out into the road. Jude's neighbour pulled out a watch.

'Dead on time, as usual,' he said with satisfaction. Turning to Jude, he asked, 'Are you familiar with this route yourself, young sir?'

Jude's heart sank. If she had thought about the journey at all, it was as a solitary experience, but now it seemed she had a sociable companion. 'Not at all,' she admitted. 'Indeed, I am but recently arrived in this country.'

At the sound of her voice he appeared even more delighted. 'And from the American colonies, I'll wager? A stranger to England! Well, you may ask me anything you wish to know, for I shall be glad to oblige you. I travel this road with great frequency, in the way of business, and I'll warrant I can answer any question you have! Jeremiah Hanway, at your service.'

Jude shook the proffered hand, which Hanway obviously took as an invitation to hold forth about his business interests in the glove trade, the excellence of Ludlow glove-making and the many bargains he had driven in that fine town. Jude listened politely and, as soon as she could, turned away to study the passing buildings and the people in the street.

Their road cut straight through the city in a westerly direction. The driver kept up a steady pace, cracking his whip at pedestrians, donkeys and carts who wandered into their path. If they didn't move, he sounded the horn – startling Jude nearly out of her wits, the first time. They threaded the old city to its limits, emerging through brick-fields and market gardens as London fell away behind them. Then they speeded up and tore magnificently along a well-made road, twice as wide as any Jude had seen either at home or in France. They passed ancient churches, busy fields, and gentlemen's houses newly built on swelling green banks, embowered in elms and chestnuts.

'These flying coaches are a fine thing, are they not?' cried Jude's new friend. 'And I'll warrant there is little more awe-inspiring to a foreigner's eye than the view from the top of a high and handsome British stagecoach! You have done well to sit outside, my lad, for you will see half of England before the journey's end.'

Their first stop was at a dingy, rambling inn announcing itself as the Three Tuns, Salt Hill. The horses were changed with practised speed, then on they went again, very soon crossing a bridge over what Hanway grandly described as 'the mighty Thames'. It was considerably less mighty here than the huge waterway that wound through London, Jude thought – but politely did not say. Below the bridge, straw-hatted boys in white were shouting and splashing and racing their boats. Soon the coach was passing through a wood; the trees grew close to the road on both sides.

''Tis as well it's broad day. There are footpads on this stretch, through the Thicket,' said her commentator with a knowing nod; but they bowled on, unmolested.

As the day wore on, Jude had to admit that the view from the top of a British stagecoach did, indeed, take some beating. The pastures and gentle hills of southern England, its little market towns and prosperous farms, passed by in the glittering sunshine, and Jude fell slightly in love with the land of her forefathers. Each stop presented a different picture: the Bull at Gerrard's Cross was an ancient timbered house overlooking a quiet village green, while the George at Woburn Marsh was undergoing major works and buzzing like a beehive as the owners installed an elegant flat frontage and modern sash windows. The builders, perched on tall ladders, sang and whistled and shouted greetings down at the travellers. Their voices had a twang that was strange to Jude, but she was becoming accustomed to the huge variety of English speech and, most of the time, she understood it.

The next inn, at West Wycombe, was in the centre of the town, right on the main street. Even here, the outside passengers did not climb down – there was no time – and by midday Jude was growing weary of the perpetual bounce and sway, the hard little seat and the sun beating on her; she needed to eat, and she needed a privy. Just as she was thinking this, she became aware that the road had started to descend steeply. The brakes squealed and the driver pulled the horses up until they began to prance and shift from side to side, showing the whites of their eyes. It felt as if the huge weight of the coach might overwhelm them and send everything careering out of control downhill.

Jude's neighbour looked amused at her obvious nervousness. 'This is nothing!' he assured her. 'I came this way in February! The mud was deep enough to drown you, *and* it was snowing. They had to put half the horses to the back of the coach to hold it – but we got through without harm. Never fear!'

And he was right. Soon they were on level ground again and the team resumed its normal pace, drawing in safely to the next inn a few miles further on, with no harm done. After that, they travelled for several miles on an older, less well-kept road. ('Avoiding the turnpike toll at Wheatley,' said Hanway, sagely.) Soon after they had rejoined the Oxford road, it veered left on a sudden and the land dropped away, showing a brief vista of towers and spires with the river glinting between. They bowled terrifyingly down a lesser but equally startling hill, and came into Oxford, a honeycomb of golden stone in the slanting sunshine.

Jude and the rest of the cramped and yawning passengers were all too glad to roll in under an ancient gateway into the yard of the Golden Cross, to stretch their muscles and bespeak their dinners. They had no time to eat them, however, before the horn was sounding again and the traces rattling outside the windows. Jude, who had been preoccupied with finding a privy whose use did not reveal her sex, had come into the dining room after the other passengers had ordered their food, so she was merely nursing a mug of cloudy cider when they were all chivvied back on board. Jeremiah Hanway scooped as much of his food as he could into one hand; the plate which he then thrust at her still held a hunk of bread and a leathery slice of something brown. 'Pity to waste it, my boy,' he said, and swarmed up, hauling her after him.

Waldon Hall sat on a slight rise, so that Annette saw it from a considerable distance as the post chaise passed between the tall wrought-iron gates and up the meandering drive through the park. The house was built of greyish stone, square and unlovely; like a prison, she thought miserably. It seemed like an hour before they drew up on the sweep of gravel in front of the porticoed steps and she climbed down out of the hated coach. She felt stiff and frowsty; the two things she wanted most at that moment were warm water to wash and space to be alone.

Neither were granted, for she was required to accompany her godmother on her inspection of the house, which had been prepared somewhat hastily for their arrival. She had a blurred impression of high painted ceilings, of walls lined with the usual dull paintings in gilded frames, of more rooms than anyone could need, leading out of each other in endless succession, full of stiff, uncomfortable furniture. At the back of the house, beyond an elaborate formal garden, the views were of woodlands, crowding close, and a heaving shoulder of barren hill. By the time they arrived at the chamber assigned to her, Annette was dizzy with fatigue and strain. She felt absurdly grateful for the sight of Peggy, already bustling about the room putting things away.

'I will leave you to refresh yourself and dress,' said Lady Waldon coolly. 'Dinner is at five. I'm sure your maid can find you something to wear that is not too crushed.' And she departed.

'Oh, Miss! How weary and sad you look!' said Peggy. 'Will I send down for some hot water now, so you can wash? And then I can do your hair.'

As Annette sank into the nearest chair, Peggy crossed to the door, opened it, looked out with exaggerated thoroughness and closed it again. 'And then,' she said in a conspiratorial whisper, 'I can tell you all my news!'

After Oxford, the Ludlow Flyer jounced onwards, through the rest of a long, sunlit afternoon and into the twilight. The houses in this part of the country were of yellowish stone, glowing the colour of honey in the sinking sun. Between these golden towns and villages, the road ran past orchards, many bearing heavy crops of apples and pears. As the moon rose and the light turned from gold to silver, it seemed to Jude that the scene took on the magic of a fairy tale. As the wayside shadows deepened, she slipped into a strange half sleep, and her mind ranged wide. Sometimes she was in touch with the real questions she needed to ask: where, in the end, could this road lead? What could she do, even if she found the house for which Annette was bound? Storm the doors, climb the ivy, as no doubt Peggy's fantastical imaginary hero would have done? Creep in by the kitchens and seize her beloved at pistol-point? But then she would drift away into the fantasy herself, imagining Annette, in Aunt Isabella's red brocade dress, opening her arms, drawing Jude into a still, quiet room with a soft heap of pillows and a flask of cool wine…

The stars were out before they reached the Angel at Pershore, on the banks of the River Avon. There were still hours of driving ahead of them, but the moon was only a couple of days from the full, so that Jude could still make out the white ribbon of the road and the outlines of trees and houses. She struggled to stay awake, not wanting to miss a single place or vista, but in spite of herself she began to nod, and finally slept. She did not see Worcester, or the winding road beyond it which crossed and re-crossed the little river Teme; she only woke when the coachman cried, 'Ludlow ahead, ladies and gentlemen!' and she looked out to see the moonlight illuminating the ruins of a fairy-tale castle on a hill. Half an hour later, the Ludlow Flyer climbed the sloping road into the town and shuddered to its final stop behind the Feathers Inn. They climbed stiffly down. It was almost dawn.

Hanbury clapped Jude on the back. 'Welcome to the ancient

county of Salop!' he cried, before hastening off into the gloom.

Jude stood, dumbfounded. Salop? Her mind whirled, racing back to Salem and the meeting in John Fell's office. *Madeley, in the County of Salop.* Shropshire was Salop? She had arrived, all unaware, in the part of England where her inheritance lay.

39

The Feathers Inn was shuttered and still asleep. Like Mr Hanway, the other passengers immediately set off, either alone or with welcoming friends, to destinations of their own; Jude was left standing in the yard. The solitary ostler walked studiously round her as he released the horses and led them away, and the driver had disappeared at once – she had not seen where to. Eventually the ostler came back with a bucket, presumably to sluice some of the dust off the coach, and stared at her.

'Beds inside, young sir,' he said, jerking his head, 'or a pint of ale. You'll have to wake the missus, though.'

'Thank you,' Jude said, 'But I think I shall take a walk first. Up to the castle.'

'Suit yourself,' he said, and flung his bucketful at the offside door.

She set off undirected; but as she had observed, it was uphill to the castle, and she did not miss her way. She stretched her legs up a broad sloping street, with upstanding new houses as well as the slouching old oak frames that had become familiar during her journey across the breadth of England. Rounding a corner, she soon came to the market hall, a fine stone building – all columns and pediments – and headed down a strong-smelling alley beside it. A cat had been busy there: it crouched, hissing, over a small black corpse. The alley led out into the market. Jude threaded her way through the twisting rows of wooden shanties and boarded-shut shops and came out in front of a high stone wall with a gatehouse. The castle, for sure. Beside it stood a very fine old house – criss-crossed again with beams, irregular and out of true, but soaring up and spreading wide, filling a whole corner of the market square. It was opulent and elegant, even to a modern eye. The leaded windows of the top storey caught the first gleam of the rising sun.

The old house had a mounting block at its door, and she sat down to think. She didn't actually want to see the castle, however romantic; it had only been a way to appear less lost to the surly ostler. What she wanted, apart from to lie down flat and take fifteen hours' sleep, was information. And if, as Hanbury had suggested, Shropshire and Salop were one and the same place, had chance brought her within travelling distance of the property that was her inheritance? Where was Madeley? And, more urgently, where was this Waldon Hall, and how could she get there?

To make all these enquiries without being too conspicuous would be difficult: this quietly prosperous town felt like the sort of place where a foreign stranger asking questions would be remarked; though it would probably be crowded enough (once it woke up) for her to move around. But a great hall... She had seen many, standing aloof from the coach road down tree-lined avenues, and knew it would be hard to approach unnoticed. Near and yet so far. A vision of Annette rose up before her closing eyes. She swayed forward and just stopped herself falling off the block, flat on her face. Shaking herself, she staggered to her feet.

Across the way, a young woman appeared from one of the alleys in the market, carrying a flat basket covered with a cloth. Seeing Jude, she paused.

'Good morning,' Jude said. 'Might you give me some information, please?'

And it was as easy as that.

The girl, frowning uncomprehendingly in the first moment, but soon finding herself charmed and delighted to be quizzed by a gentleman, told her what she needed to know, and more. The way to the village of Little Waldon, where the hall was, lay westwards – out towards Montgomery, the county town of the next county – 'In Wales, that is!' – and the way to get there was by the mail coach. But not today. The girl was not exactly sure what were all the days that it did go, but what she did know was that today, being a Thursday, wasn't one of them. No. But it went from the Angel, in Broad Street, that she did know.

'Is that somewhat like the Feathers?' Jude asked. She deduced from the rambling reply that it was indeed that kind of inn: big, unwelcoming, and no doubt shut.

But the girl was quick. 'Would you be wanting somewhere quiet-like to bide, maybe, sir, until you might go?'

Jude nodded.

'My mother keeps a good clean house, sir, down by the river, and we have a room free, and a good breakfast.' She flipped the cloth from one side of her basket; the smell of new-baked bread, warm and yeasty, wafted up.

'Lead on!' said Jude.

It was Saturday before she boarded the mail coach and set out westwards, by unfrequented little roads banked by increasing hills, through a folded green country full of sheep. Single farms tucked into the hillside were the main signs of habitation, but few people were to be seen, until the coach stopped at a wayside inn with an old board announcing the Two Crosses: the nearest stop to Waldon Hall.

Lucy held out her mug as Joey eased his bulk forward until he could reach to pull the heated poker from the fire. The hot metal hissed into the ale and the familiar scent of malt and spices rose in the steam. Most folks called mulled ale a winter drink, but she and Joey enjoyed it in all weathers. Besides, the summer heat hardly touched the inner reaches of the parlour, where a fire was still lit daily on the big hearth. The Crosses was fuller than usual today, there being little work to do at this stage of the summer, and the mail with its promise of news from afar being due, so their conversation sank into a background buzz of talk and laughter.

Joey settled back in his chair. 'We'm both still here, then,' he announced with heavy sarcasm. 'No more ghosties come to call you away?' He chuckled at his own joke.

'I didn't say it was a ghost,' snapped Lucy. 'I said it was a dream. I swear you're deaf as a post, Joey Jones! You don't hear half I say. I might as well be talking to the cat. But who else can I talk to? There's no one else remembers the old days, now, but you and me.' She stared into the fire. 'Though them as are gone seem close enough to touch, some days.'

'Like who?' Joey was interested in spite of himself. 'Who else comes to you? Have you seen Bell again?'

There was no point in telling him about Mr Brown. Her adventures with the players had happened before she arrived in these parts, and she had never spoken of those things to Joey. They had been dark times: she pushed them away, and looked up. 'Do you remember when I first came here?'

'Oh, that I do!' He laughed again. 'Couldn't take my eyes off you, girl! I'd never seen anyone with dark skin before. I thought you must have come from foreign parts, you know?'

Lucy snorted derisively. 'The people where I came from thought worse. Said my mam had laid with the Devil. Ignorant pigs, the lot of them. Mam said my father was a prince, in his own country.' She paused. 'I used to think he must have looked like the black king in the Christmas picture – in the church, you know? But now I think he was just a slave. He was coachman in a big house, and she was a laundry maid.'

Joey shook his head wonderingly. 'Well, well. All these long years I've known you, Lucy Weaver, and you never told me that before. You're a deep one, and that's a fact.'

They were interrupted by a rumbling which shook the ground under their feet. All heads craned to see the Royal Mail as it drew to a jingling halt outside. Friendly voices greeted the driver as he pushed his way in between the customers. He plonked down the mail bag on an empty chair. Its heavy lock overbalanced the somewhat shrunken body of the bag itself: people did not get many letters out here. Joey's son William handed him his customary pint of ale, which he downed where he stood, while young Ben went out with a second pint for the guard. Thirst slaked, the driver fished in his pockets and pulled out a newspaper, handing it to William with a knowing nod. 'One copy of *Jackson's Oxford*

Journal, bought in Ludlow yesterday, hot off the press. You'll want to know what it has to say about the barley harvest, no doubt. Still looking good, I gather, though it isn't all in yet, of course.'

'And won't be for a good while, here,' said William. 'Last week's paper was all news from France – terrible, what's going on there.' He laid the paper on his counter to enjoy anon, and looked over the coachman's shoulder. 'No passengers for us today, Noah?'

'Yes, now you mention it,' said the driver, 'there was one. Young lad...' He looked round. 'Don't know where he's got to.'

Those who'd come for the news glanced around too, seeking this possible extra diversion, but no newcomer had appeared. Noah shook himself, took the bag of letters William gave him and, raising his hand as if to clear the way for the majesty of the Mails, departed.

The door swung to behind him, and attention turned to William and his eagerly awaited reading from the weekly paper.

'Tell us about the Frenchies, William,' someone said.

Thus invited, the publican opened the folded news sheet. '*News from France*,' he intoned. '*All the Advices from Paris agree, that the French make very little Progress in re-establishing Order and Tranquillity among the People.*'

Heads nodded. 'Never yet met a Frenchman that was orderly and tranquil to start with!' a voice in the corner piped up.

He had probably never met any Frenchmen at all, thought Lucy crossly, but she said nothing.

'You be quiet, Ralph Tucker!' Joey called out.

'Do you want to hear all this, then?' William asked. 'There's a bit here about folk being butchered by the mob. In broad day, it seems.'

The room paid attention again, but he was drawing it out. He scanned the page, frowning. 'And here's a bit about more of them poor gentlemen arriving in England. In their droves, seemingly. Gentry, and all, but starving. Shocking!' There was some head-shaking, but this was not as exciting as the butchery of the Paris mob, really: Lucy could have told him that a gaggle of foreigners arriving on the south coast was not going to bother the Crosses very much.

William shook the paper, and raised his eyes back to the exciting paragraph. They looked at him expectantly. Behind them, straight in Lucy's view, the door opened again. Framed in the summer sunlight, a young man appeared, carrying a portmanteau. William put down his paper, and all heads turned.

Lucy, too, gazed at the young man. Her hands flew to her face. Something about him – the way he stood, the nervous bravado of his manner – brought her heart into her mouth.

There was a pause before William, remembering his calling, said heartily, 'Come in, young sir. Welcome to the Two Crosses. Can I fetch you a drink, or something to eat?'

Lucy didn't hear the stranger's reply. She had stumbled to her feet, staring at the newcomer, who was – she knew it now – the image of her long-ago hero, Mr Brown.

40

The way to Waldon Hall took Jude by field paths and over stiles, brushing through wicked old nettles and skirting packs of lolloping lambs – full-grown, but not come to years of discretion – intent upon breaking her legs. And all the way, she thought about the old woman at the inn.

As her eyes had become accustomed to the indoor gloom, and she'd looked round to see who had spoken to her, she had noticed the woman by the fire. Jude had seen black people in London – mostly servants in livery or very poor, ragged people – but this ancient countrywoman had an air of assurance, of belonging, that reminded her suddenly of her old friend Tabitha. A free woman. As if she felt Jude's gaze, the old woman had looked up, straight at her; and, with a shock of fear, Jude knew beyond any doubt that the dark eyes were staring, not just at Jude, but at Rebecca. For a few moments she had been completely unnerved, as if her mask had been torn away and her true self revealed to the whole world; but no one else in the room seemed to have noticed anything amiss. With an effort, she had regained her outward composure and turned back to speak with the innkeeper.

He had taken her bag, promised a room would be readied, and shown a courteous lack of curiosity about what she might want at Little Waldon. Several people had been keen to give her directions there, however.

'Dunna you bother with the high road, not this time o' year. ''Tis two hours' walk or more that way, but two-three miles less if you go over the top, and the paths is all dry now.'

'Off the road by the first gate – you canna miss it, there's a great holly tree there – then follow by the stiles. Straight up the bank, then all along the top, and then you come down again behind the hall, or carry on into the village.'

And all the while, as they explained, and as the innkeeper and his son bustled about to welcome their new customer, Jude had felt the old woman's gaze upon her.

The path crested a rise, and ran clearly before her along the top of a ridge: slippery whitened grass between leaning columns of faded flower stems, with the last purple bells at the top, their spotted tongues hanging out. On the horizon, great white August clouds were building against the blue sky. Then the view opened up on her right: a winding green valley of ravishing beauty in the late summer sun. Not far away – perhaps a mile – a dark copse spread up the slope towards her with, embedded in it, a glimpse of high chimneys. She strode on. Reaching the wood, she left the field path that they had said led along to the village, and turned instead into a dark track that burrowed down through the trees. She caught a glimpse of the house, quite close now, before she slid down into a dank path running along a dilapidated wall and came to a halt.

The wall was twice her height and stretched away into the trees on both sides. A dead end. Suddenly, her courage failed her. The complete futility of what she was doing – of the whole pointless, insane project – caught up with her. She sat down on the bank and stared hopelessly at the wall. Whatever had she thought she could achieve, racing across the breadth of England, with no clear end in sight? There was a neglected-looking wooden gate, with a rusted latch and a straggle of ivy over it, set into the wall a few yards away; but she could hardly push her way into the unseen place on the other side and march up to the house. She got up and peered through the gaps by the hinges, but could see nothing but a gravel path. It occurred to her that she didn't even know if Annette was there. A wave of utter desolation washed over her. She leaned against the wall and closed her eyes. After a while, she turned away from the door and began to retrace her steps uphill, back to the Two Crosses.

*

Had Jude but known, the goal of her quest was a few yards away. In a little bower against that same wall, at the end of a walk stretching out from the terrace through the formal beds, Annette was sitting with only Peggy to keep her company. The arbour was screened from the house by a thick hedge; here, she could escape for a few moments from her godmother's surveillance. She and Peggy had brought their work out into the garden with them; they were supposedly each sewing a shift. Annette was not deemed by her godmother to have anything approaching an adequate wardrobe and, out here in the wilds, as much as possible must be made at home. While Peggy's needle raced through the white lawn, Annette was making slow and inelegant progress with her wavering seam. The salons at Brillac were strewn with examples of the complicated embroidery with which her father loved to see her occupied, but she had not done any plain sewing of this kind since she was in the nursery, learning to hold a needle. The two young women had not spoken for what seemed like hours. Even Peggy was feeling overwhelmed by the crackling atmosphere of disapproval that Lady Waldon created.

'And everyone below stairs thinks what she thinks,' she had told Annette glumly. 'Or else they keep their own counsel.'

'Though there's a nice little boy who polishes,' she mused now, as if they had been talking over Lady Waldon's household just a moment before, 'and a pair of girls who might be useful, could you get them away from this – this – swamp.' She bit her thread off short.

'But what use would that be?' Annette answered wearily. 'We have no plan of escape that anyone might help us with – and nowhere to go.'

'People are always useful, Miss,' Peggy said, 'and you never know. Something will turn up, my pa always says. I've told you that Mr Wiston is on his way – and he will have a plan!'

Annette let her work drop to her lap. 'Oh, Peggy! I wish I had your faith. How could Mr Wiston find this remote place? Besides, what can he do, if he does come here?' The memory of the morning rendezvous at Wetten's, the embrace in Berkeley Square, returned in all its horror. 'My godmother would have him driven from her door.'

Peggy thought for a moment. 'Disguise!' she announced triumphantly. 'Young gentlemen in plays are always disguising themselves – as music masters, or Dutch merchants, or Lord knows what – to visit their beloved, right under the nose of her horrid old father. I'm sure Mr Wiston could easily think of something like that.'

Annette did not reply. She picked up her work and they sewed in silence for a few minutes.

Peggy tried again. 'We shall escape for a few hours, though, shall we not, tomorrow, when we go to mass?'

'Yes. My godmother says the whole household are to go to mass in the family chapel.' She frowned. 'Which is, for some reason I did not understand, within the village church. Don't ask me why. I suppose it was there before the English all became Protestants or something. But it is only a step from the gates of Waldon, so what use is that? It's worse than useless.' She let her sewing fall again. 'Lady Waldon promises me local families. Nice young men. Nice, *eligible* young men. Moneyed, landed, young men. Of the Faith. Oh, Peggy! All that parading, and ogling, and calculating – I don't know that I can bear it.' She thrust the sorry tangle of her needlework aside and impaled it with her needle. 'Let's walk,' she said. 'I'm getting cold.'

Peggy gathered up the sewing and followed her.

By the time Jude arrived back at the inn, the looming clouds had swept in on a freshening west wind, blotting out the sun, and the first few drops of thundery rain were falling. Most of the morning's customers, including the mysterious old woman, had gone home, to Jude's relief. She gratefully ate the plate of cold beef and pickles that was set before her, and accepted the offer of the loan of the *Oxford Journal*. There was a great deal of nonsense in it about the birthday celebrations of the Prince of Wales; but she also learned that Parliament had at last been prorogued, after sitting beyond its time to respond to the news from France. There was a whole column headed 'News from France' which made anxious reading, though some of it was just as bizarre as the British royal birthday. Apparently, the National Assembly had voted to dissolve all the religious houses and use them to house war veterans. Did that include the one where Annette had been imprisoned? And however many war veterans did they have? There must be dozens of convents and monasteries, even in the part of the country she had seen. The relish with which the English press reported the struggles of the French pained her, and the news itself was frightening. It really did appear that the landed gentry were on the run, arriving daily in England seeking refuge from the angry mob. She and Annette were not the only refugees. *À bas les aristos.* She shivered, remembering. What had become of her friends in Bordeaux? Of Jean-Baptiste and his family? Were they still alive? Surely, solid tradesmen like the Bonnats would be safe? She put the paper aside and rose from the table. Avoiding the huddle of regulars by the fire, she asked to be shown to her room.

It proved to be tiny and angular, with a little gable giving all the light there was, but it smelt sweetly of lavender-stored sheets and the fire below. She sat gazing out at the falling rain, and a blank gloom descended and blotted out all constructive thought. After a while she lay down, just for a moment; but whether she was in despair and denial, or exhausted from the trip to this distant place and now this unaccustomed hill-walking, or simply reverting to shipboard habits of snatching rest whenever possible, she fell deeply asleep. She woke in the dark, undressed to her shirt, scrambled into the sweet-smelling feather bed, slept again; and woke with a lighter mind.

It was early morning – assorted birds were singing fit to burst just outside her window. She rose and peered out under the shaggy gable. There was no human habitation around the inn, just the two crossing roads it was named for. It was not even what the British – she mentally tipped her hat to Mr Hanway – called a hamlet. Little Waldon was possibly the nearest village. In the light of morning, Jude felt more hopeful. She would go there again, carry on into the village this time, and see the great house from its front gate. There was bound to be another inn, and maybe people to talk to; she might find out all sorts of things, if she were to ask.

What she had forgotten was that it was Sunday. From at least a mile away, as she passed along the refreshed, dampened path and down onto the high road between still-gleaming hedges, she heard church bells ringing, rough and exuberant but recognisably like the changing patterns she had heard in London. As she made her way along the road they soon reduced to a single note and then fell silent. She walked on. Another single bell tolled. In a few minutes more, she rounded a tall hedge and the church came in sight, across the village green. As she walked towards it, she realised the service must be over. The congregation was streaming out into the sun: families in their best clothes, children subdued or running into the open; by the door, a group of gossiping old men, bent over their sticks; and, hurrying away, passing her as she walked, a couple with a child in arms. She crossed onto the green, where there was an old oak leaning its shade over a bench, and sat to watch them go. When they had all dispersed, she looked around at the widely spread cottages. She had not noticed anyone she would have identified as being from the hall, or of the better sort at all, amongst the parishioners. But no, of course not – the people from the hall would not be there: whatever mysterious forms of worship the English went in for, they were at least Protestants; Annette and her Catholic godmother would not be worshipping with them.

She sat for a little longer, wondering what to do next. She surveyed the cottages again, trying to work out the lie of the land and guess where the entrance to Waldon Hall would be – maybe that broader path, over to the right? She was about to stroll inconspicuously that way when she saw a carriage drawing up round the side of the church. Someone in a very ladylike hat began to descend, leaning on the arm of a gentleman. Jude stood up. She could see other carriages coming from two directions; and a group of young men in summer finery, silk stockings flashing, striding down the hill towards the stile to her right. Beyond were indeed the gates of Waldon Hall – she could see them opening – and there was Annette, walking beside her godmother, coming down towards the church. Jude turned away hastily, hiding her face with her hat, her mind spinning. They were all heading one way, to the church, but not to its front: round at the south side, a second, smaller door was open, and they were streaming in. Jude stepped behind the oak tree, her heart beating like a drum.

Annette passed in through the low stone arch, trying hard not to think of the Convent of the Little Angels. Her godmother, walking ahead of her, crossed herself piously. Then Annette felt a hand on her arm.

'Your handkerchief, Miss – you dropped it.' Having gained Annette's attention, Peggy dropped her voice to an excited whisper. 'Did you see?'

They followed Lady Waldon towards a big side chapel.

'See what?' She was whispering, too.

'By the tree! Mr Wiston! No, don't stand still, Miss. Keep going. He was there, outside, on the grass. It was him!'

From only a few feet ahead, Lady Waldon turned and frowned. Peggy fell back. Annette, hardly breathing, followed her godmother into the chapel, and reached blindly for the holy water stoup beside the door.

She had no idea how she endured the mass, and certainly she saw none of the glances and whispers that must have greeted her appearance there. Eventually it was over: the priest disappeared. Annette found her arm clasped firmly to her godmother's side, and was led forth into the sun. She made a blind curtsey to every face that presented itself, straining every nerve to see past them, out and away towards the tree on the green; no one was there. Her heart sank, and she smiled at another face, a florid woman speaking to her entirely incomprehensibly, though possibly in what was meant for French. Peggy must be mistaken. No one was there. They began to move slowly away from the church, towards the Hall gates. Their servants fell in behind them – but

Peggy had disappeared. Annette turned and saw her sitting on the church wall, holding up her shoe, with a comically dolorous face, talking to the boy who polished the knives. He looked up as Lady Waldon beckoned impatiently. He came running. 'The heel come off 'er shoe, m'lady.'

'Let her follow us, then,' said Lady Waldon. She turned to the red-faced woman, who was now walking with them. 'London servants, ma'am. No sense of how to behave themselves on a country road.'

41

'What time is it now?' Annette demanded. 'It *must* be three o'clock! Are you absolutely sure that's when you told Mr Wiston to come?'

'I am! And absolutely sure that he'll not fail you. Be patient just a little longer, Miss!'

For the hundredth time, Annette peered round the side of the little arbour, toward the blank, weed-choked gate in the wall. 'Oh, it *must* be time. This waiting is unbearable. Run and look at the stable clock again, Peggy!'

As her long-suffering maid rose to her feet, the gate shivered and began to scrape forward. Annette held her breath. Slowly it was forced open – and then the world stood still, because there, walking towards her, was Jude. For a moment Annette could not move or speak; then they were in each other's arms, and nothing else mattered.

'Just an hour, now!' said Peggy, as she went off to keep watch. 'Then you have to dress for dinner.'

But neither of them heard her.

The hour was not long enough. They did not speak for the first half of it, beyond the murmurs of meeting and missing and reassuring and love; and, even then, they could not bring themselves to sit and talk without holding on to each other. All their news came tumbling out at once. Annette told Jude about her miserable journey to Shropshire, and her virtual imprisonment at Waldon Hall. Jude recounted the stagecoach ride, and the incident with the old woman at the inn.

'She knew as soon as she saw me, I'm sure of it. It was terrifying.

But I think she was more frightened of me than I was of her. I have
no idea why!'

They both agreed that Peggy was a wonder, and that they
would never have survived without her. And before they knew it,
there was Peggy again, trotting towards them across the grass, to
carry Annette away.

'Wait,' Jude said, scooping into her broad coat pocket. 'I have
the money from your jewels for you.' She opened the little purse,
tipping gold into her hand. 'There's quite a lot left – though the
coach was expensive, and there's the inn – but you should have
most of fifty guineas, there.' She held it out.

Annette laughed and curled Jude's hand round the coins. 'It
was for you – to keep for us. I don't need it myself, here. We will
need it when we go.'

'Go?' Jude was still.

'Yes.' Annette held her hand closed tight. 'Yes, of course!' She
looked anxiously at Jude. 'Why have you come, if not to take me
away? We can go away, now, can't we? Away from here, to be
together?'

Jude was saved from answering by Peggy, who was suddenly
there again, fidgeting at Annette's elbow.

'You will come again tomorrow?' cried Annette.

'I will. How could I keep away?'

The lovers clung together once more, then Jude was gone.
Annette watched the gate close.

All the way back up the hill, Jude worried away at Annette's
question. *Had* she come to take Annette away? She had not let
herself think of anything beyond finding her, seeing her again,
holding her… But now, what? Could they really escape? More to
the point, where could they possibly go? They could not build a life
on love and fifty guineas: they had nowhere to live, and nothing to
live on. But she was struck by how nervous and unhappy Annette
had seemed; thinner than Jude remembered, her face pale. For the
first time, Jude began to realise how much the horrors of the last
few months had affected her. She strode on, thinking desperately.

It was becoming more and more pressing to make contact with the lawyers again and to find out about her own future – her inheritance. With a sinking heart, she understood that she was going to have to return to London.

She had no appetite for the friendly noise of the inn parlour tonight; she would go straight to her room, look again at the letter from Bartram and Speke, and plan what to say to Annette. But, as she approached the inn door, there was the bulky figure of William Jones the innkeeper, looking out for her return.

'I'm surely sorry, sir,' he said, 'but might you have time to do my father a favour? He would dearly love to speak with you. He asked me to look out for your coming.'

Jude was struck by his earnestness; it creased his gentle face with a worried frown that quite disturbed his professional jollity. She summoned up a smile. 'It would be an honour to meet your father,' she said. 'Where will I find him?'

William beamed. 'Why, just here, in the snug,' he said. 'By the fire. Go through, now, and I'll bring you an ale mug.'

The snug was a low-ceilinged room off the parlour. Wedged into a chair by the hearth was a florid old man who had clearly once been as much of a giant as his son. His face lit up when he saw Jude. 'Good evening to you, young sir! Joseph Jones, at your service.' He thrust out a hand in welcome. 'Forgive me for not rising to greet you, sir, but once I'm sat down, 'tis a great matter to get up again. Come, come and sit.'

Jude shook the proffered hand and took the settle at the other side of the fire.

'You come at the right time,' Joseph went on cheerfully. 'I was about to mull this here ale. Now that the days are drawing in, there's a chill in the evening.'

As the poker hissed into the long tankard, William appeared with the promised mug for Jude. She accepted the drink gratefully, and she and Joseph sat for a while in silence, watching the fire. The room felt hot after a day in the fresh air and the ale was unexpectedly strong. Jude had walked a long way and eaten nothing; she felt herself beginning to nod. In an effort to stay awake, she asked, 'Was there something you wished to speak to me about?'

'There was.' Joseph nodded. He paused, as if weighing up how to approach his subject. Then he said, 'William tells me that your name is Wiston.'

'It is, yes,' said Jude, puzzled.

The old man nodded again. 'Wiston. Well, well. Strange thing, to be sure.' He looked at Jude. 'I had a good friend and neighbour of that name, see? Long gone, now, I'm sorry to say, but – here's the thing – Lucy and I had been calling her to mind, just when you came in that day.' He paused dramatically. 'So, when William told me your name, I thought, well, there's a sign and a wonder!'

Jude smiled politely. She had no idea how many Wistons there were in England, but she doubted that her father's family had enjoyed sole rights to the name.

''Tis an uncommon name, at least in these parts,' said Joseph, as if answering her thought. 'And not one I ever heard of, except for her. And now you, of course.' His ruddy face took on a thoughtful expression. 'You don't suppose, now, do you, that you could be any kind of kin to Bell Wiston?'

Suddenly, Jude was wide awake. She touched the shape of the locket through her shirt. 'You friend's name was… Bell?'

Joseph nodded. 'Most folks called her Dame, on account of her being a wise woman in these parts. But we never called her anything but Bell… It was short for Isabella, you know.'

Peggy, arriving to dress Annette for dinner, announced that she'd seen a post-chaise driving away from the front door, and two servants carrying luggage indoors. Annette, in no mood for meeting strangers, came downstairs with some apprehension and found Lady Waldon in the hall, deep in talk with a man. It was with some relief that Annette realised it was not a stranger, after all, but Sir Charles, come from London at last. He did not look pleased to be home.

'We are conspicuous enough already, Waldon,' her godmother

was saying. 'Surely you see that we could not be associated with another French visitor?'

Her husband's face was like thunder. 'We have needed no excuse so far, my lady, to keep faith with our neighbours from across the water. And I fear we have no choice.' He stopped as he caught sight of Annette. Putting a thin smile on his face, he held out a hand. 'My dear,' he said in his usual distant way, 'you are looking well.'

She dropped a low curtsey. 'My lord.' Her heart was beating fast. What did he mean, *another French visitor*?

The long-case clock in the corner of the hall began to chime. 'Time to go in,' said Lady Waldon briskly, neatly stopping any further conversation. She fixed her husband with a meaningful stare. 'We can hear all your news over dinner.'

Sir Charles's promised news was not forthcoming with the soup; but, once the second course was laid on the table, he dismissed both the butler and the footman. As they disappeared, closing the doors behind them, a cold finger of fear touched Annette; it must be serious news, if it could not be talked about in front of the servants.

It was her godmother who spoke first. 'Sir Charles has brought news from town that you should know, my dear.' She paused, then went on, 'Not only from town, indeed, but from France.'

Annette's hand flew to her mouth.

Sir Charles spoke. 'Do not be alarmed, child. It is not good news, but it is not by any means the worst.' He cleared his throat. 'I have received a letter from your aunt, the Abbess Honorine.'

Annette looked dumbly at him, her mind racing. How had her aunt discovered she was here? Had Lady Waldon's letter reached Bordeaux after all? Everyone had said that France was in turmoil, that no mail was getting through… So, how had this letter come? What did her aunt want? Surely, the Waldons couldn't be intending to send her back? In panic, Annette half-rose from her chair.

'Sit down, my dear. Be calm,' said Sir Charles. 'Your aunt is safe. She is, even as we speak, in Bristol.'

This was even more incomprehensible. Annette struggled. 'Bristol, my lord?'

'Do stop calling me "my lord", child! I know it is the French custom, but it is not ours. Sir Charles will do, or simply Sir. Yes, she is in Bristol. It is the port where much Bordeaux shipping commonly comes in. She was –' he paused, finding the words – 'forced to flee.' Since Annette did not reply, he continued, 'How much do you know of what has happened since you left France?'

Annette shook her head. 'Very little, sir – nothing – I...'

'The National Assembly – you know what that is?'

She lifted her chin. Did he think her a child? 'I do. It is the newly formed assembly of the French people.'

Sir Charles looked at her with mild surprise, then went on, 'At the beginning of this month, August, the National Assembly voted to disestablish all religious houses.'

Disestablish? Annette tried to grasp what that might mean.

'The dissolution is already under way, I believe, across the country. However, in Bordeaux – and perhaps in other places – there has been some...' He cleared his throat. 'Unseemly haste. Your aunt was –' He broke off, as Lady Waldon stretched a warning hand towards him, then continued, 'Well, we do not need the details. She was obliged to leave, and in a great hurry. She took ship, in company with certain other clergy. They came into Bristol on a vessel carrying wine.'

Annette struggled to comprehend what he was saying. *Forced to flee?* Pierre had said nothing about attacking the Church. The France he had envisioned was of the three Estates united under a wise King and the new Assembly. Aunt Honorine had *left the convent?* Left France? On a *cargo ship?* It was too much to take in.

'It would appear that the family never received my letters,' Lady Waldon was saying. 'So she cannot yet be aware that you are with us, my dear.'

'Indeed,' said her husband. 'She simply wrote to us, in her hour of need, as her old friends.'

'Among other friends, I hope,' said his wife sharply.

His voice took on a reproving tone. 'She is alone in a strange land. In London society there is much solicitude and compassion for the poor *emigrés*.'

'Then perhaps London society can take pity on the Lady Honorine, too,' said Lady Waldon.

Sir Charles turned back to Annette. 'Your aunt's letter arrived at Hill Street just as I was leaving, yesterday. I was *en route* already, and saw no reason to delay my departure, so I have not yet replied.' He shot another glance at his wife, then sat back, fixing Annette with his cool stare. 'Have you questions I might try to answer?' he prompted, after a moment.

'Why?' Annette asked, at last.

'Why did she leave?'

'No. Why did they do that – to the convent? Pierre always said –' She broke off, trying to gather her wits. 'What will my aunt do now, sir?' she asked.

Sir Charles raised his eyebrows. 'An excellent question. We have need to consider it. But first, I think, we should enjoy our dinner.'

Sleep was impossible. Annette stared out of her window at the faint moon-shadows of the elm trees falling across the garden beds, and twisted her heavy pigtail tightly in her hand. The imposing figure of her aunt loomed up in her imagination – suave, sleek, ruthless. The Waldons had been careful about what they said at dinner, but Annette had formed the impression that Lady Waldon would prefer not to extend the hospitality of her house to Aunt Honorine. Milord, on the other hand, felt an obligation to help her, as a persecuted Catholic, a friend of the family and – Annette suspected – a most distinguished connection. There was no question who would win the argument. In the morning he would reply to the letter; and then, it seemed, Aunt Honorine would come here. Annette fought down the panic that threatened to engulf her: her aunt could not take her back to the convent.

'But if she comes here,' she thought, 'I will lose what freedom I have, just as surely as if I was in France. She will demand constant attendance. She will soon find out what happened to me, and I can just imagine how she will look down her nose at what Lady Waldon tells her. In the morning, they will write back, tell her I am here, invite her. And I will be shut up again.'

For a wild moment, she thought of creeping out of the house and running away over the hills, to Jude... but she did not know precisely where Jude was, or how to get there. She sank down on to the window seat. All the joy of the afternoon had been wiped away. Would she ever see Jude again? Would she ever feel truly safe? She rested her forehead against the cold windowpane.

When she arose, late and heavy-eyed, she found Lady Waldon in the morning room. It seemed important, now, to hear more of the story from Bordeaux; to understand what had actually happened to Aunt Honorine – and to the noble aspirations of Pierre and the other Patriots. But Lady Waldon simply said that she did not know.

'Sir Charles has shown me the letter. It is short, and far from explanatory. She writes in English, which I suppose might partly explain her reluctance to elaborate.' She paused and replaced her rather sour expression with a sympathetic little smile. 'But it is very clear, my dear, that whatever happened to the Abbess, it has been a terrible shock. Sir Charles is writing to her now, to invite her to come to us. I think we will all have to be very kind to your aunt.'

42

It was barely light when Jude woke. The little window of her chamber was misted with a fine drizzle. The old man had been right: the days were drawing in. She lay thinking about the unexpected revelation of the previous evening, which had raised more questions than it answered. Joseph's amazed delight at the picture in the locket had certainly been convincing; but Jude had always understood that her father's family hailed from Somerset, which was somewhere in the south-west part of England. If her Aunt Isabella and the mysterious Bell Wiston really were one and the same person, how had the fine lady in the portrait come to be living in a cottage in Shropshire? And what was a 'wise woman', anyway? According to Joseph, Bell's cottage was now the home of Lucy Weaver, the old black woman Jude had seen the day she arrived. She had been a close friend of Bell's, apparently, and perhaps could unravel the mystery. Most likely the whole thing was a figment of Joseph's imagination and would come to nothing; but there was only one way to find out, and Jude had nothing else to do until she could visit Annette again that afternoon, so she had agreed to let Joseph take her to see Lucy. The idea of meeting the old woman again was both pleasing and slightly frightening. If she had really seen through Jude's disguise, what might she say or do?

Joseph was waiting in the parlour, well wrapped up and armed with a hefty walking stick. He seemed excited about their expedition. 'I canna think when I last walked up the bank to Brynsquilver,' he said as they set out. 'Our Lucy'll not believe her eyes when she sees me!'

The rain had stopped, but cloud still sat low on the hills,

blurring the view as they followed the narrowest of the lanes leading uphill from the crossroads. After a hundred yards or so, Joseph paused, leaning on a stile in the hedge, then they climbed over it on to a steeply rising footpath. Joseph could not speak and walk at the same time, so they trudged mostly in silence between the thick hedges, with frequent stops for the old man to get his breath. The hedgerows were still green, but heavy already with unripe haws and scattered with sprays of scarlet rosehips. At last, they came to a flatter place, a narrow way between tall brambles, the blackberries shiny with rain. Jude wondered about gathering some, but not many were within easy reach from the path.

Joseph chuckled wheezily. 'Her cordial takes some beating,' he said.

Before Jude had worked out the meaning of this utterance, they came to another old stile in the hedge, which Joseph heaved himself over with a determination that rather alarmed Jude. Beyond it was a kitchen garden, and beyond that a stone cottage, set back against a small wood. It was still as they approached, the only movement the slow curl of smoke from the wide chimney into the damp air.

The sound of a voice made Jude jump.

'Joey Jones! What're you doing in my cabbage patch, you old fool? Trying to kill yourself with climbing, now?' Lucy Weaver was standing by the cottage door, just a few feet away but so still that Jude hadn't noticed her. 'Heard you coming a mile off,' she said scornfully. 'Townsfolk don't know how to be quiet. I heard you, trampling like cattle in a droveway. And as for him –' she tossed her head towards Joey – 'you could hear him gasping like a landed fish, from here to Shrewsbury.' She looked from one to the other of her unexpected guests, her head on one side. 'No, I can't guess your business. You had best come and tell me.'

She led them to a low bench by the door. A tabby cat ran away as they approached.

'See? Even the cat heard you,' she added triumphantly, 'and she's been deaf these many years.'

The extravagance of this extra flourish made Jude smile, but

Joseph looked concerned. 'You munna mind Lucy,' he whispered. 'She'm a sharp-tongued woman, but her bark is worse than her bite.'

Lucy whipped round and treated him to an exasperated glare. 'You don't need to tell him, codshead! He knows what I mean.' She turned to Jude and, disconcertingly, gave her a conspiratorial wink.

As Joseph sank down on the bench, Lucy disappeared into the cottage, returning with a three-legged stool for Jude. Then she disappeared again and came back carrying a jug and three cups.

'Just the morning for a tonic,' she said. 'I made this in June, and it's time I tried it.'

The wine was golden and delicious, its elderflower perfume a taste of summer. Jude began to relax.

'Now then,' said Joseph, relishing his role as the discoverer of a great marvel, 'Show Lucy that picture of yours, Mr Wiston.'

Jude took out the locket and handed it to Lucy, who looked at the portrait for a long time without speaking. Then she said simply, 'Bell.'

'I knew it!' cried Joseph, and he began to recount the story of his discovery.

Lucy listened in silence. She did not appear to be at all surprised. When Joseph had finished, she said, 'So that was what the dreams were about. Bell and Mr Brown. I understand now.'

'I wish I did!' Jude burst out. 'I understand nothing! How could your Bell Wiston be my Aunt Isabella? How could a gentleman's daughter have come to live here? Why would she do that?'

'As she told it to me,' said Lucy, slowly, 'they came here in a time of war, fleeing from the soldiers who had killed her father. At first, she was just sheltering here, I think, but then...' She looked out at the hills, feeling for the right words. 'She grew to be part of this place.' Seeing that Jude was still struggling to fit the pieces of the puzzle together, Lucy rose and moved towards the door. 'Come. I will show you something.'

Both Jude and Joseph had to duck their heads to enter the cottage. Inside it was small, and very old. A massive chimney beam ran the length of one wall; on the other side of the room, a ladder led to what must be a sleeping platform under the rafters. There was a chair by the fire, where the cat was now curled, and a table under the window covered with pots and bottles, but little else. Everything spoke of an orderly, frugal life with few comforts.

Lucy pointed to the great oak beam over the hearth. 'Look. There they are, see? The carvings? Feel them.'

Jude reached up and traced the shapes in the blackened timber with her fingertips.

'That's the bell,' said Lucy, 'and at the other end is an anchor. The anchor is a sign of hope. So it says, Hope and Bell lived here. See? Hope did it herself; she was good with her hands.'

Jude was losing the thread again. 'Hope?'

'Bell's dear friend,' said Joseph. 'They lived here together.'

Before Jude could take this in, Lucy fixed her with a stern eye. 'I see that you and I have much to speak of, *Mister* Wiston. More than we have time for today. Now that you know the way to Brynsquilver, I hope you will come here again.'

Jude arrived at Waldon Hall that afternoon full of the news about Aunt Isabella, and ready to make a story of it to cheer Annette; but Annette had news of her own, and was in no mood for ancient history. She clung desperately to Jude as the story tumbled out of her: the rioting in Bordeaux, the betrayal of Pierre's dreams, her aunt's arrival in England.

'She will take me and lock me up again, I know she will! The Waldons will be glad to be rid of me. They will tell my father where I am, and Aunt Honorine will take me off to some convent somewhere, and I shall never see you again! I would rather die!' She was weeping furiously.

Jude held her tight, stroking her hair, trying to soothe her. This was an unlooked-for twist; but nonetheless she needed to tell Annette about her plans for going to London. Aunt Isabella – and her 'dear friend' Hope – would have to wait.

'Perhaps it is not as desperate as you think,' she offered. 'They say that many French *emigrés* are making their way to England.

Most have left everything behind and are reliant on the kindness of their English friends. Your aunt will have nowhere to take you, and must be hoping that she can stay here.'

Annette stilled.

Jude took a deep breath. 'Last time I was here, you asked me if we could go away together,' she began.

Annette looked up eagerly.

'I want that, too,' Jude went on, 'but, my love, where would we go? We have no home, and no money until I can claim my inheritance. And the only way for me to do that is to go back to London and speak to the lawyers.'

Annette clutched her for a moment. 'Don't leave me here!'

'I must,' Jude insisted gently. 'There is nowhere else you can be safe.' She held Annette away, to look in her face. 'Listen. I believe that I own property, and in this part of England. I need to find out exactly what it consists of, and what rent it yields. In that way, we might have a secure future.'

'I have no money any more,' said Annette, soberly. 'I should have had my *dot*, my dowry, but with everything, that is quite gone. The jewels were all that was left.'

'And the jewels are still helping us. Then, if I have understood rightly, my inheritance will be enough for us both. But the letters from America that prove who I am will have gone to the lawyers in London, since I have no fixed address in England where I could receive them. I must go. It will take time. And meanwhile, you will need to stay here.'

'How long?' Annette's face was pale. 'How long will you be gone?'

'I don't know.'

'Months?'

'I hope not. But it depends on so much: on the letters, and on the property itself, what it is like, what needs to be put in hand; and then there are the lawyers, and the law's delays. But I will come back, my love. I will come back for you. I promise. And I will come and see you every day until I leave.'

43

It was several days before the messenger Sir Charles had sent to Bristol returned, saying that the Lady Honorine was on her way; but only another day after that before the rumble of wheels on gravel announced her arrival at Waldon Hall. The family gathered hastily outside to watch the postilion pull down the steps and open the door. To everyone's surprise, it was not the Abbess herself, but a younger, nimbler figure in the white veil of a novice who emerged first. Even more surprising to all those assembled was the girl's dark skin.

Annette could not believe her eyes. 'Charlotte! Is it you?'

Charlotte smiled in delight. 'Annette! When Reverend Mother told me you were here, I scarcely dared believe it. But here you are!'

They clasped hands, both speaking excitedly at once, until Annette, remembering her manners, turned to her godmother and said in English, 'This lady and I were acquainted in the convent at Bordeaux, ma'am.'

Before Lady Waldon could reply, a wheezing gasp escaped from the interior of the chaise. The broad back view of the Lady Honorine appeared in the doorway. Painfully slowly, she climbed backwards down the steps. When she turned to face them, Annette was shocked by the change in her aunt: her face was haggard, her silk habit crumpled. Standing there in the grey light of an English afternoon, she seemed diminished.

Sir Charles stepped forward, all courtesy. 'You are most welcome, my Lady Abbess.' He bent to kiss her ring, but she snatched her hand back. There was no insignia of office on her finger. Nor was she wearing the jewelled crucifix.

Somehow the luggage was brought in, the postilion was paid, and the hired chaise trundled off down the long drive to the road. Lady Honorine was shown to the guest chamber prepared for her, suggesting in a faint voice that, if it were not too much trouble, a small glass of brandy might help to restore her strength. A further bedroom was hastily allotted to Charlotte. Peggy, being the only French-speaking servant, was instructed to unpack for the Abbess, and to answer the bell for both visitors. Annette herself was expected to watch and wait, to comfort and attend on her aunt, all the time knowing that Jude would be at the gate in the wall. Peggy spent her afternoon running up and down stairs and along landings; it was all Annette could do to seize her for long enough to send her with a message to the garden gate.

By the time the family assembled in the blue drawing room before dinner, something – whether it was the rest or the brandy, Annette could not tell – had partially restored the colour to her aunt's cheeks, though she still looked unwell. Whatever had happened at the convent, to say nothing of their flight and subsequent struggles, had left its mark. Annette, thinking of that dreadful night at the bakery, tried not to imagine what her aunt and the other nuns might have gone through. Meanwhile, Sir Charles and Lady Waldon, albeit with impeccable courtesy and restraint, were doing their best to extract the full story from their visitor. They had no success. The Abbess seemed unable to speak coherently about what had happened to her. She became visibly distressed when the attack on the convent was mentioned and begged them not to remind her of that dreadful day. In spite of herself, Annette felt a pang of pity.

The gate in the wall closed; Jude heard the scrape and thud as Peggy pushed it home behind her. She stood, nonplussed, not knowing what to do. Annette could not meet her today, Peggy had said. The Abbess had arrived; everything was at sixes and sevens; Annette would be missed if she tried to get away. Jude had better not come tomorrow, either, Peggy had insisted; but by the day after, perhaps, things would have settled.

And that was that. A morning wasted in delicious anticipation and an afternoon spent in a fruitless walk. There were few enough days left before she took the mail coach to Ludlow and then post to London. She had planned to tell Annette so, today. She paced in front of the gate, desperately trying to think of other ways to see Annette – she considered scaling the wall, or simply marching up to the front door – but it was a pointless exercise and soon, defeated, she set off to retrace her steps to the inn.

The afternoon was sunny, the sky a brilliant blue, and it was impossible to stay completely gloomy for very long as she followed the now familiar grass path, shaded by oaks and wild cherry still heavy with fading summer leaves. Here and there a rowan tree, weighed down with swags of orange berries, flamed against the green; in between them, the hawthorns were purpled over with ripening fruit. Soon she came out onto the top of the hill, where the grass moved like the sea and harebells lay at her feet like little blue chips of the sky above them. Truly, Jude thought, this 'county of Salop' is a beautiful place. And that made her think of Madeley. She had hardly thought about it as an actual location. All her waking hours since she had arrived here had been focussed on seeing Annette; but ever since she had discovered that her inheritance, too, was somewhere in this county, it had been there in the back of her mind. She had no clear idea how much her inheritance was worth. Would it be enough to provide a home for herself and Annette, somewhere where no one would look for them? She could not tell until she knew more about it. It occurred to her now that the empty time until she could see Annette again might be usefully filled with some enquiries into where exactly this Madeley was. The thought cheered her a little. As she crested the ridge and came down towards the crossroads, she found she was humming one of Jean-Baptiste's sea shanties.

Although Annette shrank from imagining exactly how her aunt might have suffered at the hands of the intruders, and understood her reluctance to speak of it, she could not suppress her curiosity about what had happened at the convent. Where were Sophie and

Thérèse now? she wondered. What had become of the dreadful Madame Grimaud? It was not until next day that she had the opportunity to speak alone with Charlotte.

The time of passionate excitement that Annette had lived through at the bakery had barely touched the life of the convent, it seemed.

'There was shouting and running in the streets, quite often, but we did not know what it was all about,' said Charlotte. 'Reverend Mother knew, I suppose, but the rest of us just had to guess. Soon after I became a novice, Sister Josephine had set me to serve the Abbess, so I saw her several times a day. I expect she thought waiting on a lady was the fitting role for someone like me.'

Charlotte's small smile was wry, just as Annette remembered. She reached out and squeezed her hand.

Charlotte looked up at her. 'I knew she was becoming very anxious, but of course, she never spoke to me about matters outside the community. I could feel the trouble in the air, though. But you saw all that, yourself, before you came away?'

Annette nodded. 'Yes, I was there. It was happening all around me.' The memories were suddenly vivid: the crowds in the park, Pierre's speeches, dancing with Jude under the stars – how could Charlotte understand? 'It was so... exciting,' she said. *Excitant* – the word felt entirely inadequate.

'You were there? In the streets?' Charlotte looked wistful. 'I wondered, sometimes, where you were.'

'I thought about you, too – but I never dreamed any harm would come to you.'

Charlotte's smile was rueful this time. 'I used to wish that *something* would happen – I did not know what, but something... to change things. Our lives just went on, the same as always, everyone pretending things were normal, when you could *feel* that they weren't.'

They were sitting in Annette's chamber; Charlotte was gazing out at the dark garden, as if watching the events she described. 'After you went, most of the boarders left, one way or another – Madame Grimaud was all alone – so we had no news from outside.

And, of course, the nuns didn't talk about what was happening, ever. Reverend Mother went around in a thundercloud.' She turned to look at Annette, judging whether to go on. 'She was already furious about your escaping, before all the other trouble started.'

'I'm sure she was!' said Annette. 'After all, she had to tell my father.'

'Oh, he came to see her! He was in such a rage! I could hear his voice from downstairs. They both shouted for quite a long time. He never came again, but Reverend Mother had meetings with your other relatives, too.' She frowned. 'About you, at first, I suppose; but the Lord Lavigne, he came to see her more than once.'

'Cousin Henri? Whatever for, I wonder?'

Charlotte shrugged. 'Politics, I think. Then they had a falling out, when Milord came in the new uniform that was suddenly everywhere in the streets.'

'Uniform? Cousin Henri?' Annette could not imagine it, though of course there were lots of generals and so forth in the family portraits.

'They said it was for the new National Guard.' Charlotte paused, picking at the hem of her scapular. 'I think the National Guard were the reason the mob turned on the convent that day.' Then she was silent, screwing up the fine wool in her hands.

'You don't have to tell me about this part, it if it distresses you,' said Annette gently.

But Charlotte took a deep breath and continued, her voice carefully calm. 'It was just after the Assumption of Our Lady. After we had cleared away from the feast – changed the vestments in the choir, and the flowers and everything – so, a few days, perhaps. Then, one morning there was a lot of shouting in the streets. I watched for a time from the parlour window, but Sister Josephine made me come away and set me to cleaning the chapel silver. Now, I think she was thinking of hiding it, somehow, but she couldn't bring herself – or maybe she just wanted me to think about something other than being frightened. Then there was a great tramping and drumming outside, and we both ended up at the window. It wasn't the mob, but the new guards – they came marching into the square, and they all marched in at the gates of La Trompette and shut them. Then we saw them walking along the ramparts. It was quiet for a while, and it began to get dark, but what we didn't know was that the mob were still there, round behind the fortress – it sprawls for miles, that place – and then we began to hear fighting. Gunshots. Screams.' She rubbed her eyes. 'Then it suddenly got louder, and the people started running into the square, with the guards behind them. More and more people came from all directions, until the guards ran back inside the fortress and the people could not follow. They just swarmed into the square, more and more and more, all shouting up at the walls of La Trompette. A man got up on the mounting block on the corner, and he shouted and pointed...' She looked at Annette. 'And then they turned and came up towards us in a tide.'

Annette could feel the fear of that moment. 'What were they looking for?' she asked. 'Food? Flour?'

Charlotte nodded. 'How did you know? They said we had secret stores, hidden barrels of flour, heaven knows what. They swarmed everywhere. Some of them were women! But not all. By no means all.' She gripped her hands tightly together, but she went on. 'We ran to the chapel, thinking they would not harm us there, and they rampaged around, tearing things open – they did find some food in the kitchen, but they weren't looking for pottage. They scattered most of it about in their fury. Then they thought of the valuable things in the chapel, I suppose, and it turned into a kind of hunting, a cattle-running – we were the cattle. I don't know why I ran up towards Reverend Mother's room. When I got there, three men were in the room. I saw them knock her to the ground...'

Annette swallowed hard, pushing away the memory of Jacques, of grabbing hands, stinking breath... 'Oh, Charlotte, no! Poor, poor Aunt Honorine!'

'She got off lightly!' said Charlotte, with an expression near to contempt. 'They only took her jewellery, and called her some names, and left her.'

'But, she said –'

'Of course she did. She wouldn't want people to think she ran away from her responsibilities just because she was robbed of a few trinkets, would she? They took her ring, of course. And other things, I suppose, from her room. But she received no hurt.' She smiled a hard little smile. 'Except to her pride.'

It took Annette a few moments to absorb this version of a story she had imagined so differently. Then she said, 'But how did you get away?'

'Not easily, you may be sure,' Charlotte replied. 'When the men saw me in the doorway, they left Reverend Mother alone at once.' Her tone was bitter. 'So I suppose I did her some service, then, because I ran. And they left her, and ran after me …' She fell silent, gazing out into the dark.

Annette was silent, too.

Eventually Charlotte spoke. 'I was so frightened. Everyone thinks, because I was brought up like a lady, that I couldn't know… what men do to helpless girls. But I do.' She shook herself. 'So, I ran and hid. I had lived in that place long enough. I knew every nook and cranny of it. I lost them in the cellars and hid behind some barrels until everything was quiet again.'

Annette, who found she had been holding her breath, laughed with relief.

At that moment Peggy erupted into the room. Charlotte was needed to attend on the Abbess. Charlotte sighed and rose to her feet. At the door she turned back to Annette. 'It is so good to see you again!' She smiled. 'And I haven't told you, yet, about my adventures in Bristol. Tomorrow, perhaps.' Then she was gone.

44

Since the revelation about her kinship to Bell Wiston, Jude had been an honoured guest at the Two Crosses. That evening she found herself yet again sharing a canister of mulled ale with Joseph, and took the opportunity to ask him where Madeley was.

He sucked thoughtfully on his pipe. 'Mm... Somewhere over Severn stream way, as I recall... William! Where's Madeley?'

His son put down his napkin and the tankard he was polishing with it, and came over to the fire. 'Why, yes, you'm right, Father – 'tis just above Coalbrookdale. Two, three miles up the bank from where they've built the iron bridge. You must remember old Flora Edwards, Father? She that made my Mary's wedding dress? Well, her great-uncle George came from there, did he not? A place full of Methodies and Quakers, he used to say.' He turned to Jude. 'A fine little market town, 'tis, with some good alehouses. You have some business there, sir?'

Jude smiled. The Joneses had been scrupulously incurious about her reasons for suddenly appearing in this remote spot, and about what her business might be at Waldon; but perhaps now they felt that their growing acquaintance entitled them to a little more information.

'I might have some business there, yes. But I wondered – I do not know this part of England – how far would it be from here to there?'

They conferred, corrected each other, and arrived at a distance of forty miles.

'Or thereabouts,' said Joseph. 'Couldn't walk it in a day, that's certain.'

'But you could do it on horseback in a long morning,' added William. 'And back the same night, if you had to.'

Jude was weighing up this information when Joseph suddenly exclaimed, 'Why! How could I forget? Bell's brother lived at Coalbrookdale, didn't he?' He looked delightedly at Jude. 'Your father, then? Before he went to America. Well, well! You must ask our Lucy about it. She'll remember better than I.'

Jude needed no further encouragement to visit the cottage again. A whole empty day stretched before her. She could not go back to Waldon Hall until the day after tomorrow – hoping against hope that Annette could get away then – and there was no time, before she left for London, to put in hand a visit to Madeley. So, the next morning found her once again on the stony track that she had climbed with Joseph. She reflected as she walked that every destination in Shropshire seemed to involve climbing a slope. William had said that Madeley was 'above' Coalbrookdale: another steep hill, no doubt.

After a while, the track levelled out and she came into the wood. On the other side was the bramble brake that told her she had almost arrived. With the stick she had picked from the hedge two fields back, Jude swiped self-consciously at the nettles blocking the path to the inner recesses of the thorny brake. She smiled at herself. She was not responsible for clearing the way for the old woman's blackberry harvest – they hardly knew each other! But Jude was drawn by the memory of how she had felt on her last visit. Recognised; welcomed as her real self. After the initial shock, it had felt good.

How old was Lucy Weaver, she wondered? She had shown Jude a date carved between the symbols over the hearth that was more than seventy years ago. But that marked an event some years before Dame Weaver had come here herself: the arrival of Isabella Wiston. So maybe the old woman was only sixty or seventy; but she had had a hard life, out here. A country life, close to the rain and the sun and the snow, the earth and the storms; and at such a distance from all human contact, except with odd folk from a few tiny farms. How had she come by her knowledge, then? And how had a lady like Isabella Wiston ever learned to live here?

She reached the stile and saw the dame sitting by the cottage door. At Jude's approach she stood up and held out her hand in welcome. She looked Jude in the eye. 'What shall I call you?' she asked.

There was a pause before Jude replied. 'I'm called Jude, now,' she said. 'And you might call me that. But I am also Rebecca Judith Wiston, from Salem in Massachusetts.'

The dame snorted dismissively. 'You are welcome here without that pedigree. You shall be Jude, here; and I am Lucy. Come and sit.'

So they sat side by side on the old bench, gazing out at the valley and the hills beyond, and talked. Lucy seemed to accept that it was right and proper for Jude to be there, a matter of course. And Jude soon found herself telling Lucy all the things that she had not been able to tell anyone else. It was a strange but joyful thing, to speak out plainly. She had never testified in Meeting, back in Salem, but she thought it might feel like this – an unburdening. She talked about Lizzie, about Lotta, about learning to be a sailor, about life at the barrel-makers'; but most of all she talked about the miracle of loving Annette.

In turn, Lucy told her a different love story: how the young Isabella Wiston had run away with the girl who had once been her maid, and how they had found refuge, at last, in this cottage; how Bell had learned the lore of plants and herbs, and had become known for miles around as a wise woman, a healer.

'It was Bell who taught me,' Lucy said. 'And after Bron died, I came to live here. People know it is the Dame's cottage. There have been many of us – before me, and before Bell.' She paused, head cocked as if listening, or as if summoning up a decision. 'Come. I can show you.'

Rising from her seat, she seized a long-handled pruning hook that was propped by the door. Using the ferocious-looking implement as a walking stick, she trudged off round the house. Jude followed, along a narrow path that wound through the wood.

The graves were in a clearing, surrounded by long grass and

spent flowers, though it looked as if Lucy must have been here recently and cleared off the stones. Perhaps she did it regularly. Or perhaps just this morning, for this moment? There were five that Jude could see – the furthest ones marked only with rounded rocks, almost sunk out of sight unless one were looking for the line. But at her feet there was a neat oblong slab, with the roughly cut initials 'BR'. Beyond that lay a larger stone, flat, with 'IW' carved at the head. Isabella Wiston, Jude thought. Next to it, a matching stone bore the letters 'HB' beneath a dusty incursion of heather. Jude stepped forward and went down on her knee to brush it aside.

Lucy, meanwhile, was attending to a very small stone, hardly big enough to be a marker. With her long hook she sliced away a bramble which had crept across it. Straightening up, she came to join Jude, who was pulling at the tough heather. The hook flicked expertly at the root, cutting it clean away.

Jude snatched her hand back and stood up.

Lucy smiled. 'You are welcome here,' she said. She looked up at the sun. 'How the day runs away with talking! We should eat and drink.'

Back at the cottage, she brought out bread and a jug, and they went on talking. Lucy seemed pleased to answer Jude's questions about her mysterious Aunt Bell. She had met Jude's father too, before he left England for America. This was a part of his life that Jude knew little about, and she listened hungrily.

'I think Bell had expected never to see her brother again, but then he suddenly reappeared. And he was living in Coalbrookdale – only a day's ride from here! He'd turned Quaker there, and then he married a Quaker girl.'

Jude nodded. 'My mother. She was the birthright Quaker in our family – I did know that. And, from what you say, she must have grown up very near to the place where my inheritance is now. But she died when I was small, so I never really knew anything about their life in England. Did you meet my mother, too, Lucy?'

'Just once. Yes.' Lucy paused, searching the past. 'She was a comely girl, I remember. Quiet, but unafraid. She was already with child when they took ship for America. It was on some Quaker business or other – a bunch of 'em went. And of course, never came back. I do remember how sad Bell was, to lose her brother again so soon. But anyone could see that he doted on your mother, and Bell said she could only be glad he had found joy at last, after the unhappiness of his first marriage.'

First marriage?

Jude sat very still for a moment. Then she said, 'My father was married... before?'

The old woman looked worried. 'You did not know? Yes, Hope told me that story. It was when he was living in France.'

France? Jude's head spun. Neither her father nor her brothers had ever spoken of this. Steadying her voice with an effort, she said, 'Can you tell me that story?'

Lucy sat for a while, looking into the distance, as if ordering her thoughts. Then she said, 'It was long before I was born but, as Hope told it to me, Bell's kin – your kin – were supporters of the banished king, King James. After good Queen Anne died, this James wanted to come back and have the throne again. There was a lot of fighting about it, seemingly. But he was defeated, and all his followers were punished. Bell's own father was killed by King George's men, and she and her brothers had to flee away.' She turned to Jude. 'That was what brought her and Hope here.'

Jude did not know what to say. Lucy's story had given her the link between the aristocratic lady in the portrait and the country healer her aunt had become; but why had she heard nothing of all this from her father, or her mother? Of course, she thought, in revolutionary Massachusetts, people had little time for kings and queens: her father's royalist past would have been best forgotten.

'Go on,' she urged. 'And my father? He fled, too?'

Lucy nodded. 'Yes. Bell never spoke of her other brother, so I do not know what happened to him; but Alistair ran away to France, along with many other Jacobite gentlemen. He must have been very young, still. And it seems he fell in love with a young Frenchwoman there and wedded her.' She paused. Then, watching Jude carefully, she went on, 'They had a child, a boy. But she died, having their baby. Her family were set against the marriage. They took the child and Alistair never saw it again.'

They sat without speaking. Jude thought about her father, whom she had only known as an old man. She struggled to imagine him as Lucy had described: young, passionate for a cause, headlong in love and suddenly widowed. She thought about that other child, even older than her brothers, far away in both time and space. Her father had had another life, another family, of which she had known nothing.

The sun was sinking towards the hills before she finally took a reluctant leave of Lucy, promising to visit her again, and started off down the track to the Crosses.

Seeing Jude had been a lifeline. Deprived of that meeting even for a couple of days, Annette felt desperately lonely. Charlotte was a godsend: a friend of her own age to whom she could talk freely. As well as the leafy bower where she met Jude, Annette had already discovered other private spots that were good for escaping from the oppressive atmosphere indoors. One of them was the grotto – a fanciful little stone garden house at one end of a long pool. Nobody went in there in summer, her godmother had told her, for fear of the persistent hornets nesting in its domed roof. But there had been no hornets to be seen when Annette found it, and it was the ideal place to take refuge with Charlotte after breakfast. As their eyes adjusted to the gloom, she showed Charlotte how the inside of the grotto was decorated with hundreds of seashells, stuck into the plaster in swirling patterns. They wondered idly where they had all come from – Waldon must be, they thought, a long way from the sea.

The thought of the sea reminded Annette of Charlotte's parting remark the night before. 'You were going to tell me a story about your time in Bristol, I think?'

'I was!' Charlotte answered eagerly. 'It was wonderful. You can't imagine.'

'Tell me *everything*!' said Annette.

Charlotte, with a little frown of concentration, clasped her hands in her lap, like a child trying to recite her lesson in order. 'Well. I left the Convent at night, with your aunt, as I told you – she said I was the only one she wanted, which I suppose was true – I don't think she could have asked anyone else, anyway, but I wanted to go. She must have known about the ship. It was ready to sail that very night, full of people – frightened people, I thought. There was a little cabin waiting for her and everything. We reached Bristol next day. When we arrived, we were taken in at first by some French people – there is a surprising number of our countrymen and women there. Then, after two or three days, someone offered Reverend Mother the use of a small house. The owners were away, but the house was not shut up; the cook and some of the servants were still there, so we were well cared for. Reverend Mother did not go out at all while we were there, but I did! I walked for miles, every day!' Her eyes shone. 'Bristol is the most beautiful city, and I think it must be very prosperous – there are whole new streets being added to it all the time. In Park Street, where we were staying, there was building going on further up the hill. And everything is bustling and busy.'

'Oh, I envy you those walks! What an adventure! But it was very brave of you to go out unaccompanied – were you not afraid?'

'I was at first, yes. I was afraid that the English, being Protestants, would not like to see a religious sister – but I soon found that no one minded me. And another thing that surprised me was that there are very many black people there – far more than in Bordeaux – so that no one stared at me because of that, either. I walked and walked: I saw the waterfront with all the great ships, and the cathedral, and all manner of shops. Sometimes I got lost. That was how I met Mrs Yearsley. She was so kind – she walked with me all the way back to Park Street, because she was on her way to visit a friend who lives there.'

'And this Mrs Yearsley befriended you?'

'Yes, she did. She is a most interesting lady. Well, not a lady at all, actually – they say she was a milkmaid when she was young. And she married a farmer. But she educated herself, and now she writes the most wonderful poetry! She and her friend Mrs More are campaigning for the abolition of slavery. Look: she wrote this.' She reached into her pocket and brought out a small pamphlet, which she handed to Annette.

'*A Poem on the Inhumanity of the Slave Trade*,' Annette read. The booklet was too long for her to read all at once – she found poetry much harder than any other kind of reading in English – but she could see that it was a political pamphlet as much as a poem. Annette knew something of the horrors of the Atlantic slave trade: in another world, Pierre had made her read both Montesquieu and Diderot on the subject, and had waxed passionate about the brotherhood of all men. She looked enquiringly at Charlotte, who smiled.

'The English is quite hard for me, too. But Mrs Yearsley told me the story. It is very sad. But it is written to help people understand. Do you know, there is a whole community of people in Bristol who are working to end slavery? Mrs Yearsley invited me to a meeting and introduced me to some of their committee. She thinks I could be useful to their cause, because I was born on a plantation and could speak to people about what it was like. Oh! I can't explain how... *important* it felt.' She stopped and looked at Annette with a sudden intensity.

This is what matters to her, Annette thought. What she really wants to tell me.

'There is a lady on the committee who is trying to get all their pamphlets and published lives translated into other languages. When she heard that I know Spanish as well as French, she asked if I would take employment with her, to help.' Charlotte swallowed, and looked at her hands. 'And I thought, perhaps, I could. But then Reverend Mother carried me off here with her, as you see. I was so... disappointed. Angry, even.' She looked hard at Annette, as if she were seeing her from a great way off. 'I keep thinking that I could go back,' she said. 'I think I must, if I can. A way will reveal itself, perhaps.' She paused again. 'You see, I have begun to think that God might be calling me to this work, rather than to a life of prayer.'

Annette was doing her best to keep up. 'But – your vocation?'

she asked. 'You are a novice nun! I suppose I had imagined that you would have to go with my aunt to whatever convent she finds to give her refuge…'

Charlotte shook her head. 'No. I am not bound. I have not taken my final vows.' She hesitated, then with a decisive gesture started to pull the pins from her veil and wimple, removing them both. Annette stared. Charlotte's springy dark hair stood out an inch or more from her head; she looked like a pretty boy. 'I started to let it grow when we left France,' she said calmly, 'so that, if I had to hide what I was, I had at least some chance of succeeding. With a cap and bonnet, I could be any free black woman.'

45

'And I told her,' Annette concluded triumphantly, 'that we would pay her coach fare, and that you would see to the arrangements for her!'

Jude blinked. 'And was she pleased with this idea?'

'Of course! She is so eager to go back to Bristol. And you told me that a mail coach goes on Tuesdays. That is tomorrow. She could change at Ludlow, as you did when you came from London?'

Jude was perturbed by the vision of Charlotte – so noticeable with her dark skin and foreign accent, and dressed in the habit of a Catholic nun – making this trip alone. She tried to explain to Annette that the melting-pot of a sea port like Bristol was one thing, but Ludlow – little, provincial Ludlow – was quite another.

Annette, however, was full of confidence. 'You have no idea how *certain* she is,' she said. 'She was always self-contained, you know – and strong. Horrible things had happened to her before she came from the Islands, when she was little; and the girls at the convent were hateful to her; but she can take care of herself, she really can. And she doesn't want to be a nun any more. She showed me: she has grown her hair. In an everyday gown, no one will take notice of her.'

Jude shook her head. 'The good folk of Ludlow will find a black face remarkable enough, whatever she wears. But she will be safe once she has shed her habit, I hope. And the work she wants to do in Bristol seems to me a far better vocation than life in the convent.'

They had snatched an hour in the garden bower, and Peggy had undertaken to let them know if there was any call for Annette indoors. Rain was threatening, and they sat pressed together, sharing their warmth, Jude's chin resting on Annette's head. 'I have been hearing strange tales,' she said. 'And it has made me think about the story you told me of your grandmother. Did you say that your English grandfather was a Jacobite?'

'Yes, I did!' said Annette. 'Why do you ask?'

'A strange coincidence. The old dame up the hill, Lucy Weaver, remembers my father when he was here in Shropshire; but she told me that, much earlier in his life, he was in France with King James, too. I know there must have been quite a few young men like him, but I do wonder if he and your grandfather might have known each other. Wouldn't that be strange?'

Annette considered, fiddling with Jude's buttons. 'Would they have been something like the same age?' she said.

'They could have been – my father was older than my mother, by quite a bit; he was born in the last century. He was sixty-six when I was born, I think.'

'So how old was he when he was in France? And where – do you know?'

'He must have been around twenty. But I have no idea how long he was there, or whereabouts he was.'

'I think my grandfather was very young, also, although he got married,' Annette said. 'So, they could have been friends! How lovely! I do wish I had known my grandparents. But my grandmother died when my father was born, and I think my grandfather must have gone back to England.'

Jude sat up. 'Do you recall his name, your grandfather?' she said.

'I don't think they ever told me,' Annette said. 'I could ask my godmother, I suppose.'

Walking back, Jude could not shake the idea from her head. Should she have told Annette her guess? Surely it was just too improbable. She put her hand to the locket. She had never met her Aunt Bell; but the resemblance to Annette was clear from the portrait. So, what if her father's first wife had been Annette's sad grandmother? If the little half-brother she had never known had grown up to be Annette's father? If, in a hitherto entirely concealed romantic, royalist youth, the steady American Friend Alistair Wiston had fathered the august Monsieur Lavigne-Brillac?

Putting it out of her mind, she vaulted the stile into the lane running downhill to the Crosses, and returned her thoughts to Charlotte and her resolution to go back to Bristol. The plan was more than a little wild. The journey would be difficult, and it was not certain that Charlotte would be as welcome as she expected. But Jude had heard good things about the British abolitionists from their connections in New England. On balance, it seemed a good decision, if only the young woman could succeed in escaping undetected.

And she did. On Tuesday morning, at first light, Jude looked out of her bedroom window to see Charlotte appear in the front yard of the Two Crosses, wearing one of Annette's plainer dresses and a broad-brimmed straw hat. She must have walked out of the gates of Waldon Hall in the darkness before even the kitchen maids were stirring, following the high road until it brought her to the inn. Jude had spoken the previous evening to William Jones, who had advised on the route: after Ludlow, it would be a matter of the daily waggon down the border. Charlotte was handed into the coach by the imperturbable Noah; apart from a crate of fancy doves being shipped from Bacheldre to Chepstow, she was the solitary inside passenger.

Annette had not quite thought the plan through, she realised – at least, not from her own perspective. She came down that morning to find Aunt Honorine in full flow.

'She is gone! Gone! How *dare* she? A girl like that! Where is she? Madame, what have you done with her?' She stood in the breakfast room, amidst the cooling eggs and mutton chops, clutching her silken veil at the throat and raising her right arm to heaven; for all the world, Annette thought, like a rather portly tragic heroine from one of Peggy's dramas. Annette took one look and ducked back out of the room before she could be seized upon.

But she did not escape the consequences. After the Abbess had been escorted back to her room, and a sweep of the grounds instituted which found no trace of Charlotte, Lady Waldon sent for Annette.

'If she has left us, then so be it,' she said. 'I make no doubt she had her reasons. But she should have told the Lady Abbess where she was going. You must see that?' She fixed Annette with the bird-like stare. 'You should tell me what you know, Annette. Where has she gone?'

'I am sorry, Madame,' Annette said, 'but I cannot. It is not mine to tell.'

She maintained her refusal as the consequences of Charlotte's disappearance hardened into place. The Abbess needed constant attention. Peggy was not enough – indeed, she was dismissed as clumsy and rude, and never to answer her bell again – and Annette had to sit by her and listen to her outpourings of rage and, increasingly, of an irrational fear. Then came the *coup de grâce*: around midday a gaping footman appeared at the door to say that Sir Charles wished to see them both in the drawing room.

He was standing on the hearth rug – centre stage, as Peggy would no doubt have put it – with an opened letter in his hand. His wife was already there; she drew the Abbess to a fireside chair, then took Annette's arm, leading her to a sofa and sitting her down at her side; she was tense as a harp string, though Annette could not tell whether she was terribly worried and concerned, or simply excited.

Sir Charles surveyed his audience. 'I have news of consequence to impart,' he began.

Annette had to suppress a sudden giggle that rose in her throat. What *now*? Surely there had been drama enough for one day! Sir Charles looked at her, and she closed her lips firmly. He turned to Aunt Honorine.

'I have received a letter, Madame,' he said, 'a letter from

France. From your esteemed kinsman.'

The Abbess, sitting in an attitude of pious despair, straightened slightly, and turned her monumental head towards him.

Annette froze, her heart in her mouth.

'Monsieur Lavigne-Brillac has at last received our letter.' He glanced towards his wife. 'How long ago was it you wrote, my dear?' Giving her no time to answer, he swept on. 'He was most pleased to hear from us. Yes, indeed.'

Then he looked at Annette, who bit her lip. I will not speak, she thought.

He gave her no opportunity to do so. 'Monsieur is grateful, of course, that we have his daughter here safe. Most grateful. And he thinks, if means can be found, that it would now be safe for her to return.' He looked meaningfully at his wife. 'That is good news, is it not?'

Annette felt that she might choke. She stood up and stared at him. She struggled to find words. 'But how can I?' she managed finally. 'How can I go back to France?' Even as she spoke, she knew what the answer would be.

Her aunt's voice was as deep and reverberating, as masterful as ever Annette remembered, all trace of the morning's panic suddenly swept away. She too had risen to her feet. 'You shall go with me, of course!' Crossing herself, she added, 'The hand of God is in this. I see, now, that *le bon Dieu* in His wisdom has brought me here to aid you, my dear.' Her eyes gleamed with what looked to Annette like triumph.

They read and reread the single sheet of her father's letter, exclaiming over its battered outside, covered in broken wax and marks, scrawls and nameless stains. Inside, there was much that Annette did not understand, as when her father wrote that the countryside was 'much more settled' (after what?) and that the harvest would 'no doubt soon be begun'. It is September, she thought; the wheat should all be home and housed by now. Whatever had been happening? And then, he was full of praise for Cousin Henri and his *Garde Nationale*, for their 'grip upon the city'. What on earth? But Annette could not say any of this.

It would only appear that she was finding fault, trying to get out of going home. And it was horribly obvious to her that, for their own individual reasons, everyone wanted her gone. Lady Waldon had never forgiven her tryst in Berkeley Square; while Sir Charles, having willingly played patron for a time to the 'poor *emigrés*', was clearly relieved to be freed of the rebellious Annette and her awkward aunt, to say nothing of the uninvited and now disappeared Charlotte.

As he left the room to go about his daily business, he patted Annette's hand. 'All's well that ends well, my dear, is it not?'

The letter made no mention of the Lady Honorine, despite being dated after she had vanished from the convent; nonetheless, she embraced it as a personal directive from her family, if not from heaven. Annette quickly realised that her aunt must see the delivery of an erring daughter back into her father's hands as a way to reconcile herself to her brother and make her own position secure again. The Abbess was swelling into her former insufferable self-satisfaction as every moment passed. Pretty soon, she would have them understand that she had been only waiting for this letter, or something like it, since it was clearly meant to be that her brother would put his trust in her to rescue his dear daughter. Repatriating, patronising, guiding and shaping the dear daughter was to be her chief care and concern now – and probably for the rest of her life. 'Which will not perhaps be long,' she added, casting her eyes to heaven. 'But, His will be done.'

Annette was speechless.

At last, well into the afternoon, Lady Waldon remembered an appointment to visit a neighbour, and Aunt Honorine stalked away to her room, intimating that she was going to read the Office. What this actually meant, as Charlotte had explained to Annette, was that the Abbess wanted a glass of the brandy she was keeping beside her bed.

Annette rang for Peggy to fetch her hat and they escaped into the windswept garden.

'I won't go, Peggy!' she burst out as soon as they were clear of the house. 'I can't! Oh, what can I do? They will send me off with her! Help me!'

Peggy linked her arm in Annette's. 'Bless you, Miss, we can stop their little games!' she said. 'Come this way, now.' She steered her mistress down a path towards the stable gate. 'They might be watching,' she explained, 'so just come this way first, and then we can cut back to your little bower. He won't be here yet, surely.'

But he was. They rounded the last semi-stripped row of late raspberries – startling a cloud of pigeons out of the fruit, dripping scarlet from their beaks – and Annette saw a figure in the arbour ahead.

Jude had arrived early because she had something to say: she had reserved herself a place on the mail coach to Ludlow in two days' time. From there she would take the Flyer, which they assured her left the Feathers every morning at eight, and she could be at the lawyers' office in the Middle Temple when they opened for business on Monday. She must tell Annette all this, gently, today.

But when she saw Annette's face, her own news was swallowed up in alarm. Annette threw herself into Jude's arms, clinging desperately. 'They are sending me back!' she said. 'You must take me away, *now*!'

Over her shoulder, Jude saw that Peggy was still there. Usually, she vanished discreetly as soon as Jude arrived, but here she was, standing between them and the house, a picture of concern – and big with importance.

''Tis true, sir,' she said. 'Miss's father has writ a letter, it come this morning, sir, and she's to go home directly, so she is. That Reverend Mother is to take her.'

Annette was gripping Jude's coat. 'That's why we have to go, now!' she said. 'She'll force me to go with her, whatever it takes. I know she will. Oh, please!'

Jude held her, shushing, her heart in her mouth, and looked at Peggy for help; but the girl was nodding furiously.

''Tis true, sir, she will. She's seen her way to get back on terms with her family, if you ask me. They'll be on the next boat out of Bristol harbour.'

Annette started to cry.

Eventually they sat down and talked it through. Jude told them she was bound for London soon, and could not stay in spite of what had happened – indeed, it was the more urgent, now, that she should go. Annette wanted to go with her, of course; but between them Jude and Peggy made her understand that this would provoke pursuit, would make them more noticeable, and would make it harder to escape from the Waldons' people in London and go on from there together.

'But as soon as you are in London, sir, you can apply for special licence and be married!' cried Peggy. 'Then they cannot stop you!'

She was puzzled by their insistence that no licence, however special, existed to cover their particular case. After a moment of confusion, Annette said it was something to do with neither of them being British subjects; Jude gratefully agreed.

Peggy raised her shoulders and her eyebrows, but did not pursue the matter.

Jude went hurriedly on. She would come back, she insisted, once she had her inheritance in hand, and then she and Annette could go away, to a place where no one could follow or find them. Until then, Annette must be patient.

Annette was silent. It was Peggy who said, 'Where, then? Where shall she wait?'

Jude turned to Annette. 'You are quite sure you cannot stay here?'

Annette looked up into her face. 'I swear to you, I would not be here when you returned.'

'I see.' Jude had been thinking furiously, but only one solution had come to her. 'I will take you to Lucy Weaver,' she said. 'You recall? The old woman, up the hill, where my aunt used to live? I think she will give you shelter.'

The stable clock struck four. Annette stood up, drawing them both after her. 'So, I must waste no time. It must be tonight. Will you wait here for me, my darling? Wait by the gate until dark. I'll go in to dinner as if nothing is happening. But we will pack.' She took Peggy's hand. 'Peggy will pack for me. And as soon as I can get away, I will come to the gate, and we can go.'

It was near dark when the gate finally opened. It was Peggy who emerged, to deliver Annette's luggage. 'She's going to wear the French dress she arrived in,' she hissed. 'Better for walking. And her old boots. Lucky we kept them! Lady W would have thrown them out, to be sure.'

Jude took the portmanteau – heavy, she thought, for a few weeks' accumulation of shopping, even in London. But looking at Peggy, who was smiling with cheerful satisfaction at the conspiracy, a worrying thought came to Jude. 'Will you be safe yourself?' she asked the girl. 'They won't turn you away, out here in the wilds, so far from home?'

'Ah, don't you worry, sir. I'll be grand. They won't know I know anything about anything, will they? I shall be *so* surprised in the morning! And who's to wait on the old carrion crow and talk French to her, now both her chicks have flown?' She grinned, a flash of teeth in the gathering gloom. 'But I shan't be long with them. They'll go back to town, or I'll give warning – I might make them pay my fare, to get me to stay until they can get shut of the Reverend Mother. Never you worry over me, sir.' Tossing her curls and grinning, she began to back towards the gate.

Jude put her hand into her pocket, but Peggy shook her head vehemently.

'Oh come, Peggy, at least let me help you on your way, as you have helped us on ours,' Jude said. Catching the girl's hand in the gloom, she pressed what she hoped was half a guinea into her palm.

Peggy dropped a little bob, opened the gate and stepped through. Then, suddenly, she turned back. 'You wear the breeches better than Mrs Jordan,' she said. 'Though you're not half as pretty.'

The gate ground on the stones, and she was gone.

Jude was grateful to have the portmanteau to sit on, having

no idea how noisome or indeed noxious the night-time bugs of a Shropshire lane might be. She had plenty of time to think about Peggy's parting shot as she watched a huge harvest moon rise over the shoulder of the wooded hill, and waited for Annette to escape.

The moon hung over the valley like a great silver dish, its cold light streaming in at the window where Lucy stood. It was almost as bright as day; every plant and stone cast a clear-edged shadow. A hunting owl called from behind the house. The old cat had stayed out tonight and was hunting somewhere, too. Lucy had pulled down the bed, but not yet got into it. For most of the year, she rose at dawn and slept when it grew dark, but she knew that sleep would not come when there was such a moon. Turning from the window, she went in search of a warmer shawl.

The chest that stood next to her bed contained all her small wardrobe: the smell of dried lavender rose from it as she pushed up the lid. Underneath a neatly folded cap and shift were the warm stockings and quilted petticoat she would soon need to see her through the winter. Under those was the heavy knitted shawl she was looking for; as she pulled at it, she caught sight of the grey woollen dress that lay at the bottom of the chest. She had never worn it, but kept it carefully, shaking it out each summer and replacing rosemary and cloves in its folds to keep the moth away. On that summer day long ago when they had taken Bron from the prison, a Quaker lady had given her this dress so that she could appear before the judge with some dignity. Bron had never worn it again – it was too ladylike for a farmer – but Lucy had laid it away, a memento of the miracle of Bron's release and of the unlooked-for kindness of a stranger. She touched it now. The past was always near, these days.

She closed the lid and, with some difficulty, hauled herself up from the floor. As she pulled the shawl round her shoulders, she heard a noise outside. She froze, her heart quickening. There it was again. Footsteps. Who had come into her garden in the night? She moved towards the door and took hold of the old pruning hook.

The footsteps were nearer now and she thought she heard voices. Leaning her slight weight on the door in an attempt to hold it shut, she shouted, 'Who's there?'

'It's Jude. We need your help.'

Lucy let out a shaky breath. When she opened the door, two figures stood on the threshold: Jude, and a woman in a cloak and hood.

'I hope we didn't frighten you,' Jude was saying anxiously. 'I've brought Annette. She has run away and we had nowhere else to go...'

Lucy stepped back to let them in.

The young woman – Annette – pushed back her hood and smiled.

And Lucy stood, dumbstruck, as the ghost of Bell Wiston walked into her cottage.

46

Jude had no time to notice Lucy's reaction. Her concern over Annette's sodden shoes and scratched arms – the brambles had caught them more than once – was reinforced by a powerful urge to get under cover and hide all lights. Of course, they were not being followed, but she hurried inside nonetheless, and shut the door as firmly as she could before she turned. Annette was standing in the middle of the little room, in the light of the fire which Lucy was now stirring into life. Her petticoats were muddy and her wet curls clung to her cheeks, but she was still so beautiful that it took Jude's breath away. Jude tugged the wet cloak from her shoulders, stroking her hair, and smiled reassurance.

'Bring that here.' Lucy took the cloak and hung it by the fire, but her eyes were on Annette still; she looked almost afraid.

Jude said, 'We are sorry to burst upon you, Dame, but we are…'

'Yes, yes. It's well enough – you are welcome,' Lucy said distractedly, grasping each of them by the elbow and pushing them on to the settle beside the fire. 'Sit there and dry your feet.' She took the chair at the other side of the hearth, still staring at Annette as if she'd seen a ghost. At last, she said softly, half to herself, 'But who are you, girl? Where did you come from?'

Annette looked startled, but replied politely, as if she were in some grand drawing-room: 'My father's name is Philippe Lavigne-Brillac, and I am named Annette, for his mother.'

Since Lucy continued to stare at her without speaking, and Jude did not come to her rescue, Annette plunged on. 'I come from France. But I have English blood, too, through my grandmother.

She married an Englishman exiled with King James. But he had to leave France, and she returned alone to her family. It is a sad tale, is it not?'

Lucy was alert. She turned a questioning frown on Jude.

'Yes,' said Jude. 'I had thought of it myself.' She turned to Annette. 'It seems to me, my darling, that my father had two families. And that he and your dashing young grandfather were – well, one and the same person.'

Annette gasped. There was a moment of silence before she said, 'Oh! but that is wonderful!' Smiling, she reached for the chain round Jude's neck. She pulled out the locket, sprang it open and looked hard at the likeness of Isabella. 'So – this lady is my... some kind of cousin?'

'Well, yes, a relation of some kind, certainly,' said Jude. 'A half-great-aunt, I think...'

On the other side of the hearth, Lucy began to laugh. ''Tis no wonder, then, that you look so like her!' She chuckled at this joke until she had to wipe her eyes on the hem of her petticoat.

'Yes, yes, I do! And that is because we are kinsfolk!' cried Annette delightedly. She turned to Jude. 'And so are you and I, my darling! And so this is where I belong.'

Eventually, Lucy shook herself and turned again to Jude. 'Cousins you may be,' she said, 'but you have not told me what brings you here now. Running away, is it?'

'Well, yes, I am afraid it is,' Jude said. 'We are running away from the Waldons, and from Annette's *other* aunt, a real live aunt who is here and now, and is intending to take her back to France. It's complicated –'

'I dare say,' said Lucy, 'and I don't need to know. You're both welcome here, anygates.'

'It's only Annette who needs to hide with you,' Jude said, 'while I go to London. I have to claim my inheritance – I think I told you that was what I came to England for in the first place? I have to see some London lawyers about it. And then –' she squeezed Annette's hand – 'I can come back for her.'

Lucy considered this information for a moment, her head on

one side. Something like mischief came into her eyes. 'And are these lawyers expecting you, *Mister* Jude?'

Annette's hand tightened on Jude's, but Jude had thought of this. 'No, of course they are not. And that's something I will have to see to. I will need to be Miss Rebecca Wiston. We have some money, so I can buy clothes, I expect – the difficulty will be getting hold of them without making myself very conspicuous. But I shall manage somehow.' She turned to smile at Annette.

'Oh!' Lucy exclaimed, rising from her seat. 'How everything works together, to be sure!' She turned away into the darkness under the overhanging platform and bent to something there. 'Look what showed itself just now,' she said. 'Come and lend me a hand.'

Jude heaved up the lid of the chest, and Lucy burrowed in it, finally pulling out a bundle of cloth that wafted a soft miasma of lavender and spices. She shook it out. It was a grey woollen gown.

'Try it,' Lucy said. 'I think it will fit.'

It did. After a moment's hesitation, Jude stepped away from the light and stripped to her drawers, then thrust her arms into the narrow sleeves and pulled the stiff folds of the dress round her. It was old-fashioned in its cut and drab in colour, but unworn, firm in its stitching, the skirt smooth. It had clearly been made for a woman considerably taller than Lucy but was, if anything, a trifle short for Jude. Otherwise, it fitted well. Jude fastened the bodice and turned self-consciously to her audience. What would her lover think of this sudden appearance of Rebecca?

Annette gazed wonderingly, but did not speak.

Lucy nodded her satisfaction. 'With a good white kerchief, you will do well,' she said.

'Thank you,' Jude said after a moment. 'I will be sure to bring it back safely.' She retreated into the shadows, took off the dress and got back into her shirt and breeches. When she sank back onto the settle, reaching for Annette's arm, she could not look at her.

There was a silence. They all stared into the fire. Annette was drooping with tiredness and Jude felt exhausted herself.

For a long moment Lucy stared at them, until Jude felt her cheeks begin to redden. Then the old woman shrugged. 'Come, my chicks, never look so wild. Are you warmer now? To bed with you, then.' She pointed up the little ladder. 'You'll find it dry, but no one has slept there for an age – shake out the spiders before you lay yourselves down.'

The straw mattress with its feather bed and quilt proved to be both dry and sweet-smelling.

'Though I could sleep on bare boards, I am so tired,' said Annette, peeling off her gown. 'Since I no longer have Peggy, will you unlace me?'

They were speaking in whispers, aware of Lucy still moving about downstairs.

'What did you think?' Jude hissed, putting her mouth to Annette's ear as she loosened her stays.

'About what?' asked Annette, shrugging them off and turning to face her.

'The dress – seeing me –' Jude stopped.

'But I *have* seen you, my darling!' Annette replied. She laughed. 'All of you! Come now.' She pulled Jude down onto the feather bed and leaned across to kiss her. 'Clothes make no difference whatsoever. Except, *dear cousin,*' she smiled into Jude's eyes, 'that I do greatly prefer you without them.'

Jude came to herself somewhere a few miles beyond Worcester, on a particularly muddy stretch of the turnpike where the wheels sank axle-deep, and the six hairy horses strained and blew in the dank air. Another jolt, another sick swerve of the sky before her, dragged her to the surface from a deep reverie. Ever since she had taken up her perch between the lumpy luggage to her left and the old pig farmer squeezed on her right (no mistaking his calling, though he said not a word), she had been sunk into herself, revisiting that night at Brynsquilver in Annette's arms. Its bubbling urgency had filled her again and she relived their gasping breath, the triumphal arc of their total reabsorption into each other, as if they rose together to make a single creature, all sparking surfaces and inevitable, swooping, silky curves. Her blood had warmed again, remembering it.

But that inner warmth had faded now, and she raised her head into the pale light of an English afternoon, a white sky blown about with leaves and ragged flights of crows. She drew a deep breath and looked around her. She was amazed at how much had changed since that magical trip through the ripening summer, only a few weeks before. Now that summer was clearly over, and England was no longer a territory either surprising or particularly strange. She gazed out at the half-bare fruit trees and sodden thatches, watched the slow curl of smoke from cottage chimneys and the mist lying on the fields; but her thoughts, on this journey, were less about where she was than who she was. Around her, everything had moved on from that first stagecoach journey; but the greater change was within.

When she accepted the old dress, she had thought, at first, only about how her men's boots would show beneath it, and whether she would need to buy a jacket as well as some linen. But then, as she stood there transformed – into what? – she had seen Annette's face. What did her beloved see? Questions she had kept at bay rose up and could no longer be ignored. Their time together at Brynsquilver had reassured her that no outward appearance mattered between them, not at heart. But how would it be, in their days together as well as their nights, living here in England as man and wife – but not man, no wifehood? How would it be? She had felt strange in the dress, though it had fitted her well enough. She had sound reasons to resume that skin, to be Miss Rebecca Wiston, heiress to as yet unknown houses and lands; even, perhaps, to take up a position in the society of Coalbrookdale as an American descendant returned to her family. Were there in fact any of her mother's relatives still alive, still living there? She had no idea. And did she want to walk in to another Meeting, to face the politely curious householders and put off the calculating approaches of aspirant men, to assert the right to independence and freedom that a respectable position – and money – could give her? Or did she want to assert something else, something larger, finer? Her total freedom from their expectations of a lady, her claim to be Mr Jude Wiston, gentleman – even though it was not true? If she stayed there in Madeley, that would be difficult – and dangerous. It would mean a lifelong pretence. Would it be a pretence, though? she wondered. Is it not nearer the truth, if they should think of me as a man, rather than as a woman? But they would not understand that, when it came to the test. She could imagine moments of exposure – of accident or illness, or just the sudden surprise of a stranger hearing her high voice, or some sly underling staring at her perpetually smooth cheeks. Perhaps it was not, in the end, what other people thought that mattered. She stared down the road ahead.

It was scarcely light as Lucy blew up the fire and set the water to boil, all the while thinking about her unexpected guest, the young Frenchwoman who looked so unnervingly like Bell Wiston. She had wondered if the noise of the poker and bellows might wake Annette, but there was no sound from above. The girl must still be fast asleep. She had looked pale and tired enough last night. She and Jude had had only the two nights together before the coach carried Jude away, and Lucy doubted they had slept much. Well, there would be plenty of time to rest now. Lucy had no clear idea when they would see Jude again: a return journey to London and a visit to a lawyer's office might take as little as a week or two, but who knew what complications and delays might intervene? It was nearly Michaelmas already and the weather was growing rougher; wind and rain would soon make the roads more difficult. Meanwhile, this refugee from foreign parts was Lucy's secret responsibility.

Even though Annette had not stirred, the cat knew she was there. It stood at the bottom of the ladder, ears cocked, lashing its tail.

'Just as well your climbing days are over, you old villain,' Lucy told it. 'Or you'd be up there on that feather bed, bothering her,

I know!' She scooped it up and pulled gently at its ears. 'Let the child sleep and mend. There will be plenty of time for talk.'

Certainly, there had been little time for conversation the night the pair arrived. Annette had said very little, except for apologies and thanks. The girl had the manners of a lady, anygates, Lucy thought. The lovers had made their farewells in the garden; from the window, Lucy had watched Annette standing at the stile long after Jude had disappeared from sight. She had come indoors with tears on her cheeks, and now was no doubt pining for her absent love. How painful it was to be young! Perhaps old age had its compensations, after all. Lucy put the bakestone over the fire and went for meal to make griddle cakes. The other thing she remembered about youth was that it was always hungry.

For a second, Annette thought she heard Jacqueline's feet on the stairs. Then she opened her eyes to the dusty floor and daub walls of the cottage, and was back in the present. The noise had been Lucy moving about below. Annette turned onto her back and stared at the roof a few feet above her head. She had slept in many places since she left her turret chamber in the château at Brillac, but never in one like this. There was no ceiling here, so that she was looking straight at the rafters and laths that supported the thatch. A spider was at work building its web between the cut ends of a handful of straws. She watched it for a few minutes, unwilling to abandon the warmth of the bed. She could hear Lucy downstairs, talking to the cat, then the smell of something cooking. She should get up. But she did not move.

She still felt a little shy of Lucy. It wasn't that she was frightened of the old woman's sharp tongue – it hadn't taken her long to realise that Lucy's waspish manner covered a quick understanding and a kind heart – but she was not like anyone Annette had met before. Not the servants on her father's estate, or the turbulent working people of Bordeaux, or the hurrying, quick-spoken Londoners. Lucy was something apart; watchful, self-sufficient, mysterious. She was very old; yet she lived alone, beyond help or rescue. How could she bear it? Annette tried to imagine what it would be like to live here forever. The idea horrified her. How could anyone survive without conversation, ideas? She had thought the convent bad enough, but at least there she had been able to gather news of the world outside, and to talk sometimes with Charlotte. It was only in the Rue des Cordeliers that she had felt truly alive, caught up in the flow of new ideas and passionate feelings. Even at Waldon there had been contact, however tenuous, with politics and society; here, there was nothing. It was extraordinary to think that Jude's aunt, a lady by birth, had spent most of her life in this same cottage, and ended up belonging to the place so thoroughly that she was still remembered with affection in the district. Annette shook her head vehemently. She could never belong in a place like this – it would drive her mad.

Where *did* she belong? She had always assumed that she was a part of Brillac; but she was no longer welcome in her father's house. That life was gone, forever. She had certainly never felt at home in the convent. And, looking back, could she really pretend that either she or Pierre had truly fitted in among the *bourgeois* revolutionaries of Bordeaux? The melancholy truth was, she thought, that she belonged nowhere. Except with Jude. She thought longingly of the night before Jude went away. That was where she belonged: in Jude's arms, Jude's bed, wherever in the world that was. It was only a day since Jude had departed, and already the waiting was unbearable.

She *must* do something to pass the time, or she would go mad. So far, Lucy seemed not to need much help around the house and, in any case, Annette had few domestic skills. Perhaps she could use the time to look over the journal she had been keeping, and to write? It might do her good to order her thoughts about the momentous events in Bordeaux and in Paris, and perhaps it might interest others. If the Waldons were anything to go by, English people were endlessly curious about what was going on in France, without really understanding what the unrest was about. Annette, on the other hand, had watched the events from both sides, had wrestled with the politics and seen the suffering at first hand. If the young Madame de Staël could find a publisher, why should not she? Pleased with this idea, she rolled out of bed and started to pull on her clothes. She must ask Lucy, again, how long it would take for Jude to travel to London and return. Then she would somehow acquire ink and paper, and set to work.

47

In the end, it all depended on Aunt Isabella.

Jude walked into Pump Court, off Middle Temple Lane, in Bron's grey gown. Its outmoded cut and dowdy colour were, she had decided, perfectly suited to the colonial Quaker lady the lawyers were expecting. She announced herself to the doorman at Number 3 with head held high, and sat straight-backed under the curious stares of the law clerks to whom she had told her business, waiting until old Mr Speke could see her. He came forth at last from an inner room, a spidery little person in a grey wig and a high stock, and ushered her in to a fusty space where a single small window blinked slantwise upon the only piece of furniture, a tall desk. He took up his position of authority behind the desk, and only then turned and met her gaze.

'We have received, Madam, a letter from Salem, from a Mr Fell, and so we have had some expectation of your arrival.' He paused for effect. 'Or, as perhaps I should more correctly say, of the arrival of Miss Wiston.'

Jude watched him, but said nothing.

Clasping his hands behind him over the tails of his black coat, he continued, 'However, dear lady – speaking without offence, I hope – what I have to establish is, if I mistake not, that you are indeed she.'

There was a pause. Speke stood, and nodded, and hummed a little, until a clerk followed them into the room bearing papers: a single sheet, opened; and another, folded and sealed. Speke took them and placed them on the desk. Smoothing out the open sheet, he applied his mind and his spectacles to what John Fell had said.

Jude waited.

'I understand,' the little man said, eventually, 'that you have met with considerable difficulties in your passage here. I am sorry.' He looked up, finger on the page. 'And all your baggage, and so forth, all means of identification, were lost at sea.'

It was not a question, so Jude nodded, but held her peace.

'You left Salem, I believe, in March. Bound for – ah?' he looked at her.

Ah, thought Jude. I see. This is to be a game of questions. 'Jamaica, sir. Aboard the *Robin*. We were wrecked off the coast of the island of Cuba. It is possible that news of the wreck reached Salem, but then they would have known no more of what had befallen me, until my letters from Bordeaux arrived.'

'Yes.' He looked at her, head to toe, and cocked his head a little. 'Mr, ah,' he glanced down (for effect, she thought), 'Mr Fell informs me that you have the distinction to belong to one of the oldest families in Salem. The house of – ah?'

'Of Samuel and Barnabas Wiston, mercantile shipping. Our father, Alistair Wiston, came there from England fifty years ago.' She raised her chin, looking down her nose a little. If what he wants is pompous self-assurance, she thought, I can do that, yes indeed.

'I am sure it is a well-known house, in its own sphere. But therein lies the rub, I am afraid. For very many people might know of the loss of this ship, and of the supposed death of its unfortunate passengers. A little probing on anyone's part could reveal what you have told me. And so, my dear lady, before we can proceed to the bequest of Richard Farley, in which I am, as you know, charged with a responsibility, I must needs ask you to demonstrate that you are indeed that same Miss Wiston, of Salem. If you would be so good.'

Jude felt a shiver of fear. So near… Surely, he could not refuse to believe her now? Struggling to appear calm, she asked, 'But how might I do that? As we have said, all my papers and possessions were lost at sea.'

Mr Speke smiled a small, tight smile. Was he embarrassed,

Jude wondered, or amused? 'I am given to understand, Madam, that you might still be in possession of – let us say, an amulet? A surviving token that might attest to your *bona fides*? Mr Fell,' he tapped the page, 'mentions such an item as perhaps having been saved, when all else was lost?'

Oh, bless John Fell! Jude raised her hands and pulled on the locket's chain until she could extract it from the high neck of Bron's gown. She lifted the chain slowly over her head, clicked open the cover, and held it out. 'My aunt, sir,' she said. 'The Lady Isabella Wiston.'

She left the Middle Temple an hour later with a bundle of legal papers: if not the titles to the properties in Shropshire, then at least affidavits and indentures that would eventually, on payment of the right fees, put those into her hands; and two letters. One was from Bartram and Speke, addressed to a Mr Frederick Cranage of High Street Madeley, the agent who was to induct her into the properties. The other, still sealed, was addressed to her in the neat lawyer's hand of John Fell.

She could not open it at once. She thrust the letter and the other papers into her bag, and set off to the Bull and Mouth. The Shrewsbury Flyer, calling at Coalbrookdale for Madeley, left from their yard. Walking was not so easy now: striding out in her breeches through the London streets she had felt invisible, invincible; now every eye seemed upon her. At least her too-short skirts did not drag in the mud. She fixed her attention on the ladylike manner in which she must walk, and on the direction as she had memorised it. Within half an hour, and without too much deviation or casting about, she sighted the inn's high gateway.

Sitting in a dusty corner of the busy coaching office, she contemplated her next move. Until now, she had assumed that she was simply going to get herself to Madeley by the quickest route; but there could be something in John Fell's letter that would throw that into doubt. Perhaps she would have to go home to Salem? That would mean engaging Speke to liquidate her assets, whatever they were, collecting Annette, and taking ship before winter set in. A lump of panic rose in her throat. She shook her head at the impossibility and opened the letter.

It was heartfelt, but short and to the point. John Fell was delighted to hear of her preservation and hoped that she could now come into her rightful inheritance with minimum interferences. He trusted he had helped her to do that, by what he had told the London lawyer; he hoped she would not think such an intervention presumptuous. She smiled. He trusted, further, that the property would help her to a future amongst her new friends. As to old friends… Jude looked up, breathed deeply, and bent her eyes again to the page. As to old friends, he was sorry to have to bring her the news that her brother Barnabas had been laid to rest at midsummer. She looked up again, momentarily blinded, but she was too concerned to know the rest to pause for long. It was exactly as she might have expected. John Fell had told Samuel that she was alive, was in England, had written – it seemed that he had not been told in return that she had written to her brothers, too. Perhaps her second letter had miscarried? Somehow, she doubted it. And now her brother Samuel, apparently, sent no message. The letter concluded with other Salem news: Tabitha throve, and now styled her establishment an hotel; Abraham Brewer had married a widow. John Fell remained her devoted well-wisher and friend, and wished her every success in her new life.

Jude sat back and closed her eyes. The waters had closed over her past. There was no reason for her to return to America. She could go forward. She rose and approached the counter. 'I understand the Shrewsbury Flyer leaves in the morning?' she said.

The fire whispered and ticked; the eaves dripped; there was no other sound. Annette stood by the window, looking miserably at the sodden garden. The rain that had fallen steadily all morning had finally stopped and there was no wind. Lucy had told her that Brynsquilver meant 'a looking-out place on a hill' in Welsh, and that on a clear day you could indeed see into Wales – but not today, when the cloud was down over the hills and the cottage seemed to float in its own world, disconnected from everywhere else. Annette was alone. Lucy had gone to the inn, to see old friends and to gather news. She could not take Annette with her; no one was to know she was staying here, lest the news found its way to Waldon Hall. It was important, Lucy had explained, that no one should suspect anything out of the ordinary. So, she would be sure to make her customary visit every week, until the snow stopped her. Annette had been horrified by this last remark. She had no idea when snow might arrive in this dark, empty country, but surely, *surely*, she would not still be here by winter? Jude had only gone to London and would come back soon to take her away. She pictured Jude's back disappearing down the lane on the morning she left. Panic seized her. What if she never returned?

Before she could frighten herself further, she spotted Lucy climbing the stile and coming fast up the path, her face set in a frown. Annette opened the door to let her in and Lucy immediately turned to make it fast behind her.

Annette helped her drop the heavy wooden bar into its resting place. 'What is it?' she asked. 'What is happening? Is someone coming?'

'Not right now. But they might. Come away from the window.' Lucy pulled Annette further into the room, and only then began to unwind her damp shawl and shake out her petticoats. 'You have not gone out at all?' she demanded. 'Not shown yourself? You are certain?'

Annette assured her that she had not, and Lucy drew a long breath. 'They are looking for you,' she said. 'Joey told me the tale – he knows nothing of you, of course, but they see few strangers on foot at the Crosses and so he remembered it. A man came, two days ago, looking for news of a runaway lady, Joey said. He was asking if anyone had seen her – had she taken a coach, and suchlike questions. He was from Waldon Hall, for sure. He said it had not been many days since the young lady had been missed, and if she had not boarded a mail coach, then she might not have got far. He said she might be alone, or perhaps with a companion.' Unexpectedly, Lucy laughed. 'He didn't say a man, but that was what he meant, you may be sure!' Then her face grew serious again and she grasped Annette's wrist. 'They are hunting for you, child. We must take even more care than before. No more standing at that window!'

A knot of fear settled in Annette's stomach. The Waldons were searching for her. Surely no one would come here? But Lucy was well known – anyone might casually send an enquirer up the lane to ask a wise woman what she knew. Annette sank onto the settle. She must not go into the garden or look out from the window. She had already been in hiding; now, she felt as if she was in prison. When, oh when would Jude come and take her away?

48

Jude boarded the Shrewsbury Flyer early next morning; it was near dawn of the day after that before it came into Coalbrookdale. For some miles the turnpike road had inclined a little upwards from the Midland plain, with the light ahead increasing as they went. The sun was rising, but its pale light was no competition for the red, flickering glow into which the coach and horses now plunged. It was unlike any dawn that Jude had ever seen; as they crested the rise and began to descend into a river valley, it became clear to her that the Dale was lit up, not by the light of heaven, but by the fires of man. They danced all around the turnpike, near and far, lighting up the sky. The road under the wheels of the coach felt new, smoothly surfaced and wide enough for easy passing; but to either side strange mounds and crags rose up against the coming day. Where the road levelled a little and ran by the flank of the natural hillside, Jude could see that doors had been cut in it. Pathways strewn with cinders snaked out from the doors, each one marked with parallel lines of wood or iron. As they passed one of these openings, a low waggon piled with rock – or coal? – emerged, trundling along fast in a straight line. There were ground-laid metal rails, Jude now saw, to guide the waggon and to ease the passage of wheels on the stony ground. A master-stroke of engineering; she had never seen anything like it. Ahead of them, tall black chimneys shot out smoke and the fires burned, elongated, moving baskets of tangled orange streaks against the sky. Smoke hung overhead like a gritty blanket, lit up from below. The coachman began to curse and cough as he hauled savagely to keep the horses on the road.

Jude had not slept in a bed for three nights. The tall new building at the foot of the hill was, she realised as the coach rumbled to a halt, her destination. She climbed down in a daze, hardly noticing the river or its brand-new bridge, seeing only the glowing open door of the inn. She had little recollection, later, of what she had said to the inn's people, whose English sounded foreign to her ears, or of where she was taken. She woke four hours later from a bottomless chasm of sleep to find full daylight streaming across her face from the tall modern window, and sat up abruptly. Beside her narrow pallet was a china ewer and a surprisingly soft towel to refresh her face.

She found a stairway down to the chilly entrance hall, where a factotum in a black suit accepted her half-guinea for the room and listened to her request for directions onwards. As he translated her foreign vowels, he nodded sharply.

'Maister Cranage, is it? Reet enough. Tek a seat, wonna?'

His gesture, more than his unintelligible words, directed her to a sofa with spindle legs and plush cushioning. She sat. The man called for a boy, and the boy tipped his cap and ran; and then she was ignored. After a while, she schooled herself to calm, and turned her mind to the papers which she had only skimmed through under the eyes of Mr Speke. It seemed she had inherited several cottages, 'with the yards and brewhouses attached' and a stone 'shop'. These buildings all lay in Madeley Wood, a mile or more down river from where she was now. She would be in the agent's hands about their worth, of course, and whatever passed for their arrangements about rent and sale. If he spoke as strangely as this man, she was going to struggle.

But no. In a very short time, it seemed, Mr Cranage appeared, blue-coated and bustling, sweeping in with a blast of bracing, iron-flavoured air, bowing short and flourishing his smart little hat. He was perhaps thirty-five years of age, with a reassuring air of having everything completely under control. His smile of welcome was genuine and warm.

'Miss Wiston! I am delighted! Do please come with me!'

He seized her bag, sweeping her before him out of the door and into a smart conveyance that seemed to Jude little more than a red-painted bucket with lamps, perched high on two thin wheels, shuddering and bouncing behind a shining pony. The boy let go of the pony's head, Cranage flourished a whip, and they sprang away.

'I am so pleased you are come, Madam!' he said, turning the pony into another well-laid road and flicking the air in sheer enthusiasm. 'I had heard of course from Mr Speke, months ago, and through him from your lamented kinsman Mr Farley – with whom, of course, my father was acquainted.'

Jude was warmed by this link to Cousin Richard. 'You are a local man, then Mr Cranage? Only – forgive me – you do not quite sound like one.'

'Hah! Indeed, Madam – born in the Dale, but bred in Bristol and London. My father was forward-looking. He saw the need for wider views, contacts beyond, out in the world. He had visions, my father; it is only a pity that he is gone, before this day, when all is coming to fruition, here. This is the moment, in the Dale! Indeed it is.' He swept out his whip arm to take in the river, running now darkly beside them, and the massive new-built wharf that divided it from the road.

Much was afoot, indeed. The wharf was lined with deep barges, and men were busy loading them – with coal, Jude thought – something black and heavy, at any rate. There were stacks of timber, and sheds, and a line of waggons. Cranage pointed the other way, towards the rising hillside, and she saw more men, more carts, this time not loading but building. In front of several rows of new, raw-looking cottages ran a long excavation, with a huge heap of spoil and stacks of bricks. Behind it all, over the heads of the toiling labourers, wavered columns of smoke in place of the earlier fires, blackening the midday air.

Cranage turned the pony into a smaller track that wound between the brickstacks and began to climb. They came into the remains of a wood – scrubby land, with a few larger trees, but spaced out, and all with the worn look of much traffic. There was a layer of black dust over the surviving bushes. The track wound downwards again, and they came to first one row of small houses and then a second, running off to the left and steeply down. These looked much older than the brick cottages they had passed. They were made of squares of thin timber framing, with dirty plaster between, and thatched with blackened straw. Cranage drew rein, and the pony willingly stopped, stamping. A gaggle of very small children erupted all around them, their bare feet and legs muddy, their eyes bright with curiosity. Cranage waved his whip and they backed off a little but showed no sign of fear. In Bordeaux, the street children had been beggars almost as soon as they could walk, but Jude saw no outstretched hands here: these infants were simply curious. A man digging in front of the nearest cottage looked up and nodded a greeting, then went back to his digging. The house behind him looked barely weatherproof, but his garden plot was neat and still well-stocked at this late season. A door opened further down the row and a woman emerged. She acknowledged the visitors with a non-committal nod, then called to the children, who pelted away, noisy as a flight of sparrows.

Cranage looked down the muddy rut that turned along in front of the houses. 'Perhaps we should walk from here – that is, if you would like to see them now?'

'See what? Where?' Jude was startled.

'I'm sorry – I was not clear. I mean the cottages and workshop. This is your property, Madam,' he said. 'This is Farley's Rents.'

Jude closed her eyes and swallowed. So much for 'messuages and orchards', she thought. This grimy reality could not be further from her imaginings. But she was to be responsible for this now, and she would see it. 'Very good, Mr Cranage,' she said. 'Please hand me down.'

There were perhaps a dozen cottages, all in need of repair. Beyond them, the ground sloped steeply and soon the path brought them to the bank of a stream – the Washbrook, said Mr Cranage, which ran into the river a little way to the south. A long stone building, low to the ground, ran along the bank. Near it, a few blackened stakes stuck up from the mud. A strange round boat without stem or stern was tied to one of them, and another like it was upended on the path. A youth in a tattered shirt crouched beside the craft, working at it with a bent, tarry brush. He gazed at them without apparently thinking of standing up.

'Coracles,' said Mr Cranage helpfully. 'They are a curious craft, are they not? Quaint. Of another age.'

The sun broke through, shining on the smoothly flowing stream. Further along the bank, an older man was lowering one of the basket-like little boats carefully into the water. Cranage hailed him cheerfully. 'Morning, George. I've just brought Miss Wiston here to see the workshop.' George nodded wordlessly and returned to his task.

Mr Cranage stood back to let Jude go ahead of him, and she walked in through the wide door. Wavering reflections from the water lit up the shadowy interior. Tumbling stacks of withies and split wood took up only part of the shop, which was bigger than she had first realised. The floor under her feet was dry – the roof must be good and sound, she thought. It would be safe for storing all manner of goods, ready for transporting downriver. Excitement sparked and began to grow within her as she saw that there was other business this building might be put to. Her dreams of trading out of Salem had never come to pass, but here – now – she could be her own mistress and speculate as she wished. What was a workshop might be a warehouse. The Washbrook flowed into the Severn, and the broad Severn ran down to Bristol and the sea. She had already seen how fast manufacturing was growing in the Dale. Surely there was room to build a business – and a new life – here! There was a strange, tense silence in her head as she came out into the sun again and gazed, not at an old man and a boy squatting in the mud, but at the future. Her future – hers and Annette's. Something worthwhile to do, and somewhere to do it.

Later, when they sat in his snug office in the broad High Street of Madeley – a neat market town not unlike the picture-book villages Jude had seen across the rural shires – and she was warming her boots cautiously at his sparkling polished-iron fireplace, Mr Cranage admitted that he had intended the sudden view of the muddy dwellings to come as a shock.

'But I never thought you would get down and walk from top to bottom!' he said. 'Never more surprised.' He regarded her with approval. 'I just thought you needed to know, like. What the condition of the property is. Not to be under any misapprehension.'

'To speak honestly, Mr Cranage, I had not known what to expect.' She pictured again the rotten roofs and crumbling mortar of Farley's Rents. 'But now that I have seen them, I can – with your help – plan accordingly.'

Cranage looked at her for a moment, as if judging what more he could say, before continuing, 'I confess I had it in mind that, being a lady, and not from these parts, you might feel… shall I say, sentimental, about such things? The fact is, Miss Wiston, that our people are of an independent nature; they do not take kindly to charity, however well-meant. They do not bow their heads to rank and fortune.'

Jude thought about the men and women she had met since she arrived in the Dale. She had been treated with courtesy, but not deference. The cottagers at Farley's Rents had looked her straight in the eye. She smiled. 'You need have no fear on that score,' she said. 'Like Richard Farley, I was brought up in the Society of Friends. I was taught from childhood that there is something of God in every person, and all are of equal worth to Him. You will not find me "sentimental", Mr Cranage, nor expecting anyone to bow or scrape to me. However,' she sat forward, earnestly, 'it is clear to me that, if I keep them, the cottages will need money spent on them. You will tell me whether I can afford to do that.'

Cranage nodded approvingly. 'They do need work, it is true. But you have some funds available… and, regardless of its present condition, the property is worth, as it happens, a surprising great deal. Oh, yes. The price of land is rising fast hereabouts, and that makes all the difference.' He walked to the desk by the window and began to turn over papers. He looked up, as if a thought had struck him. 'Not sentimental, as you say. But, after this morning,

Madam, if I might venture – would you describe yourself as *enthusiastic*, perhaps?'

Jude hesitated, thinking about the whirlwind of emotions she had felt that morning as they explored her property, the shining moment that had come to her in the workshop. At length she said, 'I am an enthusiast for progress, Mr Cranage, just as you are, I believe?'

'You have me right there, Madam! So tell me, what was in your mind this morning? What were your first thoughts about Farley's Rents?'

Jude looked up at him, considering what she should say. Cranage was someone who would see as she saw; she knew that already. She needed to trust him.

'It was not so much about the cottages. They are sadly out of order – not your fault, I am sure, merely the problem of the absent landlord and the cautious agent – but they can be put to rights quite easily. Whereas the building at the end of the rows – at the bottom of the hill, by the Washbrook – it was the workshop that caught my attention,' she said.

'Aye, so I saw,' said Cranage. 'I can see that it would.'

'You said that the coracles were of another age. And quite soon, you tell me, they will be left behind by the progress here along the Severn?'

'They were developed and kept a-going by the need to cross the river,' Cranage said, nodding. 'But now, as you have seen, we can cross by the new iron bridge. It will be the end of George and his lads. And his ancient craft.'

He said it as if in compassion, but Jude saw his mouth quirk to one side. Not a sentimental man, indeed.

She pressed on. 'But no doubt his boat-builders have skills that could be redirected to new work. That seems to be what folk around here are doing, just now? The workshop cries out for a new use. It is a good, capacious building, with a sound roof, plenty of space – and the brook runs into the river, and the river into the sea. It is an ideal place for any number of trades.'

Cranage nodded thoughtfully. 'Indeed, Madam. It is a good

situation, and very convenient for the developments that are in hand – the building of the canal. Which reminds me: there is something I need to tell you about that, now that we are here.' He found the paper he had been looking for and brought it to Jude. 'This letter is but the most recent of several urgent enquiries from Mr Reynolds. He very much wants to buy your leases, to demolish and start anew. He has, as I happen to know, the building of a factory in mind, as well as the wharfs; and, in time, a whole canal basin. He could no doubt be brought to give a very good price indeed.'

Jude was surprised by the strength of her immediate resistance to the idea that she should sell out, but all she said was: 'Well, perhaps. That might indeed be the way forward, in good time. But for the moment, I think I will make use of Farley's Rents and its workshop myself.'

49

Annette sat on a little stool on the hearthstone rubbing at her one remaining brooch – a showy silver piece that was badly tarnished – and worrying, not about Jude, but about Lucy. The old woman was outside despite the cold, doing something or other up round the back of the cottage. At her age, she should not be needing to cut her own wood, or shovel the night-soil from her earth closet, or lord knew what else she was about out there. Did most people have to labour so hard in old age? Annette cast her mind back to the sun-warmed hamlet on the slope behind the château at Brillac, with its straggle of outlying cottages. She had never been inside any of them, but she had the impression they housed large families. Lucy had no family, so she must look after herself. Until she became too old…

'Hullo within? Good day to you, Mistress! Are you at home?'

A man's voice. Annette sprang to her feet.

Someone struck the door with force. 'Is anyone here?'

Annette froze. Now he was knocking his boots on the stone before the door – he would come in! She stared round. If she moved, he might hear her. She backed slowly towards the ladder.

'Dame? Are you within?' The door scraped open, letting in a column of afternoon light, and then stuck, a foot ajar. Annette dropped to the ground behind the old chest, gulping to catch back a tiny moan. She ducked her head desperately as a pale, bearded face appeared round the door, blinking at the darkness inside.

'Now then! What do you think you are about? What's your business here?' It was Lucy's voice from the garden – loud, her breathing harsh.

The man must have stepped back; the doorway lightened again. Annette buried her face in her apron and tried to still her breathing; but Lucy did not let him in. Annette could hear his gentling noises, as if to a baulking horse, and Lucy's furious croak cutting across him. Of course she had seen no young lady! What had put that fool's idea in his head? No, not a girl on her own, nor with anyone else – was he deaf? No, nobody had come up this hill last week, nor any other week either. What did he think this was, the highway to Shrewsbury? Had his mother not taught him to respect his elders? If so, he should know better than to go about the country bullying old women. She would thank him to leave her property *now* and stop frightening her cat.

The man's assurance withered under her onslaught, and finally he stopped asking questions; but it seemed an age before Annette heard him thump down from the stile into the lane, and another age before Lucy thrust back the door and strode in.

Annette rose up from her hiding place. The old woman was ablaze with righteous indignation, but clearly terrified.

'From Waldon Hall, that's for sure!' she announced. 'Did he see you?'

Annette tried to be calm. 'No, I do not think so. I hid myself. And he only looked in for a moment, before you came. He cannot have seen anything –' Annette stopped, her eyes following Lucy's to the hearthstone, where her silver brooch lay, winking and gleaming in the firelight.

The conversation with Cranage could have gone on all day, but he had other business to attend to and Jude needed space and time to think before she let her 'enthusiasm' (he was right about that) carry her away.

'There is a good inn here in Madeley,' he said. 'If I may, Madam, I will send my man to show you the way. In the morning, I will render you the account I have kept against your arrival. There is a tidy sum in ready money, of course, from some seven or eight months' rents, but also a sinking fund held over the years to meet outgoings… I will have the detail for you tomorrow.

Meanwhile, here is the prospectus of the canal venturers – most of which navigation they have carried out already – to show you what we are doing here in the Dale.'

Jude accepted the printed pamphlet and followed the 'man' – aged at least thirteen, she thought – as he hefted her bag and strode into the street.

The Three Horseshoes was a large old inn standing at the central crossroads of the place. When she came out into the sunshine again, Jude set herself to walk the town. No one stared very much, or, apparently, cared very much about an unknown lady taking the air. Madeley was larger than Salem, but not otherwise much in advance. There was building under way, as there seemed to be all over Coalbrookdale, but the High Street still had its roots firmly in the ground. Its hilly length was irregularly peppered with shops: small traders in groceries, butchers and bakers, sellers of hats and haberdashery, books and boots and shoes. Jude lingered over the bootmaker's window, concerned about her footwear, but told herself this was not the moment. She peered into other shop windows. They were not as elaborate nor as well stocked as those she had seen in London or Bordeaux, but there was brisk trade going on everywhere. The people seemed well-to-do and busy.

The houses, too, squeezed in among the shops, were obviously the abodes of prosperity. On her way back to the inn, Jude noticed only one closed-up frontage. A small garden was beginning to grow out of control and the windows were in need of a wash, but it was a neat and pleasant-looking little house, nonetheless. She began to imagine herself and Annette living in such a house. Could Madeley really be their new home, and her place of business? They could not perch forever on a remote hillside, that was certain. And here, there was something to do. Her excited conversation with Cranage came back to her. He was an agent not only for property, it seemed, but also for all kinds of trade. He was full of the powerful promise of the canal that was a-digging, and the wonders at the iron works, for which the fantastic tracery of the new bridge over the Severn was a striking advertisement.

'The iron trade is growing – all over the world,' he had said. 'The new castings serve for everything, from pumping engines to drain the mines, to handles to fasten your closet.' He had shown her the corner cupboard in his room, held shut by a tiny metal hand in a lace-cuffed glove. The glass panes of its door were framed in fine metalwork, too, sharper and thinner than any wood. 'Progress!' He turned to his window, gesturing. 'We have only to bring the means of trade up to scratch, and we will smooth our ways, and build our houses, and fill them with the new furnishings, the art and the – the – foodstuffs from all over the world. We will live in luxury here!'

'All of us, Mr Cranage?' Jude felt she already knew and liked this man well enough to challenge him. 'Even the barefoot babies in Farley's Rents?'

But Cranage smiled, pleased with her question. 'You are no doubt a reader, Madam?' He went to his bookcase and took out a creased volume. 'I am a convinced follower of the Scottish philosopher, Adam Smith – I do not know if you have come across him? This is his newest work, *An Inquiry into the Nature and Causes of the Wealth of Nations*. Here he explains how the path of free trade can bring wealth to all, improving their lot whatever their rank or station. International free trade – that is the goal! Meanwhile, the flow of goods everywhere is the only way: the beneficial circulation of wealth.'

'And you aim to aid that flow, sir?'

'I do, indeed! And if you have a mind to any such enterprise, Miss Wiston – then I am your man. Frederick Cranage is at your service!'

It was clear, the next morning, that he had been most efficiently at her service for some time. His book-keeping was immaculate; her capital was quite substantial. They went over the papers she had brought from London, and he vested the properties in her name before (at her request) stowing them in the box on his shelves marked 'Farley'. He would continue as her agent, he assured her, while she chose to employ him, and they would have many more discussions. He was a remarkable man, in that he seemed genuinely to look forward to the prospect of talking business with a woman. He introduced her to her banker; and she walked back to the office with more money in her pocket than seemed either likely or proper.

Only one matter remained – one that was growing more and more urgent in Jude's mind. 'Mr Cranage, I have to leave Madeley again for a little while – but when I come back, I think I shall seek to settle here. I will need a house of my own.'

Cranage attempted to conceal his surprise. 'You wish to set up your own household, Miss Wiston? I had assumed you might lodge with some good family, or –'

'I will not be alone. I shall need a house fit for two ladies living together. Might you find me any possible candidates for that purpose, amongst your clients and contacts?'

He rallied immediately. 'Surely, Miss Wiston,' he said, smiling. He turned towards his desk, then back again as a thought seemed to strike him. 'There is a very good house to let as we speak, in the High Street,' he said. 'It has lain empty these six weeks. I think my friend Mr Anstice is probably asking too much. I'll make enquiries, shall I?

'Thank you, yes,' said Jude, 'I think I saw that very house this morning. It might suit us well. Meanwhile,' she went on, 'and more immediately, I need your help on another matter – to make my way across this county. I am a moderate rider, Mr Cranage, but not much of a whip. Can I, do you think, find a hired conveyance?'

Cranage looked pensive and asked where she was heading. She told him as best she could, and at the mention of the Two Crosses he smiled delightedly. 'I believe I have it,' he said. 'I have to send my man to complete some outstanding business for me in Ludlow – a matter of carrying three chests of goods to a client there. I could send him tomorrow. He would need to detour only a little way to drop you at that inn.'

'And pick me up on his return?'

'Indeed, yes. I will arrange it,' said the invaluable Mr Cranage.

50

Lucy lowered herself into the chair, closed her eyes and let herself admit that she was exhausted. It wasn't that the girl was any trouble. And she was being brave enough, to be sure – she did not weep or storm – but the trance-like concentration with which she watched the door was enough to give anyone the collywobbles. Much as Lucy liked both Jude and Annette, she would not be entirely sorry to resume her old life, with just the cat for company. If Jude didn't come back soon, she thought, there was no knowing what she and Annette might do. Run mad, seemingly. This constant fear was wearing them both out. She opened her eyes a slit and looked at Annette as she sat there across the hearth – straight as a ramrod, no colour in her face, tight little fists buried in her lap. Lucy studied the pale cheeks, the tilted chin, the great dark eyes. The girl had been here days – it felt like weeks – and still Lucy sometimes saw through her face to another. To Bell. Now this Annette was running away from a world that had no place for her love, just as Bell had done before her. It must all mean something, Lucy thought vaguely, but she was too weary to work it out. Her eyes began to close.

It was then that then they heard footsteps in the lane.

Annette sprang to her feet, her face a mask of terror.

Lucy heaved herself up too, her heart pounding. The man from Waldon Hall. It had to be. He had seen Annette's brooch, after all! What could they do?

She faced the door and saw that they had not barred it after the morning's chores. It was too late now. The steps were loud and fast.

Annette, scrambling towards the ladder, froze. There was no time to hide.

As they stared towards it, the door burst open... and there stood Rebecca Wiston.

There was so much to say. At first there was no making sense of any of it, as Jude and Annette clung together, both chattering at once. But eventually Lucy blew up the fire, sat the pair of them down – Annette still clutching Jude's arm as if to stop her disappearing again – and they listened as Jude told her story. The afternoon darkened outside the window as she told over the detail of her adventures among the cottages and coal pits of Coalbrookdale. The place was a marvel, seemingly, with fires and furnaces everywhere, and all manner of wonders. It sounded to Lucy like hell itself, but she did not say so. She might have felt differently when she was Jude's age.

'We could be safe there,' Jude was saying eagerly to Annette. 'It might only be a day's journey away, but it is so different a place from the life you have known, that your godmother will never dream of looking for you there. It is a thriving town, full of life and ideas – I felt such a liking for the place! Of course, it was where my mother's people came from, though Mr Cranage did not know of any of the Beeston family still living in the Dale. I can build up a business there, and we can start a new life together in a house of our own – I have enough money now to keep us both.'

Annette laid her head on Jude's shoulder. 'And we will not be parted any more,' she said.

It was very late before Jude and Annette climbed up to bed. Mr Cranage's man would be waiting at the bottom of the lane by mid-morning to take them to their new life. They undressed without speaking; but then they fell upon each other hungrily, all the fears and pains washed away in the haste and taste of their passion. All would be well now. They could have and hold again.

After a while, they hushed and stroked each other to stillness, and began to think of the morning.

'Do you know,' Annette said, 'I shall be sad to leave Lucy now. I hate to see her struggling here alone.'

'We can come back to see her. Once we have been gone a while, and the Waldons have gone back down to London in the spring, and taken your revered Aunt with them, we can visit here. It is not so far to come, only forty miles or so. Quite easy in good weather.'

'We could come often?'

Jude snorted with laughter. 'As often as she will have us. I fancy she'll be quite pleased to pack us off and get back to her peaceful life.' Then she fell silent and rolled away in the rustling bed.

'What is it?' Annette asked.

There was a pause. 'I have been thinking to ask you something,' said Jude, at length. 'And now that we are cousins, it is perhaps easier to do. It seems to me that you might be safer if you changed your name.' She took Annette's hand. 'A Mr Wiston and a Mademoiselle Lavigne could never live respectably together. But the two Misses Wiston – cousins, sharing a home – would disturb no one. Could you consider calling yourself Wiston?'

'But of course!' cried Annette. 'How clever you are! Why did I not think of that?' She snuggled into Jude's arm. 'If you had been a man and I had married you, I would have taken your name, would I not? And now I can. That makes me very happy.' She turned and kissed Jude's breast. 'And what of your name? Will you always have to be Rebecca?'

'It will be simplest, I think. Though I have wondered about using my second name, Judith.'

Annette thought about this for a moment. Then she shrugged. 'Who cares what the world calls you? For me, *quand même*, you will always be my Jude.'

ABOUT THE AUTHOR

Jay Taverner is the author of three linked novels – *Rebellion, Hearts & Minds* and *Liberty* – spanning the eighteenth century, and a millennial spin-off, *Something Wicked*. Although the stories stretch across space and time, they all have a connection to Brynsquilver, an ancient cottage in the Shropshire countryside close to the Welsh border.

The novels are the creation of not one but two people: Jacky Bratton and Jane Traies, writing together as Jay Taverner. Jacky lives in West Sussex with her partner and their elderly cat; she also publishes academic works on the history of theatre. Jane is an oral historian who has edited two books of lesbian life stories and lives near Brighton. The inspiration for the Brynsquilver stories came from a deserted cottage that they came across many years ago, and from their shared interest in writing women-loving-women back into history.

Jacky Bratton (left) and Jane Traies
© Bronac McNeill